Sand Dollar Island

Liz Lehman

ISBN: 0983607427
ISBN 13: 9780983607427

1

EVA GRANT STROLLED UP THE BEACH, her attention drawn to a pelican swooping down in the sky to catch a live fish that had wiggled itself free from a seagull's beak.

She smiled. It was another beautiful day in paradise. The radiant, Florida sun felt good caressing her skin while the tropical breeze blowing in off the Atlantic set her spirits soaring.

The water appeared to be rougher than usual to her this morning. The waves were more powerful and they contained a lot of sand.

While she was watching the pelican settle onto a piece of driftwood, two waves crashed simultaneously, taking a chunk of beach and her along with it. Within seconds a rip current sucked her under the water, and like a ball of laundry tumbling in a dryer she rolled over and over, unable to escape it.

Terrified of water, her panic-stricken eyes bulged open. On each somersault she caught a glimpse of bright light. The light had to be the surface. If she could just break free from the current somehow, she might be able to reach it. But no matter how hard she tried, she could not escape the water's fury. She tried swimming across the current, but her arms and legs defied her will. Bubbles churned all around her and water tore at her clothes, almost ripping the pieces from her body. Terror consumed her mind, obstructing any rational thought. She knew that if she didn't get some air soon, her oxygen-starved lungs would force her to breathe, and she would drown.

Instead of her life passing before her eyes, Eva saw herself lying dead in a coffin, and her husband, Stuart, and daughter, Lorna, leaning over her with tears streaming down their faces. By now her lungs burned like fire, and she feared they might explode.

Suddenly something grabbed her foot. What was it, a shark? She panicked. Her heart stopped beating and then it began to pound so hard she thought she was having a heart attack. Her vision began to fade until the water went black.

Within moments, she regained consciousness. The fog cleared from her mind and she could think again. She had made it to the surface. But how? Did a rogue current shoot her to the top? Had a powerful wave broken the direction of the flow? The more she thought about it the more she didn't care. She was alive. Alive! She survived the nightmarish ordeal.

Eva went to inhale a lungful of glorious air, but something was constricting her chest. She glanced down and saw a man's arm around her waist. So that was how she had made it to the surface. Someone saw what happened and came to her rescue.

Petrified that another wave might tear them apart, she gripped the man's arm so tightly that her long, French-manicured fingernails dug into his taut flesh.

As she was slowly inhaling another deep breath, she glanced out to sea. Like the red buoy not too far off in the distance, she and the man kept bobbing up and down in the water.

Why was he waiting? They weren't that far out, only about fifty feet or so. Maybe he wasn't afraid, but she surely was. To her that short distance meant life or death.

She became more and more anxious. If another wave came along and tore them apart or a strong current sucked her under the water again, she knew she wouldn't survive. Her body lacked the strength and energy to fight.

For what seemed like hours, she found herself desperately clinging to the stranger. Just when she thought she might lose her mind, she felt him kick hard, and the two of them rode a wave to shore.

Like a frightened crab scurrying to safety, she broke free of the man's grip and scrambled up the beach on her hands and knees. In her haste to reach dry ground, she failed to notice that her halter straps had come undone. They dangled to the ground under her voluptuous, bare breasts. It took stumbling on one of the straps and toppling over onto her elbows for her to realize her near-nakedness.

Embarrassed, she plopped down on the sand and tied the straps behind her neck.

For several moments she breathed hard until her racing heart went back to beating normally.

Sand was everywhere, in her ears, nose and throat. Granules gritted between her teeth. She kept blinking, trying to get a few grains out of her eyes.

She said to the man. "I can't thank you enough. I would have drowned if you hadn't come along."

A pleasant, masculine voice responded. "You probably would have."

Eva squeezed excess water from her honey-colored hair, and then, as if she were parting a pair of curtains, she grabbed the hair covering her face and tucked it behind her ears.

Finally she was able to get a good look at the man who saved her life. Momentarily, she was stunned. He was extremely handsome.

"Who are you," she asked, thinking that he was probably one of the gardeners or handymen who worked regularly on Sand Dollar Island.

The man yanked his T-shirt over his head, tearing the hole under the arm more than it was already torn. "I was just about to ask you the same thing."

The flippant attitude surprised Eva. If any of the other workmen had talked to her in that manner, she would have fired them right then and there on the spot.

"I'm Eva Grant, Stuart Grant's wife." Mortified, she fussed with her hair. However, her attempt to make herself look more attractive proved futile. "You still haven't told me who you are. I'd like to compensate you in some way for saving me."

The man extended a strong hand out to shake hers. "I'm Michael Grant, Stuart's nephew. I guess that makes me your nephew, too."

Never in a million years would she have guessed that this knockout was part of the family. The Grants were nice-looking people, but none of them held a candle to this hunk. Although, the more she studied his face, she could see a little bit of her stepson, William, in him. They were built the same, and they both had dark, wavy hair. But William, being gay, was more effeminate in his demeanor, not rugged and virile like this Adonis.

"I should have known who you were, Michael. Your uncle told me you would be coming home this week. How does it feel to be back in Florida after spending a couple of months in the Himalayas?"

"It feels terrific. I missed the ocean."

"Speaking of the ocean, I had no idea the currents around Sand Dollar Island could be so dangerous. Who would think that one minute you could be walking the beach, enjoying the scenery, and the next minute you're being dragged out to sea?"

"Rip currents can do that. Didn't my uncle warn you about them?"

"Yes, he did. But I was under the impression you had to be careful in the water, not alongside it."

"You're not alone. Most people don't realize that rip currents can be deadly. That's why so many tourists end up drowning on vacation. People should pay more attention to warning flags."

"What do you think is causing the rip currents today?"

"There must have been a storm somewhere out in the Atlantic last night." Michael brushed some sand off the hair on his chest. "Are you all right?"

"I'm much better now. I just want to sit here a few more minutes and regroup."

"I don't blame you. Nearly drowning must be pretty scary."

Eva wiped under her eyes, embarrassed that her mascara may have run down her face. She drew in another deep breath and exhaled slowly. Of all the times for her to meet one of the sexiest men she had ever seen. She felt like digging a hole and covering herself over with sand. One thing was certain. He would never see her looking like a drowned rat again. The next time he saw her she was going to be wearing one of the sexiest outfits she owned.

She asked. "How were the Himalayas?"

"Pretty amazing."

"You can have the mountains and all of that snow. I'll take the sun and sand any day."

Michael picked up a seashell and studied its markings. "So you like our little island?"

"Are you kidding? Who wouldn't like Sand Dollar Island?" Eva caught herself. She didn't want to appear overly-impressed with everything. It would be a mistake to give the impression that she only married his uncle for his money, which she knew deep down inside was basically the truth. For years, while she was seeing Stuart behind his wife Sheila's back, she dreamed of being one of the island's mistresses, having everything at her beck and call, whether it be playing tennis whenever she felt like it, riding her bike on the winding trails, using the seaplane to go shopping, or just taking the wave runner, speedboat or yacht out on the water. Now her dreams had finally come true.

That reminded Eva. She held out her left hand. "Thank goodness! I was afraid I may have lost my engagement ring in the ocean."

"Wow! That thing looks like a small iceberg. How many carats is it?"

Her face beamed. "Ten."

"That's some stone."

"Yes, it is. Your uncle is a very generous man."

"Did you lose anything else? The water was really rough."

"That's a good question." Eva checked herself. "My Rolex and diamond tennis bracelet are still here. Oh no! My pearl necklace and one of the matching earrings is gone. So are my Gucci sandals. Now I'm really upset."

"Don't get me wrong, but why are you wearing all of that expensive jewelry so early in the morning?"

"I like to enjoy the beautiful things your uncle gives me."

Michael tossed the seashell into the surf. "I'm sorry I missed your wedding."

"You needn't apologize. Your uncle and I didn't expect you to drop everything and come running. Besides, we got married so quickly that it surprised everyone."

"Dropping everything and flying home wasn't the problem. We hit a blizzard that knocked out our communications for a few days. By the time word got to me, you two were already married." Michael twisted from side to side, loosening his tight muscles.

Eva watched him out the corner of her eye. It had been ages since a man affected her this way. He was one fiery spice she could add to any of her sexual entrees.

Michael threw his T-shirt over his shoulder. "How are you feeling now?"

"Almost normal."

He reached for her hand and helped her to her feet. "Come on, Aunt Eva. I'll walk you back to the house."

His strong grip sent a fiery jolt burning through her system, and how easily he pulled her up from the sand, like she was a rag doll. He was definitely going to be a priority on her sexual agenda.

She straightened the white linen shorts clinging to her shapely legs. "You can drop the aunt part and just call me Eva. Aunt Eva makes me sound like some old woman."

"You're far from being an old woman."

She took his response as a flirtatious comment. She smiled, thrilled that a gorgeous, young hunk in his thirties could be attracted to a woman pushing fifty.

Further up the beach Michael retrieved the running shoes he tore off before diving into the water to rescue Eva.

He asked her. "How's Uncle Stuart doing?"

"He's fine. He's busy working on some big business deal. I wish I knew enough about it to fill you in, but I never was much good at business matters." Eva winked, indicating that her expertise was in the bedroom.

"That's okay. It's not important. Uncle Stuart is always working on some big business deal."

As the two of them strolled slowly up the beach, Michael took in the beauty of the island.

He said. "Ever since my father died, Uncle Stuart has been like a father to me and my sister, Sam. He means a great deal to us."

"I'll tell him you said that. I'm sure he'll enjoy hearing it."

"You don't have to tell him. He knows how we feel." An expression of respect and admiration appeared on Michael's face. "I can remember when I was in high school. Uncle Stuart never missed one of my football games. I always felt so proud, seeing him up in the bleachers, cheering me on. He always stood out in a crowd, like some giant, real big and strong." Michael smiled. "I'll never forget when we won the state championship. He bought me a fire engine-red BMW convertible. Boy, did I love that car! In fact, I still do."

"Do you still have the car?"

"Yes. I drive it all the time."

The two reached a sandy path that led to a paved road circling Sand Dollar Island. Under a canopy of fluffy Australian pines they side-stepped broken seashells and roots of trees. Deeper into the botanical tunnel their presence startled several parrots which suddenly took flight, disturbing a Monarch butterfly feeding on the nectar of a yellow frangipani blossom. The insect's dark orange and black wings fluttered nervously until the parrots settled onto a palm frond.

In no time Eva and Michael had reached the paved road. Up ahead of them on the lush grounds of Michael's Grandmother Millicent's estate there were men erecting a large, white scallop-edged tent. Other workmen were standing on ladders, wrapping strands of twinkle lights around trunks of royal palm trees, getting the decorations ready for Millicent's annual birthday bash.

As they were crossing the road, a landscaping truck pulled over to park. Three Haitian men jumped out of the cab and went around to a cart they were hauling, after which they began unloading various tools they would be using to manicure the lush vegetation flourishing on Sand Dollar Island.

Eva laughed. "It's funny. At first I thought you might be a gardener or handyman."

"That wasn't such a bad guess."

"What do you mean?"

"Academically, I couldn't cut it."

"Then how did you play football? I thought you had to make good grades to play sports?"

"I almost didn't play football. But my coach thought I was a pretty good quarterback. He pulled some strings so that I could play."

"That wasn't very nice."

"Maybe not, but sometimes that's how the game is played."

"Is that why you never went to work at Grant Office Supplies?"

"Are you kidding? I'd drive my uncle crazy if I worked for him." Michael wiped beads of sweat from the top of his lip. "I've got to hand it to Uncle Stuart. When it comes to business matters, the man is a genius."

"What do you do to keep busy when you're not climbing mountains?"

"I teach climbing at my athletic club. Then I take trips with my students, where they put whatever they've learned in action. I also do some volunteer work with children whenever I get the chance."

Eva couldn't wait to get back to the house. Even in front of the workmen she felt mortified with her wet clothes clinging to her body and her hair and makeup a mess. "I'm so embarrassed," she said. "I must look horrendous."

"I'm sure those landscapers have seen a worse."

"You're a nice person, Michael."

"Don't be so sure. You don't know me that well."

A mischievous, seductive smile parted Eva's lips. "I can't think of anything I would enjoy more than getting to know you better."

The sun blazed relentlessly, its scorching rays beating down on their helpless bodies. Like moving about in a steamy sauna, their skin glistened with sweat.

Without the protection of shoes on Eva's feet, she jumped from the hot asphalt onto the grass. "Your grandfather was a shrewd businessman, buying Sand Dollar Island from the State of Florida."

"That's for sure. When I think of how he only paid a couple hundred thousand for it back in the sixties and what it might be worth today, I'd say he did really well." Michael shook his head. "I hope some of that shrewdness has rubbed off on me."

"With your looks, Michael, you have nothing to worry about."

Three mansions graced Sand Dollar Island. No other homes on the island existed. Stuart owned the estate directly in front of them. Millicent lived in the center mansion along with her servants, and the estate farthest up the road belonged to Michael's mother, Gayle.

Grateful that she had finally made it to the house, Eva took comfort in knowing that she was home safe and sound.

Stuart's house was huge. A monstrous crystal chandelier hung in the grand foyer over a shiny, white marble floor. Towards the back of the foyer, a matching pair of curved staircases joined together at the second floor, where two Greek columns stood defiant, like sentries keeping watch over a castle.

Although Eva had several servants working for her, they must have been doing their daily chores in other areas of the house, as the mansion showed no signs of life.

She glanced at herself in an ornate antique mirror. "Egad! I'm a complete mess. I hope you don't think I'm rude if I leave you to go take a shower."

"Not at all. I'm going to make a phone call, and then I'll be heading for home."

"Thanks again for rescuing me."

"No problem. You're lucky I happened to be running this morning. Be more careful from now on."

MICHAEL TURNED INTO THE DEN, his favorite room in Stuart's house. The masculine décor projected a quiet inner strength he appreciated. The dark walls set the tone with rich, mahogany paneling. In front of the window a museum-quality bust of a curly-haired Greek nobleman sat atop an antique table. A traditional leather sofa and matching chairs were ideally located in front of a fireplace that only got used on those rare chilly nights that occurred during Florida's winter season. On an antique commode behind the sofa sat a Remington bronze sculpture of an intense-looking cowboy on horseback roping a struggling steer. Over the mantle above the fireplace an authentic saber once used by a member of the cavalry graced the wall. Each piece of furniture and every work of art played its part in expressing a sophisticated man's taste and personality.

Michael slid onto the leather chair behind Stuart's desk. He had been abroad for several months so he felt compelled to talk with his attorney, David Chernoff. David took care of his private matters for him whenever he went out of town.

While he was waiting for David to come on the line, his mind rehashed his encounter with Eva. She seemed friendly enough, but what was with the winks and sexy innuendoes? Was she coming on to him? Nah! Why would she? She and his uncle just got married. If anything, it was probably her way of being friendly. Michael smirked. Stuart always was a sucker for a sexy, beautiful woman.

As he continued to wait, his eyes followed a streak of sunlight piercing through a crack in the plush, beige draperies, where it connected with an oil painting on the wall, seeming to split the work of art in two. What normally portrayed the scene of a rotting, red canoe anchored off the shore of a decaying Italian fishing village now looked like some higher power had zapped it in half with a laser gun. Michael gazed blankly at the brilliant streak until David's voice broke his reverie.

"Hey, Michael, When did you get back in town?"

"Last night."

"How were the Himalayas?"

"Tough as a bitch, but I enjoyed them."

"Do you still have all of your fingers and toes?"

"The last time I checked." Michael slid his feet off the desk. "What about you? How are you doing?"

"I'm fine, still working myself to death."

"Did anything important happen while I was gone?"

"There is one thing you might want to look into. A few weeks ago, while I was going through your mail, I opened a letter you received from the IRS."

"What did the IRS want?"

"Back taxes on the ten million dollar income you had two years ago."

The information surprised Michael. "You're kidding me."

"I'm not kidding. The IRS doesn't have a sense of humor."

"Are you sure they got the name right? Maybe they sent the letter to me by mistake."

"The social security number matched."

"I don't get it. Ten million?"

"Did you sell any of your Grant Office Supplies stock?"

"No. You would know if I did."

"I wasn't sure. I thought maybe you had another attorney handle the sale."

"This is so strange. Did you respond to the IRS?"

"No I called Stuart. I know he works with the accountant on most of the tax returns."

"Do you know if my uncle called the IRS?"

"He told me he would take care of it. Maybe you should ask him if he sent them a check. You don't need the IRS having a judgment against you or threatening you with tax evasion."

"Did you make a copy of the letter?"

"You know us lawyers. We make copies of everything. Do you want me to e-mail the letter to you?"

"Yes, and do me a favor, David. See what you can find out about this IRS thing. I don't like hearing about my possibly going to prison for tax evasion."

Michael hated the anxious feeling festering in his gut. The one thing his father stressed over and over again before he died was that no matter what happens, he, his mother and sister should hang on to their fifty percent of the stock, as Grant Office Supplies was expanding. If they heeded his advice, they would never have to worry about money, and nobody could ever force them out of the business.

David asked. "What about your mother? Doesn't she have power of attorney for you in case anything happens when you go out of town? Maybe she sold some of your stock."

"My mother wouldn't go selling any of my stock without discussing it with me first. And even if she did, it wouldn't have been my shares she sold. They would have been her own."

"Take a look at your tax return. Maybe it will clear up the confusion."

"I don't have any of my returns. Stuart keeps them locked up in his files along with the rest of the family's."

"Do you remember seeing anything about a stock sale when you signed your return?"

"No."

"In that case I'll call your uncle's accountant and get a copy of the return."

"I'm afraid to ask, David. Is there anything else I should know about before we hang up?"

"No. Everything is fine. I'm e-mailing you a report."

Either somebody had turned off the air conditioning, or the IRS letter bothered Michael more than he thought. He wiped sweat from his brow and left the den.

As he was heading for the back terrace, he heard a woman clearing her throat, as if trying to attract his attention.

No less dramatically than Gloria Swanson in *Sunset Boulevard*, his cousin, Holly, came sashaying down the staircase. "Michael dahling, you're back from climbing those huge boulders they call the Himalayas. How grand it is to see you again."

"Is that you, Holly?"

"The one and only."

"I never would have guessed. What have you done to your hair?"

She slipped out of the dramatic mode. "I dyed it black. Don't you just love it?"

"I'll say one thing. It looks better than that wild, poufy thing you used to wear. What happened?"

"I got tired of the sixties look. All of those psychedelic colors made me dizzy."

"You are dizzy, if you ask me."

It dawned on Michael that he had never seen his cousin without makeup or her hair done up in some fancy way. Even when they went swimming in the pool or ocean, she always looked glamorous. "What phase are you in now?"

"Can't you tell?"

"Not really."

"For Pete's sake, Michael, look at the lavender contacts."

He looked more closely at Holly's eyes.

"Well," she said, her hands on her hips, and the toe of her yellow pump tapping against the hard marble floor.

"Are you supposed to be Elizabeth Taylor?"

"Yeah, neat, huh?" She spun around in the yellow, fifties-style dress, the tight bodice accentuating her pointed breasts, the waist tucked and belted, and the full skirt flaring out with two cancan slips underneath it.

He teased her about her pointed breasts. "You better be careful with those things. You could hurt somebody with them."

"For your information, Einstein, this is how women back in the fifties looked. Don't you remember Marilyn Monroe and Jayne Mansfield with their big, pointed bazookas?"

"I'll say one thing for you, Holly. You have guts."

"If you think this is something, wait until you see what I'm wearing to Grandmother Millicent's birthday party. I had a seamstress make me a strapless dress exactly like the one Elizabeth Taylor wore in *A Place in the Sun.*"

"Are you bringing a date to the party?"

"Brandon Kent is the only man I know who comes close to looking like Montgomery Clift, so I invited him."

"Does Brandon know he's a stand-in for Monty?"

"No. And don't you go teasing him about it and spoiling my fun."

"Don't worry. I won't."

"Are you bringing anyone, Michael?"

"I doubt it. I hate calling somebody up at the last minute." It just occurred to him that Holly had more in her life than old movies. "How are you and your new stepmother getting along?"

"As long as Eva doesn't go sticking her nose in any of my business, we'll get along just fine." Holly rolled her eyes. "You're not going to believe this, Michael. I also have a new stepsister, Lorna. You should see her."

"Why? What's wrong with her?"

"The girl's a complete wreck."

"So?"

"She knows absolutely nothing about fashion. She always wears sloppy T-shirts and raggedy shorts, things like that. As far as her nails and makeup are concerned, forget it! I'll bet the girl has never been within ten feet of a beauty parlor."

"Not everyone dresses like some Hollywood glamour puss every hour of the day like you do, Holly. Maybe this Lorna has more important things on her mind."

"That's not it. The girl just doesn't have one shred of class."

"It sounds to me like you're jealous of her."

"Are you crazy? Wait until you see her."

"How old is she?"

"Twenty-seven. She just earned a Ph.D. from the University of Florida."

"Good for her."

"Bad for me."

"What is that supposed to mean?"

"Now that she's out of school, she'll be coming here to spend the summer with us." Holly sighed. "This should certainly prove interesting."

"Who knows? Maybe you'll enjoy having a step-sister around."

"No way, Jose. What could the two of us possibly have in common?"

Dramatically, as if once again she was Gloria Swanson in *Sunset Boulevard*, Holly leaned her head back and rested her arm against her forehead. "I think I'm getting a migraine, dahling."

"You told me you never get headaches."

"It's one I think I should be having."

Michael couldn't handle it when Holly acted like a spoiled brat. He headed for the door, eager to leave the wilting drama queen to her jealousy and fake headache. "I'll talk to you later. I want to go say hello to grandmother."

"Are you up for some snorkeling this afternoon?"

"Can't. The water's too rough."

"Shoot! Is it really?"

"It's so rough that I had to drag Eva out of an undertow."

Holly burst out laughing. "No! Don't tell me Miss Fancy Pants got her hair all messed up?"

"She almost drowned, you unsympathetic snob."

"Who cares?"

"I hope your dad never hears you talk that way."

"Are you crazy? I'm not stupid."

"Sometimes I wonder."

Holly went to punch Michael's arm, but his reflexes were too quick for her. He caught her wrist and twisted it until her face grimaced. "Too bad you missed," he said. "See you later, Liz."

As he was heading for the door, Holly strolled over to a mirror on the wall. As she admired her lavender contacts, she flipped her bangs to form two curls on her forehead. "There," she said smiling at her reflection. "That looks more like the way Elizabeth Taylor wore her hair in *Cat on a Hot Tin Roof.*"

FROM STUART'S BACK TERRACE Michael took a shortcut to his grandmother's house. As he was passing the swimming pool, a waterfall cascading over a stack of boulders into the deep end of the pool sprayed a refreshing mist on him. Down the stone path and further along he passed a white, gilded gazebo draped with fuchsia bougainvillea. From the gazebo he continued across the formal gardens to his grandmother's property.

Under the shade of a large banyan tree, he stopped to absorb the tropical splendor. Sand Dollar Island looked especially good to him today. Every time he returned home from one of his long trips he experienced this same reaction.

The royal palm trees had grown a little taller. He envisioned them someday touching the sky, which today could not have been bluer. So many flowers were in bloom. The orange and white bird of paradise appeared as though they could break free of their stems and take flight. The red and fuchsia impatiens, their dainty flowers delicate and abundant, speckled a background of lush, variegated green foliage. Orchids, bromeliads and gardenias vied for his attention along with colorful pink, coral and yellow hibiscus. A warm ocean breeze drifting over the island carried with it a blend of exotic scents created by Mother Nature's floral masterpieces. He inhaled deeply, appreciating the intoxicating aroma.

Millicent's greenhouse sat like an oasis in a desert void of sand but lush with emerald green grass. Around the exterior walls of the structure a picturesque display of diverse flowers grew. Many times Michael had visited with his grandmother here. He gazed out at the ocean. The water washing up over the rocks reminded him of the times he and his cousin, William, went snorkeling over the reefs in search of an octopus or eel.

Like everyone else in the Grant family, Michael admired and respected his grandmother. When he swung open the greenhouse door, a gust of wind blew through the windows, creating a strong draft that sent Millicent's straw hat sailing in the air. He caught the hat just before it hit the ground.

Millicent wasn't the usual type of grandmother who sat in a rocking chair doing needlepoint or crocheting doilies. Her youthfulness she maintained by working out with a personal trainer three times a week, and she enjoyed playing tennis and golf. As for her mental faculties, her mind was as sharp as the garden tools she used to stir up the soil in her potted plants. She could spot a crock of bull whenever someone tried handing it to her, and shove that same bull back down the fool's throat before he or she had a chance to realize what had just happened.

A big, warm smile graced Michael's face. "I thought I would find you here."

"Michael, dear," she responded happily. "You're back from your trip."

He handed the hat to his grandmother and gave her a big hug. "I missed you."

She wrapped her strong, youthful arms around his back. "I missed you, too." She pinched him lovingly. "My goodness, didn't you eat anything while you were staying in those mountains? You're all skin and bones."

"The mountains have nothing to do with it. You've been teasing me about being skinny my whole life."

"Why are your shorts all wet?"

"Eva got hit by a rip current. I had to jump in the water and pull her out."

"You should have let the bitch drown."

Michael laughed. "I see you're still as feisty as ever."

"That's right. And I'm going to stay feisty until the day I die."

"You're not going anywhere. You'll going to outlive us all."

"Listen to who's talking, mister physically fit."

Michael leaned against a wooden ledge lined with potted orchids. "What's with everyone around here? Why doesn't anyone like Eva?"

"Who else doesn't like her?"

"I just ran into Holly. She didn't seem too thrilled to have a new stepmother."

Millicent dug at a pile of dirt so aggressively that chunks of soil went flying everywhere. "I wish your Uncle Stuart had never met that blood-sucking parasite. Humph! Lord knows the woman only married him for his money." Millicent waved a small pitchfork in front of Michael's face. "You mark my words. Some day your uncle will regret he ever met that woman. When he least expects it, she's going to rip his heart out and hand it back to him on a silver platter."

"Is Eva really that bad? She seemed okay to me."

"What do you know, Michael? You've never been married."

"Give her a chance. I think you're being too hard on her."

"You know me. I call a spade a spade."

Michael was about to tell his grandmother about the IRS letter but changed his mind. Until he knew more about the supposed stock sale, he felt the less said the better. On the other hand, now was a good time to clear up something else that was bugging him. "Do you remember that vow my dad and Uncle Stuart made the day granddad died?"

"Why? Is something wrong?"

"No. I just happened to think about it while I was walking Eva back to the house."

"Aha! So you were being coy with me. You think she's a gold digger, too."

"That's not true. It didn't cross my mind until you brought up the subject."

Millicent went to a black wrought-iron bench and sat. She took off her gloves and patted the empty space next to her. "Here," she said, brushing loose dirt off her pale blue linen shorts. "Come sit beside me." After Michael complied with her request, she continued. "I remember that day as clearly as I can see that pink orchid over there. Besides me and your father, your Uncle Stuart and Aunt Margot were there. So was Charles Lerner, your grandfather's attorney. Here's what happened. Before your grandfather passed away, he wanted to make it perfectly clear, so there wouldn't be any question among his three children, just how he was going to split up his assets. Since your Aunt Margot didn't want any involvement in Grant Office Supplies, she got real estate holdings. As for your father and Stuart, they got a fifty/fifty share of the business.

Millicent took off her hat and fanned herself with it. "Your grandfather also made your dad and Uncle Stuart promise that if and when one of them died, they would take care of each other's family and keep the stock in Grant Office Supplies split evenly. Like me, your grandfather believed in a good sense of family."

"Did my dad and Uncle Stuart actually sign any kind of document agreeing to all of this?"

"They most certainly did, and so did I along with Charles Lerner as witnesses. The agreement between your father and Uncle Stuart is legally binding."

"That's all I wanted to know." Michael stood up to leave. "I take that back. There is one other thing."

"What's that, dear?"

"What are you doing about William? Did you invite him to your birthday party?"

"Of course, I invited William to my party. He IS my grandson."

"What about Julian?"

"I told William he can bring whoever he wants to my party, including Julian."

"Uncle Stuart is going to have a fit. He can't stand to be around William, let alone Julian."

"That's Stuart's problem. If he can't handle the fact that his son is gay, then he doesn't have to come to my party." Millicent gave Michael a loving whack on the rear. "Now get going. My plants are crying out for my attention."

Michael left the greenhouse, picturing Stuart losing control at the party and causing a big scene. He had done so in the past with William, and he could very easily do the same thing again.

The sun had slipped behind a blanket of clouds, taking the aquamarine color of the sea with it. Like the gloomy sky, the water had taken on a gray hue. It no longer looked inviting to him.

On the way to his mother's house, he experienced an old familiar feeling, one that took pleasure in grabbing his stomach and twisting it into knots. A man in his thirties should not be living with his mother. Although the mansion had eighteen rooms, six of which were bedrooms, he thought he should be living on his own, fending for himself. If he and his mother didn't get along so well, things would be different, but they kept their distance and respected each other's privacy. Every time he brought up the subject of moving, his mother always talked him out of it. She said that with his father gone, she liked having her son around, even if it wasn't on a constant basis. As for his sister, Samantha, she moved out of her mother's house after she married Tom Bryce, a successful dentist. That was over five years ago.

———

GAYLE'S HOUSE WAS the smallest of the three mansions. With its stone arches and black wrought iron-trimmed balconies, the architecture was European-inspired.

Unique furniture and artifacts family members had brought back from their journeys around the world decorated the interior. Outside by the pool a Tuscany-style portico shaded a cozy seating area perfect for relaxation or enjoying afternoon tea.

Michael took the steps to the terrace two at a time. When he opened the door to the kitchen, he smelled the mouth-watering aroma of fresh bread baking in the oven. Last night, when he arrived home from his trip, he felt too exhausted to eat. Now he couldn't wait to dig into a tasty home-cooked meal.

Arielle, the Haitian cook, stood at the sink rinsing fruits and vegetables she planned to mix together in a salad for lunch. "Lordy me," she said, "if it isn't my favorite boy! Get over here and give Arielle a big hug."

Michael went over and wrapped his arms around Arielle's waif-like waist. "You get prettier every day," he said.

"Go on! You're making me blush."

"That's why I like to make you blush. Blushing makes you even prettier."

Arielle's deep brown eyes sparkled happily. "Are you hungry, Michael?"

"Starved."

"What would you like for breakfast? How about some fresh-baked whole wheat toast or some of that cereal you like?"

"I don't know yet." He went to the refrigerator and opened its door. On the shelf before him sat the biggest, most succulent-looking key lime pie he had ever seen. "Forget about anything else. I'm having a big piece of your key lime pie."

As he was placing the pie on the speckled granite countertop, a tangy citrusy aroma wafted up his nose, teasing his taste buds. "You're an angel sent from heaven, Arielle."

"I made that pie especially for you. I know how much you love my key lime pie."

With a large carving knife he fetched from the cutlery drawer, he sliced into the smooth, pale-yellow filling. A dab of foamy, whipped-cream from the rim of the pie stuck to his fingers. He licked them after placing a quarter of the pie on a dish. The dessert looked so scrumptious that he could not wait to eat it. He had consumed enough lousy foreign foods to last him a lifetime.

Without bothering to sit, he stood at the counter and devoured his snack.

Arielle continued washing the fruits and vegetables. "What else would you like to eat?"

"Nothing right now. I want to savor the flavor of the pie a little while longer." He grabbed a bottle of water from the refrigerator. "I have some things to do, but I'll be back in a little while for lunch."

Michael left the kitchen and headed for the den. The fact that nothing in the house ever changed pleased him. He didn't like change. Change brought insecure feelings; not that he was a wimp by any means. Maybe it was because too many bizarre things happened to him when he traveled. Home he wanted to remain peaceful and stable. He smiled slyly. The antique tapestry he brought back from Nepal as a surprise for his mother was going to go nicely mounted on the bare space next to the wall of windows overlooking the Atlantic.

A custom-built maple wall unit stretched the entire length of the den. On the desk section of the unit sat his computer. He checked his e-mails, looking for the IRS letter from David, his fatigued body screaming out for rest as he did. Annoyed with the bothersome aches and pains, he ignored them. If he went back to bed for the remainder of the day, he would only feel worse.

Sure enough, the IRS was threatening tax evasion for his not paying the back taxes on a ten million dollar stock sale he supposedly made two years ago. Hoping to clear up the matter of the mystery stock sale once and for all, Michael went to speak with his mother.

Of all the rooms in the house he knew she preferred the Florida room. The charming white wicker furniture, soothing trickling fountain and colorful hanging flower baskets provided a calming atmosphere in which she could rest or read a book.

When Gayle saw Michael, she closed her book. "What are you doing up? I thought for sure you would still be sleeping."

"I was anxious to get up and go for a run on the beach."

He sat on a wicker chair. "I want to talk to you about something. I talked with David Chernoff a little while ago. He told me he opened a letter I got from the IRS while I was away. According to the government, I sold shares of G.O.S. stock for ten million dollars."

"Michael, you didn't."

"Don't worry. I didn't sell anything. I just wanted to make sure you didn't sell any stock in my name."

"You know better than that. I would never sell any of your stock. Just because I have power of attorney for you and Samantha doesn't mean I would do anything behind your backs."

"It's not possible Sam could have sold any of my stock, right?"

"Right. I'm the only one, other than you, who can sell it. Besides, Samantha has her own stock. Why would she sell yours? And you know she didn't sell any of hers, because she intends to pass some stock down to Hillary when she's of age."

"That's what I thought."

"I hope David didn't pay the taxes on it."

"He didn't, but I think Uncle Stuart did."

"You better call Stuart and tell him to get his money back."

"That's what bugs me about this whole thing. If no one sold any stock, where did the IRS come up with this information?"

"You know the government, Michael. They can't keep anything straight."

"I don't want the letter upsetting you. That reminds me. Have you started an exercise program yet?"

"No."

Michael threw his hands in the air. "You know what the doctor said. If you don't start getting some exercise, you might have another heart attack."

"I don't feel like exercising."

"Tomorrow, before the sun gets too hot, we'll go for a short walk on the beach."

"I know you mean well, sweetheart, but I'm content just sitting here."

"Look at you, mother, you're wasting away."

"So I'm wasting away. It's my life. I'll do whatever I want with it."

"You're still a young woman. You could be out dating."

"Dating? Are you out of your mind?"

"Dating, that's right. You're an attractive woman. Go to the beauty parlor and get your hair done. Put on some makeup. You should be out with some nice man having a good time."

"I couldn't care less about men. I'm beyond that stage of my life."

"Do you realize what will happen to you if you don't start exercising? Your whole system will shut down. What do you say? Let's start a walking program tomorrow."

"I promise. I'll make an effort soon."

Gayle stopped Michael as he was about to leave. "That letter bothers me. Are you going to do anything about it?"

"I don't want you worrying about it. I'm having David check things out for me."

2

THE TIRES MADE DULL thumping sounds as the old, white Honda crossed the narrow, wooden bridge onto Sand Dollar Island. Stuffed in the car's trunk and stacked on its seats were boxes and suitcases containing personal items it had taken Lorna Meade the past five years to accumulate in her furnished apartment in Gainesville.

The sunroof, which she opened after it quit raining, welcomed in the fresh air and warm sunshine. At the same time, the opening amplified the booming base of her cranked-up radio, startling the birds and other wildlife out of their peaceful cohabitation.

Lorna fidgeted in her seat, anticipating a turbulent stay on the island. Rarely, did she and her mother get along, but spending the summer on the island beat staying in Gainesville. She was sick and tired of college life and everything else that went along with it. For months she had looked forward to graduation and spending a lot of relaxing time just vegetating on the beach. The only way she could accomplish her goal was to stay with her mother and Stuart, because money was a major problem. Sure, she could have gone to Michigan and stayed with her father for a while, but after what happened the last time she visited him, she didn't think that was such a good idea. Her dad had way too many lady friends marching in and out of his house. Until he settled down and started acting like a father instead some cooped-up animal someone just let out of a cage, she refused to subject herself to his flagrant, immature behavior. Besides, Michigan didn't have swaying palm trees and an ocean nearby. Lorna smiled to hide her pain. Why the good lord blessed her with such a dysfunctional family, she would never know. Her middle-aged father acted like a horny teenager, and her over-sexed mother liked to chase sexy, young men.

Her fingers strummed the steering wheel nervously. In the next ten or fifteen minutes, World War III was going to break out. No doubt her mother was going to throw a fit over her sloppy appearance. 'Look presentable when you arrive' she was warned. 'Make a good impression on the Grants.' What a crock of bull! Why should she get all dressed up in good clothes for a five-hour drive to Sand Dollar Island? It made absolutely no sense. The green soccer shorts and white tank top she was wearing were much more appropriate for traveling in this heat.

Lorna rubbed her temples. Was it her imagination or did her headache actually get worse the closer she came to Sand Dollar Island? Maybe it was an omen telling her to turn around and get the heck out of there. She loosened the purple clip clamping her long, blonde hair together, hoping to relieve the dull throbbing pain. As she did, a few strands fell and got lodged between her and the seat. When she turned her head to marvel over a beautiful white heron strutting carefree on the grass, the trapped strands pinched her neck, creating a pain so fierce it felt like somebody had ripped out the back of her skull. She groaned as she leaned forward to free the hair.

Finally at the entranceway, she realized that she had forgotten the security code to get through the huge black wrought-iron gate. Now what was she supposed to do? She exhaled an exasperated sigh. Here she was with a Ph.D., and she couldn't remember something as simple as a security code. Maybe she could back the car into the ocean and cruise around the island to Stuart's house. The ridiculous thought amused her.

She sat there for what seemed like an hour trying to remember the code. Her purse sat next to her on a plastic garbage bag full of dirty laundry. Did she have the number written down in her wallet? No. That would have been the intelligent thing to do. Why write down something that was so easy to remember? Now the joke was on her. Furious with herself for being so stupid, she pounded the steering wheel. After contemplating for a moment whether or not she should turn off the engine, her eyes suddenly lit up as if she had just solved the mystery of the universe. 9 8 9 8, she punched into the security box.

Once through the gate, she turned left onto the paved road circling Sand Dollar Island.

Down the road she continued, passing a small lake on her right and the ocean to her left. As she was nearing one of the island's many coves, she saw Holly Grant walking with a man. They were heading towards the beach.

The man was strikingly handsome. If he had been at her mother and Stuart's wedding, she felt certain she would have noticed him. How could she not? He could give a matinee idol a run for his money. Her curious eyes followed the man as he turned onto the sandy path. Could he have been Holly's boyfriend? Lorna pondered the subject. If he was, she decided Holly could have him—him and every other good-looking man she wanted. Gorgeous guys like this one were nothing but trouble, the jerks, every one of them acting like they were God's gift to women, thinking they're stud material, always hopping from one female to the next, interested in only one thing, getting laid. No, never again. No more handsome guys for her. Lorna's grin shifted to a smirk. In a way, the man with Holly reminded her of Jeff, whom she would have choked to death right then and there if he had been with her in the car. Lorna sighed. Six months had gone by since she caught Jeff in bed with her roommate, but the pain in her heart still lingered. After that disastrous encounter, she vowed she would stay away from ladies men forever.

Her pounding headache refused to tolerate one more pounding beat. She turned off the radio, appreciating the sound of the ocean which blended much better with the tranquil surroundings.

If America had castles, in her opinion Stuart's mansion would have been ranked among them. As she approached the estate, her mind reeled over trying to figure out how much money Stuart must have had to fork over in the divorce settlement to his ex-wife, Sheila, in order to keep it.

Someone inside the house must have been testing the hurricane shutters. Big sheets of aluminum came sliding down over the windows and then went rolling back up to their original positions.

On both sides of the winding driveway leading up to the front door Royal palm trees grew tall and stately. As she turned onto Stuart's property, she cruised past a tropical garden showcasing various marble statues.

Her throat felt parched and dry from traveling. The game plan was for her to go inside and say hello first. After she got that out of the way, she would start unloading the car.

After trying the front door and finding it locked, she rang the bell.

Within seconds, Andrew, the butler was greeting her with his usual, pleasant smile and proper, British accent. "Miss Lorna. What a pleasure it is to see you!"

"It's nice to see you, too, Andrew. Is my mother home?"

"Yes. Please come in. I will inform Mrs. Grant of your arrival."

"Don't bother. Where is she?"

"Madame is upstairs in her sleeping quarters."

"Thanks. Oh, Andrew. Do you mind bringing me something cold to drink?"

"Would you prefer a glass of iced tea or lemonade?"

"Iced tea sounds great."

Lorna crossed the white marble foyer to the grand staircase. As she was ascending the stairs to the second floor, she glanced out a glass wall stretching from the floor to the ceiling.

Boats out on the Atlantic speckled a never-ending, blue sea. One, a large sailboat, listed back and forth, as if an imaginary child were rocking it. Further out in the distance, just barely visible with the naked eye, an oil tanker chugged slowly across the horizon. Like everything else about Stuart's house, even the view was spectacular.

Instead of barging right in on her mother, Lorna thought she better knock first. She rapped lightly on the bedroom door. "It's me, mother."

While she was waiting out in the corridor for her mother to answer, she braced herself for the attack she knew was coming over her sloppy appearance. As expected, her mother did not let her down.

Eva opened the door and commanded the entranceway, her hands on her hips and her head shaking. "I thought I told you to fix yourself up before you came here. What will the Grants think?"

Lorna could have screamed. "More than likely they'll think I'm some bum off the street." She pushed past her mother. "For Pete's sake! I'm sure the Grants will see me for what I am, a brain dead college graduate who just drove hours to get here. God, you kill me."

"That does it, young lady. You're coming with me."

"Where?"

"I'm taking you shopping."

"But, I just got here. I don't want to go shopping."

"I don't care what you feel like doing. You're going shopping with me today, and Saturday we're spending the afternoon at the beauty parlor. If you want to attend Millicent's birthday party, you are not going to attend it looking like that."

"Then I won't go to the party. I had enough partying at school to last me a lifetime."

"You will go to the party, and you will go looking like a lady, not some vagrant living in the streets."

"I promise I'll fix myself up for the party. We don't have to go shopping today or spend all day Saturday at the beauty parlor. I'm exhausted right now. I don't feel like going anywhere."

"I made up my mind before you got here. You will do as I say while you're on Sand Dollar Island. What else do you have to do anyway?"

Andrew arrived, balancing a silver tray in his hand. "Here you are, Miss Lorna." The butler handed her a glass of iced tea and then offered one to Eva. "I took the liberty of bringing you a refreshing drink, also, Madame."

"Iced tea sounds divine, Andrew."

Lorna rolled her eyes. Divine? Never, not once in her life did she ever hear her mother say 'divine'. The affected response nauseated her.

Eva waited until Andrew left the room. "You will be using the suite two doors down from mine on this side of the hall. It has a bathroom in it. Go take a shower."

"Now?"

"I don't mean next week."

"But I have to unload my car."

"No you don't."

"All of my things are in it."

"Everything you need for now is in the suite."

"What about clothes?"

"We're basically the same size. You can wear something of mine. Now go get ready."

"Who is going to unload my car in the meantime?"

"The servants will do it."

Lorna had only been in her mother's presence a few minutes and already she felt like leaving.

Nothing could be gained by another big fight she knew. As she walked out the door to go take a shower, she stifled an exasperated sigh.

The last time she had stayed at the mansion, she occupied a different suite. While she was getting undressed, she admired the extravagant décor. Sheer, beige netting attached to a ring on the ceiling over the king-size bed draped to four carved bedposts and down to the floor. An exquisite rustic vase on the antique dresser brimmed with bright pink peonies. In the bathroom the green marble counter tops matched the raised marble tub sitting directly under a skylight in the ceiling. Fish-shaped faucets on the tub shined so brilliantly that she swore they were plated with gold. She could not imagine living in or affording such luxury.

After driving for so long, the cool black marble felt soothing beneath her feet. From what she recalled she had never seen black marble in a bathroom, only in museums and old government buildings up north. The bedroom suite she occupied when she came down for her mother and Stuart's wedding had a pinkish-colored marble floor.

The walls and floor of this bathroom's shower were also black marble. When she stepped inside the stall, she noticed there were two separate fixtures with their own controls, obviously for two people to shower together. She turned one fixture on and allowed the refreshing water to rejuvenate her fatigued muscles.

After she showered and blew her hair dry, she wrapped a big, fluffy, green towel around her body and then went back to her mother's suite. From out of the spacious, walk-in closet she selected a sleeveless beige linen chemise with a long slit traveling halfway up her thigh, one of the more conservative dresses Eva owned. As their shoe sizes were different, she had no choice but to wear her old, beat-up, brown leather sandals.

Because her mother thrived on being the center of attention, Lorna had no desire to try and upstage her. She learned a long time ago that her mother's ego always got in the way of their having a normal mother/daughter relationship.

Eva grabbed her purse. "Let's go. I'm tired of waiting."

Lorna glanced at herself in the mirror and shrugged her shoulders. "I guess this will have to do."

Down the staircase, through the house and into the garage they went with Eva leading the way.

While her mother was deciding on which car she should take, Lorna observed her. Eva chose the cream-colored Rolls Royce convertible. Lorna expected as much. Her mother undoubtedly enjoyed people staring at the car and wondering who she was.

No sooner did they leave the mansion than they were at the same cove Lorna had passed not even an hour ago. It reminded her of seeing Holly. "On my way in this morning I saw Holly and her boyfriend heading for that path over there."

"Holly dates, but I don't think she has a steady boyfriend. What did this man look like? Was he exceptionally good-looking?"

"I guess you could say that."

"And really nicely built?"

Lorna wanted to vomit. "He was a real stud-muffin, mother, just your type."

"That must have been Michael."

"Who is Michael?"

"Gayle's son. You remember Stuart's sister-in-law, Gayle. You met her at our wedding."

"That real nice woman who was married to Stuart's dead brother, Richard?"

"That's right."

"Gayle did tell me she had a son climbing the Himalayas. Why didn't he come to the wedding? Don't he and Stuart get along?"

"They get along perfectly."

"Then why wasn't he at the wedding?"

"For one thing, we got married quickly. And another, he took a group of his students mountain climbing. From what I understand, the trip had been planned for months."

"What is this Michael like?"

"Why?"

"No particular reason. I was just asking."

"Don't get any fancy ideas, young lady."

"Like what?"

"Like dating him."

"What is your problem? Did you hear me say I wanted to date him?"

"No, and you're not going to either. One Meade in the Grant family is enough. Besides, Michael Grant would never date a girl like you."

"What in the heck is that supposed to mean?"

"I'm sure he only dates women of good breeding."

"Thanks a lot. It's nice to know I have a supportive mother."

"You know what I mean."

"No, I don't know what you mean."

"Men like Michael only associate with classy women."

"Did I hear you right? You're admitting we don't have class?"

"I have class, but you don't. You're just a young girl."

"Just so I get this straight, being young means I can't have class?"

"That's right."

"I must have been crazy to come here. Who needs this aggravation?"

"Don't work yourself up into a tizzy, Lorna. You know what I mean."

"No I don't know what you mean. Maybe you should explain it to me."

"Up until a few years ago, you were nothing but a chubby little geek, and you know it."

"Since we're reflecting back to happier times, mother, why don't we discuss how you constantly rode my back about being overweight."

"It must have helped, because look at you now. You're finally a normal size."

"Let's get another thing straight while we're at it. I didn't lose all of that weight because you wanted me to. I lost it because I got sick and tired of seeing my girlfriends go out on dates, while I sat home alone. Come to think of it, that really infuriated you when I lost all of that weight, didn't it?"

"Why would it infuriate me? You just said I rode you about it, miss smarty-pants."

"You were jealous of me."

"Jealous of you? PUHLEEEZE!"

"You were. I remember when my male friends used to come over to the house. You literally vied with me for their attention."

"And, how did I do that?"

"You would horn in on our conversations or invite yourself to watch TV with us."

"I never did any such thing."

"You most certainly did. And, the few times you allowed me to have parties, you got all dressed up in some sexy outfit and danced with every guy there."

"From what deli are you getting your baloney?"

"It's true, and you know it. Don't you remember the fights we used to have?"

"No. As a matter of fact, I don't."

"How convenient!"

"I don't want to hear anymore. You're talking like some lunatic."

"I am not. First we would fight. Then you would give me the silent treatment. We would make up, and you would let me have company again. After that, you would go and pull something else off the wall. Yes, mother. You certainly set a good example for me."

"What did I do that was so terrible? I was just being nice to your friends."

"You call walking into the living room in your bra and panties, pretending like you didn't know I had company, being nice to my friends?"

"You're insane, Lorna. I think you should see a shrink."

"If anyone needs a shrink, it's you, mother. Maybe you lost your mind when dad divorced you. Who knows? Maybe you just have raging hormones."

"I've had enough of your smart mouth."

Lorna's head still pounded from the same headache she had earlier. She leaned her head back against the headrest and closed her eyes.

For several minutes, the two women rode without saying another word to each other.

Lorna figured she better smooth things over before matters got worse. "Stuart's house is really beautiful. Are you going to change anything now that the two of you are married?"

"In time maybe, but not right away."

"How much did he have to give Sheila in the divorce settlement in order to keep it?"

"Forty million."

Lorna's eyes shot open. "Forty million? I bet that left a big hole in his bank account."

"It certainly didn't help it any."

"By the way, mother, where are we going?"

"Worth Avenue. The shops there have exactly what it takes to make a lady out of you."

3

ZUCKERMAN, Kamin, Katz and Schwartz, one of the most prestigious law firms in Palm Beach County, took up the top three floors of the Zuckerman Building, a gray granite structure directly overlooking the Intracoastal Waterway in West Palm Beach.

As Stuart Grant was riding the elevator to the eighth floor, he hoped desperately that the meeting would turn out in his favor. If it did, his life would definitely change for the better. As he straightened the knot of his blue and burgundy-striped tie, his lips curled, forming a sly grin. Soon he would be rid of Gayle and her two lazy, good-for-nothing kids.

Stuart could not wait. After years of playing mister nice guy, the good uncle, he was finally going to be rid of his late brother's family. What he should have done long ago was get rid of the lazy, inept loafers the day after Richard died, the leaches, constantly sucking money out of the company, money he broke his back to make, especially Gayle, the old hag. No other man in his right mind would have put up with the three of them all these years. Hell! He ran the business and made all of the important decisions. Why should they benefit from his hard work? He despised having partners, especially the built-in kind.

Just thinking about Gayle made Stuart's blood boil. He pictured her when she was younger. Boy, over the years did she ever change! There was a time though that she put all of the other pretty women he knew to shame. Back in college she could have had any man she wanted, yet she chose him. Inviting her to Sand Dollar Island for spring break had to be the stupidest thing he ever did. Gayle saw Richard, Richard saw Gayle, and the two of them fell madly in love. For years, seeing her and his brother together drove him nuts, even while he was married to Sheila, because for the longest time he ached for Gayle. But all of that changed when Eva came to work for him. Now he planned to get even, not with Richard, because the almighty had already taken care of that problem for him, but with Gayle for making his life so miserable for so long.

None of the children knew about him and Gayle being college sweethearts, nor did Eva. Millicent advised him to let sleeping dogs lie. Things were better off that way. Yes. Soon he would be free of the bloodsuckers. Whatever time he had left on this Earth he planned to travel the world with Eva or do whatever else he damn well pleased.

As Stuart was stepping off the elevator, a determined look enveloped his face. Enough of Gayle and her two dimwits! This morning's meeting was way too important to dwell on negativity. He had to focus all of his energy on making the deal happen.

He sauntered up to the reception desk and smiled at the attractive, dark-haired woman, her doe eyes twinkling and her smile creating dimples.

He said with an air of confidence. "Good morning, Candace."

"Good morning, Mr. Grant. Everyone involved in the meeting is already here. They're waiting for you in the big conference room." Candace got up to escort Stuart to the meeting.

Stuart motioned for her to stay seated. "Don't get up. I know the way."

He turned down a corridor, smelling the combined aroma of fresh paint, new wood paneling and expensive Italian leather. The law offices had just been redecorated. In his estimation the new look added more prestige to the firm.

At the far end of the corridor he ran into Jonathan Katz, one of the senior partners. Stuart thrust out his hand and shook Jonathan's vigorously. "With all of the money you guys make off me, I thought the furniture would look a lot more expensive."

The attorney laughed. "Are you kidding? You pay us so little, this cheap crap is all we could afford."

Stuart slapped Jonathan on the back. "I'm just kidding. The place looks great."

Although Stuart stood six-feet-two, today he wore his black leather shoes with the two-inch lifts in them. Experience taught him that towering over people in meetings intimidated others into submission, giving him the edge. He also had his hair dyed to cover the gray, number 60B, a medium brown shade he periodically got done privately in a salon. With all of the tennis he had been playing lately, he knocked off ten pounds. Now he looked more like a man in his forties instead of somebody in his fifties.

When Stuart reached the conference room, he found Jerry Zuckerman seated at the table opposite John Powers, the President of World Office Products, and John's attorney, Henry White.

Stuart pulled out the chair next to Jerry. "Sorry I'm late. Traffic was murder."

For the next few minutes the men discussed the prior evening's Marlins baseball game. The male bonding did what everyone intended. It broke the ice and put everyone at ease.

Henry White, the attorney representing World Office Products, began the meeting. "World Office Products will pay $1.5 billion for Grant Office Supplies, twenty-five percent up front and the remainder paid out in equal, annual installments over the next five years."

Stuart and Jerry Zuckerman had been working on the deal for months. For tax purposes they felt it was wise to defer payments, as they expected Congress would be lowering the tax rate on capital gains income in the next year or two. Both men expected the future payout, but not over five years.

Stuart came back at Henry White. "Two billion, a third up front, and two payments of one third each annually for the next two years."

John Powers, the President of World Office Products, responded. "That will put substantial financial pressure on the company."

Stuart responded. "What if World Office Products folds? I can't take the chance of that happening."

"Do you want it paid in stock or cash?"

"Cash."

"If you take stock, it's a tax-free exchange."

"And if the stock value drops, I'm screwed."

Afraid that World Office Products might walk from the deal, Stuart glanced to his attorney.

Jerry Zuckerman leaned forward in his chair. "There should be a penalty clause if either party breaks the purchase agreement."

The opposing attorney asked. "How much do you propose?"

"Seventy-five million. A seventy million break-up fee and five million to reimburse the other party for its costs."

"Anything else?"

"That's it."

"Give us a minute." Henry White and John Powers left the room to discuss the deal. Five minutes later they came back into the room.

John Powers spoke. "All right, but the board has to review the deal first."

Stuart stood up and shook John's hand. "Great. We'll look forward to hearing from you."

As John Powers and Henry White were leaving, Jerry Zuckerman motioned for Stuart to stick around.

Stuart poured himself a cup of coffee and waited while Jerry saw his guests to the elevator.

When Jerry returned, he handed Stuart a thick, brown folder, old and musty-smelling. "Here are the files you wanted."

"What files?"

"The ones Charles Lerner kept on your father."

"You're kidding! How did you get them?"

"It wasn't easy. I had to track down the firm that bought Lerner's business after he died."

"Who did buy him out?"

"Badgely and Haines."

"Excellent. I can't wait to get home and go through these."

"I'm sorry but you can't take the files home. I assured Hutch Badgely the folder wouldn't leave this office. But I see no reason why you can't sit here for as long as you like and go through them."

Stuart glanced at his watch. "I have about an hour until my luncheon engagement."

"While you're going through the folder, I'm going to make a few phone calls. When you're done, drop the folder off in my office or leave it with my secretary."

"Good work, Jerry. This is great. I guess you're worth the money I pay you."

The attorney laughed as he left the room.

Anxious to get to the files, Stuart sat forward in the leather chair.

The folder reeked of insect spray. He grimaced. It obviously came straight out of storage. He loosened the elastic band and emptied the contents onto the table.

As if he were a prospector searching for gold, he went through the files, hoping to find one that contained a copy of the agreement he and Richard had signed.

A quarter of the way down in the stack he encountered a disintegrating, dead roach. Repulsed, Stuart blew the roach off the page and across the table, where it slipped off the edge and fell onto the firm's new burgundy carpet.

For the next twenty minutes, he flipped through file after file, scanning the papers each one contained.

Near the bottom of the stack he ran across a legal-size manila folder marked Stuart/Richard Grant Agreement. Stuart's heart pounded. Could the old attorney's copy of the agreement still be in the folder or was he wasting his time?

As if the papers had been typed yesterday, Lerner's copy sat on the table before Stuart. He smiled. Now he had Gayle and her pain-in-the-ass kids right where he wanted them. He glanced out into the corridor. Seeing no one, he folded the agreement and slid it into his inside jacket pocket.

Before he left, he realized there might be other important papers he needed. He spent a few minutes going through the remaining files.

Nothing else interested him, so he packed up the folder and delivered it to Jerry's office.

———

LATER THAT EVENING, Stuart sat at the dinner table with Eva, Lorna and Holly. Dessert had just been served.

He scooped up a fork full of fresh berries and whipped cream. "I'm going next door for a few minutes. I have some papers for Gayle to sign."

Eva tossed her napkin onto the chair. "Give me a few minutes to change, and I'll go with you."

"What's this sudden interest in Gayle? You never wanted to go see her before."

"That's why I think I should go now. I feel guilty because I never go over to visit her."

"But, if you go with me, we'll end up spending the entire evening over there."

"I promise we won't stay any longer than you have to."

"All right then. But, I see no reason why you have to change."

"Are you kidding? I've been in this dress all day. It's a wrinkled mess."

"So what! Haven't you noticed the way Gayle dresses?"

Lorna's eyes followed her mother. "I agree with Stuart. Why change? You're just going next door to see Gayle, aren't you?" She said it sarcastically, suspecting her mother had ulterior motives about seeing Michael.

Eva glared at Lorna. "You could take a few lessons from me as far as your personal appearance is concerned, young lady. Where are all those clothes I bought you yesterday? And why do you always wear those cheap plastic clips in your hair? You don't see Holly wearing those stupid things or the raggedy, shorts and old T-shirts you always wear. And, she's your age."

Holly leaned back in her chair, a derisive expression on her face. "I would be happy to give you a few pointers on dressing and fixing your hair, Lorna."

"No thanks. I've managed this long without anybody's help."

Stuart suddenly had a change of mind. With Eva with him, Gayle would be distracted from concentrating on the papers he wanted her to sign, not that she bothered reading the documents he ever took over in the past, but tonight one document was especially important. "If you insist on coming with me, then go get ready."

"I'll only be a minute." Eva hurried out of the dining room.

Stuart, Holly and Lorna went back to eating their dessert.

As Andrew was about to clear the table, they heard Eva's high heels clacking on the hard marble floor.

Stuart got up from his chair and went to the foyer. When he saw Eva in skin-tight jeans and a white silk shirt unbuttoned so low that it barely contained her braless breasts, he gulped. "Where do you think you're going in that outfit?"

Lorna overheard Stuart making a fuss and came running out of the dining room to see what kind of wild, sexy outfit her mother was wearing. "Are you serious, mother? Aren't you a little old to be going braless?"

"How do you know I'm not wearing a bra? You can't tell."

"Bet me I can't. Your boobs are practically touching the floor."

Eva glared at Lorna. "You can be a real brat."

Holly came sashaying into the foyer. "Eva, I don't think I've ever seen you in jeans."

"That's because I rarely wear them. The mood has to hit me right."

Although Stuart loved seeing Eva in revealing clothes, the look seemed totally inappropriate for a visit next door.

"That outfit is rather sexy to be wearing to Gayle's house, isn't it?"

Lorna scoffed. "It sure is."

Eva strolled over to the antique mirror. "You can't get any more casual than jeans, can you?"

The sexy clothes aroused Stuart. "I must admit those jeans do look good on you."

"Oh pooh! You and Lorna are making a big fuss over nothing." Eva spun around. "Do I look that bad, Holly?"

"I say if you got it, flaunt it."

"Thank you. That is my sentiment exactly."

Lorna threw her hands in the air. "I give up. Go make a fool out of yourself."

———

FROM THE VERY first moment Eva met Michael, she found herself fantasizing about him. Tonight was going to be one of those rare occasions when she would get to see him, and she looked forward to adding some fun to her life. Her heart beat faster as they approached the house.

Instead of Michael answering the door, Gayle stood before them. Eva hid her disappointment. What if Michael wasn't home? She had gone through the trouble of changing and touching up her makeup, for what, a visit with one of the most boring women on the face of the earth?

Gayle welcomed Stuart and Eva into the house. "What a nice surprise! I'm so glad you brought Eva with you, Stuart." She took Eva's arm. "You look younger every time I see you. You could pass for a teenager in those jeans."

Eva lapped up the compliment. "Why thank you, Gayle. That's nice of you to say."

Like a lovesick adolescent, Eva glanced around the house, looking for Michael. He was nowhere in sight. She could have kicked herself for coming with Stuart; although, on second thought, Michael could be anywhere. The house was huge.

Gayle led Stuart and Eva into the Florida room. "I hope you two haven't eaten dessert yet. Right after you called and said you were coming over tonight, Stuart, I had Arielle prepare a fruit cobbler."

Careful not to upset a member of the Grant family, telling Gayle that they had just eaten fresh berries with whipped cream, Eva responded graciously. "Fruit cobbler sounds divine."

As Eva was about to sit, Michael came strolling into the room. "Hey, Uncle Stuart,' he said, "how's it going?"

When Eva saw Michael in his white linen shirt and tan cargo shorts, her legs almost buckled from under her. He looked like he had just stepped off the cover of a GQ Magazine. "Hello, Michael," she said, her eyes twinkling with excitement.

Michael kissed her on the cheek. "I feel great now that I've gotten a few hours sleep. How about you?"

For that brief moment Michael's moist, full lips grazed her cheek, Eva wanted to grab him and press her body against his. And when she caught him glancing down her shirt as he stepped away from her, it confirmed what she was hoping. He was attracted to her as much as she was to him.

Gayle handed Eva a bowl of mixed nuts. "Before we get started, I'll go see about the dessert and coffee."

Eva and Stuart were sitting on the wicker sofa, she with her legs crossed and he with the folder of papers safely on his lap.

Michael settled into a chair. "Uncle Stuart, how's everything coming along on that big business deal you're working on?"

Stuart patted Eva's leg. "For the sake of my lovely wife, let's not bore her with mundane business talk."

"You're totally right. That was rude of me. Just one thing and we won't talk business anymore." Michael leaned forward, resting his elbows on his legs. "I want to thank you for taking care of that IRS matter for me while I was out of the country."

"No problem." Stuart rubbed Eva's thigh. "That's enough. I said no more business talk."

Eva could not take her eyes off Michael. Each tilt of his head and expression on his face she found appealing. "When is your next mountain climbing expedition, Michael?"

"If everything goes as planned, next year."

She loved hearing that he would be in Florida for a while. With a hunk like him around, things were going to be a lot more interesting on the island. "Any other travel plans?"

"Nothing scheduled, but you never know."

Gayle walked back into the room. "Arielle will be here with the cobbler in a few minutes."

Stuart slid closer to Eva. "Here, Gayle. Sit over here next to me." He laid the folder on the coffee table and opened it. "Tell us about your trip, Michael."

While Michael was entertaining everybody with details about the blizzard he hit, Gayle began to sign paper after paper. Michael did not have to sign any. If something did require his and Samantha's signatures, Gayle had power of attorney for them both.

With everyone engrossed in Michael's tales of adventure, nobody paid any attention to the General Warranty Deed Stuart placed in front of Gayle. The document wasn't the original deed to her house, but a separate legal document that once she signed it, would transfer ownership of her house over to him.

After Gayle finished signing all of the papers, Stuart shoved the documents back into the folder. "There. That's finished. Now where is that fruit cobbler?"

As if Arielle had heard Stuart, she came walking into the Florida room with a tray of desserts.

Gayle moved to a chair, while Eva was inching closer and closer to Michael, hoping nobody would notice. A growing, empty gap now separated her from Stuart.

Whenever Michael said something amusing, Eva would laugh. When he sounded serious, she grew serious. If he sat quietly, she immediately initiated another conversation with him. She would perform subtle movements, trying to entice him. At times, her head would fall back, and she would inhale deeply, expanding her ample chest.

As Michael slouched comfortably in the easy chair, her hungry eyes followed every muscle down to his ankles. At one point, when his strong, muscular legs spread further apart, and his shorts hiked up his thighs, accentuating the manly bulge between his legs, she wished so badly that she could be sitting on his lap, running her hands over his taut skin and making love to him. For the first time in ages, she felt a sexual fire burn, a natural phenomenon she thought had vanished long ago. She also felt guilty, because here Stuart was sitting next to her. Of course she loved her husband, but it wasn't a heart-pounding, passionate kind of love, the kind that brought fire and excitement with it. Sex she performed solely for the purpose of having sex. It was an annoying service she had to provide. No. She wasn't going to let the guilt get to her. After all, Stuart got what he wanted, a trophy wife, and she got whatever, whenever she wanted it. In that respect, the two of them were perfectly suited for each other.

Stuart grabbed Eva's hand. "Are you ready to go, my dear?"

"We're not leaving yet, are we? We just got here."

"It's getting late. I have a big day tomorrow."

Gayle put her cup of decaf on the table. "Eva, if Stuart doesn't mind, you should stay and visit with us a little while longer."

Eva thought staying another hour or so was a great idea. Stuart could leave, and maybe in a little while, Gayle would go to bed. Then she would have Michael all to herself. "I might just do that."

Stuart pulled Eva to her feet. "It's late. We can visit another time."

Michael stood up and headed for the door. "I think I'll go take a look at my E-mails. See you guys later."

That's all Eva had to hear. She faked a yawn. "On second thought, I am getting sleepy."

Gayle escorted her guests through the house to the front door. "I hope the two of you will come back and visit soon."

Stuart shoved Eva outside. "We will. We will."

After Gayle shut the door, Stuart slid his arm around Eva's waist. "You seemed to enjoy your conversation with Michael."

"He's a pleasant person. Don't you think?"

"For a while there, I felt jealous."

Eva stopped and wrapped her arms around Stuart's neck. "Don't be foolish, sweetie. Michael is young enough to be my son."

"That's not true, and you know it. I'm sure there is no more than fifteen years between the two of you."

"Women have babies at fifteen. Like I said, he's young enough to be my son." Eva took Stuart's hand. "Come on, sweetie. I'm feeling amorous. Let's go for a walk on the beach."

"But it's getting late."

She slid his hand down her blouse, wishing it were Michael's. "Are you sure I can't tempt you into coming with me?"

Stuart caressed the full mounds of soft flesh. "This could get interesting," he said.

"Then come on. Let's go find some cozy, little spot and make love."

"That's what I like about you. You're full of surprises."

Hand-in-hand, Eva and Stuart strolled down the winding path leading to the beach.

Eva unbuttoned her shirt and threw it onto the sand.

Stuart had never seen his wife act this way. "What are you doing? Somebody might see us."

Eva glanced up and down the beach. "Nobody is around. Now make love to me."

4

FOR THE FIFTH TIME in twenty minutes, Lorna glanced at the clock. If one o'clock weren't such an ungodly hour of the morning, she would have gotten out of bed and gone for a jog on the beach. Something had told her not to go to bed as early as she did.

Although Stuart and her mother lived in Florida, where temperatures normally soared to the eighties or nineties during the day, heavy comforters blanketed all of the beds. Stuart claimed he slept better with air conditioning, and so did she for that matter, but the constant blowing was ridiculous.

Lorna threw back the white lace duvet comforter and slid out of bed. In only a pair of blue cotton, bikini panties, she hurried to the closet for the old, plaid flannel robe that her mother insisted she throw in the trash. No way was that going to happen. The robe was the most comfortable piece of clothing she owned, and she wasn't about to part with it, whether her mother liked it or not.

With nothing else to do, she decided she would go sit outside on the balcony for a while.

The night could not have been prettier. Gentle, ocean breezes lowered the temperature and humidity from what it had been earlier in the day. The moon commanded the sky, as if giving orders to twinkling stars to shine brighter. Frogs croaked and crickets chirped, their highs and lows harmonizing in a soothing melodious duet. If God had given Mother Nature strict orders to create the most pleasant night she could, this would have been the result.

Lorna found the night so beautiful that it depressed her. Wondrous nights like this one were made for lovers. How wonderful it would have been sitting out there on the balcony with someone she was in love with and someone who truly loved her, a soul mate, the two of them holding hands and gazing up at the stars. Maybe someday, if her luck ever changed, she would meet the right man, and they would get the opportunity to share a beautiful night like this.

As she was enjoying the salty smell of the ocean, she felt a hunger pang. The growling at this hour, she supposed, was a throw-back to her college days, when she would be up all hours of the night, eating sweets and downing cup after cup of loaded coffee, while cramming for exams. She decided eating your head off was a lot more fun than eating your heart out. She got up and went back inside to make a snack.

The house was quiet with everybody else asleep. If it were not for all the bright moonlight shining through the glass wall near the staircase, she would have been forced to turn on the lights in order to see where she was going. Then someone probably would have seen the light and gotten out of bed, spoiling her peace and quiet, the last thing she wanted to happen.

The kitchen was far enough away from the bedrooms that she did not hesitate to switch on the light.

Unlike school, healthy foods filled the refrigerator shelves, especially fruits and berries. Lorna stood with the door open, contemplating what she should eat. There was a leftover grilled chicken breast on a plate covered with plastic wrap. A nice, thinly-sliced chicken sandwich with lots of mayonnaise and a dash of salt and pepper might hit the spot. That was what she decided to do, make a sandwich.

What she liked best about having a cook in the house was the daily, fresh-baked breads and pastries. She reached for a loaf of golden, honey-wheat bread.

While she was feasting on her late-night snack, she browsed through a USA TODAY she found lying on the counter.

After she cleaned up her mess, she went to the library to pick out a good book to read.

Rows and rows of the classics, hard-cover novels and paperbacks lined the library shelves, making her selection difficult.

As she was passing Stuart's eighteenth-century desk, her robe caught on a folder, knocking it to the floor. Papers went sliding across the plush, beige carpet. "That's great," she said, aggravated over her clumsiness.

While she was picking up the papers, she noticed the folder looked like the same one Stuart had taken to Gayle's house earlier in the evening. Indifferent about what information the papers contained, she attempted to stack the pages together in their proper order. While she was arranging the papers, she could not help noticing the large print on one of the documents. TRANSFERS TITLE TO STUART C. GRANT. Lorna also noticed Gayle's signature on the bottom of the paper.

Her curiosity piqued, she wondered what Gayle had signed over to Stuart. Although she felt guilty for looking, she could not help herself.

The information took her by surprise. Gayle had signed her house over to Stuart. Why? Who would want to move off a beautiful place like Sand Dollar Island? Lorna pondered the subject. Maybe she had it all wrong. Gayle was probably still going to live in the house, but Stuart was going to own it for some reason.

5

EVA'S BLACK STRAPLESS, sequin dress accentuated the curves of her voluptuous body. With her blonde hair falling in waves down to her bare shoulders and her makeup applied perfectly by a make-up artist an hour earlier, she felt ready for the world.

She glowed with excitement, loving the fact that as Stuart's new wife she was now able to attend one of Millicent's birthday parties. In the past she could not go to any family events, because Stuart was still married to Sheila.

How she hated those times when Stuart would be celebrating holidays and special occasions with the Grants, while she sat home all alone or with Lorna, furious that she could not participate in any of the festivities. Now her eyes sparkled as brightly as the sequins on her dress.

Stuart brushed a piece of lint off his tuxedo jacket. "You are amazing, Eva. You have the body of a thirty year-old."

Although her efforts to look beautiful impressed Stuart, she cared more about seeing Michael's reaction.

She slid her skirt up and put Stuart's hands on her buttocks. "It's all yours, sweetie."

His sly grin exposed his arousal. "I'm a very lucky man."

"And I'm a lucky woman. You look absolutely divine in your tuxedo."

As Stuart adjusted each ruby stud to lie perfectly against his white, pleated shirt, his eyes devoured Eva's shapely legs. "If we were just getting ready for our usual evening dinner instead of mother's party, I would throw you down on that bed and make love to you all night."

Eva humored him. "There's nothing I would enjoy more, but it's too late for that now. If I tear all of my clothes off, I'll never be able to put myself back together again."

"Perhaps we better leave then, before I lose all self-control. Are you ready, dear?"

Eva posed in front of a full-length mirror. "As ready as I'll ever be."

———

THE GRANT FAMILY went all out for Millicent's birthday parties. Year after year, they held the festivities in the landscaped gardens behind her mansion.

This year, the decorator hired to turn the gardens into a wonderland exceeded the Grants expectations.

As guests strolled from one area of the garden to another, admiring huge vases of exotic flowers, marble statues, and golden balloons, they stopped occasionally to chat with other people they knew.

Round tables covered with gold cloths dotted the lush, green lawn. Cocktail stations, each situated under a scallop-edged canopy, supplied champagne and cocktails for those wishing to drink.

While some guests wandered throughout the tent, picking at trays of hors d'oeuvres, others strolled across the wooden dance floor spanning the center of the swimming pool.

Although Eva had looked forward to the party for weeks, she purposely arrived late. She wanted to make her grand entrance. As if she were a queen and Stuart a king, they descended the terrace steps to the garden.

Her eyes darted through the crowd, searching for Michael. When she did not see him, her fantasy of him watching her come down the steps and being awed by her beauty vanished with a disappointed sigh.

Millicent stood at the bottom of the steps with John Livingstone, an old, close friend of the family's.

Stuart kissed his mother on the cheek. "Here's the party girl. Happy birthday, and may you have many, many more."

Eva also kissed Millicent on the cheek. "You look radiant. And your gown, that shade of blue looks divine on you."

"Thank you, Eva." Millicent glanced behind Eva, looking for Lorna. "Where is your lovely daughter?"

"She'll be along any minute."

Stuart slapped John Livingstone on the back. "You're looking well, my good man."

The distinguished gray-haired gentleman shook hands with Stuart and then turned to Eva. "You look stunning this evening." He reached for her hand and kissed the back of it.

Several couples were standing in a line, waiting to speak with Millicent. Stuart and Eva excused themselves and went to mingle with the other guests.

"There's Holly," Eva said. "I don't believe it. She looks just like Elizabeth Taylor."

For hours that day, a hairdresser and makeup artist had spent in Holly's bedroom, preparing her for the party. While the professionals performed their magic, they kept a watchful eye on a DVD of *A Place in the Sun* on the television. Although Elizabeth Taylor's beauty surpassed Holly's, the experts did a surprisingly good job.

The strapless dress Holly's seamstress copied from the dress Elizabeth Taylor wore in the cocktail party scene in the movie turned out exceptionally well. The bustier brimmed with miniature flowers; their tiny petals crammed so tightly together that not an ounce of fabric shown from beneath. Additional tiny flowers dotted the top layer of tulle flaring out from her waist. If Holly could have been transported back in time, she could have been Elizabeth Taylor's stand-in for the movie.

Along with Brandon Kent Holly sashayed up to Stuart. "Hello, big daddy," she said, impersonating Elizabeth Taylor in *Cat on a Hot Tin Roof.*

"I'm not gaining that much weight, am I," Stuart said.

"You don't look anything like Burl Ives. I'm just having fun." Holly spun around for Stuart. "How do I look?"

"You look absolutely gorgeous, sweetheart."

Eva made a fuss over Holly's appearance, also. "I can't get over it. You're the spitting image of Elizabeth Taylor."

"Thank you, Eva. You look pretty, also."

Stuart shook Brandon's hand. "It's good to see you, son. Are your parents here tonight?"

Brandon Kent, a decent-looking young man whose face slightly resembled Montgomery Clift's, pointed. "Yes, sir, they're across the pool talking with the Fitzgeralds."

"Good," Stuart said. "Eva and I will make sure we go over and say hello to them."

While Stuart was chatting with Holly and Brandon, Eva spotted Michael and Gayle arriving at the party. Never, not in any movies or magazines, had she seen anyone as sexy or handsome as him. His black tuxedo fit the way a tuxedo should fit a man. Although she could not see his slim, muscular body beneath the fabric, she envisioned him naked. Nobody came close to arousing her the way he did. Everything about him devastated her. Above all, she hoped they shared chemistry, because then he would want her as badly as she wanted him.

Stuart noticed Eva smiling. "You look pleased about something, my dear. May I share in your thoughts?"

She lied to him. "I was just thinking about something Lorna said to me earlier."

Stuart's eyes followed her line of vision. "I see Michael is here."

She acted nonchalant. "He is? Oh I didn't notice."

In order that her watching Michael wasn't obvious, Eva glanced over every now and then, keeping an eye on him, while he and his mother were talking with Millicent.

When he went to add his present to the others on the table, a pretty brunette around Holly's age strolled up to him. The young woman's beaming face confirmed to Eva that she had a big crush on him.

Jealousy lingered in Eva's eyes until she saw Michael walking in their direction.

He shook Stuart's hand. "How's the party going?"

"So far so good."

Michael kissed Eva on the cheek. "You look especially lovely tonight."

"Thank you. And you look handsome in your tuxedo."

Michael unbuttoned his jacket and slid his hands into his pockets. "Uncle Stuart, do you remember that IRS matter about my owing back taxes on a stock sale?"

"Yes, I remember."

"To tell you the truth, I was surprised you sent the IRS a check."

"Why were you surprised? Don't I always pay your taxes?"

"I'm not talking about my regular taxes."

"What are you talking about then?"

"The taxes on the stock sale the IRS claims I made."

"Now why in God's name would I pay taxes on some stock sale, when I know damn well you would never sell any of your stock?"

"I was wondering the same thing, but apparently you paid the IRS. You're so busy. Maybe you forgot."

"What makes you think I paid the taxes in the first place?"

"David Chernoff said he called you about it. When he discussed the matter with you, you told him you sent the IRS a check."

"I must be getting senile. I don't even remember talking to David."

"Obviously, it's a big mistake. In any event, you better contact the IRS and get your . . ." Michael didn't finish the sentence. His eyes remained fixed on the terrace. "Wow," he said. "Who is that?"

Stuart and Eva turned to see what had left Michael temporarily speechless.

"THAT, Eva said, "is my daughter."

Lorna stood alone on the top landing. In a simple, white satin slip dress, she looked like an angel that had just floated down from heaven. Her long blonde hair fell loosely down her back, and it glowed like golden strands under the moonlight. She wore no jewelry and very little makeup. When she moved, she was regal, and as she walked down the steps, she appeared to glide.

A waiter at the bottom of the stairs offered Lorna a glass of champagne. She reached for the glass and continued walking.

Michael's eyes never left her for a second.

Eva seethed, livid with Lorna for stealing her thunder. That wasn't the dress she bought her for the party. And she obviously redid her hair.

Eva attempted to draw Michael's attention away from Lorna. "Michael," she said, "Why don't we get together tomorrow morning and play tennis?"

Stuart slid his arm around Eva's waist. "That's an excellent idea. Now that Lorna is staying with us, we can play doubles."

Although Eva meant her and Michael, she could not tell Stuart that. "Terrific! What do you say, Michael?"

Michael kept watching Lorna. "Sure, why not?"

Eva persisted in trying to distract Michael. "What time do you want to play?"

"Any time you say."

As Lorna walked over to them, Michael watched her the entire time.

Eva hid her fury. "I see you finally made it."

Exasperated, Lorna smirked. "I'm happy to see you, too, mother."

Michael smiled at the retort. "Eva, aren't you going to introduce me to your lovely daughter?"

Stuart responded. "Allow me to do the honors. Michael, I would like you to meet Miss Lorna Meade."

Michael smiled, a sexy slant to his lips. "It's a pleasure to meet you, Lorna."

Lorna brushed Michael off. "Yeah, same here."

Eva wanted to break up this potential union before it ever formed. "Lorna, why don't you go wish Millicent happy birthday."

"Where is she?"

Michael took Lorna's arm. "I'll take you to her."

Lorna pulled her arm out of his hand. "That's okay, Michael. It's not like she's lost or something. I'll find her."

"Really, I don't mind."

"No, please. Stay here and enjoy yourself."

Eva forced a smile. "That's all right, Michael. Lorna is a big girl. She'll find your grandmother."

"Really, I don't mind."

Stuart intervened. "Let them go, Eva. Young people don't like to hang around with their stuffy parents all night."

Eva forced another smile, wanting to choke Stuart. "You're right, sweetie."

About to walk away, Michael saw his cousin arriving at the party. "Here comes William and Julian."

Stuart's face reddened. "I can't believe it. He had the nerve to bring that piece of trash with him."

"Take it easy, Uncle Stuart."

William and his African-American partner, Julian, strolled up to Michael, who then grabbed William and hugged him. "Long time no see, cuz."

"It has been a while."

While Michael still had William in the clinches, he whispered. "Watch out. Your dad is really pissed."

William braced himself as he turned to Stuart. "Hello, father," he said.

Stuart exploded. "Get that bastard out of here, before I get a gun and shoot you both."

In an attempt to back Stuart off, Michael threw up his hands. "Whoa, Uncle Stuart, we don't need a family fight breaking up the party. It will be in all the society columns tomorrow morning."

"Mind your own business, Michael."

"They're not bothering anyone. Let them stay and enjoy themselves."

Stuart pointed his finger in William's face. "You heard me. Get that piece of trash out of here."

Julian grabbed William's arm. "Come on, Will. It isn't worth it."

William glared at Stuart. "Someday you'll regret this."

Michael tried to console William. "Why don't you, me and Julian get together and take the boat down to Key West for a few days?"

"Just because my father is acting like a jerk, doesn't mean you have to be nice."

"This has nothing to do with your father." It did, but it didn't. "What do you say? It has been a while since we did anything together."

"When are you thinking of going?"

"How about the weekend after next?"

"That sounds okay."

"Good. I'll give you a call."

Five minutes after they arrived, William and Julian were leaving.

Michael took Lorna's arm again. "Come on. I'll take you to my grandmother."

Lorna glanced to Eva. "I guess I don't have a choice."

Michael waited until they were far enough away from Stuart before he spoke. "I apologize for my uncle."

"Don't worry about me. I feel as badly as you do. I think it's terrible that Stuart wouldn't let William and Julian stay for the party. They deserve to have a good time like everybody else." Lorna slid the strap of her dress that had fallen down her arm back onto her shoulder. "I'm really surprised at your Uncle Stuart. I've never seen him that angry."

"He only gets that way around William. I think William's gayness makes him feel weak."

"I didn't notice any arguments at my mother and Stuart's wedding."

"Did William have Julian with him?"

"No."

"That helped." He let go of Lorna's arm. "Maybe your mother warned Uncle Stuart to behave."

Lorna studied Michael. "I can't get over how much you and William look alike."

"That's what everybody tells us."

———

MICHAEL FOUND MILLICENT sitting at a table with John Livingstone, Stuart's sister Margot, and Margot's husband Ted. Next to Ted sat Gayle and after Gayle sat his sister Samantha. Across from Samantha sat her husband Tom, who was holding their young daughter Hillary.

When Hillary, a beautiful child with striking blue eyes and long, dark curls, saw Michael approaching the table, she jumped off her father's lap and went running over to him, her frilly, pink satin and lace dress making a swishing sound as she ran.

"Unkie Mikey," she said, her arms stretched out wide, wanting to be held.

Michael scooped the child up in his arms. "Hey big girl, how've you been? Were you a good little girl while I was gone?"

Hillary never stopped smiling. "Yep, ask mommy."

"I'll do that." Michael bent over his sister and kissed her on the cheek. "Hi, Sam, Hillary tells me she's been a good, little girl while I was gone. Is that true?"

Like any other mother who has to chase after a toddler all day long, Samantha rolled her eyes. "She's been a perfect angel." Samantha reached for Hillary and gave her a big hug.

Michael pulled one of Hillary's curls. "Then I guess she gets the present I brought back for her."

"Yaayyy," Hillary said, clapping her hands happily.

Michael had not seen his Aunt Margot and Uncle Ted for almost a year. Aware of Margot's impeccable manners and snobbish attitude, he felt compelled to go over and say hello to them.

In the meantime, Lorna bent over Millicent and kissed her on the cheek. "Happy Birthday, Mrs. Grant."

"Lorna, dear, how nice to see you! Here. Come sit with us."

Michael interceded. "In a few minutes, grandmother."

"Ah hah," Millicent said, a sly twinkle in her eyes.

He winked at his grandmother as he took Lorna's arm.

"Would you like to dance," he asked.

"Not right now, Michael. But thanks."

Millicent overheard them. "What? You two get out on that dance floor right now."

Placed in a precarious situation, Lorna had no choice but to dance with Michael.

As he led her towards the dance floor, a man with a smooth, mellow voice sang into the microphone. "You stepped out of a dream. . ."

Michael slid his arm around Lorna's waist, and the two of them began to glide across the floor.

Eva watched them from her table. She gulped down the remainder of her champagne, furious with Lorna for defying her by dancing with Michael. Every now and then, Michael would look down at Lorna and obviously say something witty, because the two would laugh. Then he would pull her close to him again, and she would go back to resting her forehead against his chin, as if she had done it hundreds of times in the past. Eva fumed. What could Michael possibly see in Lorna? She would show him. She was going to get him out on that dance floor and let him experience what it felt like to be with a real woman.

Stuart nudged Eva, interrupting her state of reverie. "Come, darling. It's time for the toast."

Eva felt like strangling Stuart. That, she decided, she would save for later.

Stuart motioned for the singer to wait a moment before he started singing again.

A glass of champagne in one hand and the microphone in the other, Stuart quieted the crowd. "Good Evening, everybody. I'm pleased that all of you could make it here tonight on this festive occasion. As most of you know, every year I present my mother with a special gift." He directed his attention to Millicent. "Since you like traveling so much, mother, especially with the female members of the family, this year I'm sending all of the Grant women on a Mediterranean cruise."

The crowd cheered and broke out in applause.

Stuart continued. "Would you please raise your glass in a toast to a very special lady." He waited until everyone held his glass in the air. "Here's to you, mother. May you have many years of health and joy. We love you. Happy birthday!"

Millicent beamed with happiness.

The orchestra struck up a rousing rendition of happy birthday. While everyone sang along, two waiters wheeled out a four-tiered cake decorated with orchids and other edible, colorful flowers.

As Millicent blew out the candles, the island erupted in fireworks.

Although Eva enjoyed watching the spectacular display, she hoped the fireworks would soon end. Like a teenager attending her first party, she itched to dance with the most popular boy there.

After the earsplitting noise subsided, the music started playing again.

While some guests ate, others danced.

Eva had to do something to keep Stuart occupied. "You are the host of this party, sweetie. You should dance with your mother."

"That's one of the things I love about you, my dear. You're always thinking of others."

Eva waited until Stuart escorted Millicent to the dance floor before she went for Michael.

Her heart pounding, she tapped him on the shoulder. "Come dance with your Aunt Eva."

Michael glanced at Lorna and shrugged his shoulders.

As Time Goes By had just ended and *Moon River* began.

As Eva and Michael strolled onto the dance floor, Stuart and Millicent walked off it.

Eva waved to Stuart, who glared back at her.

Unlike the way Michael had held Lorna, he kept his distance from Eva.

She kept pulling him closer and closer until her breasts lay flat against his chest. "You act like you're afraid of me," she said. "I'm not going to bite you."

He went to say something, but she interrupted him. "Shhhh, this is one of my favorite songs."

For what little time she had with Michael, she wanted to savor every moment with and every thing about him. Without his noticing, she inhaled deeply. The clean, subtle scent of his cologne sent her reeling. Ever so slightly, she inched her hand up to his collar, where she left it brushing against his hair. How she ached to run her fingers through that hair, to grab his face in her hands and kiss those full, moist lips.

As they moved about on the dance floor, Eva etched in her mind the feel of Michael's hand, the strength of his grip and the warmth of his skin, all smooth and taut, not mushy like Stuart's.

When the song ended, Eva wanted to dance again. "Another one, Michael?"

"That's enough for me. I don't want Uncle Stuart to think I'm moving in on his territory."

In case she might not get a chance to dance with him later, Eva wanted to take the smell of his cologne with her. She pinched his cheeks. "You're a baby doll. Do you know that?"

Eva never did get another chance to dance with Michael. Stuart never let her out of his sight the rest of the night. Now the party was over, and Michael was gone. But she would be seeing him in the morning when they all got together for the tennis match. In the meantime, she figured she better be nice to Stuart. She took his hand. "Come on. I have a treat in store for you tonight."

———

IN THE SOFT GLOW of candlelight Eva helped Stuart undress. After guiding him to the bed, she propped pillows under his head. While he lay on the bed watching her, she unzipped her dress and let it slide to the floor. As if she were an exotic dancer, she lifted her hair off her neck and began to move sensuously around the room. Slowly, her hips swayed to soft jazz playing on the radio. She was on fire from being close to Michael. She ran her fingers over her open lips to get a whiff of his cologne. The scent aroused the passion inside her. In her high-heel sandals she swayed back and forth, allowing Stuart's hungry eyes to devour her body.

"You're beautiful," he said. "Come here."

Eva slinked over to the bed.

While Stuart fondled her breasts, she imagined Michael's hands caressing them. With her eyes closed she envisioned Michael's virile, naked body lying on the bed.

Stuart pulled Eva on top of him. "What has gotten into you tonight?"

Without opening her eyes, she murmured. "Don't talk. Make love to me."

Her fantasies of Michael continued. She envisioned his gorgeous face, his hard muscles and hairy chest. She fantasized about his tongue and hands all over her body.

As Stuart penetrated her, she slid her fingers into her mouth. The faster he pumped, the harder she sucked. Within minutes, she moaned in ecstasy.

Stuart rolled off her. "You're turning into a real sex kitten. First it's making love on the beach, and now you're dancing for me."

"Is that good or bad?"

"Are you kidding? It's wonderful."

"I'm glad you like it. Now get to sleep."

Eva turned away from Stuart, basking in the glow of orgasm. It may have been Michael making love to her in her mind, but it was only a matter of time before he would be making love to her in the flesh.

6

MICHAEL OBSERVED THE DARK, brooding clouds drifting over the island. After leaving the house to go running this morning, it started raining, not a serious downpour, but enough to wet him and the ground. Now the rain had stopped, but from the look of the sky, a thunderstorm threatened to strike at any moment.

He pushed onward close to the water's edge, his body moving like a greased machine.

The five-mile run he finished in forty minutes, not his best time ever, but pretty good just the same. He attributed the slower pace to the soft sand and high humidity.

For a few minutes more he kept walking until his heart rate returned to normal. Then he ripped off his shoes and socks and dove into the surf.

The cool water hit him like a brick wall. For a while he floated on the surface, allowing the refreshing shroud to lower his body temperature. Like a human cross he looked with his legs together and arms stretched out at his sides.

As he gazed up at the sky, he surmised the storm had passed over for the time being. Patches of blue appeared between lighter, fluffier clouds.

Like the clouds drifting across the sky, Michael's mind drifted back to the previous night's party. Ever since he danced with Lorna, he could not get her out of his mind. It felt so right when he held her, as though they belonged together. Was it possible to have such powerful feelings in such a short amount of time? He pondered the subject. Unlike his cousin, Holly, he liked knowing Lorna planned to spend the summer on the island, and he looked forward to getting to know her better.

Michael glanced at his dive watch. It was almost nine, time to play tennis. Refreshed and ready for more physical activity, he trudged through the water and up the beach to an outdoor shower, where he rinsed salt and sand from his hair and body.

From the beach he followed the path to the paved road, took the shortcut around the swimming pool and then strolled through the formal gardens which helped conceal the tennis courts.

Stuart, Eva and Lorna had not yet arrived. Michael went to a wooden bin alongside the fence to get a tennis racket. Although he hadn't played in months, he felt at home on the court. As he swung the racket, loosening his arm, voices broke the silence of the still morning.

Eva strutted onto the court in what Michael considered the sexiest tennis outfit he had ever seen. Both the white skin-tight top baring half of her breasts and the white skimpy shorts that hiked up her crack stunned him. And when he spotted all of her jewelry, he almost commented on how she came off as an eager amateur. Nobody he knew ever wore a truckload of diamonds to play tennis.

Lorna did not fit the norm either. But her laid-back look, an oversized white T-shirt and blue shorts, appealed to him. No makeup plastered her face like Eva's, and with her hair pulled back in a ponytail, she looked like a little girl about to play with the grownups. He sensed she couldn't have cared less about what any of them thought of her appearance.

Michael reached into the bin and grabbed a tube of neon-green tennis balls. "Good morning," he said cheerfully to no one in particular.

Eva's face beamed. "Good morning, Michael."

Stuart rummaged through the bin for three more rackets. "How long have you been up," he asked. "We just crawled out of bed."

"You just crawled out of bed," Eva said. "I've been up for hours."

"And it shows, my dear. You look like a breath of fresh air."

Michael bounced a ball on the ground with his racket. "I just got finished running the beach."

Still half asleep, Lorna slumped to a bench next to the bin. "How far did you run?"

"Five miles."

"Five miles? Boy! You can wrack a person's nerves."

He laughed. "What's the matter? You're not awake yet?"

"No."

"A game of tennis will fix that."

"That's what I was hoping to avoid."

Eva may have taken a lot of time to get ready, but her primping had no effect on Michael. His attention remained on Lorna. "Is everybody ready," he asked.

Eva rushed to his side. "I am. Come on, Michael, you and I will be partners."

Stuart took a practice swing. "No, no, my dear. You and me against Lorna and Michael."

"Don't you think it would be better if we mixed things up a bit?"

Stuart nudged her down the court. "It will be more fun, the two of us against them."

Her hopeful smile faded. "If you say so."

"That's better. Now let's kick their butts."

Relieved that Stuart insisted on Eva being his partner, Michael bent down and whispered in Lorna's ear. "This is going to be a massacre."

She dragged herself off the bench. "For whom, them or us?"

He winked. "Them."

"You better be really good then, because I don't even know how to play tennis."

"Don't worry. Stuart has yet to beat me."

As the set got underway, Michael played for both him and Lorna. Every time he served or volleyed, he nailed the ball.

"Wow," Lorna said. "You really are good."

The game continued, Michael tearing from side to side, forward and backwards. Lorna did her best to return the ball when it came in her direction. Even her faltering had no effect on their winning. Michael had racked up enough points to keep them way ahead of Stuart and Eva.

After the match ended, Stuart and Eva strolled over to the water fountain.

Michael grabbed one of the towels Eva had brought with her. "Lorna," he said. "Do you want me to help you with your serve?"

"Sure. I need all the help I can get."

He took her arm and showed her how to swing.

Eva watched them. "All right, you two. It's time for another game. Come on, Michael. You and I will be partners this time."

Stuart reached for her hand. "No you won't, my dear. We have to get back at them, don't we?"

"Okay, but I still think it would be better if we mixed things up a bit."

The four went back out on the court.

Again, Michael racked up points in his and Lorna's favor.

After losing another set, Stuart quit. "That's enough for me."

Lorna handed Michael her racket. "From now on I want you for a partner. Darn, you're good."

"You really are," Eva said. "Maybe when you're not too busy, you can give me lessons."

Stuart tossed his racket into the bin. "He's good, Eva, but he's no expert. If you really want to learn how to play tennis correctly, we'll hire a pro to teach you."

"In the meantime, maybe Michael can give me a few lessons."

Stuart grabbed her racket and tossed it into the bin. "If you're in that big a hurry, then we'll look for someone this afternoon."

"No, no, sweetie. You're busy enough. I don't want to bother you."

Michael hated being placed in the middle. He quickly changed the subject. "Uncle Stuart, what ever happened with that big business deal you were working on?"

"Why do you keep asking? You've never been interested in company business before."

The sarcastic response surprised Michael. "That's not true."

"It most certainly is true. You're always too damn busy running off to some god-forsaken country to do your stupid mountain climbing."

Michael slammed the bin shut. "It sounds to me like you're evading the subject."

"And it sounds to me like you don't trust me anymore."

Lorna intervened. "I think I'll head back to the house. What about you, Michael?"

"Yes, I'm getting hungry."

As Michael walked off the court, he glanced back at Stuart. Why did his uncle act that way with him? Something definitely was not right.

7

MICHAEL PILOTED the seaplane to a smooth landing. For a while the intracoastal waterway's choppy surface gave him a bumpy ride, but once he stabilized the aircraft, it glided right up to the marina.

Two pelicans protested the noisy intrusion by suddenly taking flight. No sooner did they leave their perches than a couple of excited seagulls swooped down to claim ownership of the weatherworn tree stumps sticking up out of the water.

Earlier that day, David Chernoff had phoned Michael, informing him that he had important information concerning the stock sale. Michael suggested they meet for lunch at *Captain Jacks*, one of his favorite restaurants.

One of the oldest waterfront eateries in the State of Florida, the place had nostalgic charm. Every time Michael went there he enjoyed studying the old photographs that depicted life in Florida before big hotels and air conditioning.

The restaurant's lounge had a nautical feeling with fishnets, anchors and buoys decorating the walls. Outside, just beyond the lounge, was a thatched-roof chickee bar that overlooked Lake Worth. Michael found sitting outdoors more fun, because unlike stuffy, gourmet restaurants, the chickee bar attracted colorful people—old salts, artists and writers. Blue-collar workers, business people and tourists went there as well, but they weren't nearly as much fun to watch.

David had arrived first. He extended his hand out to shake Michael's. "You really know how to arrive in style."

Michael laughed. "Flying beats driving I-95."

Before the men entered into a serious conversation, they waited until the waitress took their order.

As soon as the young woman left, David's demeanor changed from jovial to serious. "I know I'll be dropping a bomb on you, but there's no delicate way of putting it, so I'll just give it to you straight."

Michael squirmed. "I don't like the sound of this. What's wrong?"

"I just found out that your Uncle Stuart transferred some of your family's stock over to himself."

"I don't know if I heard right. Run that by me again."

"Your Uncle Stuart transferred some of your side of the family's stock over to himself."

The news dumbfounded Michael. "Are you telling me my uncle stole our stock?"

"Yes. Apparently, it has been going on for some time."

"I don't believe it. It's impossible."

"You look pale, Michael. Are you all right?"

"I guess so. You just threw me for a loop."

"Here. Drink some water."

Michael gulped down half of the water. "This can't be real."

"It's real all right."

"How much did he take?"

"Are you sure you're okay? You still look shaky."

"How much, David?"

"Forty-three percent."

Michael's back slammed against the booth. "You can't be serious."

"I've never been more serious."

"If what you're saying is true, then that means we only have seven percent of the stock left."

"Correct."

"Are you sure about this?"

"Positive. When was the last time you looked at the books?"

"I never look at the books. I never felt I had a reason to look." Michael's leg bounced nervously. "Do you have any proof?"

"It's all right here." David slid a folder across the table.

Michael glanced through the contents. "Where did you get all of this information?"

"It started with the phone call to Don Grayson about e-mailing me copies of your past five income tax returns."

"Are the returns in here?"

"No. Don said he couldn't e-mail me anything without Stuart's permission."

Michael understood now why he had been experiencing that anxious feeling in his stomach. "What did you say to Don after that?"

"I'll tell you, Michael. It really struck me as odd, my being your attorney and all, that Don wouldn't e-mail me the returns. Even after I told him about the letter you got from the IRS and how you wanted me to check into the matter for you, he still wouldn't e-mail me the returns."

"And?"

"Instead of e-mailing me the returns, he told me to e-mail him a copy of the IRS letter."

The waitress arrived with their grilled grouper sandwiches. David waited until she left and then continued. "I explained that I needed to see your returns, but Don kept fighting me. He said income tax returns were his job, that he would check it out himself and get back to me."

"What's wrong with that?"

"I don't know. I didn't like his reaction. It sounded to me like he was trying to hide something. Anyone else would have e-mailed the returns with no problem. Heck! Don knows me. What's the big secret?"

"If Don didn't help you out, then where did you get all of this information?"

"The court house and the IRS."

"I don't get it. If Stuart has ninety-three percent of the stock, why aren't me, my mother and sister broke?"

"You told me a long time ago that your uncle takes care of everything, that he runs the company and oversees the preparation of income tax returns."

"And he gives everyone an allowance." Michael shoved his plate of food aside. "Ever since I can remember, he has controlled the family's purse strings."

"What you did was make things easy for him."

Not only did Michael feel betrayed, he felt like a fool. "All of these years we trusted my uncle. Boy, were we ever stupid!" Michael's leg kept bouncing. "There's something I don't understand, David."

"What's that?"

"If my uncle stole most of our stock, then why is he still giving us money?"

"That's another thing I have to talk to you about."

"Now what? Enough is enough."

"While Stuart has been living off company profits, the money he has been giving you, your mother and sister came from equity liquidation. Do you understand what I mean by equity liquidation?"

"Kind of."

David flipped through the folder, looking for a stack of papers he clipped together before he came to lunch. "Here. Take a look at these." David laid the stack in front of Michael. "For the past five years, Stuart has been buying up your stock. The money he has been giving you, your mother and sister, as so-called allowances, is actually payment for the stock he took. If you notice here, each check he wrote has gone against a stock purchase."

"With only seven percent of the stock left, that means we're almost broke."

"It also means Stuart is the majority stock holder, and he can do whatever he wants with the company. None of you can stop him."

Michael stared into space, the turmoil inside him ripping his stomach apart. All of his life he thought Stuart was the greatest, most generous person in the world. To find out now that he was so underhanded devastated him. "This is a nightmare, David."

"What are you going to do?"

"Go see Stuart and demand that he return our stock."

"What if he refuses?"

"He has no choice. He has to give the stock back."

"Why?"

"Legally, he only owns fifty percent of the stock. These so-called transfers he has been making are pure stealing."

"Can you prove it in court? If not, it's your word against his."

"That's where I have him. You see, right before my grandfather died, he made Stuart and my father sign an agreement, requiring both of them to take care of the other's family if and when one of them died and keep the company stock split fifty/fifty."

"Maybe you'll come out of this okay then. Do you know if anyone witnessed the document?"

"My grandmother and my grandfather's attorney did."

"Who was your grandfather's attorney?"

"A guy named Charles Lerner."

"I don't know him. Do you have a copy of the document?"

"My mother does."

"If that agreement is legally binding, then you have a good chance of winning a lawsuit."

While David ate, Michael tried to process the information his attorney just presented. Anxious to leave, he fidgeted. He had lunched with David before, but he never realized how slowly David ate until now. His fingers tapped the table, waiting for what seemed like an eternity until David swallowed his last French fry.

Michael said. "I hope you don't want dessert. I'm anxious to get out of here."

"Go ahead. I understand. And don't worry about the check. I'll take care of it."

Michael hurried to the plane.

———

BEFORE MICHAEL WENT RUSHING to Stuart's office and blasting him about stealing the stock, he decided he would go home first and look for his mother's copy of the agreement. If she had not been on the birthday cruise with his grandmother, he would have phoned her and had the agreement waiting for him.

The flight went quickly, and in no time he was back at home.

As he passed the kitchen, he made a U-turn and headed for the bottle of aspirins his mother kept in the cupboard next to the coffee mugs. After downing three tablets with a glass of water, hoping his headache would soon leave, he hurried to the den.

Ever since he could remember, his mother kept her important papers in a fireproof file cabinet next to the desk, loosely and in no particular order.

For the next hour, Michael sat at the desk going through each and every paper. He would take out a handful, glance through them and then return the stack to the cabinet.

As he slammed the middle drawer shut, Ruby, the maid, interrupted him.

"Michael, your cousin, William, and his friend are here to see you."

"They are? Send them in, Ruby."

While he was waiting, Michael rummaged through the bottom drawer. All he found were a box of stationery, unused envelopes and about ten papers. No agreement.

William and Julian strolled into the den, both of them dressed in shorts and T-shirts.

Although Michael preferred having company when he wasn't so hassled, he enjoyed seeing them. "This is a nice surprise. What brings you guys here?"

William slid onto the white leather sofa. "We were passing the island on our way to South Beach, so we thought we would stop in and thank you for sticking up for us at the party."

"No problem. I know how your father gets."

"This is going to sound awful, Michael, but I despise that man."

Michael couldn't blame his cousin. As soon as Stuart learned about William's homosexuality, he threw him out of the house and cut off his money supply. If it weren't for his grandmother's help, William would have been living in the streets. Lately, though, William's life had changed for the better. A little over two years ago, he and Julian opened an interior decorating business, William Grant Interiors. The last Michael knew the business had acquired a string of wealthy clients.

William crossed his arms over his chest. "Someday, it's all going to blow up in my father's face."

Michael responded. "I agree."

"What's this? I never heard you talk negatively about my father."

"That's because I never did."

"Did something happen between you the two of you?"

Michael preferred not to get into it. He had more important things on his mind. "Do you remember that agreement our dads signed the day granddad died?"

"You mean the one about them taking care of each other's family and some other bullshit like that?"

"Yes. I need a copy of that agreement to prove we still own fifty percent of the stock."

"Who do you have to prove it to?"

"David Chernoff wants to take a look at it."

"Why?"

"While I was out of the country, I got a letter from the IRS. They claim I owed back taxes on ten million dollars of income. And the only way I could have had that much income was from selling my stock."

"Wow! How do you know a copy of the agreement actually exists? Maybe it was an oral agreement."

"It was both written and oral. My dad had a copy, but I can't seem to find it anywhere."

"Maybe your mother put it in the safe or a safety deposit box."

"I thought of that."

Julian sat on the sofa next to William. "Is that the only copy there is?"

"No. There should be at least four or five copies floating around."

"So what then if you can't find your mother's copy? Borrow somebody else's."

"With my grandmother, aunt and my mother on the cruise, it's not going to be that easy. I need to get my hands on a copy now."

William had an idea. "Call granddad's attorney."

"Didn't Charles Lerner die a long time ago?"

"Jeez! How did you remember his name?"

"I didn't really. When I got the call from David, I discussed the agreement with grandmother."

"Is Lerner's firm still in business?"

"I don't know." Michael pulled out a desk drawer and reached for the yellow pages. "Let's see if he's listed in the phone book." It took him a minute to search through the names. "No Charles Lerner anywhere."

"Maybe he wasn't a partner of the firm, and that's why he isn't listed."

"If he's still alive and practicing, I'm sure he would be listed individually."

"Then forget it. Ask my dad for his copy or call Uncle Ted."

"Your father would be the last person I ask."

"Something did happen between you two, didn't it?"

Michael didn't answer.

"You don't think my father had something to do with the stock sale, do you?" William scoffed. "I wouldn't put it past him."

Michael put the phone book back in the drawer. "I'll call Uncle Ted after he gets home from work tonight. If he can't find Aunt Margot's copy, I'm flying to Europe tomorrow."

Julian gaped at Michael. "Why would you go through all of that trouble? Wouldn't it be easier to call your mother on the boat?"

"You have no idea how important that document is."

William said. "I know you too well, Mike. If you need the agreement that badly, something big must be going down. Was anything else in the agreement?"

"Granddad made our fathers promise to keep the stock in Grant Office Supplies split evenly."

"And you think my dad has been taking your stock?"

"Yes."

"Son of a bitch!"

Julian leaned forward, resting his elbows on his legs. "How do you know what country the women will be in?"

"I have their itinerary."

"Like I said, why don't you call the boat?"

"For someone else to fly to Europe, it would be a big deal. It isn't for me. I'll sleep during the flight, spend a day or two resting on the yacht and then fly back to the states. Besides, I'd rather go through the hassle of flying over there and talking with my mother in person, than not having her understand something I said on the phone, and she suffers another heart attack."

———

TED DITHRIDGE HAD what society referred to as old money. His great grandfather, Theodore J. Dithridge, was one of the leading pioneers in pharmaceutical drug manufacturing. Over the years, the company and its profits grew, providing Theodore's heirs with a fortune.

When Ted and Margot married, they moved into a mansion on the beach. A man with more prestige than Stuart, Ted preferred to set up housekeeping in Palm Beach rather than on Sand Dollar Island.

The Dithridge House, a sprawling structure with three separate levels, had fourteen bedrooms, each with sliding glass doors leading to balconies facing the ocean. Eighteen luxurious marble baths, a tropical courtyard with lush foliage, a custom-designed Olympic size swimming pool, a spa, a tennis court and maids quarters added to Dithridge Estates elegance.

As Ted climbed the staircase, he could not dismiss the fact that the arthritis in his knees had worsened. If the disease progressed any further, he may have to install an elevator or move his bedroom to the first floor.

Ted stopped on the top landing to catch his breath. Angry with himself for not watching his diet more closely, he feared climbing the steps might eventually kill him.

He trudged down the hallway to the master bedroom he shared with Margot.

His joints aching, he sat on the bed for a moment while he gazed out at the sea.

After he regained his strength, he went to a dresser mirror and pressed a button behind its ornate frame. On metal tracks the mirror rose until it sat above a built-in safe.

Ted fumbled with the combination until the lock clicked open.

The safe contained stacks of money, wills, insurance policies, deeds and pieces of Margot's expensive, fine jewelry.

In less than ten minutes, Ted had gone through thirty documents. The agreement was not in the safe. He scratched his beard, doubting Margot had taken the document out for some reason. Perplexed, he went to the phone to call Michael.

While he was waiting for Michael to anser, he unhooked his belt and unbuttoned the pants digging into his stomach.

"Michael," he said, "it's Uncle Ted."

"Thanks for calling back. Did you find a copy of the agreement?"

"No, I didn't. Margot must have taken it out and put it somewhere else. I'm sorry, Michael. I have no idea where her copy might be."

"Damn it."

"The women will be back in two weeks. Can't you wait until they get back?"

"No. Thanks anyway."

8

MICHAEL THREW BACK THE BLANKET from the bed in his private mini-suite in the business class of the Virgin Atlantic plane he was taking to Italy. The cabin lights had just come on, waking him from a sound sleep. His eyes burned, his back ached, and the wine he had consumed with dinner when it was served to him after takeoff had left a sour taste in his mouth. No matter how many times he flew, he never got used to sleeping on planes.

The sun had just come up and he was anxious to feast his eyes on the view outside his window. The Alps provided a spectacular sight he did not want to miss.

Unlike mountain ranges of the United States, the monstrous Alps stretched as far as the eye could see. Dark, almost black, their snow-capped peaks pierced motionless clouds. Some of the jagged peaks appeared frighteningly close, as if the plane were barely clearing them. Michael pondered over what might happen, if they unexpectedly hit a freak downdraft.

The remainder of the flight went smoothly and in no time, he found himself disembarking the plane and hopping into a helicopter the yacht's captain had sent to fetch him.

From what he recalled, the Amalfie Coast just south of Naples had some of the most breathtaking scenery in all of Italy. Quaint towns and villages sat atop huge cliffs overlooking the Mediterranean Sea. Michael had driven the coast, but he had never flown over it.

The ride proved adventurous, the helicopter swooping down by jagged cliffs and then shooting over large boulders rising up out of the sea.

From the high altitude, the water resembled a giant mosaic, the various shades of blue forming what looked like an enormous oil painting.

Poised above the horizon, the sun blazed brilliantly. Wispy clouds, some a mere puff and others elongated with various shades of white, left dark, shadowy outlines on the surface of the sea.

The pilot pointed to a white, cigar-shaped object floating on the water's surface. Michael gave him a thumbs-up, indicating he saw the *La Dolce Vita.*

The helicopter zoomed down to the yacht, where it hovered at times and then charged forward and backwards until it landed safely on the top deck.

Michael jumped out of the aircraft, his overnight bag hanging from his shoulder. About to go see the captain concerning his sleeping quarters, he spotted Lorna lounging in the sun several decks below.

The sight of her in a bikini jolted his senses. Her long bronze legs, one stretched out in front of her and the other slightly bent, her ample breasts bulging out of her neon-pink top, and her sun-kissed hair surrounding her gorgeous face, pleased him immensely.

Her eyes were closed, allowing him the opportunity to sneak over and surprise her. "Enjoying the sun," he asked with an eager smile on his face.

Lorna jumped at the sound of a man's voice. "Michael. What in the world are you doing here?"

"I came to see my mother about something."

"I hope it's not an emergency."

"Not a medical one."

She glanced up to the top deck. "Was that you arriving on the helicopter?"

"Yes."

"I'll be darned. A little while ago, I saw the helicopter leave, never dreaming you would be returning with it." She grabbed her hair and loosely tied it into a knot.

While her head was turned, Michael checked out her body. She had smooth, flawless skin like golden satin. He fought an urge to touch it. "Where is everyone?"

"They're on Capri shopping and having lunch."

"What about you? You don't like to shop?"

"Shopping isn't my bag."

He laughed. "Very funny! I hope all of your jokes aren't that lame."

"Most of them are, sorry to say."

"Have you been doing any sightseeing?"

"Some."

"Don't you like to travel?"

"To tell you the truth, if Stuart hadn't insisted on my joining the women on this cruise, I would be on Sand Dollar Island, basking in the sun and wallowing in the peace and quiet." Lorna shielded the glaring sun with her hand. "Did your mother know you were coming?"

"No. It was a spur of the moment thing." He reached inside his bag for a bottle of water. "Other than sunning, what else have you been doing?"

"Lots of swimming. The Mediterranean is beautiful."

"How long have you been anchored off Capri?"

"Since early this morning."

"Has anyone taken you to see the Grotta Azzurra yet?"

"The what? Shoot that by me again."

"The Grotta Azzurra, the Blue Grotto. It's a cave not too far from here."

"No. Nobody even mentioned it to me."

"You should go see it."

"Why? What's so special about this cave?"

"Some of the most gorgeous water you'll ever see is inside it."

"Where is this Blue Grotto?"

He pointed. "Around that bend in the side of the cliff." Michael gulped down some water. "Since my mother won't be back for a while, why don't we go see it?"

"I don't think so."

"Why not? You'll never see anything like it again. Besides, who knows when you might be back in Europe?"

"I better not."

"You said you liked to swim, didn't you?"

"I love to swim."

"Picture this, the clearest, most beautiful, glowing aqua-marine colored water you can imagine, and you're the only one in it."

"You make it sound like something you would see in a travel brochure."

"It is in travel brochures. Come on. Come with me to go see it."

"I don't know. My mother expects me to be where she can find me."

"Your mother won't be back for hours." Michael laid the empty bottle on a teak table. "Look. You're in Europe, and the yacht is anchored off the Isle of Capri. You should take advantage of doing something unique and exciting while you're here. I'm telling you, this will be the most spectacular thing you do on this trip."

"Well . . . this is the first time I've been to Europe. Maybe I should go see the grotto. Okay. You sold me. But, aren't you exhausted from traveling?"

"I have a little jetlag, but I'll be okay."

"In that case, let's go."

———

LORNA SLID INTO her sandals and grabbed a towel. While she was waiting for Michael to change into his swimsuit, she leaned against the railing, admiring the yachts anchored off Capri.

As she turned to scan the hotels and houses perched high up on the cliff, she noticed Michael heading her way. When he strolled up to her, checking out her breasts, she felt like backing out of their planned excursion. She turned away and sighed. He probably couldn't wait to get her all alone in some dark cave. Maybe she should forget the whole thing.

Her mother's furious face flashed in Lorna's mind. A major war had started over her dancing with Michael at the party. If that was a war, then all hell was going to break loose, if and when her mother ever found out about her going to see the Blue Grotto with him. The result would be their not speaking, and that would put a damper on the rest of the trip. Was it worth the aggravation? She doubted it.

Michael stepped down into the dinghy. "Give me your hand."

Lorna decided she would go. She was a big girl. If he came on to her, she could handle the situation. "This better be good, Michael."

He started the engine. "It's going to be more of an adventure than you think."

"Now you tell me. Why?"

"You'll see."

"What did I get myself into? You're not going to get me killed, are you?"

"Let's hope not," he teased.

The boat ride alone frightened Lorna, the raft skimming over the waves and then slamming back to the water's surface. Afraid that she might fly out and land in the sea, she clung to the safety rope circling the boat.

While Michael maneuvered the dinghy around a rocky inlet, she watched intently. Nothing seemed to faze him. His courage and daring impressed her.

At that moment it dawned on her that Michael and his mother might be moving off Sand Dollar Island. A few times during the trip she meant to ask Gayle about it, but for one reason or another something always distracted her. About to question him about their moving, he pointed to shore.

"There's the cave," he said.

"Are you crazy, Michael? All I see is a rugged cliff."

"That little opening over there between those two rocks?"

"I must be blind. I don't see any opening."

"Wait until the current goes out and you'll be able to see it."

Her eyes remained fixed on the rocks until she saw the opening. "That little hole?"

"Yes."

"Listen, Michael. I didn't get a Ph.D. so I could go around the world discovering new ways to kill myself." The thought struck her funny, and she burst out laughing. "This better be good."

"Don't worry. You won't be disappointed."

When the dinghy got close to the cave, Michael switched off the engine. "Lay down in the boat."

"Why?"

"I don't want you to hit your head on the rocks."

She thought she better do as he said. That hole looked barely big enough for the dinghy, let alone them. Her heart pounded as she scooted down on her back.

Getting the raft inside the cave required tricky maneuvering. As a wave rolled towards shore, a swell of water filled up the opening, making it impossible for them to enter. Michael waited until the swell went back out to sea before he made his first attempt.

He grabbed a guide rope running from the outside of the cave to the inside. As soon as the opening widened, he pulled hard, hand-over-hand, faster and faster, until they were safely inside.

The sudden darkness frightened Lorna. As she lay in the middle of the boat, gazing up at the jagged ceiling, she expected Dracula or some other menacing creature to jump out at her. There could be sleeping bats hanging upside down. If something awakened the bats, what might she and Michael do? The mere thought of swarming, fang-toothed, flying rats swooping down at her and getting tangled up in her hair, gave her chills.

"You're right, Michael. This certainly is an adventure."

"You can get up now."

Lorna sat up to the most awesome sight she had ever seen. The color of the water seemed to glow an astonishing translucent shade of aqua. It was as if God had created the most beautiful water he could, and then he took a huge light bulb and placed it underneath the water to test its clarity.

"This is unbelievable. You were right, Michael. I have never seen anything like it. What is making the water glow like that?"

"It's a natural phenomenon. Somehow sunlight gets under the cave and lights up the water from underneath."

"But the blue is so alive, so vibrant."

"That's why they call the cave the Blue Grotto."

"How deep is the water?"

"Around Sixty feet. Do you want to go for a swim?"

"I would love to, but I'm afraid. What if there are some bad currents, like the kind that almost drowned my mother?"

"Don't worry. There aren't any currents. The sides of the cave block them."

"What about sharks or snakes?"

"Look how clear the water is. Do you see anything down there?"

"No. What about an octopus or eel? Maybe something is hiding in the rocks and it will come out when it sees us in the water?"

"There's nothing down there."

Hesitant about going in alone, in case anything should happen, Lorna wanted Michael in the water with her. "I'll go in if you do."

"I can't wait to go in."

"You're sure it's safe."

"I'm positive, Lorna. Look. If you don't want to go in, I'm not going to force you. But take my word for it. If you don't go in, you'll be passing up an opportunity of a lifetime."

"No, no. I'm going in. But you have to go in first."

"Okay, but I should warn you."

"Here it comes. I knew it was too good to be true."

"It's nothing dangerous."

"Then what's wrong?"

"If we go in together, we'll have to help each other get back into the raft, because the raft is too unstable."

He caught her off-guard in more ways than one. If he was a skin-hound, like she assumed, then why did he warn her? He could have gotten all the free feels he wanted, and she couldn't do a thing about it. She looked down at the water. It really was incredible. How could she leave without going in it? He was right. It really was a chance of a lifetime. "I'll still go in, Michael."

The dinghy floated in the center of the cave. Instead of jumping or diving into the water and possibly flipping the raft, he slid off the side.

As Lorna looked down at him, she could not believe how clearly she could see the submerged bottom half of his body.

"How is it?"

"Fantastic! Come on in. Don't be afraid."

With Michael already in the water, Lorna suddenly felt brave. "Here goes."

Just as he had done, she slid over the side.

As the warm water enveloped her body, it felt as though someone had adjusted the temperature just for her. The water skimmed over her skin like liquid satin. It tranquilized her, eliminating her fears and seducing her into wanting to wallow there forever.

When she surfaced, water skimmed through her long hair, leaving it lying sleekly against her head. No words, not a sigh, and she floated on her back, enchanted by the cave's beauty. Her long, blonde hair got caught in the gentle ripples. Like a golden halo around her head, it floated.

Michael treaded water, watching her. She looked like an exotic flower that had fallen to the water's surface from some mysterious tree, her hair the delicate petals, her bronzed body the sleek stem and her willowy arms the fragile leaves.

His eyes lingered for several moments. "How do you like it?"

"I'll never forget this, Michael. I'm so glad I came to see the cave."

"Do you want to go for a swim?"

"Definitely!"

Side by side, they swam at a leisurely pace, wanting to savor every exciting moment.

Halfway around the perimeter of the cave, Lorna frolicked like a mermaid, doing surface dives and swimming on her back.

Michael stopped again to watch her. "I think you like it here."

"By far this has been the best part of the trip. Thank you so much for bringing me here."

"Come on. I'll help you get back in the dinghy."

Lorna told herself that no matter what happened next, good or bad, she asked for it by agreeing to come with him to the grotto.

When Michael first put his hands on her waist, instead of her reacting negatively, she enjoyed feeling his touch. The last male who got this close to her was Jeff. She realized how much she missed being in a relationship.

Michael asked. "Are you ready?"

She placed her hands on the side of the dinghy. "Ready."

"On the count of three, 1. 2. 3."

Without having any leverage to help him, the fiasco turned into a comedy of errors. As he pushed, she pulled, trying her best to lift herself into the raft. Her wet hands slipped off the rubber, and they both went sinking into the water. When they surfaced, they burst out laughing.

Lorna brushed her hair out of her eyes. "At this rate, we'll be here all night."

"Sorry about that. Let's try again."

This time he sank beneath the surface, and while she struggled to get in the boat, he pushed on her buttocks. She almost made it into the raft, when her wet elbows slid off the smooth rubber. Like before, they sank into the water.

"I'm sorry," she said, embarrassed. "I'll get it next time."

"Maybe it will be easier if I tried."

"How can I help?"

"Go around to the other side of the raft and hold it steady."

She swam around the boat and braced her hands against the rubber.

After taking a deep breath, Michael sank beneath the surface and kicked hard, using his feet as a propellant. His body shot up, and before he lost his balance, he hoisted himself steady and then swung his leg over the side.

"Made it," he hollered down to her.

"Thank goodness! I was getting scared."

"Now I want you to do what I just did."

"What's that?"

"Sink down, kick real hard with your feet and then propel yourself up out of the water. I'll grab you and pull you into the raft."

"I'll try." Lorna sank beneath the surface and kicked as hard as she could. When her body shot up out of the water, Michael grabbed onto her arms and pulled her into the raft.

She sighed with relief. "I feel a lot better now that I'm back in the boat, too. I had all of these crazy visions of you leaving me here all alone, while you went to get help from the Italian coast guard."

"We better head back. It's getting late." Michael reached for an oar and rowed towards the opening.

Lorna lay down in the center of the raft. Maybe she had been wrong about him. He never once got out of line with her.

———

LOUD CALYPSO MUSIC BLARED from the deck, waking Michael out of a sound sleep. At first the strange surroundings confused him. Then he realized he was on the yacht. He rubbed his eyes and yawned. The women were obviously back from Capri.

Too tired to shower yet, he stared at the ceiling, his mind consumed by Lorna. He could still see her floating on the water in her pink bikini. Ever since he first visited the cave and fell in love with its beauty, he envisioned being there with someone special some day, the two of them swimming and enjoying the wonder of it all. Now he had a face to go with that vision, a vision he could keep locked up in his mind until he needed it on those dark, dreary nights back home or during his travels when he felt lost and lonely.

It would have been so great if he had known Lorna before he took her to the Blue Grotto, and the two of them had been lovers. He would have wrapped her in his arms and kissed her wet lips, done something wondrous and exciting to make the event more memorable. As he lay in bed, he decided that after he spoke with his mother about the agreement, he would invite Lorna to have a drink with him on Capri.

Anxious to be with her again, he rolled out of bed to take a shower.

None of the women knew about Michael being on board. Lorna never got the chance to tell them. After she and Michael returned from the Blue Grotto, she went straight to the stateroom she was sharing with her mother to take a nap.

The weather could not have been more pleasant. The temperature had dropped to the mid-seventies and calm, gentle breezes stirred the air. Wispy clouds floated in a darkening sky that stretched far out in the horizon, where it met with the sea, the two blending together with no visible line of demarcation.

Within minutes, those same wispy clouds went from bursts of gold and pink to pewter gray, while the setting sun had changed from a fiery ball of orange to crimson. As the vibrant red globe descended beneath the horizon, a string of lights draping the yacht's bow to its stern suddenly came alive.

Millicent sat on the lounge deck drinking champagne with Margot, Holly, Samantha and Eva. Gayle sipped iced tea.

When Millicent saw Michael, her face lit up with surprise. "Michael. What in heck are you doing here?"

He kissed his grandmother's cheek. "I missed you, so I thought I would drop by and say hello."

"As if somebody from the states just drops by a yacht in Europe just to say hello. Is everything all right?"

He felt the time inappropriate for a serious discussion.

"Everything is fine."

Gayle had an anxious look on her face. "What ARE you doing here, Michael?"

Again he couldn't blurt out in front of everybody that Stuart stole their stock. He told a little white lie instead "I had to come to Italy for a few days, so I thought I'd stop on the yacht and see how everyone was enjoying the trip." He kissed his mother hello.

Holly's eyes twinkled behind the retro-looking sunglasses.

"Hey, cuz. Get a load of the new me."

"A blonde now, huh?"

She pulled open the full, white skirt of her strapless outfit, revealing a fifties-style pair of short shorts. While she twisted her finger around a pearl necklace, she grasped the edge of her wide-brim straw hat. "Who do I look like now?"

It could have been any of a dozen old movie stars. "Marilyn Monroe?"

"No, you moron, guess again."

"I'm too tired to guess. Just tell me."

"I'll give you a hint."

"If you must!"

"Monte Carlo."

It had to be Grace Kelly, but he decided to tease her.

"Catherine Deneuve."

Everyone burst out laughing.

Holly threw a cashew at him. "Jeez, you're brainless. I'll give you another hint.

"I'm sure you will."

"She was married to a prince."

"I got it. Princess Diana."

Again everyone laughed, including the bartender.

Holly exhaled an exasperated sigh. "Grace Kelly, you dimwit."

"What happened with Liz Taylor?"

"It was time to try something new. I thought of Grace Kelly while we were in Monte Carlo."

"Is the hair yours or a wig?"

"A wig. The hairdresser said if I don't quit coloring my hair for a while, I'll go bald."

"Then you can dress up like Yul Brynner."

Everyone roared with laughter, including Holly.

Michael glanced around, looking for Lorna. When he didn't see her, he wondered where she might be. Wherever she was, she had to join the others soon. He went and sat on one of the two vacant bar stools next to his sister.

Samantha asked. "How long will you be staying?"

"One or two days, depending on how tired I am."

"How are things back home?"

He decided he would let his mother tell her about the stolen stock. "The same."

Eva had been standing next to the railing, gazing down at the water. Before anyone else had a chance to sit on the stool next to him, she strolled over to it. "It's nice to see you, Michael."

Although she feigned nonchalance, Michael saw right through her. He no longer doubted that she had the hots for him. He answered her for the sake of answering, not because he enjoyed her presence. "Hello, Eva. How was Capri?"

"Terrific. I had great fun shopping."

Michael's eyes shot to his grandmother, knowing how she felt about Eva. Millicent rolled her eyes as if to say 'Of course she had great fun shopping. She spent more money than all of us women combined.'

"What about sightseeing?"

"I'm only interested in sightseeing if there's something really exciting to see. Otherwise, I would rather not waste my time."

"Before the yacht leaves Capri, you should go see the Blue Grotto. Early tomorrow morning would be a good time."

"Ah, yes, the Blue Grotto. Tour guides on the island pushed it today. I thought maybe they were over-hyping it. You know how tour guides are in foreign countries. They'll do anything to get American dollars."

Millicent gaped at Eva, a 'so would you' expression in her eyes. "I suggested it to Eva," Millicent said. "But she didn't feel like bothering. I told her she doesn't know what she's missing."

Michael reached for his glass of champagne. "Every time I'm in this region, I go see it. I think the water in the grotto is one of the most amazing sights in the world."

"You talked me into it," Eva said. "Since you just got here and didn't have a chance to go see it yet, why don't you and I go see it together?"

Lorna happened to be strolling on deck and overheard them talking. "Michael already went, mother."

Everyone's attention shifted to Lorna, who looked enchanting in a long, flowing, butter-yellow slip dress.

"When," Eva said. "What time did you get here, Michael?"

"This morning. Lorna and I went to see the grotto, while you women were on Capri shopping and having lunch."

"You and Lorna?" Eva forced a smile. "That's nice."

Lorna smirked. "It really was . . . what's that word you always use now, mother? Oh, yes, divine. The Blue Grotto was divine."

Eva glared at her. "You can tell me all about it later."

Samantha swallowed a caviar hors d'houvre. "How did you get to the grotto, Mike?"

"We took the dinghy."

Holly reached for a cheese puff. "We should go check it out tomorrow, Sam."

"I'm game. How about you, Eva?"

"Sure," she said, forcing another smile. "That sounds great."

The bartender poured Lorna a glass of champagne. She took a sip and then walked over to the railing.

Michael grabbed his glass and went to join her.

Holly reached for a cashew. "I think your brother is smitten, Sam."

"Good for him. He and Lorna make a cute couple."

Eva downed the last of her champagne in one gulp and then said to the bartender, "I'll have a Bombay Sapphire on the rocks."

Millicent observed her. "How's Stuart, Eva? Did you get a chance to talk with him before we left for Capri?"

"Yes, briefly."

"You must miss him terribly."

"I do."

"Michael and Lorna make a beautiful couple, don't they?"

"I don't think they're suited for one another at all. The two of them have absolutely nothing in common."

"How can you say that? Look at them. They're glowing."

Eva drank her gin and put the empty glass on the bar. "Would you excuse me, Millicent. I have to go powder my nose."

As Eva walked away, Millicent smiled triumphantly.

———

EXHAUSTED FROM THEIR busy day on Capri, the women headed for their staterooms after dinner.

As Lorna had napped earlier, she felt refreshed. "You go on ahead, mother. I'm going to sit out here on deck for a while."

"I want to talk to you, young lady."

Lorna knew it had to be about her going to the Blue Grotto with Michael. "It can wait."

"No it can't."

She sighed. "You treat me like I'm a two year-old. I'm not coming to bed yet."

"I said I want to talk to you."

"Just say what you have to say and then leave me alone."

"I don't want to discuss it out here in the open."

"And I don't want to discuss it period."

"There goes that smart mouth of yours again. You're always causing some kind of trouble."

"You're the one who causes all the trouble, mother. Everyone else on this boat gets along just fine."

"Damn it, Lorna. I said I want to talk to you."

"Jeez, mother. Chill out! You're going to give yourself a heart attack."

"No. You're going to give me a heart attack." Eva saw Michael walking towards them. She put on her biggest smile. "I thought you went to your cabin."

He ignored her. "Here you are, Lorna. I was looking for you."

"Why?"

"I was wondering if you would like to have a drink with me on Capri."

Rather than get into a major battle with her mother, Lorna declined. "I'm sorry, Michael. I'm too exhausted."

His hopeful smile faded. "Maybe another time."

As he walked away, Eva closed the cabin door behind her. "Just what do you think you're doing, young lady?"

"What are you talking about?"

"Michael. That's what I'm talking about?"

"What about him?"

"I thought I told you to stay away from him."

"Why? So you can have him all to yourself."

Eva slapped her across the face. "How dare you."

Lorna glared at her mother. "One of these days you're going to pull a stunt like that again, and I'm going to knock you across the room."

"Do you realize how long and hard I've worked to become a member of the Grant family? You're not going to screw everything up for me."

"Listen to you, mother. You're pathetic. You sound like a jealous schoolgirl. Does Stuart know you have the hots for Michael?"

Eva went to slap her again, but Lorna caught her arm. "Enough is enough. You don't want any of the Grants to hear us lowlifes fighting, do you?"

Eva ripped her arm out of Lorna's hand. "I only have one thing to say to you. Stay away from Michael."

—

GAYLE HAD JUST SLIPPED out of her dress when she heard knocking. She put on her robe and answered the door.

"Michael," she said, surprised.

"I want to talk to you."

"Come in."

"Were you getting ready for bed?"

"Yes, but that's okay."

Michael sat on a chair. "I specifically flew to Italy to talk with you in person."

"My God! What's wrong?"

"Take it easy. There's no emergency, not a medical one that is."

"Nobody flies all the way to Europe if it's not important."

"It's important all right, but I'm taking care of everything."

Gayle braced herself for the news. "Tell me."

"Are you sure you're okay?"

"I'm fine."

"Do you remember that letter I got from the IRS? They wanted back taxes on a stock sale."

Her hands trembled. "Michael, you didn't sell any of your stock, did you?"

"Of course I didn't."

"Then what are you talking about?"

"I hate like heck to tell you this, because of your bad heart and all, but you have to know."

"Just say it Michael."

"You're not going to believe this."

She sat on the bed. "Damn it, Michael, tell me already."

"Here goes . . . Now stay calm . . . Uncle Stuart has been stealing our stock."

"What?"

"It's true. He now owns ninety-three percent of the shares."

Gayle could hardly speak. "Stuart has been so good to us. Are you sure about this, Michael?"

"Positive."

She sat quietly for a few seconds and then tears came to her eyes.

It broke Michael's heart to see his mother upset. "Don't worry. Everything is going to be okay."

"Do you realize what this means? Stuart has control over everything, the company, all of the money?"

"Yes, and I'm not going to let him get away with it."

Her eyes suddenly grew cold with anger. "That conniving bastard!"

"My sentiment exactly!"

"When and how did he do it?"

"I don't know."

"What are we going to do?"

Concerned about her heart, Michael squeezed her hand. "Are you all right?"

"I'm a little shaken, but I'll be all right." Gayle wiped her eyes. "What are we going to do? We can't just let Stuart screw us out of our inheritance."

"When I get back to the states, the first thing I'm going to do is confront him about it."

"What if he denies he ever took the stock?"

"Then I'll give him an ultimatum."

"What kind of ultimatum?"

"I'll tell him that if the stock isn't returned within two weeks, we're taking him to court."

"Take Stuart to court? Are you kidding? He and his lawyers will stomp all over us in a courtroom."

"No they won't. Maybe they will. But, a jury would end up siding with us."

"I'm not as optimistic as you are."

"We can't lose, mother."

"Okay. Say we take him to court. How are we going to prove that we never sold him the stock?"

"Easy. We never signed anything. He just can't take our stock, because he wants it."

"Oh no!"

"What's wrong?"

"I'm always signing papers for Stuart."

"I know."

"This is going to sound careless on my part, Michael, but I have never read a thing he put in front of me."

"Me neither. Talk about stupid! We handed him the stock on a silver platter." Michael sighed. "That's how he did it. He won our trust and then took advantage of us."

"I can't believe this is happening."

"Wait. Even if we did sign over the stock to him, I think we're okay. To prove our case, we have that agreement dad and Uncle Stuart signed when granddad died."

"That's true. Do you think it will get back our stock?"

"Like I said, when a jury hears the entire story, they'll have to side with us."

"I hope you're right."

"By the way, mother, where did you put dad's copy of the agreement?"

"In the file cabinet, where we keep all of our important papers."

"Are you sure? When I looked for it yesterday, I couldn't find it."

"I'm positive it's in there."

"When was the last time you saw it?"

"A year or so ago."

"You're kidding!"

"No, I'm not. I never go in the file cabinet unless I'm looking for something specific."

"Are you sure it was in the file cabinet? Maybe you forgot and put it in a safety deposit box. You have one at the bank, don't you?"

"Yes, but I only put my good jewelry in it."

"Think, mother. You could be mistaken."

"I'm positive, Michael. I was just at the bank before we left for the trip. I put the jewelry I wasn't taking with me . . . oh no."

"What's wrong?"

"I gave our copy to Stuart."

Michael slumped to the chair. "Please say you didn't."

"I did. I gave it to him several weeks ago."

"I thought you said you haven't seen it in over a year.

"I just remembered."

Michael sighed. "Why would you give Stuart our copy of the agreement when he already has one of his own?"

"He told me now that his divorce is final, his attorney wanted to take Sheila's name off of it. He lied to me. Why would Sheila's name be on it anyway? I could shoot myself."

Michael stared into space. "This just keeps getting worse."

"Did you talk with Grandmother Millicent or Aunt Margot? It's possible they still have their copies."

"Before I flew over here, I called Uncle Ted. He couldn't find Aunt Margot's copy anywhere. Now I know why."

"What about Grandmother Millicent? Did you ask her for hers?"

"No. I didn't get a chance to talk to her yet."

"Then let's go talk to her now."

"We better think this over before we do that."

"Why?"

"We can't just go barging in on her and telling her Stuart stole our stock. No mother in her right mind would want to believe her son is a thief."

"Are you forgetting that your father was her son, too? I'm sure she would be upset with Stuart and demand that he return what is rightfully ours."

"For now, I think I'll tell her you misplaced your copy, and we want to make a copy of hers. She doesn't have to know the details yet." Michael stood up to leave. "Do you realize what this will do to the family, if we have to take Uncle Stuart to court?"

"It's worse than that, Michael. If we don't get the stock back, we'll lose everything we have."

———

EVA LAY IN BED, staring out the stateroom window. When the boat rocked one way, all she saw was darkness. When the boat rocked the opposite way, she saw a string of clouds creeping past the moon. With each glimpse, the sky painted a different picture, once concealing the glow of moonlight and then creating a golden aura.

As exhausted as she felt, she could not sleep. If she hadn't seen Michael earlier or did not know that he was asleep in a state room just a few doors down, she would have succumbed to the rocking sensation and fallen asleep.

More powerful than a giant magnet, he drew her to him. Now fire consumed her body, and she craved satisfaction. How she ached to touch that lean, young body of his, to feel his hands sliding over her bare skin and have those gorgeous lips kissing hers.

In the bed next to her Lorna slept soundly, a nightlight casting a luminous aura over her shapely silhouette. Above an occasional sloshing sound of water lapping against the sides of the boat, Eva heard her daughter breathing.

She glanced over at Lorna, who looked like a little girl lying there with the crisp white sheet tucked under her chin, and her long blonde hair cascading over the side of the pillow. It dumbfounded Eva that nothing bothered Lorna when she slept. A bomb could go off, and she wouldn't know the difference. She had been that way since she was a baby. The exact opposite, she herself woke from the slightest noise or Stuart's subtlest movement. If she hadn't been sharing the cabin with Lorna, she would have slept nude. Nightgowns and pajamas restricted her freedom. It was an animalistic thing with her. Climbing into a cold bed and having her body warm the sheets felt sensual. Even her jewelry had to come off before she went to bed, including her wedding band.

As Eva lay in bed, she realized that her desire for Michael was growing unbearable. Her hands slid under the sheet to her breasts and then between her legs. Michael's hands now caressed her. She ran her tongue over her lips, craving the salty taste of his skin. When it got to the point where she could no longer stand it, she glanced over at Lorna, making sure she was still asleep. When she saw no movement, only rising and falling with her daughter's breathing, she threw off the covers and slid out of bed.

The bathroom lacked the room to move about freely. Eva closed the door quietly and switched on the light. Several minutes she spent in a cramped space in front of the mirror, brushing her teeth and gargling with mouthwash, applying makeup, combing her hair and then spraying perfume on her neck, stomach and breasts.

For once she appreciated that Stuart loved seeing her in sexy lingerie. He often encouraged her to go out and buy lovely ensembles for his pleasure.

While on Capri, she bought a peignoir set, a silver gray satin gown and matching full-length coat adorned with delicate sea pearls and lace. Cut to enhance a woman's cleavage, the gown showcased most of her breasts and it was slit up the front to reveal part of her thigh. She also splurged on the silver gray high-heeled slippers that went with them.

While Lorna slept, Eva transformed herself into a sex goddess.

The entire time she fussed, Lorna lay in the same position in which she had fallen asleep over an hour ago. To be on the safe side, Eva tiptoed past her and out the door.

After the warm cabin temperature, the cool night air felt crisp and damp. As she sneaked past the stateroom next to hers, she clutched the silky coat over her breasts. In case she happened to run into one of the Grant women out on deck, she planned to tell her that she couldn't sleep, that she had come outside to get some fresh air.

After her heated discussion with Lorna earlier, Eva had returned to the lounge, hoping to learn what stateroom Michael was occupying. As she nursed another Bombay Sapphire on the rocks, she noticed him exiting his mother's cabin and entering the cabin in front of which she now stood.

He must have been asleep, because no light forced its way between the slats. Should she knock? No. Someone might hear the noise and come out to see what all the fuss was about.

She stared at the shiny brass handle. Most likely, the door would not be locked. With only family members on board, safety was not a concern. She tried the handle, which turned easily.

Michael had not yet fallen asleep. When he heard the door opening and saw a shadowy figure slipping inside, he sat up, more surprised than frightened. "Whoa," he said. "Who is it?"

"It's me, Eva."

He flicked on the light. "Eva? What's the matter? Is something wrong?"

"No. Everything is fine."

After his eyes adjusted to the light, he saw the sexy, see-through nightgown underneath the silk coat. "What are you doing in my cabin in that outfit at this hour of the night?"

Without answering, she sat next to him on the bed.

The sheet covered him to the waist. Eva salivated over his muscular arms and bare chest. His hair may have been unruly, but it only made him look more rugged and virile. She ran her fingers through it.

Michael recoiled in shock. "What are you trying to pull? Get the hell out of here."

Her eyes closed, Eva basked in the warmth of reverie. "But, I just got here, Michael."

"I know what your intentions are, and I don't want any parts of the game." He pushed her away.

She could not resist his taught skin. It looked too inviting. She leaned forward and kissed his shoulder. As she attempted to get closer, he held her at bay. "What are you doing? Are you crazy?"

Her eyes glazed, she lay limp in his hands. "No one has to know. Think how wonderful it would be." She ran her tongue over his arm.

"Quit making a fool of yourself," he said. "I'm embarrassed for you."

As if she were a machine and he had hit the off switch, she bolted upright. "Who do you think you are?"

"You had too much to drink. Go back to your cabin and sober up."

She slapped him across the face. "You're not the gentleman I thought you were."

"And you're not the lady I thought you were. LEAVE . . . NOW."

Eva suddenly felt naked. She covered herself with her arms.

Michael threw back the sheet and climbed out of bed in his gray, athletic underwear. "Come on. I'll check to see if anyone is out on deck."

She pulled away from him, feeling spurned and rejected. "There is one thing you should know before I leave."

"What's that?"

"Before you go making a fool out of yourself with Lorna, she told me she doesn't want any parts of you. She finds you boring and immature."

"I don't think that's true."

Eva gloated, knowing that she just forbade Lorna to see him. "Is that right? Then why don't you ask her out sometime and see what happens."

"I'll do that." Michael opened the door and glanced up and down the deck. "Hurry up. The deck is quiet."

Her lips parted in a sly grin. "I don't know why you're fighting me, Michael. It's inevitable that sooner or later, we'll get together."

9

MICHAEL HEADED for Stuart's house, taking for granted that at this hour of the evening his uncle would be home. The women had not yet returned from their Mediterranean cruise, so he could not be out to dinner with Eva.

Ever since Michael learned about Stuart conning the women into giving him their copies of the agreement, his contempt for his uncle grew.

Although he felt like ripping the front door off its hinges, he rang the bell instead.

Andrew answered the door. "Good evening, Michael."

"Hello, Andrew. Is my uncle home?"

"Yes sir. Please, come in."

"He's not in bed yet, is he?"

"No sir. He is in the library. Shall I announce your arrival?"

"No."

"Is something wrong, sir? You look upset."

"I'm fine. Thanks."

Michael appreciated the fact that Holly wasn't around to bother him. He didn't come to socialize.

Stuart tightened the sash of his hunter-green silk smoking jacket. "Michael, I'm glad you came for a visit. Without Eva and Holly around, I'm bored to death. Come sit down. We'll have a glass of sherry."

Andrew had followed Michael into the library. "Shall I prepare some hors d'oeuvres, Mr. Grant?"

"Maybe Michael would like some."

"No thanks, Andrew. I just ate dinner."

"Don't bother then. I don't want anything either."

Andrew poured two glasses of sherry. He served one to Michael, the other to Stuart and then left.

Stuart took a sip of sherry. "What brings you here at this hour? You must be as bored as I am."

Michael laid his glass on the coffee table. With Stuart sitting directly across from him, confronting him was going to be harder than he thought. Until he learned about him stealing their stock, he had loved this man like a father.

Michael asked. "How could you do this to us?"

Stuart squirmed. "Do what?"

"You know damn well what I'm talking about."

"I'm sorry, but I don't."

"We trusted you."

"I hate to see you like this, Michael. Please, if you're upset about something, let's clear the air."

For the first time in his life, Michael saw the real Stuart Grant. "Look at you sitting over there, acting righteous and proper."

"What's with you tonight? I wish you would explain."

Michael gulped his sherry. "Quit playing dumb with me. It makes me want to puke."

"I beg your pardon."

"Where's the stock you stole from us?"

"What are you talking about?"

"You stole forty-three percent of our stock, and we want it back."

"After all I've done for you, how dare you accuse me of stealing your stock."

"If you didn't steal the stock, then where is it?"

"Don't you remember? You sold that stock to me."

"We never did any such thing."

"I beg to differ with you, but you did."

Michael flew off the chair. "You rotten bastard! You think you have this all figured out, don't you?"

"I don't appreciate the accusations or the name calling."

"And I'm not too thrilled that you stole our stock."

"In that case, this conversation is over."

"Not quite."

"Then say whatever you have to say and get out of here."

"If those shares of stock, and I mean all forty-three percent, are not returned to us in two weeks, we're taking you to court."

Stuart smirked. "What good will suing me do? You have no proof that you actually owned fifty percent of the stock in the first place."

"You think you have that figured out, too, don't you?"

"I'm way ahead of you, Michael."

"Then you admit that you have all five copies of the agreement?"

"Yes. I have them for a legitimate reason. I recently got a divorce, and Sheila's name had to be removed from them."

"Liar! You'll never get away with this. The whole family knows about that agreement."

"I hate to burst your bubble, Michael, but without that document, it's all hearsay." Stuart held up his glass to salute Michael. "Here's to you and your family's generosity."

Michael smacked the glass out of his hand, sending it smashing into the bookshelves. "Smile now, you dirty thief, because next year, you'll be broke."

———

STUART FUMED. Nothing was going to stop him from selling Grant Office Supplies, not Michael, not Gayle nor Samantha. If World Office Products found out about a pending lawsuit, they would have legitimate reason to pull out of the deal. Most likely what they would do, if they did learn about a pending suit, was hang around until the hearing to see if he lost. If he did, without a doubt they would insist that he cough up the seventy-five million for misleading them. No way was he going to allow that to happen. What he had to do, and do quickly, was get Michael out of the picture, eliminate the pain in the ass from the face of the earth.

Stuart hurried upstairs to change, putting his plan in motion.

Uncertain about how much money he would need, he took a wad of big bills with him. He also had a photograph of Michael in his pocket.

As he drove north on Ocean Boulevard, he glanced at the glowing green dial of the dashboard clock. Almost eleven. He expected Spinosa's Restaurant would be dead, but not the lounge. On most nights the joint jumped until one or two in the morning.

The parking lot alone was packed. Stuart had to park in front of Jeb's Bait & Tackle next door to Spinosa's. When he stepped out of the car, he heard the live band in the lounge playing *Mack the Knife.* He could only imagine what was going on inside. The people who went there to dine were pretty much like him and Eva. But the night owls who stayed up half of the night partying were in a class all of their own.

Just as Stuart expected, the dance floor overflowed with people gyrating to the beat of the music. Men and women of all ages, some married but most on the make, occupied the barstools and surrounding tables. A couple sitting in a dark corner kissed passionately and then got up to leave. Another man, dressed in an expensive, tailor-made suit, slid his hand up a much younger woman's short, tight red dress. Tipsy, she accidentally knocked over her glass, dousing him with champagne. He jumped up and blotted himself with cloth napkins supplied by an observant waitress.

Stuart squeezed between two men and then leaned over the bar.

"Where's Vince, Bobby?"

"Right behind you."

Surprised that he didn't notice Vince, the owner, on his way to the bar, Stuart turned around and shook hands with him. "You have a hell of a business here. I should invest in this place."

Vince laughed. "What brings you here this late? You and Eva usually come earlier for dinner."

"I'm here by myself tonight. Eva is still in Europe."

"Then come have a drink with me."

"No thanks. I didn't come here to socialize. Can I talk to you in private?"

"Let's go to my office."

Stuart didn't want anyone listening in on their conversation. "If you don't mind, I would rather go outside and talk."

"Come with me." Vince led Stuart out a back door to a pier.

The three fishing boats normally docked at the pier had left two hours ago. Snapper, grouper and Pompano, plus other fish that the men caught, arrived back at the restaurant by dawn.

Stuart and Vince strolled past an adjacent building, where kitchen employees cleaned the fresh catch for the chefs.

Stuart held his hand over his nose. "I've never been back here before. Boy, does it stink."

Vince smirked. "What's the matter? You don't like the smell of fish?"

"No. I never did. When Eva and I went to San Francisco recently, we visited Fisherman's Wharf. Do you know where they cook the crabs and chowders in those big vats? I almost threw up on the street when I passed them."

"If you find the smell that offensive, we should go for a walk."

On the verge of gagging, Stuart breathed through his mouth.

"I think that's a good idea."

Vince always acted friendly and jovial around his customers. Now that Stuart brought him out here to talk business, his demeanor changed, and he grew serious. "What did you want to talk to me about?"

"Do you remember the time you pulled me aside and told me that if I ever needed your help, to come see you?"

"Of course I remember. What can I do for you?"

"Someone is giving me trouble. Can you arrange to have it stopped?"

"What do you want stopped, the person or the trouble?"

"The person."

Vince lit a cigar and blew the smoke out the corner of his mouth. "I can do that. Who is giving you trouble?"

"My nephew Michael." Stuart handed him the photograph. "Here's a picture of him."

Although it was a family member of Stuart's, Vince did not flinch. "What did your nephew do?"

Stuart wanted to make it sound worse than it actually was.

"The little bastard raped my wife."

"What? The son-of-a-bitch raped Eva?"

"Yes."

"You have no choice but to get even with him. I don't care how hard a man's dick gets, he should never rape another man's wife."

"I want it done right away."

"That won't be a problem. But it will cost you."

"How much?"

"A hundred grand, seventy-five for me and twenty-five for my associates."

"No problem. It will be worth it."

"Is there any particular way you want it done? Do you want your nephew to choke on his balls?"

"Whatever you think, but don't do it around here."

"Where then?"

"My nephew is planning a trip to the Keys this weekend with my son and his friend. Now that I think about it, maybe you should waste the three of them."

"If that's what you want, it can be done."

"No, no, just my nephew." Stuart got a whiff of fish and almost vomited. "They're taking my brother's old boat, the *Grant Your Wish.* I thought maybe you could have it done down in the Keys."

"Any Key in particular?"

"Key West."

"Another five grand for expenses."

"All right."

"Consider it done."

10

CHUCK MURPHY opened a paperclip and picked the last remnants of a salami sandwich from between his teeth. His stomach felt full and bloated, and within the hour he expected to be straining to stay awake.

He burped up the taste and smell of garlic. As he wiped his bushy mustache with the back of his hand, he glanced at the four monitors built into the console. The screens displayed the same boring scenes they always did at two o'clock in the morning, lifeless shots of the three entranceways and the loading dock of Grant Place, the executive offices of Grant Office Supplies.

About to make another security round, mainly to get his blood flowing again, Chuck heard tapping on the glass doors. Out of habit his eyes shot to the monitors first.

A woman stood outside, a damn good-looking one at that. She seemed pretty anxious to get inside the building. Chuck suddenly felt energized. He slid his clunky feet off the console and went to investigate.

The woman didn't look familiar, but her uniform did. What brought someone from Walton Cleaning Company to the building at this late hour? The other cleaning people had left long ago. Maybe she forgot her purse or something.

To be on the safe side, he glanced up and down the street before he unlocked the door. The woman may have brought some hoodlum friends with her, and they planned to rob the place.

As if reading his mind, the woman shouted through the glass. "I'm by myself."

Chuck still felt nervous. "What do you want?"

She held up a dust mop and a can of polish. "Walton sent me over to do some special cleaning in Mr. Grant's office."

He hesitated. "I don't know. Nobody told me about it."

The woman added. "Maybe they forgot."

She had to be legit, because she knew the boss' name. Chuck unlocked the door. "You must be new. I've never seen you before."

"I'm not really. I do special cleaning jobs for the company." She smiled and winked at him. "The penthouse is on the tenth floor, isn't it?"

"Yeah. I'll take you up there."

"That's all right. I'll find it."

"I have to unlock the door for you."

She smiled again, a playful glint in her eyes. "Then I guess you have to come with me."

It seemed unusual to Chuck that nobody notified him about somebody coming to clean. "Why are you here so late? The other cleaning people left hours ago."

She headed for the elevators. "Like I said, I do special cleaning jobs for the company. This is my third stop tonight."

"Just what is this special cleaning job you have to do?"

"Someone from Mr. Grant's office called and complained about the paneling looking dusty."

"How long will it take?"

"With a mop, it goes real fast, about twenty or thirty minutes."

While riding up in the elevator, Chuck checked the woman out, trying his best not to get caught. It puzzled him why a hot babe like her took a job cleaning offices. With that sexy, long, blonde hair and nice body, she could be making a ton of money in one of them nude dance joints he went to on Saturday nights. Whatever her excuse was for being there, she brightened up his night.

He glanced to the floor and then her legs. As she watched the numbers light up above the door, he sneaked a glimpse of her breasts. The uniform fit tight on her, the way a dress should fit a woman. He scratched his chin. She said this was her third job tonight, yet her uniform didn't have a dirty mark on it. The thing looked brand new.

The woman caught Chuck ogling her breasts. "Here we are," she said, irritation in her voice.

Embarrassed, Chuck cleared his throat. "Mr. Grant's private office is down the hall to the right. Oh, and buzz fifty-five on the phone, if you need me. That's the number for security."

They headed down the corridor.

As Chuck followed the woman, he watched her nice buttocks moving up and down under the tight uniform. He envisioned her naked and his hands groping her rear.

When they arrived at Stuart's office, the young woman tried the door. "It's a good thing you came with me. It is locked."

Chuck slid the key into the hole. "There you go."

The woman waited until he left. She sprayed polish in the air, making it appear as though she had started working, and then she ran behind Stuart's desk.

What appeared to be layers of drawers was one fake door. She pulled on the middle knob to get at the safe. Out of her pocket she took a piece of paper. For a few seconds she studied the numbers written on the paper and then executed the combination. Her eyes glanced up occasionally, afraid that Chuck might return to check up on her. Through papers and envelopes she rummaged, her heart pounding in her chest. About to reach for the bottom stack of papers, she heard the elevator ding and the doors sliding open. She bolted from behind the desk and grabbed the dust mop.

Chuck stuck his head in the door. "How's it going?"

"Halfway done." She pointed to the wall. "How does it look?"

He couldn't tell the difference. The paneling always looked clean and shiny. "Real good."

"Do you mind," she said. "I hate to clean with anyone watching."

His eyes darted around the room, assuring himself that she did not come to rob the place. "No problem."

As soon as Chuck left, the woman went tearing behind the desk again. If she didn't find the agreements in the bottom stack of papers, she had gone through all of this trouble for nothing.

Underneath the entire stack of papers she encountered a brown, legal-size envelope. Scrawled on the front of the envelope in black magic marker was "COPIES OF AGREEMENT." Excited, she flipped the envelope over to see if it was sealed. It wasn't. She slid her hand inside and pulled out the papers. Five documents were inside. As she expected, Stuart had every existing copy in his possession. She smiled. He did have them. Now she had them.

The woman folded the agreements in three and shoved them down her dress.

The left side of the desk had real drawers. She opened the top drawer, looking for stationery. There was nothing but pens, staples and miscellaneous office supplies. The second drawer contained letterhead, blank paper and envelopes. She grabbed several pieces of blank paper and shoved them into the envelope. A devious grin lingered on her face as she locked the safe and wiped the dial free of her fingerprints.

The mop and polish in her hands, the woman hurried to the elevators.

By the time she arrived downstairs, the back of her uniform displayed patches of perspiration.

"I'm finished," she said, holding the mop and can of polish over her chest.

Chuck hated to see her leave. "Do you want to stay and have some coffee with me?"

"Sorry. I can't. I have another job to do."

"Bring your lunch with you next time. We'll chew the fat together."

"I just might do that."

11

WEARY FROM THE TRIP, Lorna could barely function. Every move she made took major effort. As she pulled her hair back into a French braid, she gazed languidly out the bedroom window. Like her, all of nature seemed to be moving in slow motion. That could not possibly be the case, she knew, but it appeared that way. From the blue jay perched on a branch to the chameleon resting on the patio railing, everything behaved lazier than normal.

Just climbing out of bed this morning had zapped Lorna's strength. Her body behaved like it ran a marathon, and her bloated stomach felt like a balloon.

Exercise or any other form of physical activity she definitely planned to postpone until her energy returned.

A pleasant, relaxing morning on the beach with a good book sounded much more appropriate for her lethargic condition.

She considered showering, but it would only be a waste of time and what little energy she had. Once she got outside in the sun and humidity, she was just going to sweat and get wet in the ocean.

In worse shape than she thought, she could barely lift her leg to put on her swimsuit. When she went to step into her bikini bottoms, her toes got stuck on the elastic, and she almost toppled on her face.

As she slid into her sandals, she sneezed. That was just wonderful. She probably caught a cold on the airplane. Why the FAA couldn't do something about the air in planes, she wondered. After all, planes flew up in the sky in the freshest air of all.

Convinced that she wasn't meant to mingle with the living today, she almost crawled back into bed. But the weather looked so perfect.

The warm sun on her lifeless body would feel so good. It might even revive her.

With what little energy she had, she threw a bottle of suntan lotion, her sunglasses, an iPod and a sports watch into a straw hat.

Like a zombie, she trudged down the corridor. From the stairs she gazed out to the Atlantic at a cruise ship making its way south. Most likely, it was headed for the Caribbean. Everything about the ship evoked fun and excitement, life and liveliness, the extreme opposite of anything she could handle at this particular moment.

When she reached the breakfast room, she stopped in the doorway and did a double take.

Holly never ceased to amaze her. Decked-out in a gold satin robe with a fluffy, ostrich-feather collar, a thick layer of frosted gold eye shadow, black eyeliner and long, false eyelashes, she looked like something someone had taken out of an old, silent movie, thrown into a reel of recent footage and then fast-forwarded the two reels until everything got so out of control that she came out looking like a cross between Gloria Swanson in *Sunset Boulevard* and Carol Channing in *Hello Dolly*, however on a very bad day.

Lorna studied Holly, disbelief written all over her face. And her mother wanted her to take pointers on dressing from this bizarre creature, this lunatic with a mind floating somewhere up near Jupiter, a spoiled brat who dyed her hair every shade of the rainbow and wore outrageous outfits like this one, trying to look like everyone but herself? Holly would be the last person she went to for advice.

Holly smirked. "What's the matter, Lorna? You don't like my new look?"

Lorna bit her tongue. "How you look is your business."

Holly held out her fingernails, also painted gold. "How do you like the new color?"

"It's blinding me."

Holly threw her napkin on the table. "Don't you know anything at all about style?"

"If that's style, I prefer to remain uninformed."

"You should try something new once in a while, reinvent yourself."

"I'll leave the reinventing to you."

Andrew served Holly a dish of scrambled eggs and bacon.

He said. "Good morning, Miss Lorna."

"Good morning, Andrew. How are you today?"

"Very well, thank you. May I serve you breakfast?"

She felt bloated enough. "No thanks. I'll wait for lunch."

Lorna assumed Stuart had already left for work, but wondered about Eva. "Has my mother been down to breakfast yet?"

Andrew refilled Holly's cup with coffee. "She went to the beach to enjoy the sun. I gather from your attire that you plan to join her."

Lorna didn't count on her mother being on the beach. Suddenly, getting a suntan sounded like a bad idea. She sighed. What was her mother doing out in the sun anyway? She hated the sun, said it dried out her skin and caused wrinkles. Lorna glanced out the window. It really was too nice out to spend the day indoors. Why should she let her mother spoil her fun? If her mother started on her, she would turn up the volume on her iPod and ignore her.

Lorna headed for the door. "See you later, guys."

Holly pushed back her chair. "Don't be surprised if you see me in a little while."

Lorna scoffed. "Believe me, Holly. Nothing you do would surprise me."

———

MICHAEL COULD NOT GET LORNA out of his mind. Ever since that day they went to the Blue Grotto, he looked forward to seeing her again. The only place he might be able to catch her was on the beach. After the crap Stuart pulled with the stock, he refused to go over the house to see her or call her on the phone. As far as his uncle and that black widow spider wife of his were concerned, Michael planned to avoid them like the plague. He threw on his running shoes and went downstairs.

When he stepped out on the patio, Gayle was having coffee and reading the morning paper.

He said. "You look exhausted, mother. Didn't you get any sleep?"

"A little. This stock thing has me worried sick."

"I haven't been sleeping very well myself."

"Did you get a chance to talk with Stuart yet?"

He hated to upset his mother, but she had to know. Worrying or knowing, one was just as bad as the other. "Yes, I did."

"I don't like that look on your face. It's true, isn't it? He took our stock."

"Yes."

Gayle sighed. "Did he actually admit to taking it?"

"No. He claims we sold the stock to him."

"What? That's ludicrous. How can he do this to us?"

"Try not to worry. I'll take care of everything."

"I don't know, Michael. Stuart is no dummy. He obviously has been planning this for years."

"I agree."

"Did you tell him we were going to take him to court, if he didn't return the stock?"

"Yes."

"What did he say?"

"He said without the agreement, we'll be wasting our time."

"Then you didn't come up with a copy?"

"No. He has all of them."

"I told you, Michael. He has this all figured out."

"I don't care what he has figured out. I'm not going to sit around and let him get away with it."

"A lawsuit will cost a fortune. What are we going to use for money?"

"I don't know."

"We have no choice. We'll have to start selling off some of our assets."

Michael felt like killing Stuart for making their lives so miserable. "We're not selling anything. We'll sit tight and figure out a way to stop him." He poured himself a glass of orange juice and drank it. "I'm going running now. I'll see you later."

Michael ran down the steps, heading for the beach.

For nine o'clock in the morning the sun felt ferociously hot, blazing down on his shoulders. Within minutes, his body broke out in a sweat. Usually he ran at dawn, but after spending all night tossing and turning over Stuart and the stock, he could not drag himself out of bed. Now he was paying the price for not getting up earlier.

The ocean looked calm, perfect for snorkeling or boating. He inhaled a deep breath. Normally, the air smelled somewhat fishy. Today a breeze carried the sweet smell of frangipani blossoms.

As he ran, seashells crunched beneath his feet. Like a gazelle, he sailed over seaweed and other ocean debris that had washed up with the tide. Occasionally, his heel would sink into a mound of soft sand, challenging his calf muscles. It must have been jellyfish season, because several Portuguese man-of-war lay dead on the beach. To avoid landing on them, he headed for drier sand.

As he drew nearer to Stuart's house, he saw a woman in a multi-colored swimsuit lying on a chaise lounge, sunbathing. He could not make out the face, but he hoped it was Lorna. The closer he came to the woman, he realized it was Eva. Sprawled out with her legs spread, she looked like a marinated slab of beef about to go on a rotisserie. A thick layer of suntan oil coated her skin, and a big, straw hat shaded her face. Luckily, she neither saw nor heard him coming. He passed by her and kept running.

EVERY TIME A COOL breeze blew over the island, Eva would lift the hat shading her face, welcoming the refreshing air into her lungs. She had just covered her face, when she heard someone fussing with a lounge chair. Again she lifted the hat. "Lorna. I didn't hear you coming."

"Good morning, mother. How long have you been out here?"

"About forty-five minutes."

"You better turn over or get out of the sun. You're getting fried on your front."

"I am?"

"Yes. You're also getting the sun on an angle. Your left side is redder than your right side."

As Eva straightened her chair, Lorna covered hers with an orange and blue, Gators beach towel.

Eva lay back down on her stomach. "Why don't you get rid of that junk you got from college? That part of your life is over."

Lorna grimaced. "Look, mother. I came out here to have a pleasant day. If you're going to start on me, I'm taking my chair and moving further up the beach."

"There you go again, mouthing-off at me. I can't say a word to you."

"That's because you never say anything nice." Lorna slid the earbuds in her ears and turned up the volume on her iPod. As the reggae beat of Bob Marley's *Jammin'* played on, she lay back on the chair and closed her eyes.

It wasn't often that Eva got a chance to study her daughter's body. As Lorna lay there with her eyes closed, she checked her out from head to toe. Unlike herself, no lumps of cellulite dimpled Lorna's skin. Flawless and taut, her skin shimmered a bronzy tan under the thin coat of oil. Her breasts didn't sag either, and her stomach sunk in flat below her ribcage without an ounce of fat.

Eva hated to admit it but she envied her daughter's youth. No matter how many times a week she exercised, she would never look that good again. In two more years, she would be turning fifty. Although she looked good for her age, nothing was going to stop nature from taking its course. Her skin was going to continue sagging and drying out, and it wouldn't be long before she looked like a prune. She considered having a face lift but didn't know whom to believe, the people who said having a facelift didn't hurt or the woman at the club who told her that if she had to do it all over again she would think twice about getting the surgery because of the pain.

Blinded by her infatuation with Michael, she felt embarrassed for Lorna. How any young woman in her right mind could go out without fixing her hair or putting on makeup amazed her.

At times Eva's own vanity drove her nuts. She could not imagine men not whistling at her anymore or ogling her body. Soon it would all stop, and people would start calling her ma'am instead of miss. She sighed. As far as her looks were concerned, her days were numbered, although there were a lot of younger men who found older women sexy. The thought brought Michael to mind. He certainly acted interested in her, maybe not on the boat, because he probably feared the whole family would find out about them, but the other times, like when she and Stuart went over to Gayle's house, and he glanced down her silk shirt. He certainly seemed interested enough in her then. Eva's mood changed for the better. She wasn't over the hill yet, and she wasn't going to let life pass her by. She blotted her forehead with a towel and closed her eyes.

———

WITH ONLY AN OCCASIONAL cloud drifting across the sky, the scorching sun persisted in baking down on Lorna's overheated body.

She couldn't stand it any longer. If she didn't get some relief soon, she would pass out from the heat. She turned off her iPod and went down to the water.

Not bothering to test the temperature, she dove into the surf. For a while she floated on her back, and then she stood up, wallowing in the liquid playground.

This really was the life. Now she knew why her mother loved Sand Dollar Island so much.

Still too hot to go back out in the sun, she tried to spot the colorful fish she knew had to be swimming around her. As she turned towards shore, she saw Michael jogging down the beach. She smiled and waved.

He glanced to Eva, who still lay on her stomach with her eyes closed. Before she spotted him coming, he slid off his shoes and socks and dove into the surf.

"So, Lorna," he said, happy to see her, "how was the cruise?"

"It was wonderful, especially the Blue Grotto."

"I saw you staring down at the water. Looking for fish?"

"Yes."

He pointed. "There's some great snorkeling down by those rocks. An old buddy of mine lives down there."

"I'm afraid to ask. Just what is your old buddy?"

"Spike, an eel. He lives in the coral reef."

"Does Spike recognize you, when he sees you?"

"Yes. Whenever he sees me or my cousins, he slithers out of his hole, looking for food."

"Do you feed him?"

"Sure."

"With your hand?"

"Yes."

"Aren't you afraid he'll mistake your hand for food some day? Those things have sharp teeth, don't they?"

"You have to be careful." He slicked back his hair with his fingers. "There are a lot of neat things like that around the island."

"It's a tough life you have here, Michael."

He laughed. "I've been pretty lucky."

"Then why is your mother getting rid of her house?" It just slipped out. Lorna could have kicked herself. How was she going to explain to him how she found out about it? She didn't want him to think she snooped through Stuart's papers.

Michael asked. "Where did you get that idea?"

When would she learn to keep her big mouth shut? Now what was she supposed to do? Tell him? The dilemma threw Lorna. It wasn't her place to tell Michael. She evaded answering honestly. "I don't know why I said that. I must be delirious from the sun."

"Where did you come up with that idea? Someone just doesn't blurt out your mother's getting rid of her house."

Worried about looking like a snoop, again she evaded an honest answer. "I don't know, Michael. I was just teasing you. Sand Dollar Island is such a great place, who would want to live anywhere else." Mortified, she splashed water on her face, trying to hide her embarrassment.

When Lorna saw Holly coming down the path, she sighed with relief. As usual, Holly looked like a one-woman circus. From head to toe she wore nothing but green. Her string bikini matched a shamrock-colored straw hat that had a big green bow trailing down her back. As if her feet had been greased with olive oil, they slid out of her green mules whenever the heels sunk into the sand. Even the patent leather beach bag dangling from her shoulder shimmered neon green in the sunlight. The only thing a different color was her black sunglasses.

They curved up on the sides and had tiny rhinestones speckling the frames, like styles worn by movie stars in the fifties.

Lorna motioned with a nod. "Here comes Holly."

Michael laughed. "What's with all the green? Does she think today is St. Patrick's Day or something?"

Holly hollered from shore. "Hey, Cuz, what are you doing here?"

"I live on the island. Don't you remember?"

"You know what I mean, silly."

Lorna saw Eva suddenly get up from the chair. Her mother would never change. She always had to butt-in on her fun.

———

EVA WONDERED JUST how long Michael had been there and why she hadn't seen or heard him coming.

As if she were a sex goddess, she posed, one leg in front of the other, with her arms behind her head and her stomach sucked in as far as she could get it, hoping Michael was watching. Then she walked down to the water's edge.

She said. "Michael, I didn't know you were here."

He turned his back to her. "Hello, Eva."

She wanted so badly to join them in the water but was afraid that she might get sucked up in another current. She stood frozen at the water's edge, agonizing over whether she should attempt to go in or not. It took a few seconds until she realized she had nothing to fear. Michael was there if she needed rescuing again.

After lying in the hot sun for over an hour, she grimaced when a swell of cold water hit her in the chest. For certain, if Michael hadn't been in the ocean, she would not be putting herself through this agony. She trudged through the surf until she stood next to him. "Where did you come from? Did you just pop up out of the ocean?"

"I was running the beach and happened to see Lorna."

Holly kicked off her shoes and went diving into the surf.

Up to their chests in water, everyone stood facing each other, Lorna about to choke her mother, Holly admiring her nail polish through the water, Eva grimacing when another wave crashed against her back, and Michael worried silly over Lorna's comment about his mother getting rid of her house.

He said. "I have to go."

Eva flinched when the water rolled up to her neck. "Let's all go shell hunting."

Lorna rolled her eyes. "You're getting fried, mother. You better get out of the sun."

"Then let's all go have lunch together in the cabana."

Holly squeezed the water out of her hair. "We just ate breakfast."

"I'm going to pass," Michael said. "I have to go take care of some business."

Eva backed up into shallower water. "Then how about a game of tennis later?"

"I can't. I'm busy."

"That's too bad, Michael, maybe another time."

He headed for shore. "I'll see you guys. Have fun."

"You can't leave," Eva said. "We need a lifeguard to protect us from the currents."

"You won't have any problems today. The water is like glass. Besides, Holly and Lorna are good swimmers."

———

DESPITE THE FACT THAT he had just run six miles, Michael jogged back to the house.

As he burst through the kitchen door, Arielle pulled a tray of fresh-baked dinner rolls out of the oven. She laid the tray on the burners.

Michael bent over the stove. "These rolls smell delicious. Can I take one?"

"Take as many as you want. There's more than enough for dinner."

Michael buttered a roll and bit into the flaky, golden crust. "These are really good." He ate the entire roll in two gulps. "Where's my mother?"

"She's in the den. Do you want some coffee or milk to go along with some more rolls?"

"No. I'll just have another one of these." He buttered the roll and ate it on the way to the den.

Gayle sat at the file cabinet, going through her important papers. "How was your run?"

"Invigorating. What are you looking for?"

"I thought I better get all of our important papers together and put them in the safety deposit box. I don't trust Stuart anymore."

"Good thinking. Did you happen to come across the deed to the house?"

"Yes. It's right here on my lap." She pulled the document out of a stack of papers.

Michael examined the deed closely. "Thank goodness! I was afraid he might have stolen this like he did the stock."

"No, it's here."

"Let me know when you have everything together. I'll take you to the bank."

12

JOHN POWERS, PRESIDENT of World Office Products, twirled a fountain pen between his fingertips. "Our final offer is 1.7 billion, take it or leave it."

Stuart had hoped they would go 1.9 or an even 2 billion. In any case, it was still a good offer. "I'll take it."

Jerry Zuckerman added. "Like we stated at the last meeting, a third up front and equal payments of one third for the next two years."

John leaned back in his chair. "Agreed."

A big smile crossed Stuart's face. "Gentlemen, you have yourself a deal."

"Great. When do you want to close?"

Stuart wanted it done as soon as possible. "In sixty days."

"That's fine by us."

Jerry pulled out a document he had drawn up in case both parties agreed to a deal. "The 75 million penalty clause." He handed the document to John's attorney.

Brief and to the point, Henry read over the document. "Are you prepared to sign now, John?"

Without answering, the company executive removed the lid from his pen.

After John signed, Jerry placed the document in front of Stuart.

Stuart couldn't wait to sign. In the back of his mind, he saw himself finally rid of Gayle.

Jerry stacked the papers. "I'll prepare a letter of commitment and fax it over for your parties to sign."

Henry answered. "That's less work for me."

Everyone laughed as they stood up to shake hands.

—

STUART WAS DELIGHTED that the meeting had gone so well. He propped his feet up on his desk and folded his hands behind his head, gloating over the fact that in a mere two months, it would all be over, no more employees, no more pain-in-the-ass customers, and best of all, no more family leeches. He glanced at the calendar. By this time next week, Michael would be floating face down in the ocean on his way to Cuba. Even if the boys didn't make it to the Keys over the weekend, Vince's men would have more than enough time to take him out before the closing. Yes sir! With the 75 million penalty clause, World Office Products wasn't going anywhere. He had them by the balls, right where he wanted them. This definitely was a moment to remember. Stuart smirked. Who else could have pulled off what he just did, nobody, not even Richard, the big know-it-all. His brother could rot forever in his grave for all he cared.

The papers Gayle had signed recently lay in a stack on his desk in his Grant Office Supplies office. Stuart leafed through them, looking for the General Warranty Deed, which he found near the bottom of the pile. As he glanced over the part making him the official owner of Gayle's house, a smug expression enveloped his face. Who was the smarter brother now?

Feeling good about himself, he reached to the safe and opened it. On the very bottom shelf beneath a stack of papers, he found the legal-size envelope containing the agreements, exactly where he remembered putting it.

He opened the envelope and pulled out the papers. When he noticed they were blank, he thought he was looking at the reverse side of the papers. He flipped the papers over. The other sides were blank, also. Like a wild man, he tore off the paperclip, his triumphant feeling turning to a state of panic. Where were they? He ransacked the safe, thinking he pulled out the wrong envelope. There weren't any other legal-sized envelopes in the safe. He checked the envelope on the desk again. He had the right envelope. Scrawled on the front of it in his handwriting was COPIES OF AGREEMENT. Blood drained from Stuart's face. The agreements were gone. Someone had broken into the safe and taken them. No. Someone didn't break into the safe. The bastard knew the combination. His mind reeled, wondering who all had access to the safe.

He buzzed his secretary. "Dawn, come in here."

Within moments, a slightly overweight brunette stood in front of his desk. "Yes, Mr. Grant?"

"Who has been in my safe?"

"No one."

"Did you notice anyone in my office?"

"No sir."

"Talk to the other employees. See if they noticed anything."

"Why? Is something missing?"

"I put some important papers in the safe, and now they're gone."

"Are you sure you didn't take the papers home with you?"

"Positive."

"Do you want me to call security?"

"Definitely! And tell them you want a list of everyone who came in the building after hours during the past week."

"I'll get on it right away."

While Dawn was checking for Stuart, he tore his desk apart. Maybe he forgot and took the agreements out of the envelope for some reason. Even if he did, he would not have shoved blank pieces of paper in the envelope. Why would he? It didn't make sense.

While he was wracking his mind, trying to remember if he had taken the agreements out for some reason, Dawn appeared in his doorway.

"I talked with everyone," she said, "and nobody was in your safe."

"What about security. What did they say?"

"Nothing unusual was reported. They're in the process of calling the night guard to ask him about it."

"Let me know what the guard had to say as soon as they get back with you."

The more Stuart pondered the subject he determined there could be no other explanation. Michael must have been in the building, or he had somebody steal the agreements for him. But where did he get the combination to the safe? Richard had the combination at one time, but he was dead. Maybe he wrote it down before he died, and Gayle kept it over the years.

Stuart buzzed Dawn again. "I need you back in my office."

The secretary came rushing into the room. "Yes, Mr. Grant?"

"Was my nephew, Michael, here while I was out?"

"Not that I'm aware of."

"What about Gayle or any other family members?"

"I didn't see any. Do you want me to ask the other girls?"

"Don't just ask the girls, ask everybody in the office. Maybe someone came in early or stayed late and saw something."

Stuart's shoulders ached, and then the pain progressed to his neck and head, as if he could actually feel his blood pressure rising. He massaged his neck muscles, trying to relieve the tension.

The agreements were nowhere on the desk. He went to the file cabinet. Sometimes when he got busy, and his mind was on the last phone call he received, he misfiled things. For several minutes, he went through the drawers. No agreements. Somebody definitely stole them.

Dawn came back into his office. "No one noticed anyone from your family in the office or the building."

"Damn it! Somebody was in this safe. Call security back and ask them if they saw Michael or anyone else from my family in the building this past week, day or night."

He grabbed the envelope again. No mystical fairy had waved a magic wand over it. Still no agreements.

While he was waiting final word from Dawn, he paced the floor. With the agreements gone, this definitely put him at a disadvantage. Stuart wrung his hands, wishing Michael's neck were in them.

As he was tearing the blank papers to shreds, Dawn returned to his office.

"Well," he said.

"I not only spoke with security, I went down to the lobby and checked the log book myself. Nobody saw anyone from your family, and none of their names was listed. But I think we may be on to something."

Stuart felt hopeful. "What's that?"

"Security said something strange happened the other night. They said Chuck, the night guard, let some cleaning woman in to polish the paneling in your office."

"So? What is so strange about that?"

"She supposedly showed up in the middle of the night. The cleaning people usually leave the building before midnight."

"If it was so unusual, why did the guard let her in the building?"

"That's what I wondered." Dawn crossed her arms over her chest. "They said she wore the regular uniform and had cleaning supplies with her. From what she told the guard, Walton sent her here specifically to clean the paneling in your office."

"Did you call Walton and ask them about it?"

"Yes. They said they never sent anyone to clean the paneling."

"I knew it. Did the guard give them a description?"

"He gave it to me. I got the number from security and called Chuck myself."

"What did this woman look like?"

"According to Chuck, she was a knockout."

"That still doesn't tell me anything. How old was she?"

"Young, in her twenties or thirties. She had long, blonde hair."

The only young person Stuart knew who fit that description was Lorna. But she wouldn't break into his safe. Or would she? Maybe she and Michael were tighter than he thought.

"You did real well, Dawn. I'm sure it was this so-called cleaning lady who got into my safe."

"Do you have any idea who she might be?"

"I have an idea. Thanks. That's all for now."

His mind in a stupor, Stuart stood at the window. While he was agonizing over what he should do next, the idea hit him. He grabbed the phone and dialed Gayle's house. Hopefully, the maid would answer, and he wouldn't have to talk with her or Michael directly.

When Gayle answered, he felt like ripping the cord out of the wall. "It's Stuart, Gayle. How are you doing?"

"Why do you care?"

"I called to apologize."

"Apologize for what?"

"Everything. I don't want a family rift coming between us." Until he had the agreements back in his possession, he had to con her and Michael to back them off from filing a lawsuit.

"I'm so glad to hear that, Stuart."

"If you and Michael aren't busy later this evening, I'd like to stop on my way home from work and apologize."

"I knew you couldn't go through with this."

"Then it's all right?"

"Even if Michael did make other arrangements, I'm sure he'll change his plans. This is more important. We'll see you later this evening."

13

MICHAEL HAD HIS SUSPICIONS about Stuart. For his uncle to suddenly have a change of heart did not sit right with him. Could he really be sorry for stealing the stock, or was it more of his uncle's scheming? The latter sounding more like Stuart, Michael was not taking any chances.

Ever since the 'Bug House,' a small shop selling spy paraphernalia, opened, Michael had wanted to go in and browse through the many gadgets the store offered for sale. Because it was not that important to him in the past, he never took the time to stop. He would drive past the place, putting it off for another occasion. Now he had an excuse to go in and look over the merchandise.

In case Stuart tried to play any more tricks on him and his mother, Michael thought it would be wise to get everything Stuart said on tape. Then, if they did go to court, he could use the tape as evidence against Stuart.

After nearly an hour of playing with and testing various items, he bought a silver, western-style belt buckle, the inside of which contained a powerful mini microphone that transmitted sound signals to a small tape recorder that could be hidden almost anywhere. With him wearing the belt buckle with jeans, Stuart would never suspect a thing. All he had to do now was get Stuart to admit he stole the stock, and he would have it all on tape.

Michael did not tell Gayle about the microphone. If she knew about it, she might keep staring at the buckle, and then Stuart might suspect something and storm out of the house, blowing a good chance to nail him.

He hid the tape recorder amongst the leaves of one of Gayle's hanging plants.

Slightly before six, there was knocking on the door.

"I'll get it," Michael said.

Anxiety-ridden over facing Stuart again, he took a deep breath and opened the door. "Come on in. My mother's in the Florida room waiting for you."

No longer feeling the warmth he once had for his uncle, Michael lacked the desire to initiate a conversation with him.

Stuart followed Michael through the foyer into the Florida room. "I'll only be a minute. I just wanted to stop by and clear the air."

Michael hoped the tape recorder was working properly. "Just what exactly do you mean by clear the air?"

"I care too much about the three of you to have this feud continue."

Michael persisted in trying to get Stuart to confess. "There's only one way this is going to end, and that's with the return of our stock."

"Your previous accusations are totally unwarranted, Michael. If anything, I should be accusing you of stealing."

Gayle gaped at Stuart. "How dare you!"

Michael put his hand on his mother's shoulder. "I'll handle this. You stay out of it."

"I'm not going to sit here and listen to him call you a thief."

"I said I would handle it." Michael prayed their words would not come out muffled on the recorder. "Just so I get this straight, Uncle Stuart, just what was it I supposedly stole?"

"Don't toy with me, Michael. You know damn well what you stole."

"I beg your pardon, but I don't."

"Then let me give you a clue, the safe in my office."

"What about the safe in your office?"

"You had someone break into it."

"What?"

"They didn't actually break into it. You obviously gave them the combination."

Michael wondered where his uncle came up with that. "Whatever you're smoking, Stuart, I want some of it."

"Someone got into my safe. And the only other person with the combination besides me was your father."

"Have you forgotten, Uncle Stuart? My father is dead. Or maybe you think his ghost did it?"

"Your father apparently wrote down the combination, and your mother kept it over the years."

"I haven't been in your office for months."

"Like I said, you must have put someone up to it."

"Since you're so smart, just who did I put up to it?"

"Lorna."

"What? You're out of your mind."

"I am not. Walton Security told me a nice-looking woman with long blonde hair showed up at the building one night, posing as a cleaning lady."

"You have obviously been working too hard. I think you're having a nervous breakdown."

Gayle threw her book on the coffee table. "For your information, Stuart, I don't have the combination to your safe. I never did."

"Well somebody has it, because they got into my safe."

"You make me sick," she said. "I want you out of this house immediately."

Stuart smirked. "Don't worry, Gayle. I'll never return to YOUR house."

Michael blocked his path. "What about our stock?"

Stuart ignored him and left.

As soon as the door closed, Michael went to the hanging basket.

Gayle looked at him, a curious expression on her face.

"What are you doing, Michael?"

"This is a tape recorder."

"You taped our conversation?"

"Yes. Slick, huh?"

"Excellent."

"The only thing is Uncle Stuart evaded my questions. Let's play the tape back and see what we got." He rewound the tape.

They sat quietly and listened. Nothing of importance. Michael hit the stop button. "He's smarter than we thought. He purposely watched every word he said."

Although Michael felt disappointed, he still had the tape recorder. Maybe it would come in handy in the future."

Gayle asked. "Who do you think broke into the safe, and what do you think they were looking for?"

"If Stuart's blaming me, something I want must be missing."

"That makes sense. It's either the stock or the agreements."

"I'll bet it's the agreements. It has to be."

"Who do you think took them?"

"I don't know."

"Do you think Lorna somehow got the combination?"

"I intend to find out."

14

WHEN STUART GOT HOME, he went straight to the patio to join Eva. He asked her. "How was your day, my dear?"

"Uneventful. How was yours, sweetie?"

"Terrible."

Eva nuzzled his face. "You poor thing! Would you like some champagne?"

"No. I already told Andrew to get me a double Scotch on the rocks."

"You must have had a really bad day. Here. Come sit down and relax."

"Where's Lorna?"

"Why?"

"I want to ask her something."

"Ask her what?"

"It's the strangest thing. Somebody stole documents out of my office safe."

"My goodness, I hope they weren't important."

"They were."

"What does any of this have to do with Lorna?"

"A security guard said a young, pretty woman with long blonde hair came to the building the other night, posing as a cleaning woman."

"And you think it could have been Lorna?"

"The description fit."

"Where would Lorna get the combination to your safe?"

"Maybe she snooped through my things and found it."

"What makes you think Lorna is a snoop or a thief?"

"I don't know. I thought maybe Michael put her up to it."

"Why would Michael put her up to it? For goodness sake, Stuart! What's going on?"

"Forget it."

"No. I'm not going to forget it. What do you mean Michael may have put Lorna up to breaking into your safe?"

Concerned about making her angry, he backed off. "I don't know. I said forget it."

"No. Now you have me wondering. Maybe we better go ask her."

———

LORNA LAY ON THE bed reading. About to turn the page of her novel, she heard rapping on the door. "Who is it," she said.

"It's me, mother. Stuart and I want to talk to you."

She could not imagine why. She laid her book on the dresser and went to open the door. "What do you want to talk to me about?"

Eva pushed past her. "Have you ever been in Stuart's building?"

"Yes. I stopped by to see it the other day. Why?"

Stuart answered. "A young woman fitting your description stole some important documents out of my office safe."

"And you think I did it?"

"Did you?"

Eva waited for an answer. "Well, did you?"

Lorna was at a loss for words. She and her mother didn't get along, but her honesty was never questioned. Instead of flipping out and choking the two of them to death, Lorna counted to ten before she answered. "Is that what you were hoping to hear?"

"Did you or didn't you," Eva asked.

Lorna had heard enough of her mother's revolting accusations. Now Stuart had jumped on the bandwagon. Exhausted from constantly defending herself, she realized she had been a fool for coming to stay with her mother and Stuart for the summer. Lorna sighed. If her mother thought that little of her, then she could think whatever she wanted. "Yes, mother. I broke into Stuart's safe. Now, will the two of you please leave me alone?"

Stuart glared at her. "I knew it. Michael put you up to it, didn't he?"

"Sure, Stuart, is there anything else you two want to know?" Disgusted, Lorna shook her head. As far as her relationship with Stuart was concerned, he had placed her in the same league with William. Suddenly, packing up and leaving this insane asylum sounded like a good idea.

Stuart's face grew red with anger. "Where are the agreements?"

"Ah, the agreements! Hey, like you said, Stuart, Michael put me up to stealing them for him, so who do you think has them?"

"No. You didn't give him the agreements."

Lorna smirked. "You two are pathetic."

Stuart's eyes filled with rage. "I want you out of this house by the end of the week."

"Don't worry. I have no intentions of staying." Lorna looked at her mother for one last bit of hope. When she got no sympathetic reaction at all, she shook her head. "You two deserve each other. May you share a sick, miserable life together!"

Eva scoffed. "You'll never change, will you? You'll always be a smart aleck."

Hurt deeper than she had ever been by her mother, Lorna started to cry. "You actually don't care that Stuart is throwing me out, do you?"

"Why should I. Ever since you came to Sand Dollar Island, you've caused nothing but trouble."

"Where am I supposed to go?"

"You're a big girl. Go bother your father for a while. Get a job. Do something productive with your life. Stop being a leech."

Tears streamed down Lorna's face. "How am I supposed to get to dad's house? I don't have any money."

"Call and get the money from him." Eva grabbed Stuart's arm and stormed out of the room.

Lorna slumped to the bed, her heart torn to shreds. For several moments, she sat quietly, too upset to move. About to go to the closet for her suitcases, she heard her phone ring. Too despondent to speak with anyone, she let it ring.

While she was emptying out a dresser drawer there was knocking on the bedroom door. She chose not to answer it.

Andrew hollered through the door. "There is a phone call for you, Miss Lorna."

"Did they say who it was?"

"Yes, Michael would like to speak with you."

15

LORNA BRUSHED THE TEARS from her eyes and picked up the receiver. "Hi, Michael, how are you?"

"I'm all right. I was wondering if you were busy tonight."

"I guess you could say that."

"Darn it! I was hoping you would have dinner with me."

Why not, she figured. Eating with him sounded a lot better than having to work her way around her mother and Stuart.

"Dinner sounds great."

"I thought you just said you were busy."

"I changed my mind."

"Terrific. When can you be ready?"

"How about ten or fifteen minutes?"

"That's fine with me. If you don't mind, can you meet me down at the dock?"

"Sure. I'll see you there in a little while."

Lorna hung up the phone and slid out of her shorts. Still upset over the altercation with her mother and Stuart, she barely brushed though her hair. A dab of nude lipstick, a stroke of blush, and then she dragged herself to the closet and pulled out her black, halter sundress.

Not long after Michael's call, she found herself tromping down the sandy path to join him.

He noticed her puffy eyes. "Is something wrong?"

"I'll tell you all about it later."

"You look like you could use a drink. Come on. I know a quiet, cozy, little place that has good food as well as a nice view."

The next fifteen minutes they spent driving the coast north. Close to Palm Beach they turned right onto a dirt road leading up to a rocky ledge overlooking the Atlantic.

"This place is charming, Michael."

"I think so. It's kind of an 'in spot' for locals."

As they walked up a path guarded on both sides by palm trees and clay pots brimming with colorful pink, white and coral impatiens, small lanterns in the grass illuminated their footsteps.

They followed the hostess through the main dining room, where candles gracing tables cast dim glows over hungry diners.

Michael neglected to make a reservation. The customers who did have reservations occupied the choice tables out on the veranda next to the railing. He and Lorna sat one row back, but they still had a magnificent view of the water.

No sooner did they get comfortable than a waiter arrived with menus and a wine list.

Michael laid both aside. "What would you like to drink?"

"I don't know. What are you having?"

"A beer."

"I'll have a beer, too."

Night had fallen, and moist sea breezes jostled willowy palm trees, no longer green but black silhouettes against the star-lit sky.

Lorna gazed out to sea. As the moon appeared from behind a cloud, a long beam of light suddenly stretched across the water and glided over flowing ripples, causing them to glisten as if they were sparkling diamonds.

The waiter returned to the table with their beers.

Both Michael and Lorna remained silent until he left.

Michael held his glass in the air. "Here's to you, Lorna."

"Why me?"

"You seem to have some kind of power over me."

She glanced away, certain that he just handed her a line. A man like him only wanted one thing from her, sex. Why should he care about a homeless, penniless nobody? With his looks and bank account, he could have some, beautiful, wealthy debutante.

"I mean it, Lorna. Every time I'm around you, I suddenly feel happier."

She wanted to believe him. It had been so long since she felt a man's arms around her, not just any man's, but the arms of somebody concerned about her welfare. She wanted to touch Michael, to sit on the beach and gaze up at the stars with him, to spend the night making love with him. No. This was wrong. His narcotic charm was intoxicating her. She had to block him from her mind.

She changed the subject. "This place really is lovely."

"No. You're lovely."

She sighed.

Michael tore a roll in half and buttered it. "The oddest thing happened the other day."

She felt better now that he stopped with the lines, trying to seduce her. "What was that, Michael?"

"Some woman broke into my Uncle Stuart's safe."

That's all she had to hear. "Here we go again."

"What? Did you hear about it?"

"Your wonderful uncle not only told me about it, he accused me of being that woman."

"Are you?"

Lorna tossed her beer in Michael's face. When would she ever learn her lesson? She should have known better when he called and asked her out to dinner. He just wanted to pump her for information. Naïve? She was the worst. After tonight, one thing was certain. It would never happen again. "Look, Michael. I accepted your dinner invitation, because I couldn't stand being in the same house with my mother and Stuart anymore, not to be cross-examined all night. I'm going home." She threw her arms in the air. "Home? Hah! I don't even have a home." Tears welled up in her eyes.

Michael grabbed her arm. "I'm sorry. Please, don't go."

She was furious. "You Grants are all alike."

He wiped himself off with a napkin. "You're wrong. We're not."

"What's so important about those damn agreements anyway?"

"You have no idea."

"Then why don't you fill me in on the big family secret."

"I will, if you'll just sit back down."

Exasperated, she slid onto the chair.

Michael leaned on his elbows, getting closer to her.

"Here's why the agreements are so important. You see, right before my grandfather died, he made my father and Stuart promise to take care of the other's family, if something happened to one of them, and keep the stock in Grant Office Supplies split evenly. Those papers that somebody stole from Stuart's safe are copies of the agreement they made. Without them, no one can prove the vow ever existed."

"Then ownership of the company would be like a free-for-all."

"That's it in a nutshell."

"Why is Stuart worried? He runs the company. Nobody is going to pull the wool over his eyes."

"That's true."

"Then why is he so worried about getting the agreements back?"

"It's not so much that he wants them back. He doesn't want anyone else to get their hands on them, especially me."

"I still don't understand, Michael. He's running the business and knows where all of the money is going."

"I'm going to tell you something, Lorna, but you have to promise me that you'll keep it to yourself."

"You have my word, Michael."

"Remember what I just said about my father and uncle keeping the stock split evenly? Well, I just found out that Stuart, that bastard uncle of mine, stole forty-three percent of our inherited stock."

"You're kidding! How?"

"He has been sneaking it behind our backs for years."

"How could he sneak it without any of you finding out about it?"

"Two ways. One, we trusted the son of a bitch and signed things for him without reading them first. And two, his attorneys and accountants handle all of the company business."

"Wow! What kind of monster is Stuart?"

"A slimy, underhanded one."

"I didn't take those agreements, Michael."

"I'm glad you told me without my having to wonder. Thanks." Michael drummed his fingers on the table. "If I could just get my hands on one of those agreements, I would be able to prove that half of that stock still belongs to me, my mother and my sister."

"Why don't you call Stuart's bluff?"

"How do I do that?"

"When he accused me of breaking into his safe, he said you probably put me up to it."

"What did you tell him?"

"I was so hurt and angry, I humored him. I told him I stole the agreements for you."

"Then he actually believes I have them?"

"It sounded that way to me."

"Why? What did he say?"

"He threw me out of the house."

"You're kidding!"

"I wish I were. I have to be out by the end of the week."

"Does your mother know?"

Lorna sighed. "She knows all right."

"And she doesn't care?"

"My mother doesn't care anything about me."

"It sounds like Stuart found a soul mate."

"That's what I told them in so many words."

"Where do you plan to go at the end of the week?"

"I guess to my father's place in Michigan."

"Do you really want to go back up north?"

"No, but I have no choice."

"Yes you do."

"What do you mean?"

"Stay with me and my mother. We have plenty of guest bedrooms in that big house."

"I couldn't do that."

"Why not? We have company staying from time to time. It's no big deal."

"It is when your hateful mother lives right down the street. She would kill me if I moved in with you."

"Do you really care what your mother thinks now?"

"I'm angry with her, but I still care."

"The way I see it, she and Stuart put you in a bind. You have to start looking out for yourself."

"I have to admit staying on Sand Dollar Island would be a lot more pleasant than going back up north."

"Then it's settled. You'll stay with us. Besides, I have an ulterior motive in mind."

"What's that?"

"You're going to help me wage war against my uncle."

16

A S SOON AS LORNA ARRIVED back at Stuart's house, she pulled out her suitcases and packed up her things. For the time being she only needed her clothes and toiletries. Her TV, stereo and a few other items she brought from Gainesville could wait for some other time. What mattered most was getting out peaceably, before her mother discovered she planned to leave tonight.

A suitcase in each hand, she stepped out the bedroom door. Right in the middle of the corridor stood Holly. Lorna wanted to scream, but then her frown suddenly turned to a grin. No more breakfasts, lunches or dinners with this absurd character that had a head full of Jell-O instead of brains.

With Holly blocking her path, Lorna had to say something.

"It's been a trip staying here, Holly."

"Where are you going? I thought you were staying the summer."

"You mean you haven't heard? I've been thrown out."

"What happened?"

"Ask your father."

"My dad threw you out?"

"That's right."

"Jeez! Where are you going?"

About to answer, Lorna saw her mother coming down the hall. If it hadn't been for Holly, she would have been out the door and on her way to Michael's house by now without any drama.

Eva eyed the suitcases. "That was quick. Did your father put the airplane ticket on his credit card?"

Lorna figured she might as well tell her the truth. It wouldn't be long before she found out where she was staying anyway. "No," she said, dropping the suitcases to the floor.

"I thought you didn't have any money."

"I don't."

"Then how did you get the ticket? Did Holly lend you the money?"

Holly shook her head no. "I didn't lend her anything. I didn't even know she was leaving until I ran into her here in the hall just now."

"Then how did you buy the ticket, Lorna, on your credit card?"

"For goodness sake, mother. I didn't buy a ticket. I'm not going up north."

"You're not?"

"No."

"Then where are you going?"

"Next door."

"What do you mean next door?"

"I'm moving in with Michael and Gayle until I'm on my feet."

"You're what? Oh no, you aren't, young lady. I'm not going to let you impose on Gayle. I'll put the airplane ticket on my credit card."

"It's already settled. Michael invited me earlier."

"When did you see Michael?"

"I had dinner with him a little while ago."

"You are NOT moving in with Gayle and Michael."

Holly smirked. "Let her, Eva. I'm sure Gayle doesn't mind. She's real nice like that."

Eva glared at Holly. "You stay out of this."

"Oops," Holly said. "I think I'll go to my room."

Eva waited until Holly closed the door. "So you're screwing Michael."

"I am not screwing Michael." Lorna picked up the suitcases. "If you want me for anything, I'll be down the street."

"You are not going to Gayle's."

"How are you going to stop me, put me over your knee and spank me?"

"I mean it, Lorna. You're not moving in with Michael."

"You need help, mother. Remember Gayle lives in that house, too."

"I'm warning you. If you go over there, I'll disown you."

Lorna rolled her eyes. "The way I see it, you've already done that." Suitcases in hand, she pushed past her mother. "Like I said, I'll be down the street, if you need me."

As Lorna walked away, she could almost feel her mother's fiery eyes burning through her dress.

17

THE *GRANT YOUR WISH* cruised south, heading for the Florida Keys.

Jake Butler, an experienced seaman who learned his craft in the navy, kept a keen eye on the water, while Billy Kent, the cook, as well as a deck hand, moved about the galley, preparing yellow-tail snapper, honey-glazed carrots and a garden salad for tonight's dinner.

Michael, William and Julian lounged on the rear deck in swimsuits. From one to the other they passed bags of pretzels and potato chips.

Michael crushed an empty beer can in his hand and tossed it to William. "Eva's daughter moved in with me and my mother the other day," he said.

"You're kidding! Why did she do that?"

"Eva and your dad threw her out of their house."

"How nice of them! Why?"

"They got into an argument."

"Over what?"

"I don't know." He knew, but did not feel like explaining the entire issue to William. "She says she doesn't get along with her mother."

"How long does she intend to stay at your place?"

"Until she gets on her feet."

"You should have invited her to come along with us."

"I did, but she wanted to work on her resume." Michael pointed to shore. "We're leaving Miami. We'll be in Key Largo soon."

William swallowed a mouthful of potato chips. "What do you want to do when we get to Key West?"

"Michael reached into a cooler for a bottle of water. "Hit some bars, go diving and just hang out."

A reggae CD that Julian bought in St. Martin while vacationing with William filtered through the sound system. The upbeat rhythm had him moving about the deck, his hips swaying and his arms waving in the air.

He shimmied over to them. "Why don't we browse Duval Street when we get to Key West?"

William got up to dance with Julian. "Sounds good to me. What do you think, Michael?"

"Okay." He motioned with a nod. "That boat over there must be heading for Key West, too. It has been cruising along with us for some time now."

William and Julian glanced over at the boat.

Julian remarked. "The more the merrier."

———

A THIRD THE SIZE OF *Grant Your Wish*, the nameless boat cruised at a safe distance. At the controls was a stunning Latin girl of twenty-two. Every so often, Lysette Vargas would refresh herself with a gulp she took from a can of orange soda.

Her twin sister, Lucia, sat on the blue vinyl seat next to her with her long, slender legs propped up on the steering console.

Orphaned at age six, the dark-skinned beauties had grown up on Rio de Janeiro's crowded back streets along with the other wild, homeless children. The hardships they endured and the scheming it took to survive laid the groundwork for them becoming specialists in the art of crime. Everything they knew about life they learned on the streets. As the girls grew older, they changed from filthy, little, snot-nosed beggars and thieves into stunning young women who used their wits and wiles to get what they wanted.

When the Vargas twins first arrived in Miami a little over two years ago, they dressed in sexy clothes and barhopped, until they made powerful underworld connections. Those acquaintances led them to Vince

Spinosa, who not only paid them handsomely for their two-on-one sexual favors, but he hired them to be his hit women. Lean, quick and agile, the twins proved invaluable to Vince. The girls feared nothing, and they loved living life on the edge.

While Lysette steered, Lucia rummaged through her purse for an insulin bottle and syringe. Instead of containing medication, the vial held a colorless, deadly poison the twins received from local natives living in the Brazilian rainforest. After a lethal dose had been administered, the victim would die without a trace of poison left in his system, appearing as though he had suffered a heart attack.

A bottle marked R for regular insulin contained the poison. Another bottle marked U for Ultra Lente insulin contained an antidote, in case they would ever need it, which until now the girls had not.

Carrying bottles of insulin proved to be smarter and more convenient than concealing guns or other deadly weapons. If the coast guard happened to stop the boat to inspect it for drugs, the officials would think one of the girls had diabetes.

Lucia slid the orange cap off the syringe and filled it with poison. While she had her purse on her lap, she reached for a photograph.

"Lysette," she said. "Where shall we 'off' this Michael Grant guy?"

"I think we should follow him and wait for the right moment to take him down."

"Whatever we do, we must not lose sight of him, or Vince will really be mad."

As Lucia pulled the photograph of Michael out of the bag, the turbulent airflow swirling around the boat ripped the picture out of her hand and sent it blowing across the steering console, where it caught against the windshield. She jumped up and grabbed for it, but the wind tore the picture loose and sent it flying into the air. Lysette lunged for it, but she, too, missed it. The photograph went sailing over the side of the boat into the water.

Lysette glared at Lucia. "I never got a chance to study the picture. I hope you will recognize this man when you see him."

Lucia twirled a curly black tendril around her finger. "Do not worry, my sister. I will know this Michael Grant when I see him."

18

TARZAN'S, A POPULAR SPOT in Key West, packed in tourists from all over the world. Spotlights lit up the outdoor bar, and multicolored twinkle lights circling tree trunks and branches provided subdued radiance over tables.

Michael, along with William and Julian, sat next to a muddy pit, watching a scruffy-bearded man wrestle a twelve-foot alligator. Every time the alligator got the upper hand, spectators whistled and cheered. When the opposite occurred, everyone booed.

William, feeling a buzz from the alcohol he drank, laughed so hard that tears ran down his face. "This place is nuts," he said.

Out of nowhere, a loud Tarzan yell echoed throughout the courtyard, and a muscular man in a loincloth came swinging down from a Banyan tree to a platform in the center of the bar. Everyone hollered and threw peanuts at him, the customary thing to do.

At the bar the twins sat watching Michael, William and Julian.

Lysette said. "The two white men look alike. Which one is Michael Grant?"

Lucia squirmed. "I think he is the one in the white polo shirt."

Lysette plopped her purse down on the bar. "What do you mean you think?"

Lucia squirmed even more. "How did I know there would be two men who looked the same?"

"Now what? What if we take out the wrong guy?"

"Do not worry, my sister. I have an idea."

Lysette smirked. "You better."

"The man we have to take out is Michael Grant, right? We will buy him a drink and send it over with a waitress. The man who thanks us will be Michael Grant."

Lysette grinned, a sly twinkle in her eyes. "You are very clever, my sister."

The twins arranged the drink with the waitress.

A Tarzan's special in her hand, the buxom redhead delivered the drink to the table. "Which one of you is Michael Grant," she asked.

Michael looked at her curiously. "Why?"

The young woman pointed. "Those twins over there bought you a drink."

William grabbed the drink. "I'm Michael Grant," he said, teasing Julian.

"Like I care," Julian scoffed. "You couldn't get it together with a woman if you tried."

"Oh yeah! Watch this." He jumped up to go thank the twins.

Julian grabbed the back of his shorts. "You keep your sexy ass right where it is."

Michael put the brakes on a quarrel in the making. "Sit down. I'll go."

As Michael stood, he noticed the girls leaving. He waved thanks, but with their backs to him, they did not see him.

William reached for a handful of peanuts. "You missed your chance, Mike."

"Yeah, thanks to you."

"Do you know those girls?"

"Maybe. I couldn't see their faces."

Another trendy place across the street from *Tarzan's* also drew a big crowd.

The twins lingered at the bar, keeping a safe distance from, yet maintaining a close eye on the man they believed was Michael Grant, the man they planned to kill.

Lucia boasted. "Was that not smart of me, Lysette?"

"Yes, you are wonderful. Now give me the needle."

"You cannot do it out in the open. Somebody might see you."

"Do not be stupid, my sister. I am not going to do it here. We will follow them and wait patiently."

For another fifteen minutes the twins sat there. About to order two more sodas, they saw Michael, William and Julian coming out of *Tarzan's*.

Without the men noticing, the girls followed them to Duval Street. Every now and then, the men would stop in front of a store to window shop. Each time they did, the girls either ducked into a doorway or turned their backs to them, as if they, too, had stopped to window shop.

As everyone made their way down the street, they heard drums approaching. A parade was drawing near.

Tourists, as well as locals, scurried to the curb and maneuvered for a good position, excited about seeing the action.

Michael strained to see the marchers. "What kind of parade do you think it is?"

William peered over Michael's shoulder. "It's probably a gay parade. I know they have a lot of them down here."

Behind a makeshift marching band, six gay men held up a banner saying MISS KEY WEST CONTEST.

A procession of convertibles followed behind. On top of the back seat of each car a drag queen sat decked out in an outrageous wig, exaggerated makeup, excessive jewelry and a flamboyant gown.

Julian grinned. "Look at them, Will. They look better than most women."

"I have to admit they look pretty good. What do you think, Mike?"

"They're a little much, but you know my philosophy, live and let live."

The parade continued to pass by, and more and more people gathered on the sidewalks, including the Brazilian twins.

Lucia reached into her bag for the needle. "Now is the time."

Lysette grabbed her sister's arm. "Are you sure? There are so many people."

"The more people the better."

With everyone watching the parade, nobody noticed the twins squeezing through the crowd.

Lucia stood behind William and flicked the cap off the syringe. She waited, pretending like she was enjoying the spectacle, and then she bumped against him, as if someone had pushed her. With the skill and precision of a trained nurse, she drove the needle through his shorts and injected him with the poison.

"Ouch," William said. "Something pinched me." Massaging his right buttock, he turned around to see who had bumped against him. His eyes lit up when he saw the twins. "Hey! You're the girls from *Tarzan's*."

Lucia looked up at him with big brown, apologetic eyes. "I am sorry. Somebody pushed me."

"You girls really look alike. I'll bet no one can tell you two apart."

"We hear that all the time."

"You have an accent. Where are you from?"

"South America"

"I thought so."

William tapped Michael on the shoulder. "Look who is here."

When Michael turned around, the twins were gone.

William shrugged his shoulders. "Those girls from *Tarzan's* were here a second ago, the ones who bought you a drink. I wonder why they left."

"I wish they would have stuck around. I'm curious as to how they know me."

"Especially since they're from South America."

"How do you know they're from South America?"

"They just told me."

The three men went back to watching the parade.

At the next street corner the twins turned left and hurried towards the ocean. Down one street and across another they ran. In a deserted alley, they saw the black Ford Mustang waiting for them.

A young punk jumped out of the car.

Lysette tossed him a set of keys. "The boat is docked at the marina, down the end of the street."

Without responding, the boy caught the keys in the air and went running.

The twins feared returning to the dock. If the police came looking for them, too many people had seen them. However, no one would be looking for a young man. He could take the boat and head back up the coast without anyone suspecting a thing.

Lucia reached to the back seat for a brown grocery bag. "Hurry, Lysette. We must change and get out of here." She tossed her sister a red wig, denim shorts and an oversized T-shirt. As fast as she herself could, Lucia slipped out of her sexy, red dress into a pair of white shorts and a yellow tank top. Her hair she piled on top of her head with bobby pins, and then she donned a curly brown wig. While her sister drove, she gathered together their sexy clothes and shoved them into a grocery bag. "Pull behind that seashell store over there," she said.

Lysette jerked the wheel to the left and drove up to a garbage bin. "Bury the bag deep."

"I will." Lucia jumped out of the car and ran to a big trash bin, the smell of rotting garbage gagging her. As she shoved the bag far to the bottom, knocking empty boxes and soda cans out of the way, her arms brushed against an old piece of pizza coated with maggots. When she pulled out her arm, slimy, squiggly worms stuck to it. About to vomit, Lucia flicked them to the ground.

"That was disgusting," she said, jumping back into the car.

Lysette threw the car into gear. "What happened?"

"Filthy maggots. They were on my arm."

"Too bad! We must get out of here."

19

FOUR DRAG QUEENS SAT on a makeshift stage, judging the Miss Key West contest.

As William waited to hear who had won, he began to feel sick. "Those drinks really hit me. I feel dizzy."

Julian took his arm. "Are you going to throw up?"

"Yeah. I'm . . ." William fell against Julian, unable to finish the sentence.

"I don't understand, Mike. I've seen Will feeling tipsy before, but I've never seen him this sick. We better get him back to the boat."

William gripped his chest and screamed out in pain. "Ahhhhhhhh. My heart is pounding so fast."

Michael grabbed his cousin around the waist. "He might be having a heart attack."

Julian asked. "How could he be having a heart attack? Maybe he has food poisoning."

"It can't be food poisoning. We all ate the same thing, and we're not sick."

"Maybe it didn't hit us yet. People react differently to food poisoning."

"Look. He keeps clutching his chest. I think we better get him to a hospital."

Again William threw back his head in agonizing pain.

"That's it," Michael said. "We're taking him to the hospital."

"If he's having a heart attack, we might not make it to the hospital on time."

"You're right. Call 911."

Julian sat William down on the sidewalk. "Take it easy, Will. We're getting help."

As William thrashed about in pain, he clutched his chest.

Julian held him steady, so that he wouldn't smack his head against the rough concrete.

Michael squatted down next to them. "They're sending an ambulance right away."

Julian's dark skin went pale. "He's getting worse, Mike."

Michael glanced up at the curious onlookers gathered around them. "Is anyone a doctor?"

No response came from any of the onlookers, only blank expressions and heads shaking no.

A police officer patrolling the streets had noticed the commotion. He rushed over to help. "What's the problem here?"

Michael answered. "I think my cousin might be having a heart attack."

William's eyes shot wide open, and then he fell limp."

Julian shook him. "Hang on, Will. We're getting help."

The police officer put his fingers on William's neck. "We better give him CPR."

"I can do it," Michael said. He bent over William and opened his mouth. While he was checking for obstructions, the ambulance arrived.

Three medics jumped out of the vehicle and rushed over to the crowd. One of them was carrying oxygen equipment. The second, a woman, had a medical bag, and the other man was hauling a blanket and a flat board.

For several minutes, the EMTs administered emergency life-saving techniques, trying to revive William. Their efforts proved futile. William lay dead on the cold, rough concrete.

One of the paramedics looked up at Michael and shook his head. "I'm sorry."

"How? What happened to him? Was it a heart attack?"

"It looks that way."

Julian clutched William in his arms. "It can't be. Come on, Will, wake up."

In a mind-numbing stupor, Michael knelt beside William. "I can't believe this."

Julian's body trembled as tears streamed down his face. "He can't be dead, Mike."

Michael helped Julian to his feet. "There's nothing more we can do."

"We can't just leave Will here like this."

"I'm sure the paramedics will want us to go to the hospital with them to fill out papers or what have you."

Julian fell against Michael. "I don't know if I can handle all this."

Michael helped Julian into the ambulance. "You have to for Will."

20

A POLITE RAP ON THE bedroom door woke Stuart and Eva from a sound sleep.

Bleary-eyed, Stuart glanced at the clock. "It's one o'clock in the morning, Andrew. What do you want?"

"I'm sorry to bother you, sir, but there is an important telephone call for you."

His mind in a fog, Stuart did not connect the phone call with the hit. "Can't it wait?"

"I do not believe so, sir."

It suddenly dawned on Stuart that it might be William or Vince. From the moment the boys left for the Keys, he had been waiting for word. "All right, Andrew. I'll get it."

Eva yawned. "Who do you think it is, Stuart?"

"I have no idea, darling." As he fumbled for the phone, he knocked a photograph of a younger Holly to the floor, cracking the glass.

Eva rolled her eyes and sighed. "I'll turn on the light for you."

When Stuart heard Michael's voice on the line, he gasped. Why was Michael calling instead of William, or why wasn't it the police on the line? He dreaded asking. "What is it, Michael?"

"Something terrible has happened."

Stuart's puffy, sleepy face turned ashen, his instincts telling him the hit had gone awry. "What's wrong?"

"It's William."

His groggy voice faded to a whisper. "What about William?"

"He's dead, Uncle Stuart."

"Dead?" Stuart felt like he might collapse, mixed emotions swirling throughout every cell of his body. Although he often scorned William for being gay, deep down he still loved him. "How," he asked, slumping against the headboard.

"You're not going to believe this, but he had a heart attack."

Eva propped herself up on her elbows. "What is it, Stuart? Who is dead?"

He found it difficult to answer. "William."

She sat up and grabbed Stuart, wrapping her arms around him. "William is dead? How? What happened?"

Stuart pushed her away. "Where are you, Michael?"

"At the hospital here in Key West. They pronounced him dead on arrival."

"I'll be right down."

"That might not be necessary. They're releasing the body so we can take it back home. Why don't you call a funeral parlor and arrange to have him picked up."

"I'll call right now. But I'm still coming down. I'll take the seaplane."

"Under the circumstances, I don't think you should pilot the plane. Why don't you get somebody to fly you down?"

Stuart unbuttoned his pajama top. "I'll be fine. What are your plans? Are you staying in the Keys?"

"I'll hang around here with Julian until you get here."

"I'll be there in an hour or so."

Stuart hurried to his closet and grabbed a pair of khakis. "I'm taking the seaplane down to the Keys."

"I don't think you should go by yourself. I'll go with you."

"Good. I could use the company."

Eva hurried to the bathroom and turned on the shower.

Stuart hollered in to her. "We don't have time to take showers. Just throw something on, and we'll go."

"You're right," she said. "I'll be ready in a second."

Eva rushed to her walk-in closet and pulled out a white blouse and black slacks. "What about Holly? Shouldn't we wake her and tell her about William before we leave?"

"I'll go tell her after I call a funeral director."

BY THE TIME STUART AND EVA made it to the hospital, almost two hours had passed.

When Stuart saw Michael standing in the corridor alive and well, he could have run up to him and choked him to death with his bare hands. He showed no signs of affection towards him.

The exact opposite, Michael threw his arms around Stuart. "It's all so terrible. I can't believe William is gone."

Like a block of freezing ice, Stuart stood with his arms at his sides. It was Michael who should have been dead, not his son.

Under the devastating circumstances, Eva stayed close to Stuart's side. "What was the official cause of death, Michael? Was it a heart attack?"

"Yes. The doctor just confirmed it."

As upset as he was, Stuart fought to contain his rage. If Vince's people had taken Michael out, the way they were supposed to do, nobody, not the police, doctors or anyone, would have suspected it had been a hit. This wasn't over yet. Vince's man might have botched the job this time, but he sure as hell wouldn't the next time.

21

A FLASH OF LIGHTNING lit up the empty parking lot in front of Spinosa's Restaurant.

As the black Mustang made its way around the side to the rear of the building, rain pelted the windshield, making it difficult for Lysette to see.

Lucia reached to the back seat for an umbrella. "Vince must have another job for us. He never calls us to come in at this hour of the morning."

"Maybe he has the rest of our money, and we are going to get paid."

"I doubt it. He never went through this much trouble just to pay us."

Lysette turned off the engine. "I was thinking. Maybe we should take a trip to Hawaii or something after our next job."

Lucia gave her sister a high five. "How does a cruise to Tahiti sound?"

"Boring. There is nothing but more sun and sand in Tahiti. I want to go someplace where there is lots of action."

"Name a place."

"How about Las Vegas ?"

"Las Vegas sounds fun. We will be able to gamble there."

"That and maybe get jobs as showgirls."

"Are you crazy? How can we become showgirls? Neither of us can dance?"

"We will become strippers then. You do not have to know any fancy dance steps to strip."

"That is true. Show me a man who cares if a sexy, naked woman can do a pirouette."

Lysette laughed as she lifted up on the door handle. "Wait here. I will come around with the umbrella."

The downpour showed no signs of subsiding. As the twins scurried to the building, they huddled closely together under the umbrella. Still, the rain soaked their legs and shorts, and their high-heeled sandals swam in the streams of water flowing to a sewer.

Two of Vince's henchmen were in the office with him. Neither girl reacted to their presence. They knew the men well.

Full of flirtatious energy, Lucia plopped down on Lefty's lap. "Hey, big guy, how is it going?"

Lefty lit a cigarette, ignoring her altogether.

His nonchalant attitude drove Lucia crazy. Like a moth drawn to a light bulb, she could not resist his cocky attitude. "What is the matter with you tonight?" She fluffed his hair. "You cannot say hello to me?"

His rigid face turned to a sneer. "Yeah, yeah. Hi, Lucy."

Although Lefty had been in her company a number of times, he never picked up on the fact that her real name was Lucia.

Lysette sat on the edge of the desk, her arms crossed over her chest, and her long, shapely legs extended in front of her, one ankle over the other. "Vince, are you going to offer us a drink?"

"Sure. Go get the girls a drink, Johnny."

"What do I look like, somebody's maid?"

Vince glowered at him.

"I'm going," Johnny said. "What do you broads want?"

Lucia answered. "Rum and coke. What about you, Lysette?"

"The same."

Johnny slid his thumbs under his waistband and hiked up his pants. "Since I have to go out to the lounge, does anybody else want anything?"

Lefty blew smoke in Lucia's face. "Yeah, get me a beer."

Lysette asked. "Why did you call us in, Vince? Do you have the rest of our money?"

"Business can wait. Have your drink first."

Lucia ran her index finger over Lefty's lip. "Do you want to come home with me after the meeting?"

"I can't tonight. My wife's expecting me."

Johnny strolled into the office, carrying a tray of glasses. He passed out the other drinks and kept a glass of Scotch for himself.

Vince puffed on his cigar. "Did you girls happen to bring that insulin bottle of poison and some needles with you?"

"Yes," Lysette answered. "Why? Do you have another job for us?"

"In a way."

"What do you mean, in a way?"

Vince twirled his cigar in a red glass ashtray, depositing a mound of dead ashes. "We'll get to that in a minute. Hand me the bottle and needle."

Lysette rummaged through her purse. "Here they are."

Vince held up the bottle to see how much poison it contained. "There's only a little bit left. How much does it take to kill someone?"

"We never measured," Lysette answered. "We just fill the syringe."

"Is there enough here to kill two people?"

Lucia squirmed. "Why?"

Vince ignored the question. "Do you have any more needles in your purse, not that it really matters, I guess."

"Yes. We always carry several needles with us."

"Good. Get me another one."

Again Lysette fumbled through her purse.

Vince motioned to Johnny. "Put some poison in the needles."

Lefty pushed Lucia off his lap and got up from the chair.

She smacked his arm. "You almost dropped me."

He shoved his hand in her face and pushed her away. "Watch it, bitch."

Lucia clawed at his eyes.

Lefty slammed Lucia to the chair. "You little whore. Try that again, and I'll break your neck."

She sprung to attack him, but Vince grabbed her. "That's enough, Lucia." He shoved her back to the chair. "Lysette, where's the ten grand I gave you two last week?"

She lied. "At home."

"Where at home?"

"Stuffed inside a pillow."

The twins never kept big money lying around the apartment. They kept it where nobody else could get their hands on it. The ten grand, plus a lot more, they stashed in a locker at Miami International Airport.

Vince flicked another mound of ashes into the ashtray. "Give Lefty the keys to your apartment."

Lysette fidgeted. "I do not understand."

"Just give him the damn key."

"Why are you doing this?"

"The money is not yours anymore."

She handed the key to Lefty. "What is going on, Vince?"

He ignored her. "Go get the cash, Lefty."

Lysette slid off the desk. "It is not fair. We did the hit. Now we want the other half you promised us."

Vince dug his fingers into her arm. "Do you girls remember Michael Grant?"

"Of course we remember him. Why?"

"He's still alive."

The twins gaped at each other, their mouths open and their eyes as big as quarters.

Lucia said. "That cannot be."

"You stupid idiots, you killed the wrong man."

Lysette glared at Lucia, envisioning the photograph of Michael sailing over the side of the boat into the water. Because of her twin's bungling, now they were in big trouble.

Lucia cringed. "I am sure we got the right man. To make certain, we had the waitress find out which of the men was Michael Grant."

"For your information, bitch, you girls took out his cousin, William. Now I have to pay back all of the money I made on this job."

"If what you are saying is true, we will give back the money you paid us. We do not mind."

"You screwed up, and I can't have any of my people screwing up."

Lysette reached for the insulin bottle. "Give me back the poison, and we will take Michael Grant out."

"It's too late for that."

"Then we will make it up to you. Whatever you want us to do we will." She strolled over to Vince and lifted her tight, red jersey, exposing her voluptuous, bare breasts.

Vince squeezed one of them. "It's a shame you girls won't be around anymore. I'll miss these babies."

She glanced at Lucia, and the two bolted for the door.

Johnny blocked their path. "Where do you broads think you're going?"

Vince aimed a gun at the girls. "Sit down. Now."

The twins clung to each other as they walked over to the sofa.

"No, not there, on the chairs."

Tears trickled down Lucia's face. "Please, Vince. Do not do this."

"Shut up. I hate whiny broads."

"Please, Vince," Lucia said, clutching the cross dangling from her neck.

"Do it already, Johnny. I want to go home and get some sleep."

Lefty grabbed Lysette's arms and held them as Johnny brought the needle to her leg.

She squirmed, trying to free herself from Lefty's grip. "No. Please," she cried out, her eyes wide with terror.

The pleas of mercy had no effect on Johnny. As cold as a rock in a frozen stream, he grabbed hold of her smooth skin and injected her with the poison.

Lucia watched helplessly, tears streaming down her face, as her eyes locked with Lysette's. "Good-bye, my sister, my friend. I will see you again, where the birds soar, on a cloud in the heavens."

With her sister dying, Lucia no longer wanted to live. When it came time for her turn, she sat motionless, her eyes closed and her arms dangling at her sides.

22

WILLIAM GRANT HAD always loved a certain cove of Sand Dollar Island. As his mother scattered his ashes over the sparkling blue water, everyone watched the sad event.

For several moments, relatives and friends prayed silently or reflected back to happier times they had shared with William.

Holly wailed uncontrollably. She took Sheila's arm, while Stuart followed with Eva, leading a procession of mourners back to his house.

Lorna noticed Michael remaining behind. "Are you okay?"

"I was just thinking about Julian and how upset he must be, because Stuart wouldn't let him come to the funeral."

"I was thinking the same thing. I feel so badly for him."

"Stuart was totally out of line."

"You're right. He's a louse. Where does he get off, treating people the way he does, as if nobody else matters?" Lorna pushed her hair behind her ears. "Speaking of Stuart, something has been bothering me for some time now. But I don't know if it's the right time, it being William's funeral and all."

Michael took her hand. "I don't care if it is William's funeral. Come on. We'll discuss it on the way back to Stuart's house."

They headed for the sandy path leading to the paved road.

Michael asked. "What has been bothering you?"

"It might upset you, and I don't want that to happen, especially today."

"Go ahead. I want to hear what you have to say."

"All right, if you insist." Lorna dodged a palm branch blocking their path. "Do you remember that day you ran into me and my mother while you were jogging the beach?"

"Sure. Why?"

"Remember I said something to you in the water about you and your mother moving off the island? That wasn't a figment of my imagination, like I let on. It was a slip of the tongue."

Michael's heart fluttered. "What do you mean?"

Lorna sighed. "I guess I better start at the beginning. One night, not too long ago, while everyone else in the house was asleep, I got up to make a midnight snack. On my way back to bed, I went into Stuart's library to pick out a book to read. While I was browsing the shelves, I accidentally knocked a folder to the floor. As I was putting the papers back into the folder, I saw a document that said, at least I think this is what it means, your mother's house had been transferred over to Stuart."

"Is that it?"

"You know about the transfer?"

"After you blurted out in the water that day about me and my mother moving, I went home and checked with my mother. She has the deed locked up in a safety deposit box."

"I don't know, Michael. Your mother might have the deed, but this could be an addendum of some kind. Maybe Stuart could take the house without having the deed."

Michael began to feel anxious. "Just exactly what did you see?"

"There were a few paragraphs on the paper, one of which stated what I already told you. Your mother was transferring title of her house over to Stuart."

"It can't be. How could he just take our house?"

Lorna noticed Michael's hands trembling. "I'm sorry. I didn't mean to upset you. I just thought you should know about it, in case Stuart was trying to pull a fast one on you and your mother, like he did with you and the stock."

"If he's trying to take the house, I'm going to kill that bastard." Michael stomped up the path. "Did this so-called piece of paper look like something an attorney would draw up?"

Lorna sighed, knowing she was about to add more insanity to his nightmare. "It looked legal all right."

"Was my mother's signature on it?"

"I don't know you're mother's handwriting, but her name was signed. Whether it was she herself who signed, I couldn't possibly know for sure."

"This is making me sick. Do you know how many times my mother signed papers for Stuart without reading them first?"

"I feel awful, Michael. I don't know what to say."

"What about witnesses? I don't know that much about real estate, but I do know that most legal documents have to be witnessed."

"There were several signatures. I didn't bother to look at any of the names, but they were there."

"This can't be happening. What am I going to tell my mother? She has a bad heart. I don't think she can take another shock. I know what I'll do. Before I go getting her all upset, I'll call my attorney and find out for sure if a document like that is legal." Michael's stomach growled.

Lorna teased him, trying to lift his spirits. "It sounds like something is alive in there. Have you eaten anything today?"

"No."

She grabbed his arm. "Come on. You can't go around without eating, especially now. You'll need your strength to fight Stuart."

"I don't think I can eat. My stomach is turning."

"Then you'll eat something light."

—

STUART STRUGGLED with his emotions, feeling the loss of a child, and guilt over causing William's death. On the other hand, his son's death lifted a load off his shoulders. For years, they hardly spoke. Everyone knew it. Maybe everything happened for the best. Without William around confronting him with weakness and other human frailties, he himself wouldn't feel so physically and mentally drained.

After hours of exhaustive, sympathetic conversation with one person after another, Stuart could not take any more. Since most of his guests had left or were about to leave, he found no reason why he could not talk business with Jerry Zuckerman for a few minutes.

He pulled Jerry aside. "Let's go in the den. I want to talk to you."

"I hope it's not about business. This really isn't the time."

"As long as I'm paying you, I'll decide when it's time."

While Stuart and Jerry were in the den talking, Michael and Lorna arrived back at the house. Neither of them realized how hungry they were until they strolled into the dining room and smelled the garlic in the penne pasta, the roasted turkey breast, baked ham and pastries all combined.

When Eva caught sight of Michael, she handed her empty wine glass to a servant and rushed over to him. "You must be starved," she said, ignoring Lorna. "Go sit down, and I'll prepare a plate of food for you."

"I can do it. Thanks anyway."

"I insist."

He glanced to Lorna and sighed. "I'm fine, really, Eva. I'd rather do it myself."

She straightened her suit jacket, a look of rejection on her face. "Well, all right. But if you want me to get you anything at all, something to drink maybe, just let me know. I'll be glad to get it for you."

As Eva walked away, Michael glanced around the room, looking for Stuart. He didn't see him.

"Your mother is really persistent, isn't she?"

"You'll have to learn to be more abrupt with her, like I am."

They wandered around the table, spooning various foods onto their plates.

Instead of sitting inside, they went out on the terrace, where they joined Gayle, Samantha and her husband, Tom.

In a wide-brimmed black hat with a long veil covering her face, Holly sat on the sofa behind them, sobbing openly. The only hint that a human being existed under the veil were her hands, which she slid out occasionally to grab fresh tissues.

Lorna opened her napkin up on her lap. "I feel so sad for Holly. She's really torn up over William's death."

Samantha pushed her empty plate to the center of the table. "I tried to console her, but she wants to be left alone."

While Michael and Lorna were eating, Sheila came outside, her eyes puffy from crying. She sat next to Holly and wrapped her arms around her.

Holly sobbed all the harder. "I don't understand it, mother. William was so young. How could he just up and die?"

Sheila's eyes welled with tears. "I don't know, sweetheart."

"It would be different if he had a bad heart. But William was the healthiest person I know."

"I guess it was like some of those athletes you hear about in the news. Out of nowhere they just drop d . . ." Sheila did not finish the sentence. She grabbed a tissue and blew her nose.

"But Michael said he was just walking down the street."

"I know, sweetheart. I don't understand it either."

Michael held back a tear. Before he started blubbering like a baby, he got up to get something to drink. "I'm going inside for a soda. Does anybody else want anything?"

Samantha sipped her iced tea. "Andrew will get it for you, Michael."

"That's okay. I'll get it." He pushed back his chair. "What about you, Lorna? Can I get you anything?"

"I'd like some iced tea, if you don't mind."

Michael decided he might as well use the bathroom before he got the drinks. As he passed the den, he heard Stuart's voice. The door slightly ajar, he saw Jerry Zuckerman sitting on the leather sofa. Michael continued walking until he overheard Stuart saying something about Grant Office Supplies and World Office Products. He stopped dead in his tracks and listened for a while. To his dismay, the conversation switched to usual company business. About to slip into the bathroom, Michael glanced down the corridor and saw Eva rounding the corner.

She called out to him. "I've been looking all over the place for you."

He exhaled an exasperated sigh. "Why?"

"I was concerned about you. I thought you could use a drink. Here. I brought you a glass of wine."

"Thanks, but I'm not in the mood for wine."

She persisted. "Take it. You'll feel better after you take a few sips."

He took the glass from her.

She wrapped her arms around his waist. "You look like you could use a hug."

Stuart had overheard her. He came bursting through the door.

"What in hell are you doing, Eva?"

"I saw that Michael looked sad, so I thought I would bring him a glass of wine."

Stuart pulled her off Michael. "What about me? Did you ever think I might like a glass of wine?"

"You would, sweetie? I'll be glad to go back right now and get you a glass."

"You just do that."

Eva left and Michael turned to go into the bathroom.

Stuart grabbed his arm. "Not so fast, Michael."

Michael glared back at Stuart. "What do you want?"

"How long have you been out here in the hall?"

"Why? Do you have something to hide?"

"I want you out of this house."

Michael gulped down the wine and shoved the glass in Stuart's hand. "I can't leave fast enough."

"And stay away from my wife."

Michael smirked. "The funny thing is I've been trying to do that ever since I came back from the Himalayas." He stormed away, heading for the terrace to tell everyone he was leaving.

When Samantha saw Michael's angry face, instead of calling everyone's attention to him, she asked quietly. "What's wrong?"

He glanced at Sheila and Holly, who still huddled together on the sofa. "I'll tell you about it later." He waved good-bye to everyone around the table.

Gayle asked. "Where are you going?"

"Home."

Lorna jumped up from her chair. "Wait for me."

She followed him down the terrace steps. "What happened? Did you and Stuart have words?"

"Let's just say the shit is about to hit the fan."

23

LYSETTE WRITHED ABOUT in agony. Too sick to care, she allowed the vomit climbing up her esophagus to dribble out of her mouth onto her wavy, black hair.

Her head flew up, hit something and then slammed back down . . . to what? She could not think. Her mind was in a fog, thick like pea soup. She struggled to clear it.

Slowly, she regained consciousness, and things started coming back to her. The poison did not kill her. Was she still in the process of dying, or had there not been enough poison in the needle to kill her?

Something poked her in the back. It hurt, and she wanted the pain to stop. Her body had been through enough. Another poke. With what little strength she could muster, Lysette lifted her arm, which felt like lead, and reached behind her. Flesh. The rounded curve of a knee, a familiar knee. "Lucia," she said, panicked. "Are you okay?" Lysette nudged her sister. "Wake up, Lucia."

Her twin sister did not move, indicating that she may not be alive. The pain in Lysette's heart far exceeded the pain in her body. She whimpered, wanting to die. Yet again, maybe Lucia was not yet dead. Like herself, maybe she would gain consciousness.

Their two bodies kept bouncing in the air. A car. That was it. They were in a car, the trunk. Lefty and Johnny must have thrown them in the trunk, and now they were taking them to dump their bodies. The car seemed to be going fast. And the tires kept hitting holes. A dirt road. They were traveling on a dirt road, a secluded one most likely.

Seeing anything inside the pitch-black space proved impossible for Lysette. She squirmed, praying the men had thrown their purses into the trunk with them. From what she remembered, Lucia had the insulin bottle containing the antidote in her bag. As best she could, she fumbled about, feeling for the purses.

Although religion became less and less important to her as she grew older, her mind prayed nonstop. Please, God, please. Do not let Lucia be dead. And, please do not let us be screwed-up mentally or physically from the poison.

Her hand brushed against what felt like straw. A purse, she had found a purse. After more groping, she located the other purse at the bottom of Lucia's feet.

Time meant everything. One second too late and surely she would not be able to revive her sister. Lysette fumbled with the purses until she found the insulin bottle. To make sure she had the right bottle, she shook it. The bottle was full. She had the antidote. Now all she needed was a needle. Lucia panicked. She could not find any needles. They gave the bag of needles to Vince, who laid it on his desk. Noooo, her mind screamed. Now what was she going to do?

Fear of dying pushed Lysette onward. She fumbled through the purses, hoping a syringe might be lying loose.

Lucia still hadn't moved or made a sound. If her sister was already dead, Lysette wondered why she should fight so hard to stay alive. Without her sister, her closest friend, her confidant, life would not be worth living.

Her will to survive overrode her negative mood. Lysette kept rummaging through the purses. Something slipped between her fingers, a slim tube. Her heart pounded with excitement. She ran her thumb over the tube. "Damn it," she mumbled. "A pen." She grabbed for the other purse again and went through it. Another thin tube. She ran her fingers over the end. The protective cap proved it truly was a syringe.

Just then the car slowed down. Lysette panicked. Of all the times for them to stop. Now Lefty and Johnny could bury her and Lucia or throw them into a canal, and they would be defenseless. This could not be happening.

Suddenly, the car lurched forward, and the tires rolled across a series of deep holes. Like two marionettes dangling precariously on strings, the girls bounced up and down, banging their heads on the trunk's interior and then slamming back to the metal floor.

Lysette tried to brace herself and dropped the syringe. Like the tires sinking into the holes, her heart sank.

Seconds later, the car hit level road and the jostling stopped, just an occasional roll from side to side. Quickly, Lysette fumbled about, trying to find the syringe.

Lucia still lay motionless, making Lysette all the more upset. On top of her, under and all around her sister she searched. Finally, lying next to Lucia's arm, she found the syringe. Lysette grabbed it, thankful the syringe hadn't rolled under her sister, because she probably never would have found it.

Anxiety-ridden over whether or not she would have time to administer the antidote before they got to wherever they were going, Lysette removed the protective cap covering the needle. More difficult to fill the syringe in the dark than it would have been under normal conditions, she completed the task.

About to inject her sister, the car came to a complete stop. Sweat poured from Lysette's brow. The temperature inside the trunk felt like two hundred degrees and probably came close to hitting that mark. Quickly, she plunged the needle into her sister's arm.

As she refilled the syringe, she heard the doors slam and the sound of footsteps coming around the sides of the car. Between bursts of laughter, she heard Lefty and Johnny discussing where they should dump her and Lucia's bodies. Lysette seethed, hoping that she and her sister would live to get their revenge. She raised the syringe and shoved the needle into her thigh. As the door opened, she slid the bottle and syringe into her pocket.

Cool, fresh, night air flooded the trunk. It felt wonderful on Lysette's sweat-soaked body. She wanted so badly to gulp in a lungful of air, but she could not. The men must not think she was alive. Her pulse racing, she found trying to hide her breathing extremely difficult.

Lucia lay closer to the door. As if she were a sack of manure, Lefty and Johnny lifted her out of the trunk and threw her onto the roadside.

When it came time for Lysette, they dragged her out, scraping her arm on a sharp piece of metal surrounding the key latch. She almost screamed out in pain, but stifled a moan. If pain was the price she had to pay to live, then so be it. The next thing Lysette knew, she found herself flying through the air, like a limp rag doll being cast aside by a bored toddler. Her right cheek slammed against the damp soil, sending pain shooting through her skull. A dull thud reverberated in her ears. Now faking death came easily, as she could not move. She lay still, the cool, damp earth soothing her pain. Never once did she chance opening her eyes.

Lysette listened as Lefty and Johnny joked about wild animals getting to her and Lucia and eating their flesh. It seemed surreal to Lysette. Here she and her twin were on the opposite end of the coin. How many people had they killed and left for dead? She and her twin were bad. Why would God let them live? At that moment, she became very frightened. She believed with all her heart that Lucia was dead. God punished them for being bad. She was probably going to survive and spend the rest of her life feeling lonely for her sister and carrying the burden of guilt.

As Lysette lay still on the ground, she heard the men getting back into the car and driving off. About to get up and try to help Lucia, she heard the car barreling in her direction. They had gone up the road to turn around. Now, finally, they were leaving.

When all grew quiet, except for wind rustling through the trees, Lysette dared to get up. Stiff and unsteady, she climbed to her knees and then stood. Slowly, she began to feel better, and some of her strength had returned. At that moment she would have paid a king's ransom for a drink of water. Her tongue felt like cotton, and the vomit in her teeth tasted putrid. Her sweat-soaked hair hanging in strands, she trudged up the road to her sister's body.

Besides a cool breeze she felt drops of rain on her skin. It had begun to sprinkle. The refreshing water rejuvenated her. "My poor sister," she said as she knelt down beside Lucia.

Lysette rolled Lucia onto her back and stroked her cheek. Gently, she slapped her sister, hoping she would come to. "Please, Lucia. Do not be dead. I gave you the antidote. Wake up, please."

For several minutes, Lysette tried to rouse her twin. Nothing she attempted helped. She picked Lucia's head up and cradled it in her arms. Why, she wondered. Why was she alive and her twin dead?

By now, the rain was coming down harder and droplets were pelting Lucia's face. For a brief moment, as Lysette rocked her sister in her arms, she thought she heard a groan. Had her body let out a sound, like some dead bodies do, or did the antidote work, and her sister was alive? She slapped her sister's face, trying to prod her to consciousness. "Come on, Lucia, wake up." When she heard another groan, Lysette became jubilant. She jostled her twin again. "Come on, Lucia, you can make it. Try, my sister. Try."

Sprinkles had turned to a downpour. Thunder rumbled from a distance, and a flash of lightning lit up the sky.

Heavy droplets stung Lucia's face, slowly reviving her. Lysette leaned back, allowing the rain to perform its magic.

Lucia moved her hand. Her eyes opened briefly, and the rain forced them shut again. "Lysette," she said weakly.

Lysette hugged her. "You are alive, my dear sister."

Lucia asked weakly. "Where are we?"

"I will tell you about it later. How are you feeling?"

"Drugged."

"You will feel better in a few minutes. I gave you the antidote to the poison."

"Ahhh, the poison." Lucia tried to sit up.

"Do not worry, my sister. I injected us both with the antidote."

"But how?"

"There was not enough poison left in the insulin bottle to kill us."

"It did not knock you out?"

"For a while."

Slowly, Lucia regained her strength. She sat up and hugged Lysette. "Thank goodness, we are still alive." Suddenly, she became frightened.

"We better leave the country. If Vince finds out we are alive, he will come after us."

"Not yet, my sister. Not until we get our revenge."

24

MICHAEL REACHED FOR the air conditioning control and turned the dial to maximum. His head pounding, he leaned back against the headrest and closed his eyes, allowing the cool air to blast him in the face. For several moments he sat quietly, encouraging his headache to leave. When his efforts failed, he switched gears to drive.

His mind felt like a tornado, the same thought swirling around and around. How could Stuart just take his mother's house? How could someone take something another person owned that easily? It was insane.

He drove away in a daze, the municipal building growing smaller and smaller in the rearview mirror.

Exactly as Lorna had said, his mother unknowingly signed her house over to Stuart, the last person in the world who should get it, the one person they trusted with their hearts and lives.

A clerk in the tax records office confirmed Michael's worst fear. The General Warranty Deed not only had his mother's signature on it, two people had witnessed the document, and it was notarized. The notary's round seal Michael saw stamped on the bottom. Two people in Stuart's office obviously signed as witnesses, and the person who notarized the deed probably worked for him, too.

Michael felt like driving the car into a canal and ending his misery. The bastard had him by the balls. How was he going to tell his mother that Stuart now owned her house? No matter what happened, he made up his mind they were not moving.

As cars, vans and semis whizzed by his BMW, Michael became livid. His foot pressed harder on the gas pedal, and the speedometer shot up to eighty-five.

Furious, he banged his fist against the steering wheel. He not only didn't have a copy of the agreement, whoever witnessed and notarized the General Warranty Deed would lie for Stuart in court or plead the fifth, because they would not want to lose their job.

Michael wracked his brain, trying to come up with a solution to his problem. After several moments of intense contemplation, he realized he had no choice. He had to go see his Grandmother Millicent and tell her everything. Maybe she would be able to knock some sense into Stuart's head and get him to return the house and stock.

Before he went and got his grandmother upset, Michael decided he would pop in on Stuart and have it out with him.

He turned right onto the I-95 ramp and headed south in the direction of Stuart's office.

The twenty minutes it took him to get to Grant Place became a blur. His mind reeled over how he should handle the situation. Would a law firm take the case on consignment? Would he, his mother and sister have to start selling their assets in order to pay exorbitant attorney fees? The overall subject devastated him. Here he was an inexperienced person who knew nothing about business or legal matters, and he was about to go up against a knowledgeable, conniving genius, the most dangerous kind of opponent anyone could face.

Michael stormed through the giant wooden doors leading to Stuart's office. Too furious to act congenially, he walked past the receptionist without saying a word.

Before he went barging in on Stuart and embarrassing himself in front of anyone who might be taking a meeting with his uncle, Michael stopped to speak with Stuart's secretary first. "Hello, Dawn."

"Mr. Grant, how nice to see you!"

"Thanks, you too. Is my uncle in?"

"Yes. I'll buzz him for you."

"Is anyone else in the office with him?"

"Not at the moment."

That's all Michael had to hear. He barged through the door.

"Your two weeks are up, you slimy bastard," he said. "In fact, it has been longer than two weeks, because I let things slide until after William's funeral."

"I still don't understand why you keep hounding me about that stock, Michael."

"Cut the crap, Stuart."

"I'm telling you, I don't understand. You have this silly notion that I stole your stock. I never did any such thing." Stuart threw his pen on the desk. "I don't know what kind of drugs you're taking, but apparently you are hallucinating."

Michael felt like storming over to Stuart and throwing him out the window. "I had a feeling you would start that crap again. If that's the way you want to play it, I'm having my attorney draw up the papers today." Michael headed for the door. "By the way, you son of a bitch, I found out about your sneaky little plan to take my mother's house." He raised his fist in fury. "You'll get that house over my dead body."

Stuart smirked, as if to say, 'That is being arranged.' Instead he said, "Don't tell me you're going to argue over the deed now. The house is mine. I have your mother's signature to prove it."

"Through what door of hell did you come, you slimy bastard? You took advantage of her trust. But I'm telling you this. Your little plan isn't going to work."

"What do you mean plan? You're talking out of your head."

"I want the stock and house back now, or we're going to court."

"Why do you insist on starting a major scandal in the family, when you know perfectly well you'll lose?"

"You son of a bitch, you conned us. How could you? We loved you. We trusted you."

"You're wracking my nerves, Michael. I didn't do anything. If you're finished now, I'd like to get back to work."

As a last resort, Michael tried a softer approach. "I was hoping we could settle this thing here and now, so we wouldn't have to file suit against you and disrupt the whole family. Are you or are you not going to return the things that are rightfully ours?"

"Why should I? Everything is legally binding."

"If that's the way you want it. I'll see you in court."

"If we get into a silly court battle, you'll only be hurting your grand-mother. I'm sure she won't want to see you making a public spectacle of the family. If you can't think of yourself, then have some respect for her and the others."

"Speaking of grandmother, Stuart, I'm sure when she hears you stole our house and stock, she'll side with us and testify against you."

"You know perfectly well your grandmother doesn't get involved in the day-to-day happenings of this business and neither does anyone else in the family for that matter. They're all too busy doing their own thing."

"I don't consider this another day-to-day happening of the busi-ness. I'm sure she's going to be quite upset when she hears about this."

"Even if she is, what can she do about it?"

"Testify in court that she witnessed that agreement between you and my father."

"If you're finished now, Michael, I wish you would leave."

"One last thing before I go. You're going down, big man."

Stuart smirked. "That will never happen."

Michael had nothing to lose, so he gave him his best shot.

"You forgot one thing. I have the agreements."

25

MICHAEL LEANED OVER a gardenia plant, its creamy, spiraling blossoms emitting a heady aroma.

"These flowers smell wonderful, grandmother."

"Aren't they beautiful? Gardenias are one of my favorite flowers."

He moved down the wooden table to admire an array of orchids. "There are so many different species. You definitely have a green thumb."

"Anyone can have a green thumb. It just takes time and effort. Plants are like pets. You have to feed them regularly and give them lots of love and attention."

"Whatever you have been doing with your plants obviously works."

"Now that I've given you your botanical lesson for the day, what's the real reason why you came to see me?"

Michael smiled. "You can read me like a book, can't you?"

"I guess that's because I know you better than any of my other grandchildren. None of them came to visit me here in the greenhouse nearly as often as you did."

"I don't know where to start."

"Is it that bad?"

"Worse than you can imagine."

"Maybe we better sit down."

"You go ahead. I'm too worked up to sit."

Millicent took off her gardening gloves and sat on the wrought iron bench. "What is it, Michael?"

"You're not going to believe any of this. You're going to think I'm making it all up."

"You're no liar. Why wouldn't I believe you?"

He sighed. "Remember that time I was in here and I asked you about the agreement dad and Uncle Stuart made the day granddad died?"

"Clearly."

"Stuart has reneged on his promise."

"What do you mean?"

"For the past five years he has been stealing our stock."

The news stunned Millicent. "What makes you believe he has been stealing your stock?"

"He doesn't actually admit to taking the stock, but he does say we sold it to him."

"Did you sell him any stock?"

"Absolutely not."

"Then how could he do it?"

"He's always having us sign things. I'm sure we signed a power of attorney form or some other legal document, allowing him to take the stock."

The information outraged Millicent. "How did you find out about this?"

"Through David Chernoff. He handles my financial affairs, which aren't many, when I'm out of town." He leaned against the table. "While I was in the Himalayas, he opened a letter for me from the IRS. They were looking for back taxes on a stock sale I supposedly made a few years ago. Since I never sold any stock, I had David check into the matter for me. What he found out was Stuart now owns ninety-three percent of the company stock."

"Are you certain about all of this?"

"Positive."

"Then demand that he return the stock."

"I did that. He refuses to give the stock back. He keeps insisting that we sold the stock to him. That's why I came to see you. Maybe you can talk some sense into him. I don't want to take him to court and get the entire family involved in a public scandal."

"You did the right thing. I'll speak with Stuart immediately."

"There's more."

"What?"

"Stuart also stole my mother's house from her."

"Stole her house? I never heard of such a thing. Are you sure about all of this?"

"Have I ever lied to you in the past? Haven't I always come to you when I had a problem?"

"Yes. But how can anybody just steal another person's house?"

"It was easy, obviously."

"I still don't understand."

"You know how Stuart always brings papers over to the house for my mother to sign? What she apparently did one day was sign a General Warranty Deed, transferring title of the house over to him. She trusted him so explicitly that she never questioned him about anything he put in front of her."

"How did you find out about the deed?"

"Lorna accidentally saw it one night while she was still living with her mother and Stuart."

"Unless you saw the deed yourself, I don't think you should jump to conclusions."

"That's just it. I'm not jumping to conclusions. I went to the municipal building and checked it out. The clerk of tax records verified that Stuart now owns the house. The deed has been recorded and everything."

"Dear lord! Does your mother know about this?"

"No. I'm afraid to tell her, because of her heart."

"Good. I'm glad you didn't say anything. I'll talk with Stuart. Hopefully, I'll be able to resolve the situation."

"What if he still refuses to return the stock and the house, and we have to file suit? Will you vouch for us in court?"

"If Stuart took your house and your stock, like you said he did, you have my word on it."

Michael hugged his grandmother. "I knew I could count on you."

26

STUART GULPED DOWN the remainder of his coffee and tossed the empty foam cup in the trash. About to leave for a meeting across town, he heard his phone buzz.

"Yes, Dawn," he said, straightening his navy blue and red-striped tie.

"Your mother is here to see you, Mr. Grant."

"My mother?"

"Yes, sir."

"Send her in."

Surprised, Stuart went to the door to greet his mother.

Dressed in a mint green Chanel suit, Millicent brushed her cheek against Stuart's so she wouldn't get lipstick on him when he went to kiss her. "I know you're probably busy," she said, "but I'm only staying a minute. I have to meet a few of my bridge ladies at the club for lunch."

"What brings you here? You never come to my office."

"Since the subject concerns business, I thought it should be dealt with here."

"I have a few minutes before I have to leave. Come in and sit down."

Instead of sitting behind his desk, Stuart sat in a chair in front of the desk next to his mother. "I'm not used to seeing you all dressed up. That color looks splendid on you."

"Thank you. It feels good to get dressed up every now and then."

"What did you want to talk to me about?"

Millicent sighed. "Michael came to see me yesterday afternoon."

Stuart sensed what was coming. "How does that concern me?"

184 L i z   L e h m a n

"He told me something that disturbs me deeply. He said you now own ninety-three percent of the company stock. Is that true?"

"Yes."

"I thought the company was to remain split evenly between you and Richard's heirs."

"They decided to sell their shares."

Millicent fidgeted in her chair. "According to Michael, you stole that stock from them."

"I didn't steal anything. They sold me the stock fairly and squarely."

"He, Gayle and Samantha want the stock returned, or they are going to file suit against you to get it back."

"I know. That's what he told me."

Millicent glared at Stuart. "The last thing this family needs is a public scandal. I insist that you return that stock. And another thing, I understand you also tricked Gayle into signing her house over to you."

"I what? Michael is out of his mind. Is that what he told you? I think he's on drugs or something. Gayle even mentioned to you with Richard gone and the kids grown, she doesn't need a big house. She's sick of the place, and you know it."

"I am not going to tell you again, Stuart. I insist that you return what is rightfully theirs."

Stuart sat unresponsive for a moment, gathering his thoughts together. He decided he would humor his mother and the rest of the family until the World Office Products deal closed. In the meantime, he would go back to see Vince and put another contract out on Michael's life. Vince still owed him the cash for screwing up the first hit anyway. If at that time they still insisted on filing suit, he would have more money than the mint could print to get the case thrown out of court.

With feigned exasperation, Stuart said. "Look, mother. I'm not the one who started this court thing in the first place."

"You may not have started it, but still you caused it."

"All right," he said, watching ever word. "I see how much this is upsetting you. I'll take care of everything."

"Just exactly what do you mean by you'll take care of everything?"

"Don't worry, mother. I'll settle things with Michael. I promise. But it's not going to happen overnight. It will take a little while."

"Do I have your word?"

"You have my word."

"I don't know. How can I be sure?"

"I promised you I would take care of it, and I never go back on my word." He patted her hand. "I mean it."

"On your dead father's soul you will do as you say?"

"On my dead father's soul."

Millicent smiled. "Good. Approximately how long will it take? I have to tell Michael something."

Stuart had to give himself breathing room in case the World Office Products deal stalled for some reason. "Two months, six at the most."

"Why so long?"

"It takes time to do everything legally. You know how slow attorneys are. They like to stretch things out, so they can bill more money."

"Are you sure you will do as you say?"

"Rest easy, I gave you my word. I will take care of it."

"That's all I wanted to hear." Millicent got up to leave. "I'm sorry I had to come in and confront you about this, but what's right is right."

Stuart continued to humor his mother. "I could not let you leave here without seeing a pretty smile on your face."

Millicent gave him a partial smile. "You may have aged over the years, but you haven't changed much. You're still as cunning as ever."

He walked out the door with her. "I'll take that as a compliment."

———

MILLICENT REACHED in her purse for her cell phone. As the limousine pulled away from Grant Place, she had Michael on the line. "I just left Stuart's office," she said.

Michael got excited. "Did you confront him about the stock and the house?"

"You'll be happy to hear that he's going to return both."

"I had a hard time believing he actually took the stock and house. Now, I can't believe he's going to return them."

"Well, he is. He gave me his word."

"I hope you're right, grandmother. I don't trust Stuart a bit anymore."

"We have to have faith that he will do the right thing. He seemed sincere."

"When can we expect all of this to happen?"

"He said it would take about two to six months."

"I guess we have no choice but to wait. However, if I sense that he's stalling, I'm going after him."

"I agree. Do you feel better now?"

"Are you kidding?"

"I feel better, too. That's all I wanted to tell you. You can go back to whatever you were doing."

"You're the greatest, grandmother."

———

MICHAEL HUNG UP the phone and went looking for Gayle to tell her the good news.

After roaming the house, looking everywhere for his mother, he found her outside in the portico having coffee and cheesecake.

His face beaming, he sat at the table with her. "I have excellent news for you."

Gayle laid her fork on the dish and dabbed her mouth with a napkin. "It's about time. I need some good news."

"Uncle Stuart is going to return our stock." He assured himself that he did the right thing by not telling her about the General Warranty Deed and Stuart taking the house. He saved her needless worrying.

"I'm so relieved. How did you get him to do it?"

"I went to see Grandmother Millicent yesterday. I told her that before we filed suit against Stuart, we should talk to her first. She agreed. She said I did the right thing coming to her about it." Michael reached for his mother's fork and took a bite of her cheesecake. "She called a little while ago and told me that she just left Uncle Stuart's office, and he agreed to return our shares. The only thing that is bothering me about this whole thing is Stuart says it will take two to six months to accomplish what he has to do. Can you live with that?"

"As long as he returns the stock, I guess we can wait a couple of months."

"Where's Lorna. I want to tell her the good news."

"She's going over the want ads down by the pool."

"Are you sure you don't mind her staying with us?"

"Of course not. She's a lovely girl."

"I think so, too."

Gayle added. "It's the little things I like about her. I don't believe she has a selfish bone in her body. And, she keeps her distance, not that I prefer that. She's just considerate of other people. To tell you the truth, Michael, I like her a lot." Gayle smiled. "Are you interested in her romantically?"

"Very. We'll see what happens."

With the weather ideal with only an occasional cloud cover, Michael decided he would run upstairs first and change into his swimsuit. While he was getting undressed, he realized how natural it felt, wanting to share his happiness with Lorna. He had never experienced this kind of feeling with any other woman, and he suspected he was falling in love with her.

27

LORNA LAY ON A chaise lounge. Finished checking the want ads, she folded the newspaper and stuffed it under the cushion of her chair so that the wind would not scatter or blow the pages into the pool.

In an old, yellow bikini she bought in her freshman year of college, she felt naked. Her body had filled out some since then and the swimsuit fitted tighter than it should. The bra revealed way too much of her breasts, and part of her buttocks hung out the bottom. Compared to the skimpy thongs some girls wore, she did not know why this swimsuit should bother her.

The sun's rays blazed down so ferociously that it felt like someone was holding hot coals close to her skin. Sweat poured down her neck and a tiny pool of oil mixed with sweat had settled in her belly button.

As she dabbed her face with a towel, she noticed Michael.

Lorna laid the towel on a table. "You look like you're in a good mood about something. What's up?"

"Let's go in the water. It's too hot to sit out here."

She loosened a plastic clip, allowing her hair to fall down her back.

Michael did a racing dive into the water.

Lorna strolled to the edge and dove gracefully into the deep end of the pool.

She swam over to Michael. "It's nice to see you happy for a change. You have such a beautiful smile."

"Thanks. I finally have something to smile about. Guess what. Stuart is returning our stock and house."

"I don't believe it."

"It's true. My grandmother went to see him this morning. She talked him into returning everything."

"That's wonderful, Michael." Lorna slicked her hair back with her hands. "You have to be so relieved."

"I just hope Stuart does what he says he's going to do. After all of the crap he has put us through, it's hard for me to trust him."

Lorna loved that Michael came outside to share the news with her. She had reached the point where she wished something would happen between them. Not once, since she moved into the house, did he make a pass at her. Now that she knew him better, she found herself becoming more and more attracted to him. He felt comfortable to be around, and she enjoyed his sense of humor. If she didn't watch herself, she could fall for him. But until he displayed any affection for her, she would stand back and let him take the initiative.

Michael hoisted himself up on the edge of the pool. "Did you find anything in the want ads?"

The question put her on the defensive. She hadn't found a job yet. She hoped she was not intruding on him and his mother. "Don't worry," she said. "I'm sure I'll find something soon."

"You make it sound like I'm rushing you. You're not intruding. I told you not to worry. In fact, my mother just commented on what a nice person you are."

"That's nice to hear."

"I hope every time I ask you about job hunting, you won't get upset over it. I'm only asking, because I care."

His lean, hard muscles and washboard stomach unnerved her. "Thanks, Michael. I'm not used to having anyone care about me."

While they were talking, they noticed Holly descending the terrace steps.

Michael pointed. "Look at this, Lorna, Sand Dollar Island's version of a sex symbol."

Lorna chuckled. "You're terrible."

Holly resembled the sexy, Hollywood bombshells of the fifties. In skin-tight, leopard-print Capri pants and a black, off-the-shoulder crop top that accentuated her tiny, bare midriff, she exaggerated her hip swinging. Her long, blonde hair hung loosely under a wide-brim straw hat, and if the occasion ever arose, she could use her black stiletto pumps as weapons.

Holly placed a long, black cigarette holder with a gold mouth-piece to her lips, pretending like she was smoking. "Bon jour," she said affectedly.

The blonde hair stunned Lorna. Holly fit the description of the woman who broke into Stuart's safe.

Lorna tightened the straps of her bikini. "I'll bet you never get bored, Holly."

"Why do you say that?"

"You must spend hours planning what you're going to wear, apply-ing all of that makeup and fussing with your hair."

"I have fun. I really enjoy it." Holly reached into her oversized faux leopard fur purse for a mirror. "Speaking of makeup, it's so hot out here, I think mine is melting." She looked at herself. "Egad! It is." She threw the mirror back into her purse. "What are you two up to?"

Michael rolled his eyes. "Who are you supposed to be this time?"

"If you don't know, I'm not going to tell you." Holly fanned herself with her straw hat. "How about you, Lorna, can you guess?"

"Are you tying to look like Mata Hari?" Lorna had no idea what the real Mata Hari looked like, but she knew she was a famous spy. Thinking Holly could have been the one who stole the agreements, she connected the two together.

Holly tapped the cigarette holder, dumping invisible ashes into the pool. "You two are pathetic. Jayne Mansfield."

Michael asked. "Who is Jayne Mansfield?"

"A movie star from the fifties, that's who." Holly kept fanning her-self. "If we ever play a game of trivia, Michael, please be on the oppos-ing team. You are the worst." Holly directed her attention to Lorna. "How is the job hunting coming?"

"I'm still at it, nothing yet."

"I'll bet you're relieved. Who in their right mind wants to work?"

"I'm looking forward to getting a job. I don't know how anyone can just sit around all day watching TV."

"Who sits around watching TV all day? Like I said before, I'm much too busy shopping and going to the beauty parlor, trying to come up with new ways to reinvent myself."

Michael splashed water at Holly. "You're the laziest person I know. If anyone should get a job, it's you."

"Are you nuts? I never want to work." She threw her hat on a lounge chair. "I'm bored. I think I'll come in the pool with you."

Holly pulled off the wig and tossed it on the chair with her hat. Embarrassed with her hair flattened against her head, she fluffed it.

When she slid down her Capri pants, exposing black lacey panties, Michael tried to stop her from making a fool out of herself. "For Pete's sake! Go home and put on a bathing suit."

"What's your problem? You've seen me in my underwear before."

"Only when I had no other choice, like now for instance."

"You're overreacting."

Perplexed over Holly's bizarreness, Lorna watched as she yanked the crop top over her head, as though it were perfectly normal to strip in front of a near stranger and an adult cousin of the opposite sex.

The expression "built like a brick shithouse" popped into Lorna's mind. The lord gifted Holly with full breasts, a small waist, rounded hips, and long, slender legs.

Without bothering to test the water temperature, Holly jumped into the pool. For the next half hour, the three of them talked and swam laps.

—

AFTER HOLLY LEFT, Lorna and Michael slid out of the water and sat on the edge of the pool to dry off.

She grabbed her bottle of water. "I couldn't wait for Holly to leave so we could talk. Did you notice the wig she was wearing?"

"How could I not?"

"Are you thinking what I'm thinking?"

"She could have been the one who broke into Stuart's safe. But I guess that doesn't matter now."

"I'm still uncomfortable about this whole thing. Something just doesn't sit right with me."

"I had that same response when my grandmother phoned me. After how rotten Stuart has been, I can't believe he's going to change all of a sudden."

"Maybe we're being too pessimistic."

"Especially since he promised my grandmother he would return the stock and house. I can see him lying to me, my mother or Sam, but not to my grandmother."

"Then he'll probably come through on his word."

"I hope you're right."

"I think it's great that you don't have to worry about the agreements anymore."

"I guess."

"Curiously speaking, do you think Holly broke into Stuart's safe?"

"I seriously doubt it."

"The description fits. It could have been her."

"Why would Holly want the agreements?"

"All I know is the woman who broke into the safe knew the combination. It wasn't me, so it had to have been Holly."

"I just can't see it."

"I would love to ask her about it sometime."

"Let's not mention anything to her just yet. Suppose Stuart reneges on his promise. If we asked Holly about the agreements, she would probably tell Stuart about it, and that would blow a good chance to nail him. Remember I told him I had the agreements. If he finds out that I'm asking Holly about them, he'll know we were bluffing. Until I get back that stock, I want to keep our ace in the hole. In the meantime, since things look like they're going to work out, let's celebrate tonight."

"That sounds fun. What do you want to do?"

"Let's pop a bottle of champagne and cook some thick, juicy steaks on the grill."

"I hope you'll have your mother join us. It's her celebration, too."

"We'll do that."

———

MOTHER NATURE MUST HAVE sensed their jubilation, because she gifted Michael and Lorna with a glorious evening for a celebration.

A full moon led the heavens in a symphony of light. As star after star vied to sparkle brighter, Venus put them all to shame, her brilliance standing out like a beacon in the sky. Orion, the celestial hunter, beckoned the big dipper to come closer, as if he were going to dip the huge ladle into the milky way and scoop out bowls of creamy light that he planned to pour over the moon to make it glow brighter.

The terrace of Gayle's house sat up high, providing a marvelous view of the yachts cruising up and down the coastline.

Lorna, in the long, pale-yellow, slip dress she wore on Millicent's birthday cruise, gazed out at the sea.

Michael sat at the table, watching the most gorgeous creature he had ever seen, Lorna. She fit so right in his life.

Gayle, was sitting across the table from Michael, seeming to lavish in her own, private Garden of Eden.

The first bottle of champagne went quickly. Michael opened a second one, while the three chatted happily over a grilled filet mignon dinner with a Caesar salad, baked potato, steamed broccoli, sautéed mushrooms and scrumptious apple pie ala mode.

After Gayle finished the last of her pie, she got up from the table. "That's enough celebrating for me. I think I'll call it a night."

Michael dabbed his mouth with a napkin. "You're not going to bed already, are you?"

"Since this whole thing with Stuart started, I haven't been resting well at night. Now that it looks like everything is going to work out fine, I feel like I could sleep forever."

Lorna kissed Gayle on the cheek. "Sweet dreams."

After his mother went into the house, Michael threw his napkin down on the table. "Would you like to go for a walk?"

"I would love to."

He took Lorna's hand.

Through the garden and around the pool they strolled.

Lorna stopped next to the diving board. "There is something so beautiful about an empty swimming pool at night. The glowing water is so inviting. It makes you want to go in it, like we experienced at the Blue Grotto."

"That's funny. I always thought that, too. Do you want to go for a swim?"

"Not tonight. Right now I would rather walk the beach."

"The beach it is then."

Michael and Lorna strolled hand-in-hand through the garden, across the paved road circling Sand Dollar Island and down the path leading to the beach.

The vast ocean rippled endlessly. Its gentle waves caressed the shore, smoothing the sand into a soft, beige carpet beneath their feet. Night breezes carried lazy clouds across a star-dotted sky, while nocturnal insects sang out, their undulating high-pitched shrill constant. The unusual lullaby continued until a passing yacht's horn scared the insects into silence. Within moments, the undulating shrill commenced without any signs of stopping.

Lorna stopped to enjoy a moonbeam sparkling like diamonds on the rippling water. Michael stood behind her and slid his arms around her waist. "I have never met anyone like you, Lorna."

"I could take that several ways. Maybe you think I'm weird or something."

"I'll show you how weird." He turned her around and crushed her luscious lips with his."

Lorna melted in his arms, returning the kiss. For several moments, their lips locked in ecstasy, their tongues probing and delving into new and exciting worlds. Neither could pull away from the other, nor did they want to. It felt so wonderful, so right. They slumped to the sand, where Michael lowered her gently to the ground, his lips demanding more of her kisses.

The damp sand felt cool against his arms. He ran his hands down her body. "I want you so badly, Lorna."

He lifted her skirt and put his hand between her legs. Her bare buttocks in the thong bikini jolted his system, sending flames of fire blazing inside him. "Tell me I can make love to you."

"Do it, Michael. Make love to me."

Nothing else mattered anymore. He became one with her. This is where he belonged.

28

STUART BURIED HIS NOSE in a handkerchief. "I purposely brought this thing because of that wretched stench. How can you stand it, Vince?"

"You really do hate the smell of seafood, don't you?"

"Seafood smells a lot different on a dinner plate than it does back here."

They walked far enough away from the storage warehouse until Stuart could breathe fresh air.

Vince pulled a cigar out of his sport jacket and lit it. "When you called and said you were coming to see me, I got the money I owed you out of the safe. To say the least, I am beside myself with grief over the awful screw-up."

"You're not as upset as I am."

"I still can't believe that my people whacked your son instead of your nephew. You can't imagine how shocked and sick to my stomach I felt while I was reading the obituary in the newspaper." Vince exhaled a mouthful of smoke. "I know nothing can replace your boy, but if it is any consolation to you, I took care of the bastards who killed him."

The information surprised Stuart. "How?"

"Let's just say they will never be able to screw up again."

"I want you to hold onto the money."

"Then you still want your nephew wasted?"

"Yes."

"It's very dangerous to try now. We should wait a little while."

"Why? What happened to my son looked like a heart attack."

"Two deaths in one family in a short amount of time will look suspicious to the police."

"You let me worry about that. Just make sure the job gets done right this time."

"I still think it would be smart to wait."

Stuart did not want to take a chance on Michael finding out about the World Office Products deal and possibly sticking a wrench into the closing. "I don't want to wait, Vince. That little prick is still sniffing my wife."

"Where does your nephew live?"

Stuart handed Vince another photograph of Michael. "He lives on Sand Dollar Island. I wrote his address and the code to get through the security gate on the back of the picture. I don't know how you plan on doing it, but maybe your man can pretend like he's a landscaper or something. So many workers come to the island. Nobody will know the difference. Oh! There's also access to the house by way of the intracoastal or ocean. I know for a fact that Michael jogs the beach at the crack of dawn almost every morning. That should provide you with enough information."

"If anyone can pull up to the island in a boat, why do you have security gates? That makes no sense."

"We have "NO TRESPASSING" signs everywhere along the shore. So far, we have only had a few minor incidences with people in boats. It's the lowlifes in cars that we're mainly concerned about."

"Do you want it done on the island?"

"I've been thinking about that. There's less chance of your man getting caught if he did it from the water. The island is real quiet at that hour of the morning, and nobody else is up other than my nephew."

Vince shook hands with Stuart. "It will be done right this time. You have my word on it."

29

BEHIND THE STEERING WHEEL of a beat up, green pickup truck, Lefty pulled close to the security box. Without having to extend his arm out fully, he punched in the security code. Within seconds, the huge wrought iron gate opened.

As he followed the paved road circling Sand Dollar Island, he checked the numbers on the houses. "Here it is, Johnny. This is the one."

Johnny flicked his cigarette to the floor and crushed it beneath his black loafer. "Pretty fancy digs, huh?"

"It must be nice to have money."

"I can't wait to kill the bastard, not because it's a hit but because he has it so damn good."

"Don't get too eager. You saw what happened with Lucy and Lysette."

"What's wrong with you, Lefty. You never could get Lucia's name right."

"Who gives a rat's ass?"

"Man! Look at those fancy little tents next to the swimming pool."

"They're not tents, jerk-off. They're cabanas."

"It ain't right that some people have this much money. Just give me half of their money, and I'd be happy."

"I'd be happy if you would just shut your trap."

Lefty was getting too close to the house for Johnny's liking. "What are you doing? We can't park in the driveway."

"Who says I'm parking in the driveway? Let's drive around the island once and check things out."

They continued on past Gayle's house.

Johnny was all eyes, soaking up the lavishness of the beautiful mansions and manicured landscaping. "I'd give your left nut to own one of these houses."

"Mess with your own damn nuts. Leave mine alone."

"Why do you care? Your nuts are so small, you would never miss them."

"And, your dick is so small, you could screw a pigeon up the ass, and it wouldn't know the difference."

They continued driving the paved road until they had completely circled the island. As both men studied the island's layout, each tried to figure out the best way to kill Michael.

Lefty grabbed his baseball cap dangling from the gear shift. "Let's pull over and go check out the beach."

"What if somebody says something to us?"

"We'll tell them we're supervisors from the landscaping company, and we're here to inspect the work."

Lefty parked alongside the road in front of an opening in the foliage.

"What if we run into this Michael guy?"

"We'll say hello and act like we're gardeners. He'll never know the difference."

"We better get a good make on him. I don't want to screw up like the twins did."

"Unless everyone on this friggin' island looks alike, I doubt that we have anything to worry about."

Although their watches said twelve minutes past two, they saw nobody from the Grant family on the beach.

As if they owned the place, Lefty and Johnny followed the coastline about thirty yards to the north, and then they headed back to the path.

Lefty spit onto the sand. "I think Vince is right. The best way to do it is by boat. We can pick him off while he's running and then keep going."

"I can picture it now. He'll be like one of those moving ducks in a shooting arcade. Fire off a few quick shots, and the guy will be a banquet for sand crabs."

"While we're here, we better check out the house better."

They stopped every now and then, pretending like they were inspecting the work done on the landscaping. At one point they measured the approximate distance from the house to the gate. If they happened to do the hit on the island instead of by boat, they had to know how much time they would need to escape.

Lefty pointed to Millicent's hothouse. "Let's go take a look."

As they approached the path leading up to the front door, Millicent appeared in the doorway and proceeded to close the door behind her.

With the audacity of cockroaches crawling through a box of homemade Christmas cookies, the two men said hello to Millicent and kept walking.

She nodded her head courteously and headed towards her house.

"The mother lode," Johnny said. "I'll bet she has more gold and money stashed away in her panty drawer than the government has at Fort Knox."

"Since we have the security code to get through the gate, maybe after we do this hit for Vince, we'll come back and go through that panty drawer."

The men made mental notes of the house's outdoor layout and then directed their attention to Stuart's mansion. As they strolled through the gardens, they noticed Eva and Holly lounging by the swimming pool.

Johnny lit a cigarette. "Look at those broads. One is finer than the other." He exhaled a lungful of smoke. "What is it with rich bitches? They always look so much better than poor broads."

"I wouldn't mind tapping that younger bitch. She has some savory, tender meat on her." Lefty had an idea. "If we don't whack this Grant guy from the boat, we can take him out from the yard next door and make it look like somebody from the family did it. Rich people do stuff like that all the time, going after each other for tappin' the other guy's wife."

"That or we could break into the house and make it look like a robbery."

Satisfied that they had seen enough, Lefty and Johnny headed back to the pickup truck.

30

THE AIR FELT as thick and sticky as a coat of oil on a dip stick. Pitch black out, Lefty and Johnny found it difficult to see anything on shore.

The wind had picked up since they left Spinosas, and they kept getting sprayed with water.

Johnny hollered over the engine's roar. "What if it starts raining?"

"That will be better yet. Less people will be out on their boats."

"Do people jog in the rain?"

"I guess if you're a diehard, you do."

"What if it starts pouring while we're out here?"

"Then we'll get wet."

"I'm wet now."

"Then it shouldn't matter, should it?"

"Did you hear that thunder? The storm is getting closer."

"We've come this far. We're not turning back."

"We can do it tomorrow, Lefty."

"We're doing it today. I didn't come all this way for nothing."

As they got closer to Sand Dollar Island, the wind had kicked up even harder.

Lefty wiped salt water off his face. "I think a real storm is headed this way."

"Would you shut up about it already? You're wracking the hell out of my nerves."

"Screw you, Lefty. Look how rough the ocean is getting."

"If you're so scared, put on a life jacket."

"There aren't any life jackets."

"Then pretend like you're wearing one."

By now the storm loomed directly off of the horizon. If it had been light out and they could see the sky, they would have noticed a sheet of rain approaching from the east. The boat kept hitting wave after wave, rising up and then slamming back down to the hard surface.

Lefty saw lights up ahead and pointed. "There's the island."

Just as Johnny was glancing at his watch, the rain hit them like a runaway truck plowing into the side of a mountain. Thunder cracked so violently over their heads that Johnny nearly jumped out of his skin. "Are you nuts, Lefty? Let's get the hell out of here."

"If it doesn't stop in a few minutes, we'll leave."

"By that time we'll be dead. One crack of that lightning hitting us and we're toast. Come on. Let's get the hell out of here."

"One more minute. If the storm hasn't passed over us by then, we'll go."

"You always were a diehard. You're gonna get us killed."

Up and down and side to side, the treacherous waves tossed the boat.

Johnny could not handle the extreme rocking and got seasick. He vomited into the ocean.

Bits of rancid bile got caught in the wind and splattered Lefty across the face.

"That's it." Lefty said. "I've had enough." He turned the boat around and headed back to Spinosa's.

———

FOR FOUR DAYS STRAIGHT it rained and poured from sunup well into the afternoon. By early evening, the rain had stopped.

On the fifth day, when the rain still ceased to let up, Vince refused to listen to any more of Lefty and Johnny's excuses. "I don't care if there's a hurricane today, I want the job done."

Johnny swallowed the last bite of his chocolate-covered donut. "That means we can't do it by boat."

"Then do it some other way."

Lefty scratched his ear with a toothpick. "You don't care how we do it?"

"At this point, I don't care if your Aunt Gertrude sits on his head and smothers him to death. Get the damn job done."

As Lefty and Johnny were walking out the door, Johnny asked Lefty. "How do you want to handle it?"

"The usual way I guess. We'll hang around outside the security gate until our man comes out. Then we'll follow him and you'll pump a few rounds in him when he stops at a red light."

"We better go steal a car."

"We don't have to steal a car this time. I still have that New Jersey plate we stole off that Cadillac last year."

"We better take your old Chevy. My Stealth is too flashy."

———

AS LEFTY PULLED into a motel lot up the street a short ways from the wooden bridge to Sand Dollar Island, he lowered the window. "I hate this part of the job," he said.

"I'm starting to hate these jobs period."

"Where else can you make ten grand in a day?"

"Robbing those mansions on the island, that's where."

"If you think robbing those mansions is going to be easy, you have another thing coming." Lefty switched on the engine. "There's a car coming through the gate."

Johnny grabbed the binoculars. "That can't be him. A rich bastard like Grant wouldn't be driving a mangled mess like that. He would be driving some fancy sports car."

"You never know with rich people."

When the old gray station wagon turned north, they saw a woman behind the wheel.

Johnny sighed. "False alarm. It's probably a cook on her way to the grocery store."

"I was really hoping it was him. I'm getting thirsty for a beer."

"Forget it. You might as well make yourself comfortable. We could be here all day."

31

LORNA HEARD A PIERCING SCREAM as she strolled into the Florida room. "Jeez, Michael. What are you two watching?"

"*Aliens,*" he answered.

She put her hands on her hips. "Well? What do you think? Do I look okay for my first interview?"

Gayle hit "PAUSE" on the remote. "Your suit looks professional. That navy color is perfect."

"Good. Did you write the directions down for me, Michael?"

"No. I decided I would take you."

"What about your movie? Don't you want to see the end?"

"I've seen this thing five or six times already."

"Are you sure you don't mind? You might get bored while you're waiting for me."

"I could never get bored waiting for you."

"Okay then. I'm ready when you are." Lorna fussed with her hair. "Wish me luck, Gayle."

"You'll do fine, dear. Don't worry."

———

UNACCUSTOMED TO WEARING a suit, Lorna could not wait to get back home and slip into an old pair of comfortable shorts again. "I don't know how I'm going to handle getting dressed up every day."

"You'll get used to it," Michael replied.

"I hope you're right."

"Don't get scared if you come out and don't see my car. While you're on your interview, I thought I would go get an oil change. I'm six hundred miles overdue."

"I feel better now that you're going to keep busy. It's so boring, waiting for someone." She glanced up at the sky. "It finally looks like the rain is going to stop. I see some blue between those clouds over there."

"If the weather is nice tomorrow, do you want to go water skiing?"

"I've never tried water skiing."

"Then I'll teach you." Michael reached for Lorna's hand. "I'm so glad you didn't go up north."

She smiled. "So am I."

"I really care about you, Lorna."

"I care about you too."

Michael pulled up to the security gate. "Just think. If your mother never married my Uncle Stuart, I never would have met you."

"If nothing else, they did something right."

———

JOHNNY GRABBED the binoculars. "Here comes a red BMW."

Lefty turned the key in the ignition. "I hope it's him. I'm sick of waiting."

"It's him. He's with a broad."

"That should make things interesting." Lefty pulled out of the parking lot behind the BMW.

Ocean Boulevard had single lanes. Lefty and Johnny were forced to wait for a four-lane road or highway to attempt the hit.

Lefty said. "They're turning. Get ready."

Johnny reached to the floor for his gun.

The two cars traveled west and then turned south towards Delray Beach.

Lefty stayed on Michael's tail. "You'll have plenty of chances to do it. Federal Highway has more lights than the Vegas strip."

"One thing is in our favor. With all this rain we've been having, the silver heads are hibernating in their fancy condos. The streets are dead."

"Quick, Johnny. The light at Linton just turned yellow."

In the far right-hand lane Michael's BMW stopped for the red light.

Lefty pulled up on the left side of the BMW. "Now, Johnny."

———

WHILE THEY WERE WAITING for the light to change, Lorna glanced over at the tan Chevy next to them. A man sitting in the passenger seat put the window down and aimed a gun at Michael. Was she seeing things, or was it real?

"Michael," she shrieked. "That man has a gun."

His reflexes quick, Michael ducked. Still, he did not move fast enough. The first bullet shattered the driver's side window, grazed his right cheek and lodged in the passenger door, barely missing Lorna. Another loud pop. The second bullet tore through his shoulder, ripped through the front seat and then got imbedded in the back-seat upholstery.

Michael slumped forward, his head landing on Lorna's lap. His foot slipped off the brake pedal, and the car began to drift through the intersection.

The Chevy peeled around Michael's BMW and made a hard right. Lorna strained to see the license plate. The car was on too much of an angle. All she caught was 6 and J. But, the color and make she etched in her mind for the police.

Like a video moving in slow motion, her movements seemed exaggerated, her mouth hanging open, as she gasped at the sight of Michael's blood splattered all over her skin and clothes. Her hand floated to the steering wheel and guided the car across the brim onto the grass, as though somebody else were driving it, not she.

"Michael, are you all right," she heard herself saying. "Please don't be dead."

He moaned in pain. "My shoulder."

She grabbed the cell phone and dialed 911.

"Hang on, Michael. I'm calling for an ambulance and the police."

While they were waiting, Lorna applied constant pressure to Michael's wound, trying to prevent him from possibly bleeding to death.

It took the paramedics five minutes to arrive. The time span seemed more like ten hours to Lorna.

While the medics were tending to Michael's wound, an elderly couple who had witnessed the shooting stepped out of their Lexus. They went over to the police and told them about a tan Chevrolet with a New Jersey plate. Everything had happened so quickly, neither of them had gotten a good look at the license number.

The paramedics loaded the flat board with Michael on it into the ambulance. As Lorna stepped inside the vehicle with Michael, a tow truck pulled up to take the BMW to the police pound.

32

LYSETTE AND LUCIA VARGAS meandered through the convenience store aisles, dumping food into their basket.

Besides eggs and bacon, they selected orange juice, a box of powdered-sugar donuts, a loaf of whole wheat bread, a package of hot dogs, buns, an onion and a bag of potato chips.

In case they had to pack up and leave Florida quickly, they decided they would buy their groceries on a day-to-day basis.

While Lysette was waiting for Lucia to pay the cashier, she browsed through the magazine rack. About to reach for a tabloid, touting an article about a famous male movie star who dressed up in his gorgeous wife's sexy lingerie and then invited his gay lovers over for private parties whenever the wife went on location to make a movie, she spotted the headline of the Miami Herald. SHOOTER TAKES SHOT AT PALM BEACH SOCIALITE. She grabbed the paper and read the article.

Her mind reeled. Vince had put another contract out on the Grant guy. He survived, and so far, because the police had no suspects, no arrests had been made. An elderly couple had witnessed the shooting and told police about a tan Chevrolet with a Jersey plate. Everything had happened so fast, neither he nor his wife got a good look at the license number.

Lysette rushed over to the counter and told the cashier to charge them for the newspaper along with the groceries. In her haste to inform Lucia about the hit, she almost knocked over a display of candy bars.

As soon as they stepped outside, like water running out of a faucet, the information poured from Lysette's lips. "Vince put another contract out on Michael Grant. Look. It is here in the paper."

"I am not surprised. Did the police get Lefty and Johnny?"

"No. And, you know they never will."

Lucia stopped to read the entire article.

"I hate those bastards for what they did to us."

"We should do something about it."

"It is funny you said that, Lysette. For a while now, I have been thinking we should settle the score."

"I knew you were going to say that."

"How do you feel about going after them?"

"What is that old, American saying about paying the bitch back?"

"You mean payback is a bitch."

"That is the one."

"You realize we will have to be extremely careful and finish the job right, or Vince's wrath will come down on us."

"Then the rest of our lives we would spend looking over our shoulders."

The twins hurried back to their apartment. After breakfast, they prepared for the hit and leaving Miami. What little belongings they possessed went into suitcases they shoved inside the trunk. The old Buick they had stolen a while back had no retail value. They thought nothing of abandoning the car at the airport.

The girls had two airplane tickets in their purses, one to Brazil under their real names and another ticket to Las Vegas under aliases. They also carried a fake I.D. under their new names, Carmen and Dira Spanos. If the police came searching for them, they would conclude the girls fled the country.

Friday nights were always big party nights for Vince and his henchmen. They hung around the restaurant for an hour or so after closing, and then they went to an after-hours club. Unless their routine had changed for some reason, the twins expected to find all of the men in Vince's office.

Because their movements had to be quick and precise, the girls wore flexible stretch pants, down the waistbands of which were .9 mm handguns. After their shaky experience with the poison, they were not going to take a chance on any of the men surviving.

They pulled into the lot of a closed gas station across the street from Spinosa's and parked. As they hurried to the trunk, a fire truck went speeding down the street, its loud siren magnified by the stillness of the night.

From out of the trunk they lifted a mesh dive bag containing three weight belts made of lead.

About to cross the street, the twins spotted a state police car cruising their way. They scooted behind a row of hedges and waited until the car drove out of sight.

They had agreed earlier that they would approach the office from the back of the building. Ever so lightly they stepped, trying not to crunch the loose seashells littering their path.

As Lysette sneaked up to the office window, Lucia hid behind a banyan tree.

Through the glass Lysette heard Vince yelling at Johnny for screwing up the Grant hit. She peeked inside. Lefty was nowhere in sight. That presented a problem. The plan was for her and Lucia to kill all three men. Why hadn't Lefty shown up for their usual Friday night partying? Maybe he had, and Vince killed him. Now it was Johnny's turn. In either case, she would find out soon enough. Ready to make her move, she heard footsteps coming up the driveway. At first she thought it was Lucia, and then she recognized Lefty's hacking cough. Quickly, she dashed to safety on the side of the building.

As soon as Lefty went inside, Lucia crept up to the porch.

The girls took for granted that Lefty left the door unlocked, because the men would be leaving soon.

Lysette nodded to Lucia. It was time. Her gun in hand, she burst through the door, catching the men off-guard.

As if the girls had risen from the grave, the men froze in disbelief, their eyes wide in wonder and their mouths hanging agape.

When it sank in that the twins indeed had survived the poison, Vince sprang for the gun in his desk drawer.

As for Lefty and Johnny, they had no reason to anticipate trouble. Their guns were in their cars.

Lysette shoved the .9 mm into Vince's stomach. "Do not even think about it, you fat freak. Go open the safe."

"Like hell I will."

"Do it I said."

"No, you little whore."

Lysette clipped Vince across the head. "Open the safe, or I will blow your brains all over this room."

A welt forming on his forehead, Vince opened the safe.

While Lucia kept her eyes fixed on Lefty and Johnny, Lysette put her gun to Vince's head. "All of the money," she said, shoving wads of cash down her top.

Concerned that someone might be able see inside the office, Lysette flicked off the light.

Moonlight poured through the windows, providing adequate visibility.

Johnny asked. "How can you two broads still be alive?"

Lucia answered. "We are not alive. We are dead. You are looking at two ghosts."

"I don't understand."

"The one thing you pigs never asked us about was the antidote for the poison."

Vince glared at Lefty and Johnny.

Lefty glared right back at Vince. "How were we supposed to know they had the antidote?" He glanced up at Lucia. "Get that gun out of my face, before I wrap it around your neck."

She spit on him. "Shut up, pig."

Vince began to sweat. "What do you girls plan to do?"

Lysette answered. "Kill the three of you bastards."

"You'll never get away with this."

"Watch us."

Lysette frisked Vince, looking for the keys to the office, which she found in his jacket pocket. As the girls had taken one of the boats down to Key West, she suspected the key would be in the desk drawer. She grabbed the key and went to the door. "Keep an eye on them, Lucia. I will check outside to make sure no one else is around."

Lysette opened the door and walked out onto the porch. Not a soul was in sight. She went back inside the office. "You first, Lucia. I will follow behind these pigs."

Lefty hesitated. "I'm not going anywhere with you broads."

Lucia swiped the gun across his face, splitting his lip. "I am sure you will go now." She waited for Lefty to get up, and then she walked backwards, facing him, Vince and Johnny. Lysette brought up the rear.

Once outside, Lucia pointed to the dive bag. "Johnny, pick up the bag."

Lysette locked the office door. When the police eventually came to investigate, the girls wanted it to look like the men left on their own volition.

Lucia kept her distance from the three men. "To the boat, all of you."

Lysette glanced at her watch. "It is almost one-thirty. The fishermen will be showing up soon to take the two bigger boats out on the ocean. We better hurry."

Lucia said. "Johnny, put the dive bag down on the pier. I do not want you accidentally on purpose dropping it into the ocean."

Lysette stepped down into the boat, her gun aimed at the men. "All of you, into the boat."

Lucia waited until the three men were inside. Then she dropped the dive bag into the boat, far enough away from the men so that none of them could grab it.

With one of the twins in front of them and the other one behind, the men remained passive.

Lucia read their faces.

Lefty made a sour expression, as if his ulcer was acting up. Johnny had a desperate look in his eyes, as though he was thinking about his kids and how distraught they were going to be when their daddy did not come home today. Vince had a glib look on his face, as if he knew he would eventually come up with a clever idea to get himself out of his dire situation.

Lysette put her foot up on the railing and pulled a pair of latex gloves out of her black socks. With Lucia's gun fixed on the men, she did not hesitate to put her gun down to slide her hands into the gloves.

With a thunderous roar, the engine started. Lysette guided the boat slowly away from the pier.

Under different circumstances, the girls would have enjoyed the endless starlit sky and warm, tropical wind blowing through their hair.

Lysette saw several lights further out on the water. She disregarded the fishing boats. Nobody would think twice about seeing their's. Anxious to get the job done, she headed for deeper waters.

Johnny jumped up and swung his leg over the railing.

Lysette fired, hitting him in the head. As if someone had yelled timber, his rigid, dead body fell back on Vince.

Vince panicked. "I'll give you girls anything you want. A hundred grand, two hundred grand, half a million, it's yours. Just let me go. I don't care about Lefty. Do whatever you want to him. Only take me back with you. I promise I'll never bother you. You have my word on it."

Lysette laughed. "You can shove your word up your fat ass. You are going down, big man."

Lucia shoved her gun in Lefty's face. "So I was never good enough for you, huh?"

"You know I always had a thing for you, Lucy. I just like to give you a hard time. Come here, baby, and give me a kiss."

"I will give you a kiss. Here is one right on your dick." Lucia aimed lower and fired. The muffled pop was overrun by the engine's roar.

Lefty looked down at his crotch, his eyes frozen in disbelief. As he fell to the side, his head hit the metal railing, and then he slid to the floor.

"Please," Vince said, "let me go." He pulled out a wad of money and handed it to Lucia. "Here. There's over ten grand there. Take it. I'll get you more. Anything you want. Just let me go."

Lucia shoved the money down her top. "Thank you, Vince. This will come in handy."

"Then you'll let me go?"

"No. But, we will give you a choice."

"Of what? I'll do anything."

"Do you want to be dead before or after you hit the water?"

"You bitch." In a last ditch effort to save himself, Vince lunged for the gun.

Lucia fired, hitting him in the neck. Blood spurted out of his carotid artery, creating a big red arc.

Like Johnny, Vince now lay dead. Lefty was still alive, but he could not move. A big, bloody hole replaced his male genitalia.

The previous afternoon, the girls had studied a map of the ocean's floor. The water beneath them plunged over a mile deep.

One by one, Lucia wrapped the lead weights tightly around the men's ankles.

Lysette turned off the engine. "Hurry, Lucia."

"We better get rid of our guns, too. Slide your gun down Johnny's shirt and then button the shirt back up to his neck. I will slide Vince's belt through the trigger hole of mine.

The girls fumbled with the two dead men until they were capable of rolling them over the side.

When it came time for Lefty, he tried to resist, but he was too far gone. As his legs went over the side, his hand gripped the railing. He dangled by his fingertips for a few seconds, and then, like a heavy sandbag he plunged beneath the surface, the lead belt dragging him to the bottom.

Lysette grabbed a flashlight out of the dive bag. She zippered the bag shut and dropped it into the water, an extra chunk of lead dragging the bag to the ocean floor.

Using an old rubber bucket the men used for fishing, Lucia kept refilling the bucket with salt water and pouring it over the bloody stains. In a steady stream reddish liquid drained from the boat into the sea.

Their task completed, the girls headed back to shore.

33

MICHAEL SWITCHED ON THE COMPUTER. While he was waiting for it to boot up, the phone rang. He slid into the chair and reached for the receiver. "Grant residence," he said.

Lysette responded. "I would like to speak with Michael Grant, please."

"This is Michael Grant."

"I read about your accident in the newspaper."

"You mean the shooting?"

"Yes."

"Who is this?"

"It does not matter."

"Maybe not to you, but it does to me."

"I am sorry, but I cannot tell you who I am."

"Then why are you calling?"

"I wanted to ease your mind about something."

"I don't understand. Ease my mind about what?"

"Somebody put a contract out on you, but now you do not have to worry."

"What is this, some kind of sick joke?"

"No. I am quite serious."

"You're saying it wasn't a random shooting."

"That is right."

"Why would someone put a contract out on me?"

"I honestly do not know. If I did, I would tell you."

"Do you happen to know who did put a contract out on me?"

"No. But I used to work for the people that person hired to kill you."

"Tell me their names."

"Their names do not matter anymore. Those men have . . . shall we say . . . been taken care of. They will never bother you again."

"How do you know about all of this?"

"I just do. That is all I can say."

Lysette could not tell Michael about William and the poison. If the police arrested her and Lucia for some reason, and Michael found out about it, he might put two and two together and connect them with his cousin's death. Then they might get the electric chair or spend the rest of their lives in prison.

"It is the truth," Lysette said. "Believe me."

"Who are you?"

"Like I already told you, I cannot say."

"Why do you care so much about me?"

"Because the same men hired to kill you, tried to kill me."

"Then go to the police with me."

"I cannot. That is impossible."

"If you're telling me the truth, which you have to understand I find it hard to believe, then you're saying I have nothing to worry about now, right?"

"Yes."

"Is there anything else I should know?"

"No. That is all."

———

MICHAEL STARED AT THE PHONE, too stunned to react. Was the call real or a crank call? The woman sounded authentic. He immediately dialed the operator, who informed him that the call came from a pay phone in Miami. That figured. Now what was he supposed to do? If the woman was being straight with him, then somebody had actually put a contract out on him. Why? What did he do? The whole thing was insane. It couldn't be true. But what if it was? He couldn't take any chances. He had to call the police. No, not just yet. He would talk the matter over with Lorna first.

Michael hurried to the sunroom, his mind reeling from the phone call.

Lorna was sitting next to the window, working on her resume.

"What's with you, Michael? You look like you've seen a ghost."

"Come outside with me. I have to talk to you."

"What happened?"

"I just got a really weird phone call."

"From whom?"

"Some woman."

"What did the woman want?"

"I don't want to talk about it in the house. My mother might hear me."

Lorna followed Michael out to the terrace.

He kept walking. "Let's go down by the pool."

Without questioning him, Lorna followed Michael down the steps.

He sighed. "Wait until you hear this. The woman who just called informed me that what happened the other day was no random shooting. She said somebody put a contract out on me."

"You can't be serious."

"I'm dead serious."

"Are you sure it wasn't a crank call? People do strange things when they read about stuff like that in the newspaper."

"That's what scares me. She sounded really authentic."

"This is horrible. Did she say anything else?"

"She said I don't have to worry anymore. The people hired to kill me have been taken care of. It sounded to me like she meant someone killed them."

"Are you sure she dialed the right number?"

"She knew my name and about the shooting."

"Did she give you her name?"

"No."

"Did you try to trace the call?"

"I called the operator. The call came from a pay phone in Miami."

"Who do you know in Miami?"

"Nobody. Do you think I should call the police?"

"Absolutely. This is your life you're talking about."

"One good thing! If it wasn't a crank call, and the woman was being straight with me, I guess I don't have to worry about anyone else coming after me."

"I would still call the police. The hit men might be out of the picture, but what about the person who put the contract out on you? He or she might still be alive."

"I didn't think of that." Michael sat on a lounge chair. "This is wild."

"Think," Lorna said. "Who hates you enough or wants to get even with you enough to put a contract out on you?"

"That's just it. I don't have any enemies, at least none that I'm aware of."

"That's not entirely true." She sat next to him. "What about Stuart? If he had the guts to steal your stock and your mother's house, I hate to say this, but he might have the guts to put a contract out on you."

"Why would he? All of that stuff is behind us now."

"All I can say is Stuart has been doing a lot of rotten things lately. Maybe it's not over. Have you gotten any of the stock back yet?"

"No, but he promised my grandmother."

"I just can't let it go. Something doesn't sit right with me."

"Now that I think about it, Stuart has been acting overly friendly lately."

"It makes you wonder, huh? When people start acting real sweet and friendly, they are usually covering up for something. Let's play detective a minute."

"I just thought of something, Lorna. What if you're right? What if Stuart lied to my grandmother, and he doesn't intend to return the house and stock? Maybe he does want me out of the picture, because I've been fighting him every step of the way." Michael gasped and bolted off the chair. "I just realized something. The woman who called me had a Latin accent."

"So? Half of the people in Miami have Latin accents."

"What I'm thinking couldn't possibly have happened."

"What are you talking about?"

"William's death."

"What does William's death have to do with anything?"

"The strangest thing happened in the Keys." Michael reflected back to that moment. "There were these two girls, twins. They sent a drink over to me. They knew my name, but I didn't recognize them."

"Maybe you met them once, and you just don't remember."

"Take no offense, Lorna, but if I had seen these girls before, I would remember them."

"I still don't understand. What point are you trying to make?"

"When the waitress brought the drink over to our table, she asked which one of us was Michael Grant. If those girls knew who I was, the waitress wouldn't have had to ask. The twins would have told her."

Lorna shrugged her shoulders. "I'm completely lost."

"William grabbed the drink out of the waitress's hand. Those same twins were standing behind us, watching a gay parade. Not too long after that, William had a heart attack."

Lorna rubbed her arms. "You're giving me chills. You're not inferring that there might have been foul play connected with William's death."

"While we were watching the parade, William mentioned that the girls were from South America. The Latin accent, maybe this is all tied together in some way." Michael sat back down next to Lorna. "The woman knew about the hit men who shot at me. What if William's heart attack was a hit that got bungled? Maybe these so-called hit men mistook him for me, and I was the one who should have died."

"Do you think these twins had anything to do with it?"

"It's possible."

"Then you should tell the police about them."

"You're right. I'll give Detective Rogers a call."

"Are you going to mention anything about Stuart?"

"No. There might be a leak and the press would get hold of it. I'll wait a while and see what happens."

"If . . . now bear with me a minute here . . . If what happened in the keys was a botched hit, and the shooting was a botched hit, there could be another attempt on your life." Lorna put her hand on his leg. "I'm not trying to scare you, but you should keep that in mind."

"But that woman said those guys won't bother me anymore. She said they tried to kill her, too—for me not to worry, because they have been taken care of."

"Jeez! You didn't mention that they tried to kill her, too."

"I just remembered."

"Then we can assume that whoever put the contract out on you lost his source. That makes me feel a little better."

"Who knows? They may go to a new source."

"Let's back up a minute. If William's death was a botched hit, whatever they did made it look like a heart attack, so nothing could be traced back to whoever did it. The shooting is a different story. I don't think anyone would be stupid enough to try something again, at least not for a while. Besides, I don't think it would be that easy to come up with a contact who provided hit men for contract killings."

"You're smarter than I thought."

"If I'm so smart, then why don't I have a job?" Lorna scratched her arm. "Hey, I just thought of something. William was cremated. If push comes to shove, you won't be able to exhume the body for an autopsy. You'll never be able to prove his death was a botched hit."

"The doctor who examined him, when they brought him in, confirmed William died of a heart attack. The death certificate even showed a heart attack as the cause of death."

"The more I think about it, if William's death was a botched hit, these so-called twins probably had something to do with it."

"That's why I'm calling Detective Rogers."

"Unless the police ever find the twins, you'll never be able to prove William's death was a botched hit."

"This thing is thought out so well, you almost have to believe that Stuart had something to do with it."

"Do you realize, Michael, if Stuart did put a contract out on you, and William's death was a hit that got bungled, he killed his own son."

The thought proved so overwhelming that neither of them could speak. They sat quietly contemplating the matter.

After several moments of silence, Lorna grabbed Michael's hand. "If you're not going to tell the police about Stuart, I think you should hire a private detective to spy on him."

Michael wrapped his good arm around Lorna and kissed her. "You gave me an idea."

When she put her arms around his neck, she accidentally bumped his sore shoulder. "I'm sorry. I didn't mean to hurt you."

"Don't worry about it. Your kind of hurt feels good."

She smiled and kissed the tip of his nose. "What is this idea I gave you?"

"You and I are going to play spy."

"We are?"

"We're going to hide a tape recorder in Stuart's house."

"And, how are we going to do that?"

"Easy. I bought a special belt buckle with a mini-microphone in it. What we'll do is hide the microphone and the tape recorder in his bedroom. A lot of important things are said during pillow talk."

"What if we hide them, and he doesn't say anything that implicates him?"

"We'll do it more than once. Hey. It's worth a try. What do we have to lose?"

"You're right."

Michael and Lorna hurried into the house for the belt buckle and tape recorder.

As it was a weekday, they expected Stuart would be at work. Holly might be home, but she could easily be distracted. If they happened to run into her or Eva, Michael would distract them, while Lorna went upstairs, pretending that she had left something behind the day she moved out of the house, an ear- ring maybe. When Andrew and the maids weren't looking, she would sneak into Stuart's room and plant the microphone and recorder close to the bed.

As they crossed the foyer of Stuart's house, they heard music blaring from the exercise room, the deep thumps of the bass guitar and the pounding rhythms of the percussion instruments in Earth, Wind and Fire's *Boogie Wonderland* vibrating in their chests.

Michael said. "Holly must be exercising. Did you ever work out with her while you were staying here?"

"I never got the chance. Besides, she never invited me to work out with her, and I never suggested it."

Michael and Lorna stopped at the doorway and watched Holly, who glittered in a silver, one-piece bodysuit, silver socks and silver athletic shoes covered with rhinestones. A silver band held her hair back in a ponytail, and although sweat poured from her brow, her exaggerated, waterproof makeup never ran. As if she were a Las Vegas showgirl, she moved about the large, airy space, gyrating to the music. She would leap high in the air, as though she was reaching for the skylights, and then spin, shimmy and dip, her voluptuous body becoming one with the rhythm. So wrapped-up in her dancing was she that she never noticed Michael or Lorna standing in the doorway.

When the song ended, she went to the ballet barre. As she slid her heel down the barre, stretching her leg muscles, she noticed their reflections in a wall of mirrors behind a row of exercise machines.

"Hey, you guys," Holly said, delighted. "How long have you two been standing there?"

Michael replied. "A few minutes."

"Go change, Lorna. We'll work out together."

"That did look fun. I could use a good workout."

"Then go change."

"Not today, Holly. Will you be working out tomorrow?" She and Michael would probably be coming back over to change the tape. It would give them a good excuse to return to the house.

"Probably."

"Call me if you do."

"What are you guys doing here anyway?"

Lorna yanked on her ear. "I can't find one of my good ear- rings. I thought I might have left it upstairs in the bedroom."

"I'm sure Andrew would have called you, if one of the maids had found it."

"That's true. But I thought I would come over and take a look anyway."

Michael humored Holly. "Put on another song. I want to see you dance some more. I never realized it before, but you're pretty good."

Holly's face beamed. "Okay. Watch this. I've been making up a routine to *Move Like Jagger* by Maroon Five." Holly waltzed over to the massive stereo system stacked on shelves in the corner of the room and changed the CD. "Stick around and watch, Lorna.

"I will when I get back."

"Hurry up then." Holly flicked on the stereo.

Lorna hurried upstairs, the belt buckle and recorder in her pocket. Just as she arrived at her former suite, she ran into her mother.

Eva scowled. "What are you doing here?"

"I can't find one of my good, silver earrings. I thought maybe I left it behind in the bedroom."

"Wouldn't the maids have found it by now?"

"Probably, but I thought I would take a look anyway." She had to get rid of her mother, so she could hide the recorder. "How long has it been since you have seen Michael?"

"I don't know. Why? Is this another one of your sick, trick questions?"

"No. For your information I was being nice. He's down in the exercise room with Holly. I thought you might want to say hello to him."

Eva spoke less aggressively. "You know, I've been thinking. Maybe you should move back in with me and Stuart."

Lorna sighed. Not too long ago, her mother told her she never wanted anything more to do with her. Why the sudden change? It had to be because her living with Michael and Gayle was still eating away at her. Move back into this loony bin? She would rather live in Siberia. Instead of blasting Eva and venting her frustration on her, she responded nicely. "I don't know. We'll see."

"You can move in today if you like."

She wished her mother would get out of her face. "If you're going to say hello to Michael, you better do it now. I don't think he's staying very long."

Eva headed for the stairs "Think it over. It would be best for everyone concerned if you moved back in with us until you're on your feet."

"We'll see."

As soon as Eva started to descend the stairs, Lorna headed down the corridor. She glanced over her shoulder, looking for Andrew or the maids and then ducked into the master bedroom.

From memory she had the layout of the room pictured in her mind. It made hiding the devices easy for her.

The headboard of the bed, an elaborate scroll design, formed a peak in the center, like a crown. Made of cherry wood, the thick frame stuck out slightly from the wall.

Lorna taped the microphone to the back of a scroll, close to her mother and Stuart's stacked pillows.

Not far from the bed, among the bushy leaves of a philodendron plant, she hid the recorder. The high tech machine impressed Lorna. A tiny, little gadget like that could sustain hours of conversation, and it made no noises when it came on or shut off. If a device like this was available to the public, what were real spies using? She wondered.

Like a secret agent on a clandestine mission, she crept to the door and peeked up and down the corridor. All was clear. She sashayed nonchalantly downstairs to the exercise room.

When Lorna saw her mother doting on Michael, it nauseated her. How a person could change so drastically from being passive and bored, like she was upstairs, to perky and excited confounded her. She, herself, had only experienced such a feeling once or twice in her life, most recently also with Michael.

Although Lorna no longer liked Stuart, she almost felt sorry for him, because of the deceit her mother brought to their marriage. If and when she ever got married, it would be for love, not money, not security, just love.

Lorna waved good-bye. "I'm leaving now."

Michael pulled away from Eva. "Wait up, Lorna. I'm leaving, too."

———

SOON AFTER MICHAEL LEFT, Eva went back upstairs to take a hot bath. She lusted so badly from just being near him that she needed privacy to release her sexual tensions.

Almost in a trance she slid out of her clothes and draped them over a chair.

A fluffy black towel with hers and Stuart's initials scrolled in gold hung neatly on the gold-plated rack. She grabbed the towel and laid it on the green marble ledge surrounding the elevated tub.

As she turned on the gold-plated faucet, she gazed at her nude body in the mirror, envisioning Michael in the bathroom with her, naked and on fire, just as she felt. The two of them were making love in a tub filled with bubbles, and the room softly glowed from candlelight, lots of candles, and champagne, sipping the wine as they touched and kissed wildly and passionately.

In a dreamlike stupor, she accidentally bumped a Baccarat vase brimming with yellow roses as she slid into the tub, almost knocking the vase to the green marble floor.

Like a coat of velvet sliding over satin, the water skimmed over her bare skin, the warm bubbles frothing around her, like miniature soft pillows cushioning her every muscle.

Eva pulled her hair up on her head, unconcerned about the tendrils left cascading down her neck.

At that moment she realized that if she was ever going to seduce Michael, it had to be soon. Until then, she would have no peace. She hated herself for being so weak, but she could not help it. Her desire surpassed her self-control. Like air to lungs, she needed to make love with him. If she did not, she felt like she would die. If and when that day ever came, she desperately hoped she would discover that the chase had been more exciting than the capture, that the powerful spell he cast over her would no longer exist. Then, and only then, could she continue on with her life in a normal fashion, appreciating Stuart for the man he was, not someone she went to bed with only because she felt it was her duty.

Eva rested her head against a bath pillow and closed her eyes, allowing her thoughts to float wherever they dared, but never once leaving the image of Michael.

In her reverie, she envisioned the evening she went with Stuart to Gayle's house, and how Michael's shorts kept hiking up his thighs as he sat on the chair. Clearly, as if it were happening now, she pictured his legs cut with muscles, his gorgeous face and those full lips she longed so badly to kiss. Her tongue slid over her lips, imagining Michael kissing her. She could almost taste the moisture on his lips. Her fingertips fondled her breast. Michael was fondling it. When she could stand it no longer, she got up on her knees and reached for the hand shower. Between her legs she directed the warm water. Faster and faster she rubbed herself, the pulsating rush of water taking her to ecstasy. It was Michael making love to her, not herself nor the water. He was inside her, pumping her, kissing her. When her body had reached the point of no return, the fire consuming her burned so fiercely that she thought she might faint. Enraptured, she almost toppled over onto her side. She braced herself against the tub, not daring to move. The slightest distraction would scare away the heavenly vision of Michael—take away that wonderful glow she felt inside.

Her body still tingling from orgasm, she slid down into the warm water. For several moments, she lay with her head against the pillow. With the image of Michael's face dominating her mind, she began the process all over again. Only this time, her body did not crave release. The next four times she climaxed were pure indulgence.

———

LATER THAT NIGHT, when Stuart wanted sex, Eva sighed. "I know this will sound like some stupid cliché," she said. "But I have a bad headache, sweetie."

"Look, Eva. It isn't every night that I get in the mood. Those times are getting fewer and farther between."

"I realize that, dear, and you know I never turn you down. Let's wait a few minutes. Maybe my headache will go away."

As the two discussed whether or not they should have sex, the tape recorder picked up their conversation. When they spoke, the machine recorded. When they lay quietly, the tape stopped.

Eva changed the subject, hoping Stuart would forget about having sex. "How was work today?"

"Excellent. Remember I told you this morning that I had another meeting scheduled with World Office Products today?"

"How could I forget? That's all you ever talk about anymore."

"I can't help it. I'm really excited about getting out of the business. You know that."

She played with the hair on his chest. "I didn't mean to sound sarcastic. How did the meeting go?"

"It looks like the deal is going to close on schedule. By the week's end, I'll be a retired man."

"I can't wait. Just think of all the fun we're going to have, taking the trip around the world that we've been talking about all these months and doing whatever else we want."

"You still haven't mentioned anything to anyone about my selling the company, did you? I don't want anything screwing up the deal."

"I haven't told a soul."

"Not even Holly?"

"Nobody."

"What about Lorna?"

"Absolutely not. You told me not to tell anyone about it, and I didn't."

"Good. I never wanted anything to happen so badly in my life."

She rested her head on his chest. "My goodness! What are we going to do with all of that money?"

"You let me worry about that."

"I'll bet Michael, Gayle and Samantha are going to be sick they ever sold you their stock, when they hear about the profit you're going to make when you sell the company."

"That's their problem. What's done is done. Now, enough business talk." Stuart put his hand between her legs.

She flinched, still sensitive from the five orgasms she experienced earlier that afternoon.

"That must have felt good. You're sensitive to my touch." Stuart kissed her, his tongue probing her mouth.

After Eva thought about it, she figured she better accommodate him, or he might not be as generous with her as he had been, especially now that the World Office Products deal was about to close. Having sex might also ease the guilt she suffered over her infatuation with Michael.

She jumped out of bed. "I'll be right back."
Stuart reached for her. "Where are you going? Come back here."
"I'm going for the jar of lubricant, sweetie."

34

THE TELEPHONE WOKE LORNA. Half asleep, she fumbled with the receiver. "Hello," she said, about to yawn.

"It's Holly. You told me to call you about working out this morning."

"Work out? I can hardly open my eyes, let alone work out."

"Come on. You can sleep later."

Without thinking, Lorna almost declined Holly's invitation, until she remembered that she and Michael had to go over to Stuart's house and switch the tape in the recorder. Besides, some aerobic activity would do her good. All she had been doing lately was lounging by the pool, scouring the wanted ads.

Lorna rubbed her eyes. "Okay. I'll be over in a few minutes."

Fancy leotards did not exist in Lorna's sparse, inexpensive wardrobe. It was her Gators shorts and a T-shirt or nothing. About to slip the T-shirt over her head, she suddenly remembered owning a T-back athletic top.

Through the drawer containing casual things she rummaged. As she expected, nothing in the drawer came close to resembling an athletic top. Her nerves getting frazzled, she ransacked three more drawers. About to give up, she found the top among her socks and underwear.

Aware that Michael and Gayle might be waiting to have breakfast with her, she pulled herself together and went downstairs.

When it wasn't storming, breakfast was usually served on the terrace. Lorna slid open the sliding glass door and bid them good morning.

Michael's face lit up, when he saw her. "Where are you going?"

"To work out with Holly."

"Did she call you this morning?"

"Yes, a little while ago."

Lorna appreciated Gayle's genuine caring and looked at her more as a loving mother than her real mother. She bent over Gayle and kissed her cheek. "How are you today?"

"Just fine, dear. How did you sleep?"

"Like a log."

"Would you like some breakfast before you leave?"

"No. It's not good to work out on a full stomach. But I'll have a glass of juice. I could use a quick burst of energy."

Michael swallowed a bite of multi-grain toast. "I'll go with you."

"Oh no you won't. You're not going to sit and watch me make a fool out of myself."

"I promise I won't laugh."

She pretended like she was going to punch his sore shoulder. "Okay. You can come with me. But if I see any stupid grins on your face, you're out of there, pal." She knew he had to go with her, because they had to replace the tape with a new one.

"Deal," he said.

On the way to Stuart's house, Michael discussed the tape recording with her. "We can't keep going over there every morning, or it will look fishy."

"I know. I thought of that, too. Why don't we do this? If there's nothing important on the tape today, we'll leave the next one for about a week."

"A week is too long. Let's give it three or four days and see what happens."

She snickered. "I feel like James Bond or something."

"If you're James Bond, then I must be Pussy Galore."

"Michael. That was terrible." She couldn't hold back. Her stern expression broke into a wide smile.

———

HOLLY DID NOT LIKE it when anyone looked better than she did. Jealous of Lorna, she dressed in her most expensive exercise outfit, a dazzling pink-sequined crop top and pink shorts.

She didn't have to go through much effort to dress better than Lorna, because when it came to clothes, Lorna provided no competition for her. Yet, Lorna possessed a beautiful, simple, classic look that irritated Holly.

She strutted over to the stereo system, delighted that any minute now she could show off in front of Lorna, bringing some excitement to her day.

While scanning the wide collection of CD's, Lorna arrived with Michael.

Holly popped a *Dance Hits* CD into the player. "Hi, guys," she said.

Lorna gawked at her outfit. "I had no idea they made work-out clothes with sequins. Where did you find them, I'm sure in no regular athletic store."

"I bought these in Beverly Hills. You would be surprised at some of the things you can buy on Rodeo Drive."

"The sequins are a little too glitzy for me, but you look really great in them."

Holly eyed Lorna's outfit. Although the shorts obviously came from the University of Florida, she could not dismiss the long, shapely legs, tiny waist and voluptuous breasts. Seeing Lorna's face without a trace of makeup, those stunning emerald eyes, the perfect nose and pouty lips, and that long blonde hair looking like she never brushed through it, yet still sexy, stunned Holly.

"Are you ready," Holly said, anxious to impress Lorna with her dancing.

"As ready as I'll ever be."

"How about you, Michael? Do you want to work out with us? It will be fun."

"Thanks, but no thanks. I'll leave the dancing to you girls."

Lorna squatted down to tighten her sneakers. "Has my mother been down to breakfast yet?"

"She has been down to breakfast and long gone already."

"Where did she go?"

"The beauty parlor. I hope you don't need her for anything important, because once she goes to the beauty parlor, she is there for hours."

"I was just curious."

Holly noticed Michael leaving. "Where are you going, cuz?"

"I'll be back in a minute. I'm going to get a drink of water."

"There's a small fridge right over there, dodo."

"I changed my mind. I think I'll get some lemonade or a glass of juice."

"Suit yourself, but hurry back."

As Michael was walking out the door, Holly flicked on the CD.

Michael crossed the foyer, feeling for the tape in his pocket. On the way up the grand staircase, he ran into Andrew.

"How's it going, Andrew," he said.

"How good to see you, sir! It has been a while since you came for a visit."

"Yes. It has been a while."

"Is there something I can do for you, sir?"

"No. Lorna can't find one of her good earrings. She thinks she lost it somewhere in the bedroom. I came up to look for it, while she's working out with Holly."

"Allow me to help you, sir."

"You're busy enough, Andrew. I'll look."

"I insist, sir."

"No. Really. I don't need any help."

"Please, sir. Give me the pleasure of assisting you."

"All right then. I appreciate it."

Andrew led Michael down the corridor and then opened the bedroom door for him.

For the next five minutes, they searched through drawers, on the bookcases and under the bed.

"It's not here," Michael said. "I guess she lost it somewhere else."

"I'll have the maid go through the vacuum sweeper. Maybe the sweeper picked up the earring while she was vacuuming the area rug."

"You go ahead, Andrew. I have to use the bathroom."

"By all means, sir."

Michael went into the suite's bathroom, waited a minute and then flushed the toilet.

As he walked out of the bedroom, he looked for any maids who might be cleaning the upstairs. None around, he ducked into Stuart and Eva's bedroom and switched the tape in the recorder.

———

LORNA HAD DONE DANCE AEROBICS before, but she never had the luxury of doing them in her own, private exercise room, the way Holly did. She followed along, allowing Holly to act as the instructor.

At the peak of the workout, their heart rates pumped at their highest.

Intent on showing off, Holly behaved like a wound up toy somebody had just sprung loose.

It got to the point where Lorna could not keep up with her. "You go ahead, Holly. You're in much better shape than I am."

Lorna jogged in place to the beat, while Holly went spinning and leaping across the floor.

About to stop altogether and begin doing some cool down exercises, Lorna noticed Michael walking through the door. When Holly wasn't looking, she gave him an okay signal with her fingers, wondering if he got the tape.

He nodded yes. "Looking good," he said, shouting over the blaring music.

Lorna strolled over to Michael. "Holly is too good for me."

"That's because she gets more practice."

Michael and Lorna watched Holly as she did a series of ballet moves that she had learned in dance school when she was a kid. Pirouettes, leaps and tour jetés she executed skillfully to Ricky Martin's *Livin' La Vida Loca*. Across the floor and back, and then into a series of spins she went, getting so carried away that she lost her balance and tripped over her foot. Down to the floor she slammed.

Her ego more bruised than any body parts, she jumped back up on her feet. "I guess that's enough for today. Come on, Lorna. Let's do some cool down exercises."

———

LIKE TWO MISCHIEVOUS CHILDREN who had just sneaked into the closet to play dress up in their mommy and daddy's good clothes, Michael and Lorna raced upstairs to his bedroom to listen to the tape.

"With my luck," he said, shoving the tape into the player, "this thing won't have anything important on it."

"With my luck," she said laughing, "it will all be sex."

"I thought of that, too. If we hear any sex, we'll fast forward over it."

"I was wondering, Michael. Isn't it against the law to record somebody without their permission?"

"Probably, but I don't care. It's illegal to steal somebody's stock and house, too."

"You're right." Lorna slid onto the chair next to the window. "I'm pretty sure that, even if Stuart incriminates himself on the tape, none of it will be admissible in court."

"Are you sure about that?"

"I'm pretty sure. I think the only way a recorded tape would be admissible is if you or your mother was on the tape with him. One of the parties involved has to know he's being recorded. At least I think that's how it goes. You'll have to ask your attorney."

"We probably didn't get anything important anyway. Here goes nothing." He hit the "PLAY" button.

As soon as they heard Eva and Stuart's voices, they became spellbound. They also rolled their eyes while they listened to Eva explaining to Stuart how her head pounded with a headache, and she didn't want to have sex.

The disgusted look on their faces suddenly switched to astonishment. Stuart and Eva were discussing his retirement and the big profit he was going to make on a World Office Products deal. When it came to that part of the tape where Stuart and Eva began to have sex, Michael switched off the recorder. "He's selling Grant Office Supplies to World Office Products, and then he's retiring. No wonder he stole our stock." Michael slammed his fist against the pillow. "That lowdown, scum-sucking bastard! No wonder he told my grandmother it was going to take a few months to return the house and stock. He wanted to make sure the deal closed, before anyone from my side of the family screwed up the deal." Michael slumped against the headboard. "He probably did put a contract out on me to get me out of the way. That does it. I'm going to see my attorney."

"Should I come with you?"

"It might be a good idea. Maybe David will want to question you about something."

Not more than an hour later, Michael and Lorna were sitting in front of David Chernoff's desk.

While Michael explained his situation, Lorna listened.

After David listened to the tape, Michael sighed. "I don't think Stuart ever intended to return the stock."

"I agree with you."

"How about suing him?"

"You could get him for securities fraud, breach of fiduciary duty and unlawful conversion of assets. You can also charge him with racketeering under the civil code of the Racketeer-Influenced and Corrupt Organizations Act.

"How long would all of that take?"

"It won't happen overnight. It could take years."

"That's all well and good in the long run, but what about now? Do you think I should go see World Office Products?"

"Again, it's your word against Stuart's. All he has to do is provide them with the documents your mother signed, and that will be enough proof for them. They'll look at you like you're some jealous relative and go ahead with the deal."

"What if I showed them the suit we filed against Stuart? Won't that back them off?"

"It might. It's worth a try. The best thing you can do in the meantime is come up with a copy of the agreement. Present that and show the people from World Office Products the pending lawsuit, and I think they will definitely back out of the deal or at least postpone it."

"Those damn agreements! I have no idea where they could be."

"Talk to everybody you can think of. Maybe you'll come up with something."

"Stuart thinks I have them in my possession. I'll bluff World Office Products."

"What would you show them as proof?"

"I'll show them a phony agreement."

"That's fraud, Michael. You don't want to commit a felony and wind up in prison."

Michael ran his fingers through his hair. "Wait a minute. I have my grandmother. She'll vouch for me."

"Think about it, Michael. Put yourself in Stuart's shoes. If you did have a copy of the agreement, you would have produced it by now. You wouldn't need your grandmother or anyone else vouching for you. You would have all the proof you need in that agreement."

Lorna concurred. "He's right, Michael."

Michael sighed. "Damn it. Isn't there anything I can do? Is Stuart just going to sell the company and pocket all that money, our money?"

"It's simple," David said. "Come up with a copy of the agreement."

Michael slumped to the chair, frustration nearly choking him. "I was wondering, David. Is there some way you can find out what happened to Charles Lerner's files? If they're still around, I'll bet we'll find a copy of the agreement among them."

"I'll have one of my paralegals get on it right away."

35

EVA TOSSED A PAIR OF Stuart's socks and underwear into his leather, overnight suitcase. "I don't know where I caught this flu bug, but my stomach feels awful." She feigned a cramp, giving Stuart the impression she was sick.

"Here let me get that. You go back to bed." Stuart zipped the suitcase shut and dropped it to the floor. "I'll miss you. I hate traveling alone."

"I'll miss you, too, sweetie, but it's only for one night. You'll be back before you know it."

"If World Office Products hadn't called this special meeting, I wouldn't be going."

"I hope they're not backing out of the deal."

"No. Everything is fine with the deal. They just want to go over some details of the contract with me."

Eva acted interested. "Couldn't you have handled the details by e-mail or fax?"

"I wanted to do it face to face. I don't want any last minute problems at the closing."

Stuart slid into his navy blue blazer. "I wish you hadn't given Andrew and the maids the night off. What if you get sicker?"

"I like total peace and quiet, when I don't feel well."

"All you have to do is tell the servants not to bother you, and they won't."

"You know how considerate Andrew is. It would bother him not to bother me. And, that's just what I don't want, people doting on me, when I'd rather be left alone."

"You're really going to be alone. I'm not even going to be around, and that bothers me."

"I'm not that sick, Stuart. You go and have your meeting. I'll talk to you on the phone when you get to your hotel."

"Should I tell Holly not to go to the club tonight?"

"Stuart, please. How many times do I have to tell you that I want to be left alone? Besides, Holly loves the dances at the club. I don't want to deprive her of having a good time."

Stuart bent down and kissed Eva. "I'll call you when I get to Atlanta."

As soon as Eva saw the Jaguar pulling out of the garage, she called the airlines to verify that Stuart's plane was scheduled to take off on time. Satisfied that there were no problems with the flight, she dialed Gayle's house.

———

MICHAEL WAS ABOUT to go upstairs to ask Lorna if she wanted to take a moonlit stroll on the beach, when the phone rang. He went to the den and answered it. "Grant residence," he said.

"It's Eva, Michael."

She never called the house. He figured it must be some kind of emergency. "Is everything all right," he asked.

"Can you come over? I have something important I want to discuss with you."

He didn't trust her. "Where's Stuart? Does he want to talk to me, too?"

"No. He had to go out of town."

"Where did he go?"

"Atlanta."

"When is he coming back?"

"Tomorrow."

"Then I'll come over tomorrow, after he gets back."

"I need to talk to you now."

"About what?"

"I don't want to discuss it over the phone. It's too important."

"Where's Andrew?"

"I gave him the night off."

"What about the maids?"

"The entire household staff has the night off."

"Then you are over there by yourself."

"Yes. It's not the first time, and it won't be the last." She hesitated a moment and then said. "Look, Michael, if you're not interested in hearing what I have to say, then forget it."

For all he knew, she might be on the level. He had no choice. "I'll be right over."

"And, don't bring Lorna with you. Her birthday is coming soon. I want to discuss that with you, too. It's a surprise. Don't even tell her I called."

"I'll see you in a few minutes." Michael hung up the phone.

Gayle was sitting in the Florida room with Michael and heard his end of the conversation. "Was that Eva, dear?"

"Yes. I'm going next door for a little while."

"Is everything all right over at Stuart's house?"

"Everything is fine. Eva says she has something important she wants to discuss with me. I'll be right back."

———

WHEN MICHAEL ARRIVED at Stuart's house, he had second thoughts . About to leave, he heard Eva calling his name.

"Where are you," he said, following her voice to the foyer.

"Upstairs."

The house was so dimly lit that he could barely see her on the second floor. He felt like a defenseless fly buzzing around a black widow's web. One false move and he was dead. "Come down here," he said. "I don't want to talk up there."

"You act like I'm going to bite you or something."

"Aren't you," he said under his breath. "If you want to talk to me, come down here."

"I can't take the chance of somebody walking in and hearing us. Please, Michael. It's important."

He sighed through gritted teeth. "All right, but this better be good."

Eva hurried back to the bedroom to wait for him.

In a red silk blouse, the top buttons of which she left open to expose her cleavage, and a pair of tight, black leather pants, she stood in the doorway and motioned with her hand. "In here, Michael."

"I don't like this one bit, Eva."

She led him inside the room. "I'm sorry. I'm not trying to make you angry."

He glanced at the two chairs draped with clothing. The only place to sit was on the two-seat sofa. "I'll stand, if you don't mind."

"Please, sit down, Michael. You're making me nervous."

He didn't trust her for one minute. "No. What did you want to talk to me about?"

She went to the liquor stand. "We'll talk in a minute. Have a glass of champagne with me first."

Michael just wanted to hear what she had to say and get out of there. "Why wait? Talk to me now."

"It's a delicate situation."

"Then let's talk about Lorna. What were you planning for her birthday?"

"What's the hurry? We'll get to all of that in a minute. In the meantime, sit down. You're making me a nervous wreck, standing there like you're afraid of me."

"I am afraid of you." He sat on the sofa. "All right, I'm sitting. Now talk or I'm leaving."

As she handed him a glass of champagne, she ran the back of her fingers down his cheek. "You're remarkably handsome."

He pulled away from her. "I don't know what you're trying to pull, but whatever it is, it's not going to work."

She touched his wavy, dark hair. "Relax. You're too wound up." With her back to him, she unbuttoned her blouse lower. "I'll tell you in a minute." She went to the stereo and dialed the tuner to a soft jazz station. The sensual, soothing sound of a saxophone filled the room.

The whole scene had the earmarks of a den of iniquity. Michael suspected all along that something like this was going to happen. "I'm leaving, Eva."

"No. Wait."

"Then speak."

"I will, but first I have to use the bathroom."

As soon as the bathroom door closed, Michael went for the hidden microphone and tape recorder. Now that he knew about Stuart selling Grant Office Supplies, he thought he better get the devices out of there before one of the maids found them. He grabbed the devices and sat back down on the sofa.

Eva came out of the bathroom, her nude body wrapped in an ivory satin robe. "Those leather pants were too binding. I hope you don't mind that I slipped into something more comfortable."

"I wish you hadn't done that. Stuart is going to be furious if he ever finds out about this."

She took a sip of champagne and then sat down next to him. "You worry too much."

"I have every reason to."

"How is your shoulder?"

"It's fine."

"Will you be able to use it normally after it has healed?"

"Yes. The doctor said I should expect a full recovery, a little scarring, but that's it."

Eva stared down at Michael's muscular, hairy legs in the linen shorts. Closer and closer she brought her hand to his leg until her fingertips touched his taut skin.

"Here we go again," Michael said. "I'm out of here." As he stood up, she grabbed his sore arm and pulled him down to the loveseat.

Pain shot through his shoulder, almost blinding him, and he fell on top of her.

Eva trapped him in her clutches and kissed him.

At that moment, Lorna walked into the bedroom. "You sick bastards," she cried out when she saw them.

Michael struggled to get up. "Wait, Lorna. You have this all wrong."

"I should have known you were like all of the others." She left, slamming the door behind her.

Michael felt like punching Eva. "You're nothing but a cheap tramp."

Eva reached for him. "No, Michael, Don't go."

He ignored Eva and went running after Lorna.

Across the lawn and through Millicent's garden he chased after her. At Gayle's swimming pool, he caught up with her.

Michael grabbed her arm. "I love you, Lorna. Would you please listen?"

"Actions speak louder than words. You didn't look like a man in love, when you were kissing my mother."

"I wasn't kissing your mother. She was kissing me."

"As soon as your mother told me that you went over to Stuart's house, because my mother wanted to talk to you, I knew something like this was going to happen." She broke away from Michael. "It's obvious that you're no different than any of the other men I've known. Sooner or later, you all end up following my mother around like a puppy."

"You don't understand. Your mother told me she had something important to tell me. I was hoping it had something to do with the World Office Products deal."

"Take a good, hard look at me, Michael. Do I look stupid or something?"

"Your mother tried to seduce me. You have to believe me, Lorna."

"More than anyone I know what my mother is like. I'm sure she did try to seduce you."

"Then why are you angry with me?"

"Just answer one question. Did you know Stuart wouldn't be home?"

"Your mother told me she couldn't talk to me with him there."

"And you believed her."

"Not really. I had my doubts."

"And you still fell for her crap, after everything I've told you about her."

"Like I said, I thought she might have some important information about the World Office Products deal."

"Please tell me you didn't know Andrew or any of the servants weren't going to be there."

His defeated expression answered her question. "You probably got a cheap thrill out of going over there to see my mother."

"You're wrong."

"No. You're the one who was wrong. I'm packing up and leaving tonight."

"Where can you go? You don't have any money."

"By the time I get through talking to that sick mother of mine, I'm sure she will supply all the money I'll need." Lorna stormed away from Michael.

———

INSTEAD OF GOING INSIDE TO PACK, Lorna headed back to Stuart's house. With none of the servants there to overhear them quarreling, now was the perfect time to have it out with her mother.

The back door was still unlocked. Lorna charged through the kitchen and up the stairs to the bedroom.

As she turned the knob, she hollered to her mother. "It's me, I'm coming in." Without waiting for permission to enter, Lorna stormed into the room.

Eva gulped the last of her champagne. "What do you want?"

"Money to get an apartment."

"Why should I give you anything?"

"Just think, mother. I'm moving out of Gayle's house. Aren't you thrilled?"

"Why should I care?"

"You care plenty, and you know it."

"Why are you always coming to me for money? Call your father for a change."

"We've been through this before. Are you going to give me the money or not?"

"I'll give you enough money to fly to Michigan, and that's it."

"I don't want to live with dad."

"That's too bad? You should have thought of that before you started this whole commotion. I warned you not to get involved with Michael."

"Speaking of Michael, what in hell were you trying to prove tonight? Do you have to spread your legs for every good-looking, young stud you see?"

Eva slapped Lorna across the face. "How dare you! Get out."

"Not until you give me money to get an apartment."

"I don't care if you have to live on the street. I'm not giving you a dime."

"Oh yes you will."

"Like hell I will."

"If you don't, I'll tell Stuart about your little escapade tonight and what a tramp you were while I was growing up."

"He would never believe you."

"After I was through giving him every sordid detail, he'll believe me all right. Even if he doesn't at first, the seed will be planted."

"You little bitch! How much do you need?"

"Twenty thousand."

"Twenty thousand?"

"Why do you sound surprised? To you and Stuart that's chicken feed."

"Why twenty thousand? What kind of apartment do you intend to get?"

"Say I have to spend a thousand or two a month, I figure by the time I pay the first-month's rent, the last month's rent and a security deposit, and I get the bare necessities I'll need, plus an extra month or two of rent money, in case I don't find a job right away, it will take that much."

"I don't have that kind of money on me right now."

"Then give me money for a hotel room tonight, and I'll come back tomorrow."

Eva went to her jewelry box. From a secret compartment under the satin pad, she pulled out several one-hundred dollar bills. "Here's four hundred dollars."

"What time should I come back tomorrow?"

"I don't want you to come back."

"How far do you think four hundred dollars will get me?"

"I'll write you out a check for the rest. You can take it to my bank and cash it tomorrow."

———

MICHAEL WAITED IN THE DEN, where he could not miss Lorna. When he heard the front door opening, he jumped up to go talk with her. "Did you go see your mother," he asked.

She brushed past him without answering.

"You're not really going to leave, are you?"

"Oh yes, I am."

"Don't go, Lorna. Please."

"You should have thought about this, before you went to see my mother."

"I don't want you to go."

"That's too bad."

36

MORE SO THAN at any other time in her life, Lorna felt alone. Lonely was one thing, but being alone meant something altogether different. When somebody was lonely, they craved love and fulfillment. They still had friends and family members around to keep them company. But, alone meant singular, no friends, no lovers, no family, no coworkers, nobody with whom she could share her life, good or bad.

She said her good-byes to Gayle and thanked her for her generous hospitality. She explained that her mother had given her money to get her own apartment. If Michael cared to give her the sordid details of his and her mother's tryst, he could do so. She saw no need to hurt or upset Gayle with the information.

As Lorna drove south on Ocean Boulevard, it bothered her that she might have overreacted. The World Office Products deal was extremely important to Michael. But with him constantly in her face, she could not think. She did the right thing by moving out. At least she hoped she did the right thing. She needed time to get her head together. After all, she could not stay at Gayle's house the rest of her life. It was only a matter of time, before she had to move out and get her own apartment. Now she would be paying a price for moving out, loneliness. But then again, things could change. Maybe she would get lucky and find a good job right away. Working would certainly take her mind off her troubles. She might even meet some nice people wherever she moved, hook up with some neat women around her age and build friendships.

Lorna drove further south, passing up different hotels and motels. With the twenty thousand-dollar check in her purse, plus the four hundred in cash her mother gave her, she decided she would stay somewhere nice tonight, a place that lifted her spirits and made her feel safe.

After driving two more miles down the road she pulled into the Palmetto Inn, a quaint motel on the beach. From the well-cared-for look of the building and the beautiful landscaping, it had to be clean and safe.

When she went inside to register, her instincts proved correct. Everything, from the glass hurricane lamps flickering with burning candles to the white wicker furniture and spotless terracotta Mexican tile floor, the lobby personified the type of place she would feel comfortable in tonight.

The rooms started at three hundred dollars a night, also confirming her impression of the place. As she planned on leaving the first thing in the morning to go apartment hunting, she would not be staying to enjoy the pool or the beach, so she took the standard room at the base rate.

The entire night she tossed and turned, upset over her fight with Michael. By seven o'clock in the morning, she had showered, eaten breakfast and checked out of the inn.

One apartment complex in particular caught her eye, a place called Ocean Breezes. She went up to the rental office and met with an on-sight, leasing agent. From the congenial woman Lorna learned that Ocean Breezes appealed to people of all ages, not just senior citizens like some of the other developments. The woman took her on a tour through model apartments, one furnished and the other unfurnished.

Lorna immediately fell in love with the place. One of the things she especially liked was the safe feeling the complex provided. A gated community with a security guard posted at the entrance, only residents and pre-approved visitors could pass inside. After being shot at that day with Michael, she did not want to lie awake for hours worrying about anyone breaking in during the night.

There were several rental complexes in the area; however, she lacked the patience and right disposition to make a big ordeal out of moving. To her surprise and delight, a furnished apartment was available for immediate occupancy. She happily signed the lease and paid two months rent plus a security deposit.

Piled up in the car, on the seats and in the trunk, were all of her belongings.

She drove past a small lake, in the center of which was a fountain shooting water high into the air. A little further down the road she made the right turn into the parking lot in front of her apartment.

The scarlet red bougainvillea vines draping over her second-floor patio railing brought a trace of a smile to her sad face.

To and from her apartment she went, anxious to get all of the boxes inside before it grew totally dark. All evening she planned to spend putting everything away in its own, special place.

On her fourth trip back to her apartment, she dropped her car keys. About to put down the box and get them, she heard a man's voice.

"I'll get them for you," he said.

When she turned around to thank the man, she immediately recognized him. "Julian."

"I'm sorry," he said. "You look familiar, but I can't place the face."

"Lorna Meade. You remember. Eva Grant's daughter. You know, Stuart Grant. I met you at Millicent's birthday party."

"Sure. Now I remember." He handed her the keys, a pleasant smile on his face. "It looks like you're moving in."

"As a matter of fact I am."

"Any more boxes in the car?"

"A few."

"Is the car unlocked?"

"Yes."

"I'll help you. What's the apartment number?"

"203."

"Go on ahead. I'll be right up."

No sooner did Lorna get upstairs and put the box in a corner than Julian arrived with another box.

"There are two more left," he said. "Come on."

"You don't have to help me, Julian. I can get them."

"I have nothing else to do."

Lorna followed Julian down the stairs. "Do you live here, or are you just visiting somebody," she asked.

"I live downstairs, number 101."

"That's terrific! I was hoping I would get to know my neighbors. Now I don't have to worry about that anymore. When did you move in? I know you were living with William."

"I moved in here not too long after he died. I couldn't stand being reminded of him constantly. It hurt too much."

"I can imagine."

They got the last two boxes out of the car and took them upstairs to her apartment.

After stacking the boxes on top of the others, Lorna grimaced. "I can't even offer you a soda."

"You're just moving in. What do you expect?" He glanced around him. "I see you took a furnished apartment."

"I had to. I can't afford to go out and buy all new furniture right now."

"It's not too bad."

"Is Ocean Breezes a nice place to live in?"

"I haven't been here that long, but so far I like it." Julian leaned back against the kitchen counter. "How is everybody on Sand Dollar Island?"

"You wouldn't believe what all has been going on."

"If Stuart has anything to do with it, I would. That man was downright cruel to me and William."

"As a matter of fact, he is at the center of the trouble."

"What did he do?"

"He pulled a fast one on Michael, his mother and his sister. Believe it or not, he stole most of their Grant Office Supply stock, so he can sell the business and retire."

"That was real nice of him," Julian said sarcastically. "Are they going to try and stop him?"

"Yes. They filed a lawsuit against him."

"When William and I stopped to see Mike before the accident, he was looking for a copy of an agreement his dad and Stuart made a long time ago. He seemed really pissed at Stuart. I'll bet it had something to do with the stock, because he went to Europe chasing his mother down over it."

"That's when this whole thing started."

"Did he ever find a copy of that agreement?"

"No."

"That no-good Stuart probably has them all."

"That's the strange part. Stuart did have them, but they were stolen from his office safe."

"You mean somebody broke into his safe and took them?"

"Yes and the person who did it knew the combination."

"I'll be damned."

"Michael has been looking everywhere for those agreements. He said without a copy of one, he won't be able to prove that they own half of the stock. Even if he doesn't find the agreements, he's going to try to stop Stuart from selling the business."

"How's he going to do that?"

"I believe he's going to show World Office Products, the company that's buying the business, a copy of the lawsuit they filed."

"That should do it."

"It might and it might not. There's a chance Stuart will convince the bigwigs from World Office Products that Michael is a lunatic who is trying to start trouble."

"Stuart is bad news."

"I still can't believe he didn't let you come to William's funeral."

"That man will get what he deserves someday. What goes around comes around."

"I totally agree with you."

"He's your stepfather, right?"

"Yes, I'm sorry to say."

"How do you get along with him?"

"I keep my distance. I don't like him."

"Your poor mother!"

"I have mixed emotions over her. I guess I love her, because she's my mother and all, but she treats me so terribly. Maybe she and Stuart deserve each other."

"Is that why you moved out?"

"This story never ends."

"What do you mean?"

"Are you sure you want to hear all this?"

"The people on Sand Dollar Island fascinate me."

"If you insist. I didn't move out of Stuart's house, I moved out of Michael's."

"No kidding? You were living with Mike. You two were getting it on?"

"We were, but that's not why I moved in with him. My mother threw me out of Stuart's house, and I didn't want to go up north and live with my dad. I didn't have any money, so Michael invited me to move in with him and his mother, until I found a job and got on my feet."

"Where are you working?"

"I'm not. I didn't find a job yet."

"I don't understand. These apartments aren't cheap."

"I blackmailed my mother for the money."

Julian laughed. "You're right. There is no end to your saga."

"That's it. I'm not boring you with any more."

"You have to finish. You can't keep me hanging. It's too interesting."

"I busted my mother and Michael together."

"I don't believe it. Mike isn't the type."

Her explaining everything to Julian helped open her eyes. "He's not, I guess. I think my mother tried to seduce him."

"That pissed you off, so you told her you would tell Stuart on her."

"Right. That's it. The end. Now I'm here at Ocean Breezes."

"Too bad I'm not a writer. This would make a good book." He checked his watch. "I better run now. I have an appointment with a woman in St. Andrews Country Club."

"Are you still in the decorating business?"

"Absolutely. It seems those rich, white women like hanging around with a talented, gay, black decorator. They think it's chic and cool. You should see. They invite me to all of their fancy soirees, on their yachts, to Europe, everywhere."

"I hope you're making a lot of money."

"Honey, if those money-honeys can afford me, they can hang with me."

"I'm glad everything is working out for you, Julian."

"Before I leave, you have to tell me if you're still seeing Mike?"

"No. I got so angry when I saw him with my mother that I broke it off."

"You just said it was your mother's fault. She tried to seduce him."

"I know."

"Then why are you taking it out on Mike?"

"I need time to think."

"Take it from me, sweetpea. I know men. That guy is a good catch. He's a decent person, and he's no skirt chaser, if you know what I mean. Besides, if he gets all of that company business straightened out, he'll be worth a ton of cash." Julian kissed Lorna on the cheek. "Come down and see me anytime." He reached inside his white silk shirt pocket for his business card. "My home number is on there. It might be better if you called first. I'm usually out during the day." Julian waved good-bye. "Ta Ta, darling. You must come down for dinner sometime. Gays are great cooks."

"I'll do that. Thanks, you brightened up my day."

37

MICHAEL ALMOST WISHED he had never met Lorna. Ever since that night she walked in on him and Eva, it felt like part of him had died. His insides ached for her, and everything beautiful about life now seemed meaningless. She never phoned him after she left to tell him where she was living, which was almost a week ago. He even broke down and called Eva to see if she knew anything. She didn't, or so she let on. Calling information proved to be a waste of time. Lorna either got a new cell phone number or her home phone number was unlisted. When he talked with the operator, he learned there was a list of Meades, none of them a Lorna Meade or L. Meade. She could have used another initial with her last name, because she did not want anyone bothering her. He eventually went down the entire list, calling each and every name, hoping to find her. None of the parties who answered even came close to sounding like Lorna. The remaining Meades he found were not at home or answering their phones. He also checked the internet for information but he found nothing there either.

As Michael was walking into David Chernoff's office, he wondered if he would ever see Lorna again.

"How's it going, David," he said.

"Not too badly, Mike. Have a seat."

"Did you get a chance to go through Lerner's folder?"

"Yes, but I'm sorry to say I didn't find a copy of the agreement."

"Damn it. If I didn't have bad luck, I wouldn't have any luck at all."

"I think it's a matter of being too late. Hutch Badgely told me Jerry Zuckerman borrowed the folder from him a good while back."

"You have got to be kidding me. That means he probably went through the folder for Stuart, or Stuart went through the folder himself."

"That's my guess."

"I wonder if Stuart still has Lerner's copy, or if it was stolen out of his safe along with the other copies."

"I thought of that while I was over Badgely's office. I asked him when Jerry Zuckerman borrowed the file. From what Hutch remembers Jerry borrowed it before the copies were stolen."

"Then there's a good chance Stuart still doesn't have that copy. They're all still missing."

"I believe so."

"What do I do now?"

"From what I gather, you never came up with a copy of the agreement either."

"No. Did you get the chance to call Jerry yet and ask him about the World Office Products deal?"

"Yes. But just as I guessed, he wouldn't divulge any information."

"Wonderful!"

"But, I did do some investigating of my own and found out they're closing the deal this Friday."

"That's four days from now.

"I know."

"I have to do something. I can't just sit here and let Stuart get away with this."

"You have no other choice. You have to come up with a copy of that agreement."

"And if I can't?"

"I don't know, Michael."

"I have an idea. I'll make a big stink. I'll hire a bunch of people to stand out in front of Grant Office Supplies and picket the place. I'll make big banners saying what a bum my uncle is and how he stole half of the family business."

"That would be a mistake."

"Why?"

"It will kill business."

"Why should I care?"

"You'll care plenty if and when you ever get the stock back. Nobody will do business with you. You'll wind up bankrupt."

"You have a point."

"Do what you want, but if it were up to me, I would handle everything as quietly as possible."

"It's killing me that I'm just sitting here with my hands tied."

"Go hunt down those agreements."

"When I don't find them, then what?"

"I have to think about it. Don't forget we filed suit."

"But, you said it could take years to get to court. By then, Stuart will have all of the money locked up in some Swiss Bank account. Wait a minute. I know what I'll do. Whether I come up with those agreements or not, I'll surprise my uncle and attend that closing Friday."

38

MICHAEL PULLED UP TO his mother's house, wondering whose black Oldsmobile was parked in the driveway. Lorna had a Honda. It wasn't her car.

As he stepped out of his convertible, he noticed a man taping a piece of paper to the front door.

Michael hurried up to the man. "Can I help you with something?"

"I knocked on the door, but nobody answered."

"Who are you looking for?"

"Gayle Grant. I was going to serve her with this notice." The man put the role of tape back into his pocket. "Who are you?"

"I'm her son."

"Here. It's all there, written down."

"How did you get on the island—through the security gate?"

"A Mister Stuart Grant provided that information."

The man got into his car and left.

Michael wondered why Ruby, Arielle or his mother didn't answer the door. Somebody was always home. He glanced at his watch. It was close to one. Ruby was probably serving his mother lunch out on the back terrace.

Michael read the paper in his hand. "What in hell?" He stomped through the house to the terrace.

Gayle laid her tuna fish sandwich on the plate. "What's wrong, Michael? You look upset."

"Prepare yourself for bad news."

"How bad?"

"Nobody died. It's just more legal crap we have to go through."

"Is it about the stock? Did Stuart change his mind, and he's not going to return it?"

"No. It's something else entirely."

"Thank goodness it has nothing to do with Stuart."

"It does have something to do with Stuart, I'm sorry to say."

"Now what?"

"It's something that can be settled, so don't get all worked up."

"I took my pill. I'll be fine."

"It's about the house." Michael sat across from his mother. "I better go back to the beginning." He sighed. "Do you remember all of those times Stuart brought papers over to the house for you to sign?"

"My heart may be bad, but my memory isn't."

"Among one of those papers was a General Warranty Deed. Without your knowing it, you signed the house over to Stuart."

"Dear Lord in heaven! That can't be."

"It's true"

"How? Somebody can't just take another person's house."

"Oh yes they can and Stuart did it."

Gayle froze in disbelief. "How do you know about all this?"

"Lorna accidentally saw the deed, while she was still living with Eva and Stuart. I checked it out, and it's true."

"When did all of this take place? I thought everything was okay between Stuart and us, that he was returning the stock, and we were friends again."

"It's far from being over. The bastard is evicting us. According to this notice we have a month to vacate the premises."

"He can't do this, can he?"

"I'll call David. If he can't help us, I'm sure he will refer us to a good real estate attorney."

"I never would have believed Stuart could be so underhanded."

"Now that I already have you upset, I guess you should know everything."

Gayle sighed. "What more can there possibly be?"

"Stuart is selling Grant Office Supplies. That's why he stole our stock in the first place. He wants to pocket the money and retire."

Gayle gasped, scaring Michael.

"Are you all right?"

She nodded yes.

"Don't worry, mother, everything is going to be okay."

"What are we going to do?"

"Kill the bastard."

"Quit talking so crazy, Michael. I'm serious."

"I'll go call David now. Will you be all right? Do you want another pill or something?"

"I have enough medicine in me to stock a drugstore." She sighed again. "Do you happen to know when Stuart is planning to sell the company?"

"The closing is Friday."

———

GAYLE FEARED SHE MIGHT suffer another heart attack if she didn't lie down and get some rest. She spent the rest of the afternoon in her bedroom.

When evening came, she could not stomach the thought of eating, so she skipped dinner. The only thought fixated in her mind was having it out with Stuart once and for all.

She walked into the den, where Michael was sitting, checking his e-mails on his computer. "I'll be back in a little while," she said.

"Where are you going?"

"To see Stuart."

"Are you serious?"

"I most certainly am."

"I don't think you should. He might get you worked-up."

"By the time I'm finished with him, he'll be the one who gets worked up."

"I wish you would let me handle this."

"It's time I got involved. Where is that eviction notice?"

Michael grabbed the document from the desk and handed it to his mother. "I don't think you should be going over there. It's too risky."

"I'll be fine."

"If you insist on it, then I'm going with you."

"Maybe you shouldn't. It's going to get ugly."

"Then I'm definitely going with you. You'll need all the support you can get with that bastard."

"All right then. Come on."

"How do you know Stuart will be home?"

"I don't."

"Why don't we call first?"

"And have him duck out on me. Not on your life."

———

GAYLE TRIED the front door, finding it unlocked. She stomped through the house with Michael following behind her.

She glanced in the den and library. No Stuart. Across the foyer and down the corridor she marched to the dining room.

Stuart was in the midst of eating dinner with Eva and Holly.

Gayle stormed up to him, the eviction notice crunched in her hand. "Damn you, Stuart. What is this?"

Both Eva and Holly gaped at Gayle. Neither one of them had ever heard her swear.

His mother's assertive attitude even surprised Michael. Not once since she suffered the heart attack had he seen her so aggressive.

Stuart threw down his napkin. "How dare you barge in here like this, while we're eating dinner!"

Gayle was livid. "Go to hell, Stuart."

"I demand that you leave this instant."

"If you think you can just throw us out of our house, you have another thing coming."

Eva grabbed Stuart's arm. "What is Gayle talking about?"

"Never mind. It's none of your business."

Holly laid her fork on the dish. "What's going on, dad?"

"Shut up, Holly. You stay out of this, too."

His incessant condescending attitude nauseated Gayle. "What's the matter, Stuart? You don't want them to know what a louse you are."

On his feet now, Stuart glared at her. "Enough, Gayle."

"Screw you, Stuart." Gayle turned to Holly. "Do you know what your father did? He stole our house and forty-three percent of our stock. Now he thinks he's going to sell the business and pocket the money, half of our money."

Stuart scoffed. "I can do whatever I want with the business. I'm the one who built it in the first place. It took a lot of guts, stress and pressure to get that company where it is today. You certainly didn't help any. You were so inept at business matters that I had to throw you off the board. And that lazy son of yours over there, all he ever wants to do is travel the world, playing in the mountains. There's nothing either of you can do about it. I'm selling the business."

"Why are you doing this? Is it because you're still holding a grudge against me after all these years?"

"I wouldn't go there if I were you."

"Why? Are you embarrassed?"

Michael stayed close at Gayle's side. "What are you talking about, mother?"

"Do you know why Stuart has been doing all of these rotten things? He's angry, because I dumped him for your father."

Michael, Holly and Eva's faces froze in disbelief.

Stuart sloughed it off. "You're making up stories. Look at you. What man in his right mind would want an ugly hag like you?"

The insult angered Gayle, and her heart began to pound. "It's the truth, and you know it."

"Get out of my house, hag."

Her heart pounded harder. "You won't get away with this. We're going to give World Office Products a visit and stop the sale."

"Don't you dare." Stuart shoved Gayle out of his way.

Michael grabbed Stuart. About to punch him with his good hand, his mother started gasping for breath.

"Stop it," she cried. Her eyes opened wide, and she clutched her chest.

Michael caught his mother and lowered her gently to the floor. "Hurry, Holly. Get an aspirin. I think she's having another heart attack. Eva, call 911." Michael glared at Stuart. "She better be all right, or I'll kill you."

Holly came running back into the dining room with the aspirin. "I hope she'll be all right."

"She better be."

"What's going on, Michael? I don't know a thing about anything."

"Not now, Holly. Go open the gate and wait for the ambulance. Direct them in here."

Gayle kept clutching her chest. Michael put the aspirin in his mother's mouth and told her to chew it. All of a sudden, Gayle took a huge gasp and quit breathing.

Michael quickly started administering CPR with his one hand.

Eva came rushing into the dining room. "The paramedics are on their way." She knelt down beside Michael. "Is there anything else I can do?"

He didn't answer. He kept up with the CPR.

The paramedics showed up a short while later. After administering the proper life-saving procedures, doing their best to help Gayle, they rushed her to the hospital.

39

EVA LAY BACK AGAINST the pillows, upset over the evening's events. "What was Gayle talking about tonight, Stuart? Were you two lovers before she met Richard?"

"I don't want to discuss it."

"Then it's true."

"Just because I don't want to discuss something doesn't mean it's true."

"Well you're acting like it is true. If it wasn't, why would you be so defensive about the whole thing?"

"If you want to dredge up some dark, dirty secret, dredge up one of your own. I'm sure you have plenty buried away somewhere." He slid the blanket off and got out of bed. "With men falling all over you your whole life, I'm sure you have done some things you're not too proud of."

"What has gotten into you all of a sudden? You're being so mean."

Stuart sat back down on the bed next to her. "I'm not purposely trying to be mean to you."

"Then talk to me. Were you and Gayle lovers at one time?"

"No. Are you happy now?"

"Then why did she say those things?"

"Because she's angry she sold me her stock and won't be getting any of the proceeds from the W.O.P. deal."

"But she seemed so sincere."

"Who are you going to believe, me or her?"

Eva didn't know what to believe. The entire subject frightened her. If Gayle meant what she said, she planned to take Stuart to court. That is, if she survived her heart attack. Eva turned onto her side with her back to Stuart. If they did go to court, there could be a trial by jury. Gayle might win and be awarded a big settlement with punitive damages. It could wipe Stuart out, leaving them penniless. The thought unnerved Eva. Stuart could wind up in prison for the rest of his life, and she would be forced to go back to work. No. Never would she return to work. She would commit suicide first. She envisioned seeing Stuart behind bars in a baggy jumpsuit, the kind inmates wear. Could fate play that cruel of a trick on her, taking away this wonderful life of wealth and leisure and replacing it with poverty and hardship? She shuddered under the covers.

While Stuart was in the bathroom, another negative thought tied Eva's stomach into knots.

When he returned to bed, she rolled over next to him.

"Are you really throwing Gayle and Michael out of their house?"

"It's my house now. She signed it over to me."

"But she said you took the house from her."

"How could I take the house from her? How do you take somebody's house?"

"I don't know."

"She has wanted to move off the island ever since Richard died."

"That's funny. She never mentioned it to me."

"Damn it, Eva. If you want to believe I'm the bad guy here, then go ahead. I'm not going to put up with two lunatic women in one night."

"I was just asking."

"Instead of doubting everything I say and do, why don't you have more faith in me?"

Eva sighed. Was Gayle lying about the house, too? It had to be as Stuart said. Gayle realized that she had made a big mistake by selling him the stock, and she was just trying to cause trouble for Stuart. Nobody could just take somebody's house. Did she actually think she would be able to get away with such an outlandish accusation? Eva grinned. Gayle deserved everything she was getting for the things she tried to pull with Stuart. From this day forward, if Gayle was lucky enough to survive, she would never speak to her again. And, she would do whatever it took when they went to court, make up stories about

Gayle and Michael or perjure herself if it came down to that, to help her husband.

"I'm sorry, sweetie," Eva said.

"Forget it." Stuart stood up and headed for the door.

"Where are you going?"

"Downstairs to get something to eat. I've had enough of your needling."

"How can you be hungry? We just had dinner a little while ago."

"You just had dinner. I was busy arguing with Gayle." He stormed out the door.

Andrew and the maids had already gone to their rooms to retire. Stuart went to the library and poured himself a stiff drink. As he was settling into an easy chair, Holly strolled into the room.

"What are you doing up," he asked.

"I'm upset over what happened tonight. Do you think Aunt Gayle will be all right?"

"I'm sure she'll be fine, honey."

Holly curled up on her father's lap.

Stuart gave her a warm hug. "How's my baby girl?"

"I love you daddy."

"I love you, too, sweetheart."

"Can I ask you something, daddy?"

"Sure, anything."

"What did Aunt Gayle mean when she said you're throwing her out of her house?"

"I can't take any more." Stuart pushed Holly off his lap.

She picked herself up off of the floor. "What's wrong? What did I say?"

"Everyone around here thinks I'm the bad guy. Enough is enough."

"I don't think you're a bad guy. I was just wondering."

"Go back to bed and leave me alone. I'm done. Do you hear me? Done."

Holly trudged out of the room, her shoulders drooping and her slippers scraping the floor.

Stuart drank half of his vodka cocktail and then reached for the newspaper.

The headline on the front page piqued his curiosity. LOCAL RESTAURATEUR MISSING. Stuart gulped down the rest of his drink. The article was about Vince Spinosa. Stuart sat there, frozen in his chair. Vince and two acquaintances seemed to have fallen off the face of the earth. Their wives reported to police the men went out Friday night and never came home the next morning. The last person who saw Vince was the bartender. They talked in the office about twelve-thirty, and then the bartender left for home. Cops are investigating, but so far they had no leads. Officials weren't ruling out the possibility of a mob it, because all three of their cars were left in the restaurant's parking lot.

Stuart sat there in disbelief. Were the three men really dead or did they flee the country, because things got too hot for them in Florida? Where did all of this leave him? After thinking about it for a minute, he realized there was nothing he could do about putting another contract out on Michael now. He didn't know anyone else like Vince. Maybe it was just as well. After reading about the men's disappearance possibly being a mob hit, he didn't want to go near another mobster again.

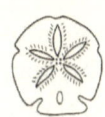

40

MICHAEL GLANCED at his watch. All night, he and his sister had waited at the hospital while their mother was having open-heart surgery.

How much easier it would have been on him if Lorna had been there beside him. "Why are all these awful things happening to us, Sam? What did we do so terrible in our lives that we're paying for it now?"

"They say everything happens for a reason, Michael."

"What God, if there really is a God, which I'm beginning to doubt there is, would make us suffer so much? Why aren't terrible things happening to Stuart? How can he keep going on reaping all of life's rewards, while mother is in there fighting for her life? Nothing makes any sense."

"I guess nothing is supposed to make any sense. It's part of the mystery."

Michael sighed. "Damn that Stuart. I hope he rots in hell for eternity after he dies."

"I'm sure he will."

Michael's head pounded so badly that it felt like a construction worker was standing on his shoulders, trying to break through his skull with a jackhammer.

Sam motioned. "Here comes Doctor Kaplan now."

They braced themselves in case of bad news.

A tall, thin woman with salt and pepper-colored hair, Doctor Kaplan spoke calmly and reassuringly. "The surgery went well."

Sam brushed tears from her eyes. "Is my mother going to be all right?"

"The next day or two will be critical for her, but I'm optimistic about her recovery."

The cardiologist questioned them. "Do you happen to know what brought on her heart attack?"

Michael answered. "She was having an argument with my uncle."

"With her heart condition, that will do it. Why don't you two go home and get some rest now."

He asked. "Can't we wait here?"

"You can, but there's no need to. We'll call you if there is any change in her condition."

After the doctor left them, Michael hugged his sister. "Go home. Hillary probably misses you. I'll give you a call later to let you know how mother is doing."

———

EXHAUSTED FROM BEING up all night, Michael rubbed his eyes. About to go for a cup of coffee, he saw Lorna walking down the corridor. They looked at each other and without saying a word they embraced.

"Where have you been," he said. "I've missed you so much."

"None of that matters any more. I'm here now."

"To stay?"

"Yes, to stay."

He squeezed her tighter. "I love you so much."

"I love you, too."

They gazed into each other's eyes, tears flowing down both of their faces.

Lorna wiped her tears. "How's your mother? Is she going to be all right?"

"I believe so. How did you find out about her?"

"I called the house, looking for you. Ruby told me. I came as soon as I heard."

"Why did you call?"

"I had a lot of time to think things over."

"And?"

"I care too much for you. No matter if you did or didn't go to see my mother for personal reasons, I want to believe in my heart that you only went over there hoping to get information on the World Office Products deal."

"On my mother, Lorna, that's the only reason."

She started to cry again. "I needed to hear you say that."

He brought her hand to his lips. "I honestly do love you."

All of the hurt and longing faded, and their hearts felt peaceful again.

The rest of the day Michael and Lorna stayed with Gayle, keeping vigil over her while she rested.

As the sun began to set, they left to get dinner and some much-needed rest.

Out in the parking lot Lorna took Michael's hand. "Do you want to see my new apartment?"

"No," he teased. "I want you to come back and live with me."

"Come on. I'm too happy to talk about that now."

"Then let's go see this apartment."

Michael got in his car and followed her.

When they arrived at Ocean Breezes, she made him park, and then she drove him in her car to see the clubhouse, spa and swimming pool.

Her face beamed as they passed the lake with the fountain of water shooting high in the air, the little wooden bridges spanning narrow canals, and the clock tower that resembled Big Ben.

Michael did not want to spoil her fun, but he knew the place well. A girl he once dated had lived in Ocean Breezes before she decided to move to Colorado.

After the tour, they headed back to her apartment.

Lorna said. "Oh. I forgot to tell you. Guess who lives downstairs."

"I have no idea."

"Julian."

"You're kidding! You saw him?"

"Yes. He helped me move in."

"What a coincidence. How's he doing?"

"He's doing great. He said he couldn't take living in the apartment he shared with William—too many memories. He thinks very highly of you, Michael."

"Julian is a good guy. Now that I know he's living here, we'll have to invite him up for dinner."

"I can't cook worth a darn."

"Then we'll invite him for cocktails some evening."

Lorna stood out on the front stoop, her back to the door. "Close your eyes." She unlocked the door and led him inside. "You can open your eyes now."

Michael did not expect the apartment to be furnished. "This is nice. Is the furniture yours?"

"No. It came with the place."

Fluffy cushions covered in a tropical leaf pattern gave the rattan sofa and matching chairs an island feeling.

From the living room they strolled through the dining room, where Michael stopped to admire a brass light fixture hanging over the round, glass table. Down the hallway they went meandering through the bedroom and bathroom and then out sliding glass doors to a small balcony overlooking the lake.

Lorna put her arms around Michael and gave him a peck on the lips. "Well?"

"It's really nice, but I'm still upset that you're not going to be living with me."

"If we love each other, the way we say we do, then everything will work out fine."

"You're right."

"How's your shoulder?"

"Just about normal."

"Any more pain?"

"Only once in a while."

"I've been checking the paper every day to see if that woman on the phone was telling you the truth."

"Apparently she was, because it seems the police are at a dead end."

"Isn't it amazing that the police didn't find the car, after that old couple came forward as eye witnesses. Although, I was there too, and I didn't get the number of the license plate either."

"I still wonder if it was Stuart who put that contract out on me. I may never know the truth."

"Let's not think about that anymore. The woman said you have nothing to worry about now."

"After getting shot at, it's hard not to worry."

Lorna changed the subject. "I have a bottle of champagne chilling in the fridge."

"And who were you planning to share that with?"

"You. Thank goodness my plans worked out, or I would really be upset."

"Come on. Let's go open it."

While Michael fussed with the bottle, Lorna prepared a dish of grapes, cheese and crackers. They took their little party outside onto the balcony.

Lorna sipped her champagne and then slid onto a chair. "What's new with Stuart?"

"Everything is still a mess." Michael placed his glass on a rattan end table. "Are you ready for this? It's not bad enough that he still has the stock. We just got an eviction notice to get out of the house. That's why my mother had the heart attack. She went over to Stuart's house and had it out with him."

"No."

"Yes. And, you should have heard her. She was great. When Stuart tried to lie in front of your mother and Holly about being the person causing the eviction, she told him to go to hell."

"That doesn't sound like your mother. She's so sweet and low-key."

"Get this. From what she was saying to Stuart, they dated or went together before she met my father."

"Yuk. Thank goodness she married your father." Lorna sighed, a pensive expression on her face. "What did my mother have to say?"

"Everything happened so quickly. Stuart went to grab my mother, and I grabbed him. Then my mother had her heart attack. After that, there was complete chaos with me giving my mother CPR and Eva and Holly racing around looking for aspirin and calling 911."

"Stuart is such a scumbag. I don't know how my mother can stand him."

"He has a way of fooling people, including your mother."

"Do you really have to move out of the house?"

"Who knows? We're going to fight Stuart in court. In the meantime, I hope to come up with a copy of that agreement."

"Is Stuart still selling Grant Office Supplies?"

"Yes. The closing is in two days."

"Boy! That was quick. What are you going to do?"

"Show up at the closing like we talked about with David Chernoff, and try to stop it."

"Even if you don't find the agreements?"

"Even if I don't find them."

"I have an idea. Why don't we make a list of people who could possibly have taken the agreements and go talk with them. You can take half of the list, and I'll take the other half."

"What about work? You didn't find a job yet?"

"I have gone on a few interviews, but so far nothing. I'll be able to help you with no problem."

"I have to find them, Lorna. I dread what the future holds if I don't."

"According to what we already know, whoever took the agreements had the combination to the safe."

"And it was a nice-looking woman with long, blonde hair."

"We already know it wasn't me. The only other woman I can think of with long, blonde hair is Holly. I'm talking about when she wears her wig. Can you think of anybody?"

"No. We'll put her at the top of the list."

"You better talk to her, Michael. She might flip out on me, if I ask her if she took them."

"I'll go see her tomorrow. Who else?"

"Somebody from Stuart's office maybe?"

"Why would anyone from Stuart's office want the agreements?"

"Are you kidding? Say it was an executive secretary or someone who earns a good salary at Grant Office Supplies, and they know your uncle is selling the business. Whoever it was won't want to lose their job, because it would be too hard to find another one that gives them status and pays a good salary. Or maybe Stuart had an affair with one of the women, and now they're angry with him about something."

"Since I'm going to see Holly, why don't you go down to the office and snoop around."

"I'll go first thing in the morning."

"What if Stuart sees you?"

"I'll be low key and make sure he doesn't."

"I have a better idea. You are looking for a job, aren't you? Fill out a job application. That way if Stuart does happen to see you, it will look perfectly natural."

"We're getting pretty good at this."

"Back to the subject, how would someone from the office know the combination to Stuart's safe?"

"People close to the boss always have special privileges. They are the people who hold down the fort while the boss is out of town."

"Why would this woman come in at night? Couldn't she take the agreements, while she was at work?"

"Maybe she was afraid of getting caught, so she posed as a cleaning woman. That's how she knew the name of the cleaning company."

"Wouldn't the security guard have recognized her?"

"Not if he worked nights, and she came in after he was off duty."

"That's true. What if the guards rotate duties and he works days, too."

"There's only one way we'll find out."

"I'll call the building and see if the guard that actually saw and talked with the woman is working tonight."

After searching down the number of security, Michael got the guard on the line. To his surprise, Chuck was working tonight, and he would be pleased to have them come down and break the monotony of his watch.

Within the hour, Michael and Lorna were at the building.

When Chuck got a look at Lorna, he sucked in his gut, stuck out his chest and straightened his hat.

"Let's see your ID," he said to Michael through the glass.

Michael pulled out his wallet and held up his driver's license for Chuck to see.

Chuck checked up and down the street and then unlocked the door. "I'm sorry I had to ask for some ID, Mr. Grant. It's the new rules around here."

"I understand. No problem."

"Do you two want some coffee? I just made a fresh pot, knowing you were coming to see me."

The hour being one in the morning, and he was fighting lack of sleep as well as the after-effects of the champagne, Michael went for a cup. "Coffee is just what I need. How about you, Lorna?"

"I would love a cup, cream and one packet of artificial sweetener, please."

"And you, Mr. Grant?"

"Make mine black."

"I'll be back in a second." Chuck went to a back room, leaving them for no more than a minute.

"Come have a seat," he said, handing them each a foam cup of steaming hot brew. "I know what you want to talk to me about, so ask away."

Too hot to drink, Michael put his cup of coffee on the console. "The woman from the cleaning company, did you ever see her before that night?"

"Nope, never did."

"Then you don't know if she works in the building."

"She might. I only switched to daylight a couple of times, when one of the other guys got sick. There were so many people coming and going, I never really noticed."

"From what I understand, the woman had long, blonde hair and was nice-looking."

"That's the funny thing. She looked a lot like you, miss."

The comment caught Lorna by surprise. "In the face and everything?"

Chuck couldn't tell her he mainly looked at her body. "She was tall like you and built about the same."

Michael questioned him further. "This woman said she was from the cleaning company. But, we all know now that she really wasn't. You said she had on a Walton's uniform."

"Yeah, that's what I told Mr. Grant's secretary. I should have known something was up, when I saw how clean and new it looked. There wasn't a mark on it."

"She could have been new with the company or ruined her old one. Did she act like she knew where she was going?"

"She knew exactly where she was going. Now that I think back to that night, she tried her damnedest not to have me go upstairs with her."

"But you did."

"Yes, sir, I did. And, I even checked up on her once. She faked me out good."

"You're not saying then that she definitely doesn't work in this building."

"Like I told you before, I only worked daylight a few times. She could."

"If you thought this woman was so attractive, wouldn't you have remembered seeing her before?"

"Do you know how many people come and go during the day? At night, it's a different story. I can tell you this much, she stood out like a sore thumb from the other cleaning ladies."

"Would you do me a favor, Chuck?"

"Fire away."

"Would you stick around for a little while after work this morning and watch everyone that comes into the building. If you happen to see this woman again, would you give me a call?"

"I'll stick around until lunch time."

"That's not necessary. Most office hours start between eight and nine o'clock. Stick around until ten and then you can leave. In fact, call me either way. I'll be anxious to hear what you have to say." Michael got up to leave. "Do you have a piece of paper? I'll give you my home and cell phone numbers." He jotted the numbers down for Chuck. "Can you think of anything else, Lorna?"

"No."

"Then I'll wait to hear from you later this morning, Chuck. By the way, you might see Lorna. She's coming down to fill out a job application."

"Do you want me to tell her, if I happen to see that woman?"

"I would appreciate it."

41

WITH THE CLOSING TOMORROW and time shooting by way too fast for his liking, Michael rushed to Stuart's house, looking for Holly. He found her down at the pool doing morning laps.

She noticed him coming and asked. "How's your mother doing?"

"She's better. The doctor said she's going to be okay."

"I'm glad to hear that. I'm going to stop at the hospital this evening on my way to the club."

"I'm sure she'll be happy to see you."

"What brings you here?"

"I wanted to talk to you."

"About what?"

"I might as well be direct. I was wondering if you took those agreements out of your dad's office safe?"

"What agreements?"

"You mean after all this time you still don't know about the agreements?"

"I don't have a clue."

"The agreement, you know the one signed by my dad and your dad about that vow grandfather made them take right before he died."

"I know about the vow, but I never saw any agreements."

"Actually, there is an original and several copies. Did you take them out of your dad's office safe?"

"What makes you think I would do a thing like that?"

"Some woman with long blonde hair supposedly stole them from the safe."

"Since when do I have long, blonde hair?"

"I've seen you wearing a long, blonde wig. It could have been you."

"Read my lips, Michael. I did not break into my dad's office safe or anyone else's safe for that matter. What's the big deal about that agreement anyway?"

"My mother wasn't kidding around the other night when she said your dad stole our stock. We need a copy of the agreement to prove half of the business is really ours."

"My father actually stole your stock?"

"Yes. He also stole our house."

"How do you expect me to believe you? He's my father, for Pete's sake."

"It's the truth, Holly."

"You mentioned something about copies. If that's the case, doesn't anyone else have a copy of this so-called agreement?"

"In your father's overall scheme of things, he made sure he had all of the copies in his possession before he made the deal with World Office Products."

"Then your mother wasn't making up stories the other night. My dad really is planning to sell the business?"

"Do you mean he never mentioned it to you?"

"Not a word."

"He probably wanted to keep you out of the loop because he was afraid you might mention something to me."

"When is all of this supposed to happen?"

"Tomorrow."

Holly got out of the pool and began to dry herself off with a towel. "I can't believe it. How could my father do something so rotten? He always treated you guys so well. He loves the three of you."

"You heard the way he screamed at my mother. If that's love, I don't want to see hate."

"He did call her some pretty nasty names." Holly adjusted her swimsuit straps. "Do you think my dad and your mother were sweethearts?"

"It sounded that way to me."

She chuckled. "Just think. If they had gotten married, you and I would be brother and sister."

"That's a scary thought!"

She gave him a dirty look. "I wonder why they always kept their relationship a big secret."

"You got me." Michael ran his fingers through his hair. "I hated coming over here and confronting you about this. That's why I never said anything to you about it. I didn't want to turn you against your father."

"I don't know what to think. I can't believe my father could do such awful things."

"I understand how you feel. It took me a long time to accept all the crap he's trying to pull, too."

"This whole thing is turning my stomach."

"Since you didn't take the agreements, can you think of anyone else who might have?"

"I don't have the vaguest idea, Michael. Honestly."

He checked the time. "I have to go."

"Where?"

"To the office."

———

LORNA FILLED IN the last item on the application form and laid the pen on the clipboard.

While she was waiting for the personnel manager to get off the phone, she glanced around the office to see if there were any women with long blonde hair. Three brunettes, a redhead and a blonde. None of the women came close to fitting the description.

The minute the personnel manager got off the phone, Lorna went to the desk and handed her the form. "I appreciate your letting me fill out a job application, my not having an appointment and all."

"No problem. People drop in unexpectedly from time to time."

As Lorna walked past the different departments and work stations on her way out of the office, she kept an eye out for a long-haired blonde. No luck on that floor, but Grant Office Supplies had several more floors of employees. If anyone questioned her presence, she would tell the person the truth. She had just filled out a job application, and while she was there, she decided to take a tour of the building.

After checking the other floors, she felt disappointed that none of the blondes she had seen matched the right description. With her luck, such an employee existed, but she was either in a meeting, had stayed home sick or she might be in the ladies room. Lorna glanced at the time. Not quite ten. Chuck might still be downstairs.

When she stepped out of the elevator, she noticed Chuck at the information desk. Michael was with him.

She rushed over to Michael, a happy grin on her face. "I didn't expect to see you here."

"I couldn't stand it. I had to know if Chuck saw that woman."

"Did he?"

"No."

"Darn it!"

"Any luck upstairs?"

"No. What should we do now?"

"Did you eat breakfast this morning?"

"No. I didn't get a chance."

"Me neither. Let's grab a quick bite and discuss our options."

Down the street from Grant Office Supplies there was a Jewish delicatessen that served the best breakfast in town. Since morning rush hour was over, Michael and Lorna did not have to wait in line for a table.

Lorna's mouth watered. "Doesn't the corned beef smell wonderful?"

"If my stomach wasn't so upset, I would get a plate of corned beef with a couple of potato pancakes."

While they were waiting to be served, they discussed the morning events.

Lorna covered her navy blue skirt with a napkin. "Did you see Holly?"

"Yes. It wasn't her."

"I was hoping so badly that she had the agreements."

"In a way I feel sorry for her. How would you like to find out your father was a thief?"

"Believe me! My mother pulled a few lousy stunts on me."

"Yeah, but they weren't criminal."

"Maybe not, but they were mean and hurtful."

"I never had anything like this ever happen to me. My parents were kind and loving."

"You're lucky."

"No long, blonde-haired women in the office?"

"No. Chuck was right. I didn't see anyone who came close to fitting his description. I take that back. There were some attractive girls, but their hair color didn't match."

"Think hard, Lorna. Who else could possibly have the agreements?"

"I've been wracking my brain all morning. I don't know."

"If we ever find out who has them, it will probably be so obvious that we will kick ourselves in the rear for not thinking of them sooner."

"I'm sure that will be the case." Her eyes lit up. "I just thought of something. Have you ever seen any of those people who go on TV to complain about something, like shoddy work done to their house by a repairman, or somebody they know was missing? Maybe you could get on the news and make a plea for the agreements."

"Television, I don't know about that. Besides, remember what my attorney said. We shouldn't draw the public's attention to big trouble or problems at Grant Office Supplies."

"You don't have to mention a thing about Grant Office Supplies. Make a plea on behalf of the entire Grant family. Say someone stole some important documents out of a safe, and you would like to have them back. Then you can leave your name and phone number. You can even offer a reward. If it was an employee who did it, you can guarantee them that they won't be prosecuted, and they would be able to keep their job."

"If an employee of mine stole something out of my safe, I wouldn't want to keep them on my payroll."

"Then you'll guarantee them that they won't be prosecuted and offer them a reward."

"I don't know. TV. That's really putting yourself out there."

"But that's the whole point. Think of the consequences if you don't get your hands on a copy of the agreement or you lose your lawsuit in court."

Michael pondered the subject for a moment. "Maybe you're right. I don't see where I have a choice." He got out his credit card to pay the waitress. "Let's go visit some news stations."

"No. That will take too long. I think you should invite the reporters to Sand Dollar Island."

"Better yet, if you don't mind, let's invite them to your apartment. We don't want Stuart seeing any news trucks on the island."

42

THE USUALLY PEACEFUL COMMUNITY of Ocean Breezes had suddenly turned into a frenzy of news vans, curious onlookers and security guards.

Earlier that afternoon, Lorna had left word with security guards at the gatehouse to allow anyone displaying a media pass to enter the complex, as she and a friend had called a news conference at her apartment.

Reporters with camera crews from four local television stations and reporters from three different newspapers crammed her small living room, anxious to hear what a member of one of South Florida's most prominent families had to say.

Michael sat on a chair next to an end table. A vase full of fresh-cut flowers sat on the table, and behind him, slightly off-center, was a Japanese palm. One of the news crews had arranged the flowers and plant to add warmth and color to the makeshift set.

With hot, bright lights shining in his face, Michael could barely make out the people standing in front of him. They looked surreal, like black and white cardboard cutouts.

Lorna leaned over him. "Julian is here. He was on his way home from an appointment and noticed the commotion."

"Tell him to stick around if he's not too busy."

"Are you nervous?"

"A little. Now I know what it feels like to be on TV."

"You'll do fine. Just keep reading from the cue card we made." She stepped off to the side of the camera and held the cue card in front of her.

As soon as the lighting had been suitably adjusted for the shoot, Michael heard a man's voice say. "We're ready to start rolling when you are, Mr. Grant."

"Is this going to be live?"

"No. We're taping it for the evening news."

"So, if I goof up, we can stop rolling?"

"Yes. But we prefer that you keep going."

"Do I have to say my name or anything?"

"No. The reporter will do a lead in."

"Are we ready?"

"The cameras are rolling. Begin whenever you want."

Michael looked at the cue card and began. "Not too long ago, somebody broke into a safe and stole some important documents. Whoever took the papers had the combination to the safe, so we know the person wasn't a burglar looking for money. It was obviously someone we know and see on a regular basis. If that person is watching, I give you my word you will not be prosecuted in any way. We, the members of the Grant family, just want the papers returned. They are legal documents and cannot be replaced. If you prefer to remain anonymous, you can have the papers delivered by courier with no questions asked. The documents can even be picked up from a third party. We just want them returned tonight. If anyone has any information at all about the stolen documents, I am offering a ten thousand dollar reward. Please. The papers have no importance to anyone but members of my family. You can reach me at 561 555-7543. Thank you."

Michael did the take in one shot. "How was it," he asked nobody in particular.

A male reporter responded. "You did just fine, Mr. Grant. Okay, guys, it's a wrap."

All of the cameras stopped rolling except one. A woman reporter shoved her microphone in Michael's face. "Mr. Grant. How is your arm?"

The bright lights left tiny, little dots floating in Michael's eyes. He could barely make out the reporter's face. "My arm is much better."

By now, the other crews had their cameras rolling again, also hoping to get more information from Michael.

The woman reporter continued asking him questions. "Will you recover full use of your arm?"

"I believe so."

"Do the police have any leads on the shooter?"

"No. From what I understand, the police are at a dead end."

Another reporter questioned Michael. "Any ideas who took those documents from the safe?"

"If I did, I wouldn't need you guys." Michael held up his hand. "That's enough. No more questions, please. Thanks a lot for coming."

The woman reporter persisted. "Just one more question."

"One more and that's it."

"What was on those documents?"

"Like I said, it's personal, family business. Why anyone else would want those papers is beyond me."

A male reporter pushed his microphone in Michael's face.

Michael turned his back to all of the reporters. "I'm sorry, guys, no more questions." He glanced around the room, looking for Lorna and Julian, who were already approaching him.

Lorna kissed Michael's cheek. "You did great."

Julian shook Michael's hand and gave him a manly hug. "It's good to see you, buddy. What's going on, man?"

"Not now with all of these reporters here. Can you stick around for a little while?"

"Sure."

A lot quicker than it took the crews to set up the lighting, they packed up their equipment and left.

Michael went to the refrigerator. "I need a drink. That was nerve-wracking. How about you guys?"

"Not me," Julian said. "I have another appointment this afternoon."

"Lorna?"

"No. I want to keep my head clear."

Michael grabbed a beer and joined them in the living room. "What's new with you, Julian? I haven't seen you in a while."

"Same old, same old." He grinned. "I see something is new around here."

"What do you mean?"

"The last I heard, you two split. Are things okay now?"

Michael smiled at Lorna. "Things are great. I have my girl back."

"I'm glad to hear it."

Julian leaned forward, his elbows resting on his legs. "So you never came up with a copy of the agreement. That's why you're going public."

"Yes. That bastard uncle of mine is selling the business tomorrow. I need a copy of the agreement to try and stop him."

"Lorna told me all about it. Maybe when you tell the guys buying the business about the lawsuit you filed against Stuart, they'll back out of the deal."

"It's all I've got for now. We'll see."

"Where is the closing? In Florida or out of town?"

"That's a good question."

Lorna reached for the phone. "That's a really good question. Let's call Stuart's secretary and ask her."

Michael took a sip of beer. "What makes you think she'll tell us?"

"I'll pretend I'm a secretary from World Office Products."

Lorna dialed information and got the number. While she was speaking with the woman, Michael motioned to her, his finger pointing to his watch. "Find out what time."

As Lorna was disconnecting the call, she smiled slyly. Ten o'clock in the morning at Stuart's office."

Julian slid back in the chair. "After Stuart sees you on TV, I'm sure he's not going to let you get anywhere near that closing."

"My uncle has no right to stop me. We're still part owners of the company."

"You might get into the building, but I'll bet he stops you from getting into the meeting."

"He can call in the National Guard if he wants to. I'll get into that closing somehow, come hell or high water."

"Stuart really pisses me off. He's so mean and underhanded. I hope you get those agreements and put that man in prison." Julian stood up to leave. "I wish you luck. Somebody has to put that jerk in his place."

"After this is all over, we'll get together for dinner some night."

Lorna walked Julian to the door. "I really am glad I have you for a neighbor."

"You know where to find me, if you need anything."

She closed the door and went back to the sofa where she sat next to Michael again. "I think it was a good idea that you used my phone number instead of yours. Now Stuart won't be able to do anything about it. He has no idea where I live."

———

A FEW MINUTES BEFORE SIX, Michael turned on the television set. Lorna sat close to him, her legs tucked under her and her hand gripping his arm. "This is so exciting. I can't wait to see you."

"I've never seen myself on television. I'll probably throw up."

"Shhhh. Here it is."

They sat quietly, their eager eyes glued to the screen. The reporter did the lead in, explaining who Michael was, giving viewers some background on Grant Office Supplies and the latest information from police on the shooting. Then Michael made his appeal to the public. Within moments their segment of the news was over.

As soon as the news anchor switched to the next story, Lorna turned down the volume with the remote. "I hope a lot of people were watching and someone calls about the agreements."

"You and me both."

———

HOLLY'S STOMACH GROWLED as she switched from channel to channel. During her switching, she saw a man who looked like Michael, but disregarded it, thinking it could never be he. Her curiosity piqued, she flicked back. It was Michael. She let out a shriek and hollered into the library to Stuart and Eva, who were having a pre-dinner cocktail.

They came rushing into the den.

Stuart asked. "What's wrong?"

"Shhhh. Quiet." Holly pointed to the television.

Stuart and Eva stood there in shock as they watched Michael make his plea.

When the news anchor went on to the next news item, Stuart exploded in anger. "Damn that Michael! What's he trying to pull?"

Holly clicked off the television. "He came over this morning and asked me if I had the agreements."

"Why didn't you tell me about this earlier?"

"What does it matter? I obviously don't have them. That's why Michael was on TV."

"How dare he exploit the family's personal business!"

Eva smirked. "He is obviously desperate."

"I don't care what he is. If he screws up that closing tomorrow, I'm going to choke him to death with my bare hands." Stuart grabbed the phone.

"Who are you calling?"

"That number you saw on the screen. I want to see who answers."

———

WHEN LORNA'S PHONE RANG, Michael grabbed for it. "Hello," he said, hoping to hear good news.

"Who is this," Stuart said.

"Michael Grant."

"You son of a bitch! How dare you go on television and divulge our personal business."

Michael realized it was his uncle's voice. "It's too bad if you don't like it, Stuart."

"Where are you?"

"None of your business."

"You'll pay for this, Michael."

"What are you going to do, hire another hit man to shoot me again?"

"You have obviously lost your mind."

"Back off, Stuart, or I'll call the police and have you arrested."

"You're in deep trouble, Michael."

"Not as much as you are, STUART." Michael hung up on his uncle.

Lorna sighed. "I was hoping it was somebody about the agreements."

Michael seethed. "I'm really getting to hate that man."

"Don't waste your energy on Stuart. He's nothing but garbage."

Michael began to pace the floor. "Come on, somebody, call."

The phone never rang.

By one o'clock in the morning, Lorna could not keep her eyes open.

Michael felt sorry for her. "Go on to bed. You've been through a lot today."

"What about you?"

"I'm too disgusted to sleep."

"Then I'm staying up with you. I'll go put on a pot of coffee."

"You don't have to stay up. I know you're tired."

She hugged him. "From now on, your problems are my problems. We're in this thing together."

"Why couldn't someone have called? It seems so unfair. Now, Stuart will probably have his closing, and we will have nothing."

"Don't overreact. You don't know what's going to happen tomorrow. World Office Products might have seen you on TV, gotten cold feet and postponed the closing. By then, you'll probably have all the copies of the agreement you need."

"I know you're trying to make me feel good, and I appreciate it."

"I didn't say that to make you feel good. You have to have faith, Michael. You have to make things happen. Go down to that office tomorrow and make a big stink."

"You heard what David said. It will be bad publicity for the company."

"I'm talking about the meeting. Get in somehow and expose Stuart for the piece of garbage he is." Lorna locked hands with Michael. "I've been thinking. Maybe I should go down there with you. You'll need all the support you can get."

"Are you sure you want to? You don't have to, you know."

"I'm going."

"If you insist, come witness the slaughter."

43

JULIAN STUMBLED into his apartment and reached for the light switch. His fingers slipped down the wall and back up again, finally grabbing hold of the switch.

He had consumed one too many drinks tonight. That Mrs. Kingsly never knew when to quit. Every time he went over to her house to discuss decorating plans with her, she always got him in trouble. The next time he has to go over to her place, he was not staying for cocktails. Where she put all of that booze he had no idea. She could drink his Uncle Curtis under the table, and that was saying something. The old man was the biggest lush he knew.

Julian glanced around the apartment, the alcohol magnifying his already depressed state. He started mumbling out loud. "Why did you go and die on me, Will? I miss you so much. It's lonely down here without you."

He picked up a photograph of himself and William on a yacht, their arms wrapped around each other and big, happy smiles on their faces. "You hurt me bad by dying, Will."

He laid the picture on the table and staggered down the hall to his bedroom.

Ever since William's death, grief prevented Julian from going near any personal mementos of William's and the life they once shared until now.

From out of the closet he pulled a big box and dragged it across the carpet to the bed. He needed to feel William close to him again, to see and touch William's things. Whether it was because he saw Michael earlier in the day, or maybe he just drank too much alcohol. For whatever reason, he needed to bond with William spiritually, to sense William there in the room with him.

A tear trickling down his face, Julian opened the lid of the box and reached inside for some photographs. For several minutes, he went through the pictures, sobbing at times as he reminisced about William.

After he went through the photographs, he pulled out a small red and gold box. "Look here," he said aloud. "We hunted high and low for this Cartier stud and cufflink set." For the first time since Julian got home, he smiled. "These looked so good with your tuxedo, Will."

Further down in the box he dug. "Get out of here! The ticket stubs from that Cher concert we went to in Vegas. We sure had a blast that night."

He laid the stubs on the bed and reached for another box. "Now what do we have here?" He opened the box and pulled out a brown, leather billfold. "Look, Will. It's one of your old wallets." He glanced in the air as if William was in the room with him.

When Julian bent down to grab the next item, he felt something soft and fluffy in his fingers. "What's this? Oh, it's that red boa you wore to that Halloween party. I've been looking all over the place for this thing."

Something glittery in a plastic bag caught his eye. He shoved a few items aside to get to the bag. "I haven't seen this gold watch in ages. I thought I saw everything I packed up. This must be one of the boxes I threw some of your stuff in after you died. What else do you have stashed away in here?"

Near the bottom of the box Julian touched something furry. Frightened, he jerked his hand away. "What the hell was that? Better not be a rat." He shook the box. No rats or mice jumped out at him. He shook the box again and tilted it under the light. The fuzzy thing looked like hair. Julian grabbed a few strands and yanked whatever it was out of the box. "What the hell? A blonde wig? I don't remember seeing this. Where did this come from, Will? Were you going to surprise me on Halloween with this? Now isn't that a shame. I would love to have seen you in this. You really have me going now, buddy. Let's see what else you got in here." Julian reached inside the box yet again. "What's this, a shirt?" He opened the garment up. "A woman's dress. No. It's not a dress. It's a uniform. Walton Cleaning Company? You were going to dress up like some cleaning lady?" Julian laughed. "You always were full of surprises."

More loose photos, pantyhose, a bra with foam falsies, a Barbra Streisand CD, two pairs of shoes, frayed denim shorts, a plastic bag containing a bottle of liquid foundation, a box of loose powder, eye shadow, blush, a pair of fake pearls and a tube of black mascara were in the box.

Julian looked down inside, finding the carton now empty. He shook the box. Anything that belonged to William he didn't want to lose. He gave the box another jiggle. It sounded like something was sliding back and forth on the bottom. Half-blinded by the alcohol, he almost missed the manila envelope. "Okay, Will. Let's see what you're going to surprise me with now." Julian reached inside the envelope and pulled out several papers. "Huh! These look like some kind of legal documents." His vision blurred by the alcohol, he had trouble focusing his eyes on the printing. He lay back on the bed, trying to read the papers and then gave up. "I'm tired now, Will. I'll check these papers out in the morning."

44

MICHAEL STOOD UNDER the shower head, allowing the warm water to massage his exhausted body.

Twice during the night he almost fell asleep but both times he forced himself to stay awake. He would have all the time in the world to rest after the closing. For now, he needed every minute to think.

While he lathered his body with soap, he pumped himself up, as if he were getting ready for one of his college football games. Negative thoughts kept trying to squeeze their way into his mind, but he fought hard to stifle them. And the ugly knot in his stomach persisted in reminding him that, when it came to business matters, he didn't stand a chance against Stuart. Before the day was over, he was going to be pounded into the ground and stomped on until there wasn't a single trace left of him.

When Lorna heard the water stop running, she poured two cups of coffee and took them with her into the bathroom. "I thought you could use this." She set his cup on the counter.

Michael reached for the cup. "Whew! Look at you in that dress. Get a load of that body."

A short, black dress hugged her slender curves. "I thought we agreed that I should wear something sexy."

"Nice legs in those high heels."

"Enough about me. How do you feel?"

"Like a mule kicked me in the stomach."

"Nervous, huh?"

"More anxiety-ridden than nervous."

"What time do you want to leave?"

"Right away. I want to be in the building before office hours. Are you ready?"

"I just have to grab my purse."

Michael reached for his toothbrush. "I still can't believe we didn't get one phone call about the agreements."

"Whoever took them must be afraid."

"I'll bet those copies are lost forever." Michael sighed. "I better not dwell on that right now."

"I agree. You're going down there and whipping Stuart's butt."

45

JULIAN LAY CURLED up on the bed with his head resting against his arm. The alarm on his watch went off, and its constant beeping sounded like a fire engine's horn blasting away in his ear.

He sat up and rubbed his temples, which were pounding so hard that he feared he might vomit all over himself.

A few of the items he took out of the box sat on the bed next to him. The rest had fallen onto the floor while he was tossing and turning in his sleep. The items puzzled him. He held the wig in the air, and then everything slowly came back to him. Although he felt like he had been run over by a herd of stampeding buffalo, he couldn't help smiling.

One by one Julian tossed William's items back into the carton. He had to get moving. He told Mrs. Kingsly he would stop back over today and help her pick out a fabric for her chairs. He groaned. No alcohol for him. If she wanted to drink, she could drink until cows started producing chocolate cookies with their milk. He was off booze for a while, at least until his stomach quit acting like he had just swallowed a stick of dynamite.

When he bent down to pick up the remaining items off the floor, his head pounded all the harder. It felt like his brain had fallen forward, and it lay smashed against his eyeballs. He rubbed his temple as he reached for the papers, which he then threw into the box.

The urge to urinate suddenly hit him. He hurried to the bathroom to relieve himself.

As he was flushing the toilet, he decided he better go back to the bedroom and take a look at those papers again. They looked like legal documents, and they could be important. But if they were important, then why were they mixed in with a bunch of old junk.

Julian reached for the papers. There seemed to be five documents in all. One looked like the original, while the other four looked like copies. He glanced over the original. It had Stuart Grant's name on it. And Richard Grant's name. Intrigued, Julian sat down on the bed. Richard Grant was Michael's father. As Julian was reading over the wording, his bloodshot eyes grew bigger and bigger. These were the copies of the agreement Michael was looking high and low for.

He sat there stunned, his mind trying to fit the pieces of the puzzle together. How did William get the agreements? Suddenly the puzzle came together. William was the one who broke into Stuart's safe. That's why the wig and uniform were in the box.

He had to get the agreements to Michael right away. Julian ran to the phone. Maybe Michael was still upstairs at Lorna's.

The phone rang and rang, but no one answered. About to hang up the receiver, Julian glanced out the window and saw Michael and Lorna getting into a car. He raced to the window and opened it.

"Mike," he hollered. "Lorna." He waved his hands in the air, trying to get their attention.

The car pulled out of the parking space.

Julian went running through the apartment and out the front door. By the time he made it to the curb, the BMW had driven out of sight.

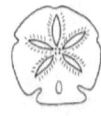

46

JUST GOING ON eight o'clock, there were only a few cars occupying spaces in the Grant Office Supplies parking lot.

Michael pulled into a space and turned off the engine. "I'm a wreck. My stomach feels like I swallowed a cement mixer."

"A few hours from now, this will all be behind you."

"Good or bad."

"Things will work out, Michael. You'll see."

"I have a tough time sharing your optimism." He lifted up on the door handle. "Come on. Let's go."

"Don't forget the lawsuit."

"I must be a wreck. I forgot all about the lawsuit." He reached to the back seat for a thick, blue folder.

They headed for the building.

Michael checked out the front entrance. "I don't see any security guards."

"Maybe this isn't going to be as hard as we thought."

He stopped abruptly. "What if they changed the location of the closing at the last minute?"

"You're overreacting again. It's still early."

Michael and Lorna entered the building without a problem.

He said. "I don't like this. Something isn't right. I'll bet the closing is taking place somewhere else."

"Keep a level head. Let's not blow everything by jumping to conclusions."

A security guard sat behind the information counter. He jumped up when he saw Michael and Lorna walking towards the elevators. "Excuse me, folks. What floor are you two headed for?"

Michael's instincts told him not to say the tenth. They could always reach Stuart's office by way of the stairs.

"Ninth."

"Okay. Go ahead."

"Why do you ask?"

"The tenth floor is closed to the public today."

"Why is that?"

"I can't say for sure, just following orders."

Michael and Lorna stepped into the elevator.

He pushed the button for nine. "I guess the closing is going to be here after all."

"Smart move. I didn't think of fooling him. I was ready to blurt out the tenth floor."

"Thank goodness you didn't."

The doors slid open and they stepped out of the car.

Michael glanced up and down the corridor for the stairs.

"This way," he said.

Like two cat burglars about to pull a major heist, Michael and Lorna sneaked past a dark office and through a metal door to the stairs.

In high heels, Lorna hurried to keep up with Michael. "What are we going to do once we're in the office? You don't want Stuart seeing us, do you?"

"I don't care if he does see us."

"He'll call for security and have us thrown out. I think we should stay out of sight until the meeting starts."

"Any suggestions where?"

"How about the restrooms?"

"What? You want to wait for nearly two hours in the bathroom?"

"There or a utility room."

"Maybe you're right. The important thing is we're in the building. We can always figure out a way to sneak into the meeting. When we get to the tenth floor, we'll go straight to the restrooms. At ten o'clock, we'll meet out in the hall."

"It's going to be boring as all hell waiting, but I think it's the only way."

Michael grabbed the doorknob and attempted to turn it. "I don't believe it."

"What?"

"The door is locked. Damn it! So much for planning."

"Now what?"

"We'll go back down to nine and take the elevator up."

"I just thought of something. What if the door locked behind us? If it did, we're stuck in here."

"Don't even say that." Michael ran down the stairs, his footsteps echoing throughout the narrow space.

When he grabbed for the knob and it turned, he let out a huge sigh. "The door is open."

Lorna came clomping down the steps. "That's a relief. Can you imagine being stuck in this stairway all day? For sure I would have a panic attack."

"Now that I think about it, we didn't have any reason to worry. We could have kept going down the steps until we reached the lobby. The guard or somebody else would have let us out when they heard us pounding and yelling."

"The guards must have purposely locked that door, so nobody could get into the office."

"You mean me, so I couldn't get into the office. My conniving uncle has thought of everything."

"What are we going to do now?"

"Let's go back to the elevator and try to get up to ten."

Michael and Lorna hurried down a corridor that was slowly becoming active with people.

He pressed the elevator button. "It's almost eight-thirty. Time is flying by way too fast. I'm getting really nervous."

"Keep your cool. We don't want to make any mistakes."

"Thank goodness you came with me. If I were here by myself, I would be a wreck."

When the doors slid open, a man got off and headed for his office.

Michael followed Lorna into the elevator. When he pressed the button for the tenth floor, they heard an annoying buzzing sound. He kept pushing the button. Nothing but more buzzing. "We're not going anywhere. This thing has been programmed to stop at nine."

"Look, Michael. There's a keyhole for the penthouse."

"That's probably how Stuart is going to get up to his office."

"What are we going to do now?"

"We have no choice. We'll have to go back downstairs and wait until the people from World Office Products get here." He pressed the lobby button.

Lorna straightened her dress. "What happens when they do?"

"I don't know. Maybe we'll jump on the elevator with them."

"Do you know what any of these people look like?"

"I have no idea."

"Then how are we going to know it's them?"

"I might have that figured out. Most people come into the building by themselves or they run into someone they know along the way. These guys should stand out. They'll be coming as a group, like they're the president's entourage or something. We won't be able to miss them."

"I hope you're right. What do you want to do in the meantime?"

"Maybe one of us should go downstairs and wait in front of the elevators. Stuart might park down in that lot and take the elevator from there."

"I'll go, Michael. You stay in the lobby. If either one of us sees him, we'll call on our cell phones."

While Lorna pressed the garage button, Michael got off the elevator.

For the next hour, a stream of people came into the building, some taking their time and others rushing.

Michael grew more and more anxious as the hands on the lobby clock ticked away. If he didn't have an ulcer by now, he never would.

The stream of people dwindled down to stragglers hurrying to their offices.

He glanced at the clock again. It was twenty minutes to ten. Stuart should have been there by now. Where was he?

As the seconds ticked away, he felt more and more anxiety-ridden. Something definitely was wrong.

Michael pulled out his cell phone and dialed Stuart's office, all the while keeping a watchful eye on the lobby, just in case the people from World Office Products arrived.

His nerves frazzled, he had to wait while the receptionist tracked down Stuart's secretary, who informed him Stuart was in his office, but he couldn't be disturbed.

Michael jumped on the elevator and went back downstairs.

As soon as the doors slid open, he called over to Lorna. "Come on. Stuart's in his office."

They went back to the lobby and hurried over to the security guard.

Michael pulled out his wallet. "I'm Michael Grant, one of the owners of Grant Office Supplies. If you don't believe me, take a look at my ID."

The man glanced at the license. "I believe you, sir. What can I do for you?"

"Take us upstairs to Stuart Grant's office."

"I'm sorry, sir, I can't do that."

"Why?"

"I have strict orders not to let anyone upstairs, family members included."

"Damn it. I said take us upstairs."

"It will cost me my job. I'm sorry, sir. I can't."

"What's your name?"

"Don, sir. Donald Miller."

"I'll remember that. Tell me, Don. How did Mr. Grant get up to his office? We've been standing in front of the elevators all morning and we haven't seen him."

"He probably took his private elevator, sir."

"His private elevator?"

"Yes, Mr. Grant."

"Where is his private elevator?"

"Down in his private garage."

"Did you see a private garage, Lorna?"

"No."

"Where is his private elevator, Don?"

"Downstairs in the parking lot."

"But she was just downstairs."

"The private garage is behind the building. Mister Grant redid the freight elevator into a private elevator. It's in his private garage."

"What's the fastest way to get there?"

"Probably the elevator, sir."

Michael grabbed Lorna's arm. "Come on."

"Didn't you know Stuart had a private elevator?"

"No. Talk about egos. He even has his own private garage. I wonder how much of our money he spent on that."

Michael pushed the garage button. "We're never going to make it. We only have thirteen minutes until the meeting starts."

"Maybe someone else will be late."

"If anything, people come early for important meetings like this, male bonding over coffee and all that crap before they get started."

Michael and Lorna tore out of the elevator.

He stopped abruptly, his eyes shooting to the rear of the building.

Way in the back he saw what appeared to be a large, enclosed parking space. In front of the space five men and two women stood talking with a security guard.

Michael yanked Lorna's hand. "That must be them. Come on."

"You go ahead. I can't run fast in these shoes."

Michael took off like a gazelle, tearing past the rows of cars, his soft-soled loafers barely making a sound on the oil-stained concrete.

He yelled to the executives. "Wait."

A metal door slid down, and all that remained visible by the time Michael got to the private garage were the people's shoes. Then the door closed completely with a thud.

Barely out of breath, Michael hurried over to the guard. "I have to get upstairs."

"There are public elevators in the back of the garage."

He yanked out his wallet again. "I'm Michael Grant. I have to get up to my Uncle Stuart's office. It's very important."

"I'm sorry, Mr. Grant. I have strict orders not to let anyone other than the parties involved go upstairs."

"I'm involved. I'm one of the owners of Grant Office Supplies."

"I hate to tell you this, sir, especially because you are a Grant, but I was specifically told not to let you, your mother or your sister upstairs."

"Do you want your job or don't you?"

"I don't mean any disrespect, Mr. Grant. I have nothing against you. Your uncle told me I would lose my job if I let you upstairs. I've been working for him a long time, and I've never seen you before. I'm sorry, sir. I have a couple of kids at home to feed."

Michael knew it was a losing battle.

Lorna came rushing up to Michael. "What's wrong? Won't he let us upstairs?"

"No."

She turned to the guard. "Don't you realize who this man is? He's Michael Grant, a stockholder in the company."

"I know exactly who he is, miss. I'm sorry I can't do anything about it."

Michael had about three hundred dollars on him. He pulled the money out of his wallet. "Here. It's yours if you let us on the elevator."

"I was told you might try to bribe me. Please, sir. I don't want your money."

"Come on. Cut me a break."

"For the last time, sir, I'm sorry. Now if you don't leave, I'll have to call security, and I don't want to do that."

"Never mind. I'm leaving."

As Michael walked away, he sighed. "It's over, Lorna. Stuart won. We lost the company, the house, everything."

47

MICHAEL AND LORNA headed for the outdoor parking lot. As they passed row after row of cars, she noticed a black woman leaning on the BMW. "There's some woman leaning on your car." Lorna looked more closely. "She must be a model. She's so tall and pretty."

"I don't care if she's the Queen of England. I just wish she would get off my car."

"Look. I think she knows you."

Dressed up in a long, black wig, navy-blue blazer, gray skirt, white silk blouse, stockings, high heels, and her makeup applied to perfection, Julian said to Michael. "I've been looking all over for you guys."

Michael and Lorna still didn't recognize him.

Julian rolled his eyes. "It's me, damn it, Julian."

Michael gasped. "Julian?"

"Where in hell have you two been?"

"Trying to get upstairs to the meeting. What are you doing here?"

"I have something for you." Julian handed Michael the documents.

When Michael unfolded the papers, he could not believe his eyes. "The agreements."

"Yes. I found them among William's things."

"This is fantastic."

"I thought you would be pleased."

"But how did William get hold of them?"

"He was the one who took them from Stuart's safe."

"You mean he dressed up in drag, so he could pull it off."

"Yes. I'm just as surprised as you are. He never mentioned anything to me."

Lorna squeezed Michael's arm. "This is terrific. You're a lifesaver, Julian."

Michael's happy expression diminished. "Thanks, Julian, but we're too late."

"What happened? Did they close the deal already?"

"I don't know. We can't get upstairs to Stuart's office. We tried every way possible, but the security guards won't let us."

"I figured that. That's why I'm dressed this way. Come on I have some things for you to put on."

"What are we going to do?"

"You'll see. Don't worry. I'll get you upstairs to that meeting."

Michael glanced at his watch. "It's almost ten. We don't have enough time."

Lorna grabbed his arm. "Darn it, Michael. You have nothing to lose. Just do it."

"When you're right, you're right. What are you going to do in the meantime?"

"I'll wait in the car."

Michael asked. "Where are we going, Julian?"

Julian opened the back door of a black Lexus parked next to Michael's BMW.

"Jump in. I have tinted windows. Nobody will see you changing."

Lorna stood by the door. "Do you need my help for anything?"

Julian replied. "Honey, no insults intended, but I can apply makeup better than any woman I know."

The two men got inside the car.

Afraid of the answer, Michael hesitated to ask. "Just what did you bring me to wear?"

"We'll save time, if you don't fight me, Mike."

"You're right. I'll do whatever you say."

Julian handed him a padded bra. "Take off your shirt and put this on."

Michael rolled his eyes and quickly did as he was told.

"Now what?"

"Put your shirt back on and tuck it into these blue pants. But first, put on these dark nylons."

"What? I'm not wearing any stockings."

"You have to do it right, Mike, or the guards might notice your hairy feet and not let you go upstairs."

"Give them to me." Michael slid the pantyhose up to his waist. "I just put a runner in them."

"Who cares? You won't see the runner under the slacks."

After Michael slid into a tan blazer, he tried on three different pairs of women's shoes. A mid-heeled black pair fit him best, so he went with them.

Julian reached for a makeup bag. "It's a good thing you shaved this morning."

Michael leaned his head back against the headrest. "Make me beautiful, Julian."

"You're so pretty, it will be easy."

"Don't get too turned on. You're scaring me."

Julian quickly applied a thick layer of foundation to cover Michael's skin, taupe eye shadow, black mascara, a rosy blush and lipstick. "Here. Now put this on."

"I'm glad you see me as a blonde."

"Do you realize where that came from?"

"Is it the one William wore when he broke into Stuart's safe?"

"That's right."

Michael stared into space. "So he was the good-looking blonde."

"Yes."

"And you never knew it."

"Not for a minute. Will didn't like to dress up in drag. I never suspected a thing."

"He was way ahead of us all."

"He sure was." Julian reached for a plastic bag. "Here. Put this bracelet on. Unhook it first or you won't be able to get it over your knuckles."

Michael did not resist. "Is that it?"

"Put the agreements in this folder. It will look more legit. I'll carry my briefcase."

"I hope this works, Julian."

"Since I've had more practice talking like a woman, let me handle it."

"Be my guest."

"Okay. That's it. Let's go."

When Lorna saw Michael get out of the car, she jumped out of the BMW and started laughing. "I don't believe it. You really look good."

"Do I look like a woman or some man trying to look like a woman?"

"Didn't you take a look at yourself in the rear view mirror?"

"I was afraid to. It might inhibit me."

Julian fussed with his wig. "Come on. We have more important things to do than stand around admiring you."

Lorna handed Michael the blue folder containing the lawsuit against Stuart. "Go get them, guys."

Michael almost tripped. "You mean girls."

Julian held Michael steady. "You have to try harder than that, Mike. If one of the guards sees you wobbling in those shoes, he's going to suspect something."

"These things are murder. They're killing my feet."

"Quit complaining. If we pull this off, it will be worth it."

Michael took a deep breath, threw back his shoulders and began to walk more like a woman. "Is this better?"

"Don't overdo it, feminine but nice."

Through the lobby they went. "My uncle has a private garage and elevator in the downstairs parking lot." Michael checked the time. "It's a few minutes after ten. They're probably up there signing away right now."

He led Julian to the elevators, avoiding possible eye contact with the security guard.

Down they went to the parking level.

In Michael's haste to get out of the elevator, the heel of his shoe got stuck in a narrow slit between the concrete and the metal doors. When he lifted his foot to walk, he slipped out of the shoe, leaving the shoe lodged in the slit. "Damn it. These things are a pain in the ass."

"You'll get used to them."

"Who says I want to?" Michael bent down and pulled the shoe out of the slit.

"Who knows? You might find out you like dressing up in drag."

"Not on your life." Michael shoved his foot back into the shoe. "We better hurry up. We have to go way in the back."

Except for their heels clicking on the damp cement, the only other sound came from a big, exhaust fan sucking out smelly fumes left behind by people parking in the garage.

Michael made a serious effort to act more like a woman. "That's the guard we talked to earlier. He's all yours, Julian."

"Good! He's black. He'll be putty in my hands."

They walked up to the guard.

Julian's voice suddenly changed octaves. "Hi there," he said. "We have important papers my boss and Mr. Grant need for their meeting this morning."

"I'm sorry, miss. I was told not to let anyone upstairs."

His feet killing him, Michael felt like ripping off his shoes and beating the guard over the head with them.

Julian stuck out his chest and gave the man a sexy smile. "They're important papers, and they must be delivered immediately."

"Then give them to me. I'll deliver them myself."

His teeth gritting, Julian forced another sexy smile. "We were told not to let these papers out of our sight. It's confidential information. You understand."

"Why does it take two of you?"

"Because we just finished making some important changes our bosses wanted made before their meeting. She has to be there to explain her changes, and I have to be there to explain mine. It's all so involved, if you know what I mean."

"I don't know. I was told not to let anyone else on the elevator."

Julian dropped the sweet tone. "Look, honey. If Mr. Grant and my boss from World Office Products find out we were here and you wouldn't let us upstairs, come tomorrow, you'll be standing on line in the unemployment office."

The guard hesitated and then said. "Okay."

Julian smiled sweetly again. "You're doing the right thing."

The guard took out a remote control and aimed it at a sensor above the door, which slowly began to rise.

The luxurious marble, gold trim, and beveled mirrors infuriated Michael. "Look at this, Julian. This is Stuart's garage."

"I wonder who designed this for him. Whoever it was, I'll bet he made a nice commission."

"If we pull this off and everything works out, you'll be my personal decorator from now on."

"Let's get this show on the road then."

48

MICHAEL WHISPERED to Julian. "This is it. I hope we're not too late."

Both of his feet had developed blisters. He stifled the pain as Julian spoke with the receptionist.

"We have important papers for Mr. Grant's meeting this morning."

The sophisticated-looking brunette smiled. "Here. I'll take them."

Julian held onto the papers. "There's a big explanation involved. We'll have to go with you."

"Follow me, please."

Michael wanted so badly to run. He pictured the meeting over and everyone involved shaking hands and patting each other on the back.

His heel twisted on the carpeting, and he almost fell out of the shoe for a third time. The receptionist didn't notice. He glanced around to see if anyone else had seen his obvious clumsiness. A balding, middle-aged man stood at the water cooler getting a drink. Michael smiled and put his hand up to his face as if he were embarrassed. The man looked Michael up and down and winked. Michael could have puked.

When the receptionist stopped at the conference room door, Michael had to contain himself. He felt like throwing the door open and barging into the room. But the receptionist might holler for a security guard if he did.

The woman rapped lightly on the door and then opened it.

Everyone seated around the conference table looked up at them.

Stuart put down his pen. "What is it, Theresa?"

"I'm sorry to interrupt you, sir, but these women from World Office Products have important papers for your meeting."

Everyone looked at John Powers, President of World Office Products, expecting an explanation.

Before John had a chance to respond, Michael spoke.

"Thank you, Theresa. You can go now."

She left, closing the door quietly behind her.

Michael already knew who Jerry Zuckerman was. The other men had to be from World Office Products.

"This is extremely important," Michael said. "I hope you didn't sign any papers yet."

When everyone around the table heard a man's voice coming out of what appeared to be a woman's mouth, they gaped at Michael.

It still hadn't dawned on Stuart who Michael actually was.

He said. "What's going on, John?"

The president of World Office Products shrugged his shoulders. "I have no idea."

John's attorney intervened. "Let me take a look at those papers." He reached for the agreements and glanced over them. "I don't understand," he said to Michael. "What do these have to do with the closing?"

"Before I explain, tell me if you signed anything yet."

The attorney replied. "No."

Stuart exploded when he finally recognized Michael. "Why you little . . ." He glared at Michael and then went to the phone. "Dawn, call security."

Michael ripped off the wig. "Stuart here is my uncle. He stole stock- -my family's stock, so he can sell Grant Office Supplies to World Office Products."

Stuart grabbed the agreements. "Don't listen to him, John. My nephew here is drug-addict. He's trying to worm his way into the deal, so he can get more money to feed his habit."

"That's a lie," Michael said. "What's true is the content of this agreement. My father and Stuart signed it years ago on my grandfather's deathbed. They promised to keep the stock in Grant Office Supplies split an even fifty/fifty. For years my Uncle Stuart has been stealing my side of the family's stock."

Two security guards came bursting through the doors.

Stuart pointed. "Get these two drag queens out of here."

Julian brushed the guard's hand off him. "If you know what's good for you, you'll back off."

The other guard grabbed Michael's arm. "Let's go."

Michael yanked his arm away and slammed the guard against the wall.

Stuart glared at the guards. "Do something. Get them out of here."

One of the guards pulled out his gun.

"Stop it," John powers said. "I think I better take a look at that document."

Stuart shoved the agreements into his breast pocket. "They're meaningless, John. My sister-in-law sold me their stock fair and square."

Michael clenched his fist at Stuart. "You liar! You stole that stock from us."

Stuart motioned to the guards. "I told you to get them out of here."

Michael turned to John Powers. "Look. Would I go through all of this trouble, dressing up like some woman, if it weren't true? Please. You must believe me. If you have any doubts at all, call a doctor and I'll take a blood test. I'm not on drugs. I'll even take a lie detector test."

Julian spoke up. "The man is telling the truth."

Stuart smirked. "Who are you? You have no business here."

Julian strolled over to Stuart, his chest out and his hips swishing from side to side. "Why are you pretending like you don't know me, doll?" Julian turned to John Powers. "For years Stuart here has been going down on me." Julian ran his fingers through Stuart's hair.

Stuart jerked away. "Get away from me, you pervert."

Julian walked over to John Powers. "Take it from me. This guy is a conniving lowlife. He'll do whatever it takes to make a buck."

John held out his hand for the agreement. "I would like to take a look at that document, Stuart."

Stuart resisted and held onto them.

Michael anticipated that all of the copies might end up back in Stuart's hands. He had a copy on him, and he left another copy at Lorna's apartment. "Here's a copy for you to look at. You should also know my family has a lawsuit pending against Stuart."

John took the agreement from Michael. "Is that true, Stuart?"

"Hell no! It's not true. I told you the man is a trouble maker."

John turned to Jerry Zuckerman. "Is there a lawsuit pending against Stuart?"

Jerry's legal reputation was on the line. "Yes. It's true."

"Then there is nothing more to discuss. When you people get your personal differences straightened out, come see me. Until then, the deal is off." John got up to leave. "By the way, Stuart, if what your nephew here says is true, you owe me seventy-five million dollars."

Stuart slumped to the chair.

Michael shook hands with John Powers. "Thank you, sir. I've saved us both a lot of trouble and aggravation."

"Time will tell, son. Come on Henry."

The men from World Office Products, their attorney and secretaries packed up their things and headed for the door.

After everyone left, Julian smirked. "You still don't have any idea who I am, do you, Stuart?"

"I couldn't care less who you are. Get out of this office, you weirdo." It suddenly hit Stuart. "You're that drag queen from Delray."

"I was your son's partner."

"I told you to get out of here. You're smelling up my office."

"I'm going. But there's something I want you to know before I leave. William took those agreements from your safe. That's right. Your one and only son took them, because he had a feeling you would try to pull something like this someday. He was way ahead of you. It's ironic, isn't it? He got even with you from his grave."

49

STUART GLOATED. "Gayle doesn't stand a chance," he said, his comment resounding throughout the large, empty courtroom.

Matt O'Brien, his new attorney, responded. "We have her signature right here to prove it."

"I wish this thing would get started. I told my wife I would meet her at the club for lunch."

"I thought maybe you were going to bring her with you for support."

"Why subject her to this nonsense? Besides, this should be over quick. I saw no reason to get her out of bed." Stuart fidgeted, anxious to get on with the hearing. "I thought for sure Gayle would be here by now."

"Maybe she won't show."

"She'll be here." Stuart glanced at his watch. "It's almost ten."

The court reporter came through a side door and began to set up her machine.

Stuart kept turning around and checking the back door. "Chernoff just walked in. He's by himself. It looks like my cowardly nephew sent his attorney to fight their battles for them." Stuart gave David a smug look, as if to say, 'You're wasting your time. You don't stand a chance.'

David ignored Stuart. He laid his briefcase on the table and opened it.

While Stuart was settling into his chair, he heard a commotion behind him. He turned and saw Michael, Gayle and Samantha entering the courtroom.

They looked pathetic to Stuart, and it boosted his confidence. He said. "Matthew, my good man, we have this thing in the bag."

"I don't know. Judge Weinberg is one of the toughest judges on the bench. You never know how she's going to rule." Matt motioned with a nod. "I think they're ready. There's the bailiff."

A tall, stocky man with gray hair and glasses glanced around the room and then went back out into the hall.

Matt reached for a pitcher of water and filled two glasses, one of which he placed in front of Stuart, and the other he drank.

While Stuart was reaching for his glass, he saw Michael getting up and waving to someone in the back of the courtroom. Curious to see who it was, he turned in that direction.

Lorna hurried up the aisle and sat in the spectator seats with Michael and Samantha.

Stuart found Lorna's presence annoying. None of this concerned her. She had no business being in the courtroom, period.

About to turn around and face the bench, Stuart heard high heels click/clacking down the marble corridor. When he glanced at the door, anticipating paralegals, he almost dropped his glass of water. In his wildest dreams he never expected this would happen. What in hell were they doing here?

Matt asked. "Who are those people, Stuart?"

"My mother, my sister Margo, and her husband Ted. Michael brought the whole damn family with him."

"Why are they here? They have no relevancy to the case."

"Michael probably brought them to try and intimidate me."

Millicent glared at Stuart. About to approach him, she took a seat instead when she saw the bailiff enter the courtroom.

The bailiff stood beside the bench. "Would everybody please rise."

Everybody stood up and waited while Judge Judith Weinberg, a petite woman with a boyish haircut and wire-rim glasses, took her seat behind the bench.

The bailiff spoke up again. "Will the plaintiff and the defendant please remain standing and raise your right hands."

As everyone else sat, Stuart and Gayle remained standing.

The bailiff continued. "Do you swear to tell the truth, the whole truth, and nothing but the truth, so help you God."

In unison, they both said, "I do."

The bailiff motioned with his hand. "You may be seated."

As this was not a full, blown-out trial, Judge Weinberg was going to hear arguments instead of trying a case. The jury box sat empty.

Stuart whispered to Matt. "She doesn't look old enough to be a judge. She looks like she's barely out of college."

"Don't let her looks fool you. She's one of the brightest judges in South Florida."

After the formalities between the judge and the attorneys were out of the way, David Chernoff began to speak. "Your Honor, the plaintiff, Mrs. Gayle Grant, is here today, because she believes the defendant, Mr. Stuart Grant, has stolen real estate property that legally belongs to her. We are seeking a motion to bar eviction."

Judge Weinberg opened the folder in front of her. "Continue Mr. Chernoff."

"Thank you, Your Honor." David paused a moment to collect his thoughts. "The defendant, Mr. Grant, holds an executive position in Grant Office Supplies. Approximately once a month, he would gather together company documents that required the plaintiff's signature and take those documents to her home for her to sign because she was a partner in Grant Office Supplies. On those occasions, when the defendant would bring with him to the plaintiff's home the company documents that required her signature, he knew from previous experience that she would be signing those documents without her ever reading the contents, because over the years he had gained her trust."

David took a sip of water. "On one of those occasions, without the plaintiff's knowledge, the defendant had Mrs. Grant sign a General Warranty Deed, which after she signed the deed, the title to her house was transferred over to the defendant. Now the defendant is trying to evict the plaintiff from her rightful property. Your Honor, the plaintiff is here today, hoping you will rule in her favor."

David reached for a copy of the lawsuit Michael, Gayle and Samantha filed against Stuart. "Your Honor, this is a copy of a pending criminal lawsuit the plaintiff and her two children filed against the defendant. I believe you have a copy there in your file. They are accusing the defendant of securities fraud, breach of fiduciary duty, unlawful conversion of assets and racketeering under the civil code of the

Racketeer-Influenced and Corrupt Organizations Act. This General Warranty Deed the defendant had my client sign is just the tip of the iceberg."

Matt pleaded his case. "But, Your Honor, the deed has been witnessed and notarized."

Judge Weinberg questioned Gayle. "Mrs. Grant, why didn't you read the documents the defendant brought to your home before you signed them?"

"At the time I trusted Stuart. Now, all of that has changed."

"Were you present when the General Warranty Deed was notarized and witnessed?"

"No, Your Honor. Stuart obviously had people from his office notarize and witness the deed."

Judge Weinberg directed her attention to Stuart. "Is that true, Mr. Grant?"

"Your Honor, ever since my brother died, my sister-in-law has wanted to move off the island. All of a sudden now, she is changing her mind."

"Answer the question, Mr. Grant. Did you have people from your office notarize and witness the General Warranty Deed?"

Stuart hesitated, but he knew he better not perjure himself. "Yes, Your Honor," he said.

Judge Weinberg sat forward in her seat, her arms resting on the bench. "Is there anything else, Mr. Chernoff?"

"Yes, Your Honor. When Mrs. Grant found out that the defendant was evicting her from her house, they argued about it, and she had a heart attack. If she wanted to get off the island and she had signed that deed, knowing full well what it was, she wouldn't be here. The bottom line is the defendant took advantage of Mrs. Grant, knowing she trusted him. Maybe she was wrong in signing that deed without reading it first, but that is no reason why Mr. Stuart should be able to take possession of her house."

"I agree."

Matt stood up to plead Stuart's case. "But, Your Honor."

Judge Weinberg cut Matt off. "The General Warranty Deed was not witnessed and notarized in Mrs. Grant's presence. I am ruling in favor of the plaintiff, granting the motion. Mrs. Grant can remain in her house." She picked up her mallet. "This court is adjourned."

Stuart was furious. "What the hell?"

Matt shoved his folder into his briefcase. "I'm sorry, Stuart. I told you she was tough."

Michael hugged Gayle. "You did it. Now all we have to do is win the criminal lawsuit."

Stuart glared at them, his teeth gritting angrily. He had always won and hated losing. As he was heading for the door, Millicent stepped in his path.

She said. "I never dreamed a son of mine could stoop this low."

"Save the speech for another time, mother."

"How dare you speak to me in that manner."

"Get out of my way."

"I will not."

"If I have to pick you up and move you, I will."

"There's a meeting at my house one hour from now. Be there."

"What do I care about your Mickey Mouse meeting. I see whose side you're on."

"I'm doing what is right and you know it. I'm warning you, Stuart, if you want future participation in Grant Office Supplies, you better be there."

50

MICHAEL SQUIRMED in his chair. "I'll bet Stuart isn't coming." For the past ten minutes, Millicent kept her eye on the time. "He'll be here all right. He witnessed something unique in that courtroom today, all of us joining together in making a stand against him."

Margot straightened her long strand of pearls. "I don't know, mother. If Stuart had the nerve to take Gayle's house and stock, he might not care what any of us do." Margot turned to her husband. "What do you think, Ted?"

"Stuart is a businessman. I believe he'll be here."

Millicent paced the floor. "What did you tell Lorna, Michael?"

"I told her I didn't think she should attend this family meeting, her being Stuart's step-daughter and all. If for some reason things don't work out between us, I want her to have somebody she can turn to; although, her living with Stuart and Eva again is highly unlikely."

"You did the right thing," Millicent said. "After all, Eva is her mother. Where is Lorna in the meantime?"

"She went back to her apartment."

"I like that girl, Michael. She would make you a good wife."

Samantha spoke up. "I agree, Michael. The whole family likes her."

Michael smiled and changed the subject. "What are those attorneys and their assistants doing in the other room?"

"Maria is feeding them. Remember. I don't want any of you letting on to Stuart that the attorneys are here. I don't want him leaving without my having a chance to say my piece." Millicent motioned to

Sam. "Pour me another cup of coffee, please, a tad of cream and one sugar."

Sam got up and went to the table. While she was biting into a freshly-baked lemon square, Stuart and Eva entered the room. She gulped down the rest of her pastry and rushed the coffee to Millicent.

Stuart disregarded everybody and with a pompous shrug went for something to eat.

Eva greeted everyone politely and then sat on the empty sofa.

Millicent waited patiently, trying to avoid an outburst, while Stuart took his time putting butter on a slice of banana bread.

He ate the banana bread and then a mango Danish. "Well, mother," he said, pouring a cup of coffee. "Are you just going to stand there all day?"

"I'm waiting for you."

"I have ears. Speak."

"Damn it, Stuart, would you sit down."

He took the coffee and another piece of banana bread with him to the sofa and sat next to Eva. He sipped some coffee and then looked Millicent straight in the eye. "Are you happy now?"

Millicent ignored his goading.

Stuart took a bite of banana bread and laid the rest on his dish. "What is this all about?"

"You realize that if and when you, Gayle and her children go to court, we will all be there as witnesses for them."

"You made that obvious this morning."

"You will never win against all of us."

"Is that what you thi . . ."

She interrupted him. "If you don't mind, Stuart, would you please let finish."

"Go ahead. Be my guest."

"Do you realize what will happen to you when you lose? You will go to prison on felony charges."

"And if I win? That is a possibility, you know."

"No jury would acquit you."

"Look what happened with O. J. Simpson."

"You're foolish if you think you can win. Don't forget I witnessed that vow you and Richard made."

"Is that it? Are you done now?"

"No, and I would appreciate it if you would quit being so belligerent and condescending with me." Millicent stirred her coffee with a spoon. "Under the circumstances, Gayle, Michael and Samantha are willing to be quite generous with you."

"They don't have a pot to piss in. How can they be generous with me?"

Millicent shook her head. "You've turned into a horrible human being, Stuart."

"Whatever you say, mother."

"Do you want to hear what I have to say or not?"

"Do I have a choice?"

"They're willing to drop the lawsuit against you."

"On what condition?"

"They become the majority stockholders with sixty percent of the stock."

"Never. I made that company what it is today."

"If they take you to court and you lose the case, a jury might award them with the entire stock. Not only that, you will rot away in prison for a very long time."

Eva squeezed his hand. "Please take their offer, Stuart. I couldn't stand the thought of you going to prison. What would I do without you?"

Millicent continued. "Let me finish, and then the two of you can go out on the terrace to discuss it."

"We'll sleep on it," Stuart said, "and then I'll get back to you tomorrow."

"No. The offer only stands now with all of us here present."

"What else did you want to say?"

"From what Michael tells me, when World Office Products saw the agreement you and Richard signed and the pending lawsuit Michael, Gayle and Samantha filed against you, they backed out of the deal."

"So?"

"Since you wanted to retire, and Gayle, Michael and Samantha have no desire to run the company, they are willing to sell Grant Office Supplies and share the profit with you. That is a mighty generous offer, if you ask me. However, the money that they lost and you made on their stock, will be paid back to them along with thirty million extra, ten million each, for their pain and suffering."

"How did they suffer? They haven't lived too shabbily."

"What's fair is fair. By taking Gayle's house, you caused her to have a heart attack. What is your answer?"

"I don't know."

"One last thing. We all want you off Sand Dollar Island by the end of the month. Michael will move into your house until we figure out who is eventually going to get it."

"Are you insane? Not on your life. I'm not moving off the island."

"Oh yes you are. Now you and Eva can go out on the terrace to discuss it."

Eva jumped up off the sofa and reached for Stuart's hand. "Come on."

As soon as Stuart and Eva left the room, Millicent nodded to Michael. "I think he'll go for it."

"When we discussed this last night, you never said anything about the thirty million."

"I saved that for a surprise. After all, he put you three through hell. You deserve the money."

Samantha held up crossed fingers to Michael. "That's a nice little bonus."

"Don't spend it yet. You never know what that louse will do."

Ted loosened his tie and unbuttoned the top button of his shirt. "Stuart would be out of his mind if he didn't take your offer. More than anyone he realizes he could spend a fortune on lawyers getting ready for the trial and then end up losing. Then where would he be, rotting away in prison for the rest of his life. No. He'll be in here in a few minutes accepting your offer."

—

EVA PLEADED with Stuart. "Please take their offer. I couldn't bear it if you went to prison. What would I do? What would you do? We would have no life."

"You're not showing much faith in me. What if I win?"

"Why take that chance? Even if you sell the company and split the profits, we'll have a great life together. There's still a lot of money involved. If you lose, you'll end up broke in some prison cell."

"Would you leave me if I got convicted of a felony and went to prison?"

"Honestly?"

"No, Eva. I want you to lie to me."

She clenched her fists. "Sometimes, you are really difficult to get along with."

"Well? Answer the question. Would you leave me if I went to prison?"

She evaded the question. "What you did, taking Gayle's house, was wrong. Take their offer."

"You still didn't answer my question."

"All right, I'll answer your question. If you are stupid enough to go to court, then yes, I'm done. We can still have a good life. In fact, we can have a very good life. Why jeopardize it?" She looked him straight in the eye. "It's me or going to court."

"You don't mean that."

"Which is it, Stuart? I'll leave Sand Dollar Island right now. I'm not kidding."

He wrapped his arms around Eva. "I couldn't live without you. Okay, if you insist I'll take their offer."

Eva threw her arms around Stuart's neck. "Thank you, darling. Thank you."

They went back into the house.

Michael took off his blazer and draped it over a chair. "Here they come, grandmother."

Millicent placed her coffee cup on the table. "Did you and Eva come to a decision?"

"Yes. Against my wishes, my wife wants me to take your offer."

Michael and Samantha grinned at each other.

Millicent smiled as she stood. "Wait here a minute, Stuart."

"Why?"

"I want this in writing."

"No problem. I'll have my attorney draw up the papers."

She stopped in her tracks. "I said this would be settled today, and I meant it."

"Where are you going?"

"I'll be back in a minute."

While Millicent was gone, nobody said a word. As if they could read each other's minds, they realized that one of them might say something to upset Stuart, and he would change his mind.

When Stuart saw Millicent walking back into the room with two attorneys and two paralegals, he did a double take. "What is Jerry Zuckerman doing here? I fired him."

"And, I hired him. You were wrong for firing him in the first place. The man has ethics."

Millicent handed Stuart a pen. "Go sit down at the table."

He sighed. "Yes, mother."

"All right, gentlemen, you can take over now."

David Chernoff put a series of documents in front of Stuart. "Sign at the tabs, Mr. Grant."

"I want to read these first."

Millicent grabbed Stuart's ear lobe and twisted it. "That is why I have your attorney here. He already reviewed the papers for you."

Jerry Zuckerman confirmed it. "Everything is just as you agreed. You can sign the documents."

Stuart shrugged his shoulders. "Here goes."

Millicent stood over Stuart's shoulder, watching him sign each and every paper.

She patted him on the back. "Good work."

"Can I go now?"

"No. We're not finished."

"Now what?"

She called into the next room. "Margot and Ted, get in here."

They came right away.

Millicent turned to David. "Where do you want us to sign?"

"Beside the blue arrows."

One after the other, they each signed as witnesses.

Stuart got up to leave.

Millicent stopped him. "One more thing."

"I'm losing my patience, mother."

She looked at the two attorneys. "Which one of your people here is a notary?"

Jerry pointed. "Jill is."

"Do your thing, Jill."

Her seal in hand, the young woman notarized the documents.

Millicent sighed with relief. "Now you can go, Stuart."

He went to walk away.

Again she stopped him. "Wait. One more minor detail."

"Make it quick. You're getting on my nerves."

"Go over and make peace with Michael and Samantha."

"That I will NOT do."

Michael said. "Yes, you will. Come with me to the library. We have some unfinished business."

Stuart looked at Millicent and shrugged his shoulders. "I'll be back in a minute." He followed Michael to the library.

Michael closed the door behind them. "I just want to get one more thing straight."

"Make it quick. Eva is waiting."

"We both know we despise each other now."

"Is that all?"

"No. I suspect you're the one who put that contract out on me. I'm not going to pursue any legal action, because I'm sure you'll suffer enough guilt over William's death."

Blood drained from Stuart's face. "I don't . . ."

"Be quiet," Michael said adamantly, "but if you so much as pull any more of your underhanded stunts or upset a member of this family again, I will go straight to the police and tell them about my suspicions. Do you understand?" Michael didn't wait for an answer. "Now get out of here. You turn my stomach."

51

MICHAEL TOOK ANOTHER SIP of his champagne. "It's finally over, Lorna."

"You won. How wonderful!"

"No. You're wonderful." He bent over her and kissed her, a long passionate kiss. "You make me weak in the knees. You're like Delilah, draining my strength."

"But I never touched your hair."

He looked at hers glowing in the moonlight. "You're so beautiful. I love you so much. Come on. I'm so happy, I feel like running."

"I thought you said I made you weak."

"That was a second ago, while I was kissing you. Now I feel like running. Come on, I'll race you."

They put their glasses on a rock and went tearing up the beach.

"Yeehaw," Michael hollered.

"Wait," Lorna said. "I think I twisted my ankle."

He stopped and ran back to her. While he was examining her leg, she pushed him over onto the sand and started running again. As fast as she could, she ran along the shoreline, her feet splashing up water on her shorts and top.

Michael tore up the beach and tackled her to the sand.

"Foul," she said. "I win. I get a great big kiss from you."

"You keep it up, and you'll get more than a kiss."

He lay on top of her, his hands pinning hers over her head. "Now what are you going to do? How are you going to get out of this one?"

"Who said I wanted to get out of this one? Now kiss me, you fool."

He rolled her on top of him and kissed her. Again and again, they kissed.

When they finally came up for air, Lorna saw a crab scurrying on the beach. "I think we better get up."

"Why? I like you on top of me."

"How would you like that crab over there on top of you?"

Michael threw her off and jumped up, pretending like the crab scared him.

As they were strolling up the beach, Michael saw something in the sand. He reached down for it, and with his back to Lorna, he fussed with it.

She tried to look over his shoulder. "What is it?"

"You're not allowed to see it."

"Come on. What is it?"

His back still to her, he brushed sand off the thing. "Wow," he said. "I don't believe it."

"What did you find?"

"This is really amazing. I didn't know you could find something like this on the beach."

"Forget it," she said, teasing him. "I don't want to see it now."

"Okay. I'll not only let you see it, I'm going to give it to you." He handed the thing to her. "Here."

She took it from him. "Big deal! It's nothing but a dirty clam shell."

"Check out what's inside it."

Her eyes lit up. "You didn't find a pearl, did you? You couldn't have. Pearls come in oyster shells."

"Open it and see."

She lifted the top and saw the most dazzling diamond engagement ring she had ever seen. "Is this what I think it is?"

"Yes. Will you marry me?"

"Yes, yes, yes."

Michael slid the ring onto Lorna's finger and then lifted her in his arms.

TROPICAL HEAT

LIZ LEHMAN

**A preview of Tropical Heat
on the following page**

TROPICAL HEAT

TAINE WOKE with a come-hither smile on her face, thinking it was her boyfriend Breeze who just whispered in her ear. When she saw the maniac who kept staring at her earlier, she couldn't breathe.

He grabbed her head and clamped his hand over her mouth. "Don't scream or I'll hurt you."

She was so terrified that she thought her pounding heart might explode through her chest. How could this slimy creep have broken into her hotel room and be sitting right next to her on the bed? His eyes were so crazed. They still had that same penetrating look she remembered. They pierced right through to her core, frightening her so badly that she immediately left Club Boca.

What might happen to her in the next few minutes paralyzed her with fear. Knowing she might be raped or even murdered caused her to breathe faster and she started to hyperventilate. At the same time, her mind was racing wildly, trying to think of something she could do. Could she fight him? After looking him over, she knew she didn't stand a chance. The white shirt and jeans clinging to his body displayed muscles underneath. This guy looked fit, like the type of guy who worked out regularly at the gym. Scared half out of mind, she pulled the sheet up to her neck and gripped it so tightly, she could feel her fingernails digging into the palms of her hands.

Coming soon

Liz Lehman's ownership in a chain of boutiques led her to the fashion capitals of the world. For lifestyle magazines she penned monthly columns on beauty and fashion. Characterized as credible, experienced and controversial, she appeared on television as an appearance expert. She has one son, Michael, and three step-children, Suzanne, Jonathan and Julie. Licensed in real estate, she and her husband, Jerry, own a Florida real estate brokerage company.